MISSION TO SECTOR ZZ 1219

MISSION TO SECTOR ZZ 1219

Creative Texts Publishers products are available at special discounts for bulk purchase for sale promotions, premiums, fund-raising, and educational needs. For details, write Creative Texts Publishers, PO Box 50, Barto, PA 19504, or visit www.creativetexts.com

MISSION TO SECTOR ZZ 1219
By Jerry D. Young
Published by Creative Texts Publishers
PO Box 50
Barto, PA 19504
www.creativetexts.com

The following is a work of fiction. Any resemblance to actual names, persons, businesses, and incidents is strictly coincidental. Locations are used only in the general sense and do not represent the real place in actuality.

ISBN: 978-0-578-42022-6

MISSION TO SECTOR ZZ-1219

JERRY D. YOUNG

Prolog

"Gunderson! Disengage! Disengage! Re-group! Don't…"

It was too late. Gunderson's F-321 Fleet Space Fighter disintegrated.

"Bogeys are dispersing, Captain! Should we pursue?"

"Negative, Claymore Three. Negative. Claymore Flight form on me. Claymore Five, hustle it up. You are way out of position. You just saw what happens out here when you leave formation. Now close up!"

The radios stayed silent after the Captain's harsh order. The four remaining F-321 combat craft of Claymore Flight maneuvered into a tight formation with the sleek Dominator Attack Craft flown by Captain William Butler in the lead.

It was a subdued group that met for the debriefing.

"Look, Cap," said Charlie, "you took out three of them before Gunderson got pulled away…"

"Captain," called out a harried looking Spaceman Two-Stripe rating, "Ops wants you on deck, on the double. Supposed to let Lieutenant Chambers handle the debrief."

"Now what?" muttered the Captain. "Very well, Spaceman. Tell the Commander I will be right there. Charlie, take over. And I don't consider losing Gunderson as worth getting three of them."

"Bill, I did not mean…"

"I know, Charlie, I know. Look, go over protective formations and cover fire with everyone again. No telling how long this is going to take."

Charlie nodded and Captain Butler followed the Spaceman rating, still talking on his communicator.

He had left the flight helmet with Charlie to put in his gear bag to bring to the Officer's quarters later, but he did not take time to change out of the flight suit. Even in the flight suit the Captain presented a striking sight as he entered the operations center for the Confederation Space Navy base.

His tall frame was lean, without an ounce of excess fat. His face showed some signs of his near exhaustion, but only to those that knew him very well. To everyone else, the wide spread blue eyes and sardonic smile on his face spoke only his determination to make the sector safe from whoever was making the attacks on not only military and merchant fleet targets, but civilian targets as well.

His sharp salute put a slight smile on Base Commander Vice-Admiral Calhoun's face. "At ease, Captain." The smile faded. "I heard we lost another craft and pilot."

"Yes, sir. Gunderson. Just a kid. Got too eager. He is…was…good. If he had been in a decent combat craft, he would probably still be alive and the Ecronians would be down at least one, if not two, raiders."

The Commander frowned. "Captain, you know the Governor has stated emphatically that we are dealing with pirates, not Ecronians."

"Yes, sir," Captain Butler said, rather sharply, drawing another deep frown from his commander. "But we both know that some of the activity is not pirates. It is Ecronian."

"I do not know that, and neither do you. It would behoove you, Captain, to keep those kinds of comments completely to yourself."

"Yes, sir," replied the Captain. "The Spaceman said my presence was requested."

Brusque now, the Commander said, "Yes. Apparently one of your requests for equipment has been approved by the Governor."

"She going to let us have toilet paper for the enlisted quarters?" popped out before Butler could prevent it.

"That will be enough, Captain!" Commander Calhoun said.

"Yes, sir. My apologies, sir."

"I don't want your apologies, Captain. I want and expect the performance of your duties as directed, without comments."

Stiffly Captain Butler responded, "Yes, Sir!"

"Now," Commander Calhoun continued, as he led the way toward his office, "you are to receive two Triple Seven combat craft and an experienced pilot to train your squadron on them."

"Yes, sir," Butler replied. Two craft to replace the fifteen they had lost the last year. The Triple Seven was a newer model combat craft than the F-321, but he knew it had significant weaknesses for the type of action it would see in the sector.

It was useless, even counterproductive, to voice the thoughts, so he kept them to himself. Instead, he asked, "When can we expect delivery, Sir? And do you know who is being sent to do the training? McCormick was an ace in the Triple Seven during the Transition Campaign."

"I don't know who it is, but I do know it's not McCormick. He was pulled Earthside to assist in the Transition. As to when they are to be here, assuming the pirates don't take out the trader's ship, delivery should be in less than three weeks, last report I had."

"Yes, sir. Next week, Sir. Is that all Sir?"

"No, it is not." Commander Calhoun sat down behind his desk and looked up at Captain Butler. "I would suggest you improve your attitude toward Governor Myers. She has requested you to be her escort at the Inaugural Ball."

"Sir, with all due respect," Captain Butler quickly said, "she simply had her appointment as sector governor re-approved. This inaugural ball is not appropriate. If someone must attend as her escort, it should be Admiral Wainshaw, as Base Commander."

"Not only did she request you personally, Captain, but General Wainshaw and I are both married and will be attending with our wives."

"I respectfully decline the invitation, sir," Captain Butler replied, standing at attention before the desk.

"It is not an invitation, Captain. You will be at the Governor's Mansion, two days prior to the ball for protocol instruction. You will be ready to escort the Governor, wearing your dress uniform three hours prior to the scheduled start of the ball. Do I make myself clear, Captain?"

"Yes, Sir."

"Very good. You are dismissed." It was more a wave of the hand than a salute that sent Captain Butler out of the Commander's office. The captain saluted, turned sharply on his heel, and marched out.

When he met up with Charlie in the BOQ, the Bachelor Officers Quarters, where the unmarried Officers lived if they did not have their own accommodations, Charlie could tell his friend was even less happy than usual. He gave a low whistle when he heard the explanation. "Come on, Bill, drop planetside and go in to *Smokey's* with us. It will do you good to have a night out."

"Charlie, I'm patrolling with Scimitar Squadron tomorrow. I need to get some rest."

"You can't fly every mission with every squadron, Bill," Charlie said quietly.

"I know, I know… But the guys are so inexperienced. We're losing them faster than they can send them out here."

Captain Butler ran his hands through his rather shaggy, light brown hair. "Okay, Okay. I'll go in with you for a little while. But don't get insulted if I don't drink."

"Just getting you off this base for a few hours will do you good. There's supposed to be a real live female type singer at *Smokey's* now."

"You say that like it's a good thing, Charlie. You do remember the last time he brought in live… uh… talent…"

Charlie laughed. "Still, she was female. There aren't that many of them out here, you know. You may be a confirmed bachelor, but I'd kind of like to find a nice…"

Captain Butler shook his head went into the bathroom to shower, cutting off what Charlie wanted to find.

Bill let the hot water beat down on his head, neck, shoulders, and back, trying to ease the tension. He was weary beyond anything he had felt during the entire initial wars, and then the Transition Campaigns. And the Confederation was ostensibly at peace.

Another patrol under his leadership had engaged the enemy, losing members of the squadron to better equipment and training. And, even knowing he fought harder and better than the enemy and his own pilots, and that they held off the force again, he still felt the pain of losing people, knowing that things will be the same the next day. And the day after that. And the day after that…

Only his personal craft that had shipped out with him, a state-of-the-art Dominator, had kept things from being worse. He smiled ever so slightly, remembering when he had gone to the Scanlon Galactic plant to pick it up.

One of his assignments near the end of the war had been serving with the military development group working with Scanlon Galactic in the development of the new craft, before being assigned to the Governor's sector, ZZ-1219.

He had made some good friends in the corporation, and with some of the Quartermaster's Corps people also working on the project. Captain Butler was very well liked and respected, so had been able to not only take the test bed Dominator with him, but managed, still, to get a few limited special resupply items through outside channels.

"Maybe the Triple Sevens will make a difference," he thought, though was not really counting on it.

Eyes closed, he thought back to those earlier days in his career. Having started in the Triumvirate military forces as a raw Spaceman No-Stripe recruit, he had advanced quickly, his intelligence and drive allowing him to excel at every task assigned during his training. His first attempt in the flight simulator caught the attention of the Commander of the Training Academy.

His experiences as a youth working with his father in the Earth Asteroid Belt, piloting jumpers for his father's mining company, had served him well for the military space forces. He was already a Lieutenant JG in the Fighter Wing of one of the Triumvirate's huge System Defense Carrier groups, serving on the main carrier itself, when the Ecronians made their first incursion into Earth controlled space.

The fights were long and bloody, but the Triumvirate was able to fight the Ecronians first to a draw and then enough to drive them out of the area completely.

But even though the military Triumvirate's rule had been fairly benevolent, almost from day one, and had successfully fought off the worst danger Earth had ever faced, the long war had turned many of the citizens more than a bit anti-military.

The military Triumvirate had always been intended as a short-term solution to earlier problems, with promises and other assurances that the military would see to it that honest, open elections were held at some point.

It would be up to the citizens to decide on the form of government they wanted permanently, and then to elect those that would be a part of it. So, not long after it was clear that the Ecronians had actually fled, the process of changing over to a civilian government from the Triumvirate began.

Not everyone was as in favor of that plan as others. Always fighting on the side of the Triumvirate and the future official government, now Lieutenant Commander William 'Telstar' Butler made even more of a name for himself during the initial steps of changing forms of government, and then the Transition Campaigns right after the Constitutional Confederation was formed and officially took over.

Those wanting a return to military rule had been only a rather small portion of those that did not want the Confederation. There were many more issues and beliefs at stake, not all of which ever became common knowledge.

By the time he became Captain, Bill had become very aware of some of them. And that even the Confederation had some issues that were not at all to his liking. Corruption seemed to be part and parcel to every human government that had ever existed, and this one was no exception.

Though the transition was nearing completion, with local elected governing bodies in almost all sectors of the human inhabited Milky Way Galaxy, there were still a few on the very edges of the areas humans controlled that were still under the leadership and control of Triumvirate appointed Governors.

On each Sector Capitol World, a planetside combination Space Navy & Space Marine, Global Army, and Civilian Space Merchant base supported the government, and with only a couple of exceptions, each Capital world boasted one or more Bastion High-Mass-Core Moon-Ship bases in orbit around the world with similar arrangements.

Around many worlds, both Capitol Worlds and simply allied worlds, there were often several more of the Moon-Ship Bases. Some civilian, some corporate, some specialized military planetary defense bases. There also many Galactic Trader Family bases supporting the multitude of Galactic Trader Family Gravity-Wheel ships plying space, doing a significant portion of the commerce between systems and planets.

Unfortunately, in Captain Butler's opinion, Sector ZZ-1219 was one of those that had only the one small combination Moon-Ship base. The military parts were poorly equipped and staffed. Planetary defenses were essentially non-existent, with the exception of the lone Space Navy Space Fighter Wing attached to the base.

The Space Fighter Wing was the most ill-equipped and staffed of all the units. And Captain Butler had begun to suspect it might be intentional. As unlikely as it sounded, he even wondered at times if the hand of the Sector's current Civilian Governor, Governor Meyers, might be part of it.

Many of the other outlying sectors, that had suffered Ecronian attacks and barely survived intact, had made sure such a thing would not happen again. And in doing so, with the patrols and readiness to take a fight to anyone, Ecronian or otherwise, to include the Pirates that had proliferated during the final days of the war and subsequent confusion of the transition, were maintained adequately at the very least, and often as well as the primary sectors.

It was difficult to believe that any human would cooperate in any way with Ecronians, but the idea of an official of the Confederation would do so was almost unthinkable. Captain Butler, whenever the Governor entered his mind in relation to that, quickly put it out of his mind. It really was inconceivable.

Hopefully.

And there was mounting evidence of collusion between someone at some level in the government and at least one of the Pirate groups operating in the sector. In the early days of the rather precarious peace, Captain Butler had been dispatched to Sector ZZ-1219 to command the Fighter Wing, to help re-equip and improve it after the devastation it suffered fighting off the Ecronians.

Despite the orders from High Command on Earth, Captain Butler had been stymied at every turn. It did not take him long to realize that both General Wainwright and Vice-Admiral Calhoun had been posted to Sector ZZ-1219 to get them away from any of the rebuilding of the military forces, where their lackluster command qualities could be a major problem.

Both were well aware that High Command knew they were not very good officers. And, they knew they were in their last commands, and now even less willing to create any waves of any kind. Essentially rubberstamping any action Governor Meyers made. Both kept a low profile, waiting for their commissions to end so they could head for Earth and a cushy retirement.

With only mostly outdated Confederation military equipment available, and what seemed to be the lowest qualified personnel being transferred to the sector as replacements to those lost or leaving the service; the chances of Sector ZZ-1219 surviving intact another Ecronian incursion was slim, thought Captain Butler.

With the High Command distracted by the central governments' belief that extended war was inevitable, despite the recent peace agreement, and steps being taken to build up military forces, but so far only in areas that are most at risk, very little attention was paid to Sector ZZ-1219, since it did seem to be in good hands.

Captain Butler had not even an inkling of the depth and breadth of the real plans being made in the sector by those that were keeping the sector weak as could be.

Captain Butler shook his head, aware that he was not going to solve the problems of the sector in the shower, and turned off the water, ready to get dressed to go planetside with his friends and military companions.

Captain Butler was still muttering to himself, "Live female singer! Sure. I'd have to see genetic test results to be sure of that; and calling her… it… whatever… a singer is like calling a… Geez! I can't even think of a suitable bad comparison," when he left *Smokey's* to take a jumper back up to the base less than an hour after arriving.

Chapter One

-

"How come you're riding with us instead of that cruiser in orbit?" Sydney asked Johnny.

Johnny did a quick scan of the instruments over Clyde's and Sydney's shoulders.

"What cruiser?" Johnny asked, a tiny smile curving his lips.

"That one over there," Clyde said pointing to a spot of light near the planetary horizon.

"See, here it is on radar," Sydney said, indicating the computer display.

"I don't see a cruiser," Johnny said, projecting himself backwards from the cockpit with a tiny motion of his hand against the bulkhead.

"But it's right… Oh." Sydney said, cutting a glance over his shoulder.

"But Syd, it's…" Clyde was protesting.

Sydney reached over and punched him on the arm and shook his head when Clyde looked at him. He gave a head nod back toward Johnny and put what he hoped was a knowing look on his face.

"I get it," Clyde said, glancing quickly over his shoulder at the tall, lanky man who seemed so at ease in the null gravity as he floated slowly feet first toward the hatch at the end of the corridor.

Stopping his journey with light pressure on the corridor wall, Johnny floated into one of the niche berths in the crew corridor and fastened one of the five restraining bungees across the opening.

"I don't suppose you can tell us where you're going or what you're doing, huh?" Sydney asked.

"Sure, I can," Johnny said.

The two men in the cockpit exchanged another glance when the silence continued.

"Uh… But you won't?" It was obviously a question Sydney asked.

"Correct," replied Johnny. He slipped a tiny device from its hidden pocket in his tunic and checked it quickly before slipping it back into hiding.

"Well… Uh… You know, you're kinda famous in these parts."

"Don't believe everything you hear," Johnny said.

Both men heard the humor in Johnny's voice when he added, "Or read, see, or are otherwise informed."

"Yeah, but everyone knows what you did out on the Rim." Both men turned to see Johnny's reaction and response to Clyde's comment. But he was in the niche and they could not see him. They did, however, hear his soft comment.

"Everyone is usually wrong, you know. Or so I have found."

"Uh… Yeah…" Clyde said. The two men exchanged yet another glance and then quickly turned their attention to the controls of the cargo shuttle ship.

There was silence for a while, and then Sydney said, "You asleep back there?"

"Nope," replied Johnny.

"You're not mad at us, or anything, are you? We… Uh… would not want you to be mad at us."

"More of that *Everybody knows it stuff?*" Johnny asked.

Again, the humor was obvious in Johnny's voice.

"Well… Yeah… Sort of," replied Sydney.

"Don't worry. I'm not mad at you. Or anything," Johnny said.

"You married? Or involved?" Sydney asked. He winked over at Clyde. Johnny heard Clyde's subdued groan.

"No. To both," Johnny replied.

"Want to be?"

"You have someone in mind, I take it," Johnny said.

"Well, since you mentioned it, my sister has been looking for a husband. She would probably settle for a boyfriend." Sydney grinned over at Clyde.

"She's actually not that bad looking. Not my type, of course, even if she was not my sister."

Clyde groaned again when an obviously angry, obviously female voice said quite menacingly, "Syd, what did I tell you I was going to do to you the next time I caught you trying to marry me off to some passing pilot?"

"Wait a minute, Sis, I…**Ow!**" Sydney clapped one hand to the back of his head. "What is that?" he asked, pulling something from his hair.

"A little gift from our good friends planetside. They did not have everything sealed properly. Stuff oozed and hardened. I got it all over me sealing things up. If it did not cost so much I'd turn us around and go back to have a little chat with our trading partners."

"Oh, Jeez!" Sydney said. He flicked the hardened wad of whatever it was to the vacuum recovery inlet.

"**Ow!**" Sydney exclaimed again, as another hard ball of material hit him in the back of the head.

Johnny had to admire the woman's aim and power. The bits of material she picked from her jump suit were flicked expertly and accurately.

"After I get changed, we're going to have a much more detailed discussion about you trying to marry me off. But for the moment, you get right back on that communicator and tell whoever it was you were talking to that I'm not available."

"But, Sis, I…**Ow!**" Another bit of the hard material hit Sydney in the back of the head.

"I was not talking to anyone on the communicator! I was talking to Johnny Oneshot back there!"

"Don't give me that, Syd. There's no one back here. Much less Johnny Oneshot. I think he's just a legend, anyway." She had unfastened the jumpsuit and was about to take it off.

Johnny made a quick sound. "A-hem."

She looked up at the sound. She always oriented herself with the seats in the cockpit when they were in null gravity or low gee acceleration. That meant the niche Johnny was in was over her head. "Why, I ought to…!" She fell silent and quickly began refastening the jumpsuit.

"Who the hell are you?" she asked when she had her clothing adjusted.

"Wilhelmina, I told you…**Ow!** Would you stop that? **Ow!**" Two more balls of hard material had hit Sydney, one after the other.

"Willi, I mean! Willi, that's Johnny Oneshot," Sydney quickly said.

She looked up at the face hanging a foot or so from hers. The head nodded.

"You normally change your clothes right out in the passageway?" Johnny asked.

"The lavatory is tiny. Sydney is my brother, not to mention he knows what I would do to him. Clyde would die of embarrassment if he saw me. Not to mention he also knows what I would do to him if he tried to look."

"I see," Johnny replied.

"Not in this lifetime you don't," came the quick response.

Johnny smiled. "Bad choice of responses. You are a mess. I'll turn my back and close my eyes if you want to go ahead and change."

"And why would I believe you would do that?"

Willi saw a slight change in his eyes. "Because I said I would."

"Yeah…Well…I'll go change in the lavatory."

"That's all right. No need. I'll go down to the cargo hold. You can call me back up when you're done."

"No," Willi said quickly. "Just…Just keep your eyes down that passageway.

"Sydney, Clyde, painful deaths await you if I even think you're turning around."

Reaching into one of the niches, Willi opened the locker built into the wall and pulled out another of the soft gray jumpsuits. She quickly changed, her eyes lifting often to Johnny. She noted that he had turned almost completely around in the niche, but had kept his head turned so she could see that he had to be looking where she had directed.

"Okay," she said when she was dressed again.

Johnny smiled when he turned and saw Willi give a slight push with her foot to sail up to the cockpit and thump Sydney in the back of the head with her palm.

"**Ow!**" Sydney said.

"You know better than to call me Whi…" She cut a look back down the passageway. "You know better than to call me that." She thumped him again, eliciting yet another '**Ow!**' "And you also know better than to try to marry me off," she added.

"Well," Clyde said, "At least he wasn't trying to sell you, this time."

Clyde got a thump then, and Sydney another.

"Don't help me, huh?" Sydney told Clyde.

"Why did I not know we had a passenger?" Willi asked them then.

"Well, he's not actually a passenger," Sydney said, this time dodging the thump. "He's *sort of* a supernumerary," he added. "The *Trinity Home* contacted us while you were off-board and said he would be coming back with us."

"Supernumerary, huh?" Willi glanced down the passageway. "Okay. You should have used the private com-link to let me know."

Before Sydney could answer, Johnny did. From right beside Willi. She started slightly when he spoke. She had not had a single sensation of his approach.

"They were told no communications about me. The incoming was a coded burst transmission, encoded to sound like a routine communication from your parent ship."

"But..." protested Willi.

"I'm sorry, but I really cannot say more," Johnny told her, meeting her clear blue eyes with his own.

Suddenly he seemed small, and she realized he had pushed off and was drifting back to the niche he had been in before. With a startled shake of her head she turned back to the cockpit and started to strap herself in the third seat. She reached over and thumped Sydney and Clyde both again.

"What was that for?" Sydney asked, rubbing the back of his head, again.

"Just because," Willi said, glancing back down the passageway. Apparently, Johnny Oneshot was back in the niche, for she could not see him. "Man, he can move quick and soft!" she said mostly to herself.

Johnny smiled in the niche. He had the comm device in his hand again. It had picked up her words and displayed them. He flipped it closed and concealed it once more. Fingers interlaced on his chest he let himself drift into a light sleep, restrained in the niche by one single bungee.

When Willi drifted past a few minutes later, headed to the lavatory, she saw that only one restraint was up. When she very quietly started to fasten the others into place Johnny's hand was suddenly gripping her wrist.

His eyes were on hers, again only inches away. "I don't like to be confined."

"If we have to maneuver…"

"The alarm will sound. I will be braced before the maneuvers can take place."

"No one is that quick. At least, not waking from a sleep."

"I am," Johnny said.

Willi stared for a moment, and then just nodded. His grip had not been that tight to start with, and now it slipped away completely from her wrist. Willi reoriented herself from the position the contact had shifted her into and floated down the passageway again, toward the lavatory.

As the hours turned into days, Willi had to admit, to herself anyway… she would never admit it to Johnny Oneshot, Clyde, or Sydney… that their non-passenger was no trouble at all. She actually tended to forget he was aboard. Except when he was in her sight, which was not often.

Willi smiled suddenly, remembering the meal they had enjoyed the prior evening. It was another of Johnny Oneshot's contributions. She still did not know what he had done to or with their regular rations to make the meal so good. They had good food aboard, it was a trader tradition, but he had made it especially…

Suddenly she was frowning. Willi was not going to let herself be mesmerized by his cooking skills. Or null gravity skills. Or those blue eyes. Or… Willi shook her head and whispered, "Where is he now, anyway?"

Still under very low g acceleration, headed on a rendezvous course with *Trinity Home* for cargo transfer, Willi floated toward the hatch opening into the cargo hold of the shuttle. Often as not she would find him doing isometric exercises there when he was not sleeping or doing whatever else it was that he did when he was not studying on the craft's library computer.

When she eased into the hold, silently closing and dogging the hatch, Willi looked around, hoping to catch sight of Johnny before he did her. She had yet to accomplish it. He was the only person she had ever met that could move as quickly and silently as she in null and low gravity.

She could not keep the wry smile from her face when she saw the flash of grey shoot across the one sizable open space in the hold.

Johnny waved at the young woman, knowing from past experience it would annoy her, as he leapt across the open space in the hold. He loved null gravity, but knew he had to keep up an intense regimen to stay in the shape he needed to stay in to be able to do the things he must do when in a gravity field.

Fortunately, it was often fun. He ignored the thought intruding suddenly that it was more fun than normal when Willi joined him in this particular exercise.

"Thought I'd get a few calisthenics in before we go to watch and watch in the Belt. Won't have much chance after that," Willi said, matching his trajectory perfectly as he sailed again across the open space.

Willi cut her eyes over to Johnny. "You do know what watch and watch is… I hope…" She frowned.

She saw the sardonic smile, as Johnny Oneshot replied. "Yes. Watch and watch. Four on four off, repeat, if I am not mistaken. Not the usual four on and eight off."

Grudgingly, Willi nodded, adjusting for her landing.

"Great minds, huh?" Johnny said. He tucked and flipped over, to push off in a slightly different direction this time, just to see if she would compensate and do the same. She was nearly as good, if not just as good, as he was in null gravity. "I find it important to stay in shape, when I can."

"Yeah. Sure," Willi said, frowning again when she noted the placement of his feet when they contacted the crates. He was going to do another of those tricky pattern sets she had seen him do before. He never did the same thing twice. She adjusted her own landing and pushed off to stay with him, automatically increasing her speed, unconsciously knowing he would speed up on this leap.

Soon they were performing what amounted to an intricate dance, their bodies twisting and spinning in unison as Willi duplicated every move that Johnny made during the energetic exercise.

The two came to rest with neither bounce nor need for adjustment beside Sydney where he stood by the hatch. His mouth was hanging open. "What's the matter with you?" Willi asked, wiping a sleeve across her forehead.

"You two... I never saw anything like that, except the Games... You two could compete in the pairs!"

A quick sideways glance at Johnny, and Willi growled, "Shut up, Syd. Clyde got us ready for the Belt?"

"Yeah. Sure." Sydney was staring at Johnny. The man was not even sweating heavily. Sydney had never seen anyone move the way he did. He quickly turned his eyes toward his sister. "Uh, yeah. Everything is ready. How about here?"

Willi frowned. "What do you mean, here?"

"Well, if we have to take evas..."

"Sid, this cargo was secure for hard maneuvering the day after we lifted off the planet. Have you ever known me to leave anything to chance?"

She shoved him slightly toward the hatch. "Un-dog the hatch. I want to shower and change before we go to watch and watch. And get something to eat. You got the galley set?"

"Of course!" Sydney replied. He cut a look over his shoulder. "Are you going to man one of the arms consoles?"

Willi spun around at Sydney's question to Johnny.

"Oh," Johnny said, that sardonic smile once again on his face, his eyes going to Willi's, "I think this ship is in capable hands without any interference from me."

"You can damn well bet it is!" Willi said, mostly under her breath. She turned and went into the lavatory.

A few minutes later Willi floated up the corridor to the control station. "I'll take the con, Clyde. I want you on weapons when we go in. Sydney, Scans and Countermeasures. I got a bad feeling about this one. They hit *R-2's* shuttle their last trip through, and *Sandusky's*, too.

"Of course, *Sandusky's* shuttle did not have any trouble turning them away. They're almost as good as we are." Johnny hid his smile at that, as Willi continued, "But the *R-2* team took heavy damage and lost their cargo. That is not going to happen to us. Damn pirates!"

Clyde looked at Johnny as he floated up, and then Sydney. For once, Sydney was subtle. He just shook his head slightly and strapped himself in to the seat beside his sister. Clyde nodded and took the third seat, at the primary weapons control console.

"You're the best pilot in space, Willi," Clyde said. "I got no worries. I'm just here because it's regulation."

"Damn straight!" Willi said, turning an appreciative glance on the young man. He was shy and rather retiring, she knew, much the opposite of her brother. But she had seen him in action on the weapons systems in training and in action.

He was as uncanny as Sydney was on the Scanners. Willi knew it was not simply braggadocio when she admitted to herself that she might not be the best pilot in space, but she probably was very close to it. Other than a crew from the *Sandusky* and one from the *Infinity*, they were undoubtedly the best shuttle team in space.

"Where do you want me?" Johnny asked quietly.

Willi started to tell him to strap into a sleeping niche, but hesitated. He had been no trouble and did seem to know the workings and procedures of small craft. "Take the Systems Console. We're ninety percent capacity. Shouldn't be any problems… never have been… but… take the Systems Console."

"Aye," came the soft response.

It did not really register on Willi, but Sydney turned his head and saw Clyde's lifted eyebrow. Again, Sydney managed to keep his foot out of his mouth, by saying nothing.

They had been into the Belt for only a few minutes when Sydney said, "Blip on long-range, bearing Zero, Zero, Zero."

Johnny's lips curled just slightly as he monitored the System Console as requested; but felt the shuttle change course and accelerate. He was sure he could not actually feel or hear the weapons system come to bear on whatever was creating the blip on Sydney's scanners. He did know that Clyde had the weapons targeted and ready.

Sydney's voice was still calm, but Johnny knew, just as did Willi and Clyde, that he was concerned when he said, "Bogey, Zero, Zero, Zero. Bogey, ten, zero, zero. Bogey, zero, ten, zero. Bogey…We got a blockade ahead, Willi."

Before Willi could respond, Sydney spoke again. "I'm getting blips all around us at long-range." He lifted his eyes from the monitors to look at Willi. "They've got us surrounded! I can't believe it! The pirates have never done anything like this before! There must be twenty ships out there!"

"Heat'em up, Clyde," Willi said softly. "They must have heard about the shipment of fissionables. Damn it!"

"They're all small attack craft," Sydney suddenly said. "One seaters. All closing. Incoming! We've been ambushed!"

"Okay, Clyde," Willis said. "Fire at will!"

Johnny continued to monitor the ship's systems control panel, but he was able to watch the expert crew do everything possible to escape the ambush. Sydney was using every countermeasure the ship had, Clyde was using every weapon the ship had, and Willi was using the craft itself. They were as good as Willi had inferred.

The ambush had been well planned, and well executed. Any other crew would have lost the battle immediately and probably have inflicted few, if any, losses on the ambushers. When the ship lost main drive power to a hit in the generator pod, Johnny knew that despite the best efforts of Willi, Sydney, and Clyde, the shuttle would be boarded within a short time, despite the fact that only half a dozen of the attackers had escaped Clyde's weapons.

"Sis," Sydney said suddenly. "I want you in a suit and on the back side of that asteroid with all our oxygen. They are not going to get their hands on you."

"No way, Syd! We still have our small arms. We'll..."

"Willi, you've heard what happens to women that fall into the hands of the pirates. I'm not going to let..."

"There is one other way," Johnny said softly. "Drift us to the asteroid like he said. I have a fighter aboard. I can use it to take out the rest of them that Clyde did not get."

"What? A fighter! What the hell are you talking about?" Willi was glaring at Johnny.

"Not enough time to explain. Just drift us past the asteroid with the maneuvering engines. They won't try to board until they know Clyde is out of weapons or power. There's enough time for me to assemble the fighter and get it launched."

"You're crazy!" Willi said.

"He's Johnny Oneshot, Willi," Sydney said, looking back at the slender blue-eyed man. "She's my sister… whatever it takes, man… Could she fly it and get away?"

Johnny nodded. "Yes. That will do. I'll just have to destroy the other one."

"You're telling me there are two fighters on this shuttle?" Willi asked.

That sardonic grin was turned to her again. "Only one is fueled and armed."

"Holy Mother! Fueled and armed! On my shuttle! You know what could happen if we took a hit in the cargo hold?"

"They want the cargo, remember?" Johnny said, heading for the hold hatch at high speed. "And I'm sure it's for the fissionables you're carrying, not the fighters. They would have just destroyed us if they had known about them."

"Sydney, drift us over! I'm going back there with him!"

"Good. Take that fighter and get away from here, Willi. We'll be… Just get away, Sis."

"Like hell," Willi muttered. She registered the fact that Clyde had fired again and Sydney's confirmation of the destruction of another ambusher as she dove through the hatch behind Johnny.

He was already opening the largest of the crates in the hold. Willi's eyes flared when she saw the sleek Dominator Attack Craft. It was a new model, she saw, taking in the changes from the last small craft briefing she had conducted herself for all the crews aboard *Trinity Home*.

"One hit in here and we'd be little specks of dust, you know," Willi said as she helped Johnny open another large crate. Working expertly with him, she helped install the few projecting parts that would have made the crate too big to fit into the shuttle if the Dominator had been left fully assembled. Twice more they sensed the launch of weapons from the shuttle. Sydney and Clyde were giving them all the time they could.

"Okay," Johnny said. "You shouldn't have any trouble with the controls. "I'll suit up and open the hold doors for you. Get in."

"No," Willi said stubbornly. "I'm staying." She looked toward the hatch into the rest of the ship. "I'm not going to leave them behind." She turned her eyes back to Johnny. "I can't just run away. Can you… can you really take them all on and win?"

Johnny gave a slight nod.

"Do it. I'll suit up and open the doors." She looked at the craft and the cargo hold exterior door. "But…"

"I'll have to suit up, too and help ease it out the doors. Let's go."

It took only a couple more minutes for both of them to be in space suits. Willi heard Johnny ask Sydney through the commlink, "Any of them where they could get a visual or scan of the cargo doors?"

"Negative."

Willi saw Johnny's motion toward the cargo door controls. She hit the button to open them, and then moved to join Johnny near one of the other crates. He touched helmets with her so he could talk to her without using the commlink. "I'm going to jettison the other Dominator. It can't fall into the hands of the pirates."

She nodded and helped him ease the crate out the open door, and then watch as he very carefully gave it a nudge to head it in the direction he wanted it to go. He watched it for a moment, and then turned to the Dominator. Willi moved to the other side of the Dominator; and watched Johnny. When he motioned to her, she duplicated his movements and eased the craft out the door. It just barely fit.

He touched his helmet to hers again. "I'm going to have to ease out and around them to make sure there aren't more lying in wait. I will be back in time."

Willi did not say anything, but Johnny felt the helmet move, as if she was nodding. He pushed off and entered the tight cockpit of the Dominator.

Willi watched the canopy close. She watched the craft drift, still without power, until it disappeared behind the asteroid as they drifted past the other side. Quickly she closed the cargo hold doors and hurried back to the shuttle cockpit.

"Willi!" exclaimed Sydney. He and Clyde had both taken time to put on space suits. "You were supposed to get away!"

Willi saw him look past her to the cargo hatch. "If anything happens to you, I'm going to kill that Johnny Oneshot!"

"He'll be back," Willi said as the power died.

"Yeah," Clyde said. "You know what they say about him."

"I used to believe it," Sydney replied. "Maybe there's still time to get you hidden on the astero…"

"No," Willi said. "I would not, even if there was enough time. And I insisted he go. He was going to let me use the fighter. And after we get out of this, we are going to have a little discussion about you letting a fully fueled and armed fighter aboard without me knowing anything about it."

"Uh…gee, Willi," Sydney stammered, "I didn't know about it either. It was just two crates. Big ones. And the one smaller one. But he didn't tell us what was in them."

"Yeah. Well. For the moment, let's just get ready. I don't intend to let them have our cargo, much less this shuttle. Clyde, you have any tricks up your sleeve?"

Clyde grinned. "A couple. But they have to be closer. Visual range."

"Do it. I want to buy him some time to check things out and get back to us."

"You really think he'll be back?" Sydney asked. He suddenly could not see through the faceplate of Willi's helmet. She had activated the flash protection so he could not see her face.

"He'll be back," was what came over the commlink. Sydney decided he would be safer not reading anything into the words or tone.

Maybe she was right anyway. Johnny Oneshot was rumored to have pulled a few rabbits out of hats before.

The pirates had given up trying to board the shuttle, thanks to Clyde's actions as three of the remaining attack craft had come closer, their instruments showing the lack of power in the shuttle.

Finally, another craft launched a grapnel line, from maximum distance and managed to snag one of the ripped open power pods. They were being towed, obviously toward the pirate's mother ship.

From the radio traffic Sydney was able to monitor, it was not going to be much longer before the shuttle would be taken aboard that mother ship. "That's weird," Sydney suddenly said, making some adjustments to the communications panel.

"What?" Willi asked.

"Just lost the main ship signal in mid word."

"Look!" Clyde yelled, looking out the flight deck window. They were being towed with the cabin three quarters away from the line of travel. One of the pirate attack craft had been trailing them. It suddenly was no longer there. Only a rapidly expanding ball of debris.

Willi lunged toward the viewports and tried to look toward where the other ships would be. She saw only what looked like another debris cloud.

"I've lost every signal!" Sydney said, again making more quick adjustments.

"It's him!" Willi said, suddenly pushing back from the cockpit windows as the Dominator Attack Craft eased carefully up to the shuttle cockpit.

"I'll raise him on the commlink," Sydney said, reaching for another control. He decided then and there that Johnny Oneshot could pull a rabbit out of a hat that was not even there.

Willi put her hand on his shoulder to stop him. She was staring at Johnny, in the cockpit of the Dominator. He had a finger to the helmet where his lips would be, in the quiet sign. When he saw that Willi had seen it, his right hand went to his forehead in a small salute, the sardonic smile just slightly curling his lips. Then the Dominator, and Johnny Oneshot, were gone.

"That guy is spooky," Clyde said softly.

"Hey," Sydney said, having left the communications console to join Clyde and Willi to stare out of the cockpit windows. "What is that?"

There seemed to be something attached to the cockpit window. Quickly Willi grabbed her suit helmet and fastened it in place, and then headed for the nearest airlock. Sydney and Clyde knew better than to try to stop her.

She handed them the note when she came back inside, and then headed toward the cargo hold again. Clyde and Sydney recognized the look on Willi's face and her posture. Willi was not a happy camper.

Both looked down at the note in Sydney's hand and read the few words there.

You'll be picked up in less than a day. Thanks for your help, guys. And the less said about it, the better. Check crate JOV010101. I hope it will alleviate some of the aggravation. Please give Lady McKindrick my thanks and my apologies. This message will self-destruct in five seconds. More or less.

"What's he mean, it will self...?" Clyde suddenly exclaimed when the paper suddenly disintegrated into tiny fragments.

"Wait," Sydney suddenly said to Clyde. "How did he get that there?"

Clyde said nothing, just shook his head, one more rumor about Johnny Oneshot in the making.

Sydney and Clyde looked around when they heard Willi. She was muttering to herself as she floated toward them.

"What was in the crate?" Sydney asked.

"Luxury items," Willi growled. "A fortune in luxury items." She stopped, her nose inches from Sydney's. "Did you know he knew Mother?"

"He knows Mother? But how?" Sydney looked down at the tiny fragments that was all that was left of the note.

"So, you didn't know, either," Willi said, looking thoughtful as she let herself drift away. "I intend to find out. But for the moment, let's see what we can do to get under way, under our own power. I don't intend to be found drifting helplessly, if I can avoid it."

It did not take as long as they thought it might. They did not have much power, but they were at least controlling their direction, and had some way on, when another shuttle from *Trinity Home* pulled alongside them twenty hours later.

The other shuttle was not alone. It was escorted by a naval corvette. Sydney, Clyde, and Willi were justifiably proud when the Captain of the corvette commended them for their defeat of the pirates, even if it had resulted in the damage they had sustained. They exchanged quick glances when not one word was mentioned about Johnny Oneshot or the Dominator having destroyed the last five of the pirate attack craft.

Casually, Willi inquired about the probable mother ship of the craft that had attacked them.

"That's why we're here," replied the Captain. "We know it has to be out here somewhere. Still don't know why it didn't try to take you. You must have put the fear of the Almighty into them, destroying all their attack craft that way."

The Captain of the corvette shook her head. "For a while, we thought you had destroyed it. We found debris, but it was too far from where you were. And to be honest, not even as good as you are, could you have destroyed it with the weapons on your shuttle.

"The debris must have been from something else, some time ago. There isn't another naval vessel anywhere close, and there isn't anything else in this quadrant that could have destroyed anything larger than your shuttle that way. We'll keep looking, but the chances are that your actions chased them back to their base."

Again, the three exchanged knowing looks. Suddenly, Sydney smiled and said, "Sounds like something Johnny Oneshot could have done."

Sydney dodged the sideways kick Willi aimed at him.

"Possibly," the Captain said. "If he was in the area. The man saved me and this corvette out on the rim a couple of years back. Not to mention half of the rest of the fleet. I really hope I get to meet him someday so I can thank him personally."

"I think the guy is just a legend," the Captain's XO said.

"I know Naval Command's official version of what happened, Lieutenant. But I was there. I saw the live tracking scans." She shook her head. "Never mind. I am not going to officially contradict Naval Command." She looked at Willi. "If you and your shipmates can rig up what you need to get you back to your mother ship, we'll be on our way. I want to continue searching for that Pirate Mother Ship."

"We can handle it from here," Willi said.

Chapter Two

-

Three days later Willi stood before her mother, commander of *Trinity Home* and leader of the trading clan that called it home. "And you really don't know him?" Willi asked.

"No, child," Arabella McKindrick replied. "Of him, of course. It was he… or so it is said… that ran the blockade to bring us the fissionables that allowed the *Trinity Home* and a dozen more ships to escape destruction by the Ecronians during the Incursion."

"That was years ago," Willi said. "I was barely twelve. He would not have been much older than that himself, then."

"It was said that the pilot was a man-child. A mere boy with the maturity and skills of one much older. He never entered the ship, merely jettisoning the materials as he passed by."

"The histories say he attacked the Ecronians then, to give time for everyone to refuel and power up so they could get away," Sydney said. "People always say that he claimed that he did very little. That others did most of it."

"So, it is said," Arabella said. "It is true that he was not alone in that. Others came to our aid."

"But he was the primary cause of the total effect."

Arabella smiled. "So, I believe. Because of that, when the coded communiqué came in, I could not refuse the request. I did refuse any payment, however." She frowned slightly as she continued. "I am not pleased that he sent along that gift. And I am even less pleased that he had our communications parameters. I've yet to determine how he acquired them. He will not reveal how he acquired the knowledge."

With a sigh, Arabella added, "He did assure me that it was not from within our organization."

"Well, how else could he have got our codes and all?" Willi asked.

"I don't know," her mother replied. "But I have no reason to doubt him. Everything I've ever heard about him indicates that he would never lie."

"Leave out whole planet loads of information, but not lie," Willi said with a snort. "I cannot believe you condoned his loading an armed and fueled…" She looked around suddenly.

Arabella was smiling and Sydney grinned, despite the danger to which doing so exposed him. "I'm sure we are secure, dear," Arabella said.

Willi flushed slightly. "Of course," she said. "Still… best not to speak of some things, I suppose."

Though Sydney really did not notice, Arabella knew immediately that Willi was concealing something when her daughter's eyes dropped slightly as she said, "Considering everything that's happened, Mother, I thought I might take a break from the routine. You've said before that I work too much. I'm thinking about just going away for a while to… relax. Get away from things."

"I see," Arabella replied, studying her daughter's face for a moment.

Willi's eyes met her mother's for a quick moment, but then flicked away even more quickly. Willi frowned a bit when Sydney pitched in with his comment.

"Mother, it would be good for her to get away from things for a while. You know what the pirates might have done if she had been captured. Let her get away from these runs. I know equality is equality, but women really are at much more risk on some of these runs that we do."

Hating the thought, but deciding it would help with her plan, Willi bit back her retort. She would let them think what they might.

Seeing the flicker in Willi's eyes, Arabella was absolutely sure that Willi was up to something. Something that had nothing to do with avoiding danger. Probably quite the opposite. And quite probably something to do with the dashing and daring young Johnny Oneshot.

Sydney and Clyde had been lavish in their praise of him. Willi had acknowledged his actions, but not the way her brother and her friend had.

"Yes," Arabella said softly. "Time for you to… get away… for a while. What arrangements would you like Alfred to make?"

"Oh," Willi said, quickly, "I can handle things myself. I'm not sure exactly where I want to go, anyway."

"Of course, dear," Arabella said. "Whatever you want. Draw as much as you need from stores, and payroll."

With a quick kiss on her cheek, Willi thanked her mother and hurried from the room.

"Thanks, Mother," Sydney said, watching his sister leave, a fond smile on his face. He turned back to look at Arabella. "She was great. But I was so scared for her." He looked at his mother for long moments. "Something has to be done about the pirates, Mother. And the rumors about the Ecronians…"

He shook his head. "Clyde and I… we've been talking about it since the attack. The navy needs some experienced people. Three-year terms…"

"Of course, Syd. You must do what you feel is correct."

"I just don't like leaving you…"

"Careful, young man," Arabella said, her eyes twinkling, "Best not to imply this clan and the operation could not operate without you. Might just have to find out another way that we can manage for your term of service."

Sydney grinned and hugged his mother. "Yes, Ma'am. I'll go find Clyde, and a few others that have been thinking the same thing. I assume we can be shuttled in to enlist when we pass the closest Naval Station."

"Oh, I think it might be arranged." Though he had released her and stepped back, Arabella pulled her son to her for another hug. As she held him she said, "I'm proud of you, son. All the traders operate as independent entities, but we are part of something larger. I am glad you are willing to contribute to the safety and well-being of all."

"Aw," Sydney said as she released him. "It's not that big of a deal. I just… well…"

"I know," Arabella said softly. "You just go have your adventures and come back to me safe and sound. All of you."

Sydney was grinning again suddenly. "I have to. Can't let Willi take over without me here to give her some advice from time to time."

-

It took Willi some time to work out in her mind the probable destination Johnny Oneshot had planned on taking the two Dominators. She wondered from time to time what might have happened to the one they had jettisoned.

She almost decided to go back and try to find it, but knew that it would be impossible to find something that size among the huge asteroid swarm if it did not have a beacon, and they had not taken the time to attach one. Johnny had not wanted it found by the pirates. "Oh, well," she said, "no use worrying about it. Let's just see if I'm right about where he was going and take it from there."

Not wanting anyone to know where she was ultimately heading, Willi booked passage on a commercial liner headed back to the inner systems. From the huge transport center that served the inner systems she began her real journey toward the sector she had decided was the most likely that Johnny was headed toward. Sector ZZ-1219.

"It's the only thing that makes sense," she told herself as she settled into the small cabin aboard the fast liner that would take her on the first outward leg of the journey. "He was taking two Dominators somewhere secretly. No way was he joining the pirates. And he would not be aiding the Ecronians."

There were occasional rumors of serious problems in several border sectors, but Willi had decided on the one that a large portion of the rumors said was a hotbed of pirate activity, with some rumors stating the problems were not pirates, but the Ecronians taking advantage of the still rather tenuous presence of the Confederation since the Transition.

The last, rather long, leg of the journey, was aboard a cargo ship with a handful of passenger cabins. Willi was pleased to have a female companion aboard the ship. With a smile, she joined the woman at the small table they had made their own in the dining room. She had decided ahead of time to adopt an alias for the journey and she was comfortable now with the name she had chosen to use for the trip from the inner systems, *Marilyn Monroe*. It had caught her eye in one of the histories that Clyde was always reading on their shuttle trips. With the resources available to the trading clans, it had been no problem to create the travel documents she needed to use the name.

"Captain," Willi said, "were you able to check the cargo you are accompanying?"

Naval Space Forces Captain Janet Echart frowned. "No. They would not let me in the hold. I shouldn't say anything, I suppose... Naval Command is always right..."

Willi laughed, drawing a smile and shake of the head from Janet. She found herself drawn to the personable young woman, so different from herself.

Janet's short bob haircut of dark brown, nearly black hair, contrasted with Willi's long blonde locks.

While Janet's figure was trim, it was obvious she was in excellent physical condition. Willi looked sleek and willowy. Perhaps it was the fact that they were the only two women aboard. From what she had seen of Willi, Janet really thought it was more the fact that they seemed rather kindred souls, despite Willi's looks.

There was some steel in that backbone. Janet had seen it in the way Willi dealt with the two rather obnoxious male passengers, and a couple of the crew that were outright letches.

"I really shouldn't say anything, Marilyn," Janet continued, "but I need to vent and I really do think I can trust you not to report me to my superiors.

"I simply cannot understand why they decided to ship these craft commercially and with the contents marked plain as day. Not only are the crates marked Naval Property, but Combat Craft, no less. It doesn't make any sense. The pirates would love to get their hands on them. It's just asking for trouble doing it like this."

Janet shook her head then. "But I am an Officer and a Lady, and I do follow orders. Even ones like these."

Willi was comfortable now with the name she had chosen to use for the trip from the inner systems. It had caught her eye in one of the histories that Clyde was always reading on their shuttle trips. With the resources available to the trading clans, it had been no problem to create the travel documents she needed to use the name.

"Well, I suppose someone had a reason for it," Willi/Marilyn replied.

"Oh, I'm sure of it. I just don't have a clue what it could be. I'll just be glad to get to the base with them. I know the guys out there need the equipment.

Though I would think they would be sending them…" Captain Echart's words stopped quickly. "Sorry. I really can't discuss this anymore. I shouldn't have said what I have. I hope you understand, Marilyn."

"Sure," Willi replied. "But I have to say, I think I probably agree with you. I know you can't really discuss it, but I would think Dominators would be better for what the rumors say is happening than Triple Sevens."

Willi watched Janet's reaction closely. She could tell that Captain Echart agreed, but that she really was not going to discuss military matters. That was probably actually a good thing, Willi decided.

She would like to learn more, but quite a few rumors were surfacing that there was at least some collusion between whoever was causing all the trouble and some governmental people, either intentionally or through carelessness.

Janet, a bit surprised that Marilyn seemed to know the difference, decided to try to find out if she might know even more than she was letting on. Being beautiful did not make you stupid, despite what some people might still think.

"I'm surprised you even know the difference. Not many do."

Realizing she had let slip more than she should, Willi thought quickly. "I was on a ship attacked by pirates. It was a Dominator that saved us. I saw Triple Sevens patrolling around the Transport Center. Just don't look like they could have done what the Dominator did."

Willi hoped Janet would accept the explanation. Being beautiful did not make you stupid, despite what some people might still think. Janet did not get where she was in the Naval Space Forces being a dummy.

"Oh. You've survived a pirate attack? That must have been frightening."

"I'll say. I'm just glad there are people like you looking out for people like me." Willi smiled brightly.

Janet nodded, leaving it at that. She was definitely going to have to be a bit more careful in what she said. Marilyn Monroe seemed innocent enough, but it was a bad habit to get into, anyway.

Willi had similar thoughts. She would have to be more careful about what she said. She turned the conversation to that night's supper, which was actually quite good. The ship did have a good cook.

When she saw the look on Janet's face the day before they were to dock at the High-Mass-Core Moon-Ship base in geosynchronous orbit around the Capital Planet of Sector ZZ-1219, Willi knew something was drastically wrong. Captain Echart was ashen.

"What's wrong? What happened?"

Janet sighed and said, "They finally let me into the hold to check the Triple Sevens. They've been sabotaged. I don't know how or when, but both crates have been infected with mice. I don't know how much damage has been done, but it is extensive."

"Mice?" Willi cringed. The two-centimeter-long mechanical devices were a favorite sabotage implement. They took quite some time to inflict damage, but when a few were placed into any type of mechanism they began to cut tiny slits in anything they contacted. Everywhere they moved, something was damaged.

Any given point of damage was small, but every bit added up. Given enough of them they could totally destroy even a solid block of high density alloy. Their tiny power plants only lasted a few days, but even one could do enough damage to put sophisticated equipment out of commission for days, if not forever.

"It looks like it was only the Triple Seven crates they were put into. There'll be a team from the base meeting me at the transfer station."

"It's not your fault, Janet," Willi said. "They were out of your control from the minute they were loaded."

"I know. But I still feel responsible. I should have insisted on inspecting them. Maybe I could have found the mice and deactivated them. Something…"

Willi knew there was little, if anything, that she could say that would make Janet feel any less responsible. She tried a few more times over the next day; but had no more success than the first time.

Having said good-bye to Janet the evening before they docked with the transfer station, Willi was the first passenger off the ship. It took only moments to arrange to drop to the planet's main port.

A few inquiries at the busy terminus and she headed to a busy business section just a few minutes from the port's main entrance. Just another port dive, Willi decided, as she looked over the exterior of the building housing *Smokey's*.

It was the name that had come up consistently when she had been asking where the Naval Personnel hung out. It had not bothered her… much… the looks she usually got when she asked the question.

Willi took a deep breath, and then entered *Smokey's* with determination. Or tried to. The front doors were locked. It dawned on her that a place like *Smokey's* probably did not open until lunch, if then. "More likely early evening," she muttered to herself.

Despite having been in and out of more ports than she could probably remember, all of the crews from *Trinity Home* usually just went in and out. Very seldom did any of them hit the local places. At least, not in the outlying sectors.

With a slight shrug, Willi walked around the side of the building, knowing that while they might not be open for some time, it was likely there was someone inside, working.

She was right. It was not all that difficult to get a job, just as she had intended, she found. It just was not the job she had planned on, as a server or bartender. The only openings they had for her, so said the little runt that was Smokey, was entertainer.

Or, "*Entertainer!*" he said again, winking and leering at her. "We have an arrangement with the establishment next door, sweetie. We get ten percent, they get ten percent and you keep eighty."

"I think I will just stick with singing," Willi said firmly.

"Don't mind him," said the more or less normal looking man that suddenly joined them from the doorway just past where they stood talking. "Go get the main room set for tonight, Slick."

He turned to Willi after watching the man shuffle away. "Sorry, Miss. Slick oversteps his bounds from time to time when someone such as yourself enters."

Willi felt herself brighten considerably. She had thought that her singing ability, slight as it was, would probably be adequate in the place, but perhaps there was another position available.

"I understand." She held out her hand. "I'm Marilyn Monroe. I'm looking for a server or bartending position."

The man shook her hand firmly. "Nice to meet you, Marilyn. I'm the real Smokey. And sorry. The only position I have open is for a singer. And of course, B-girls. I doubt you'd have any trouble getting licensed."

"Oh. But I thought…" She made a slight motion to where the runt had disappeared.

"Slick doesn't have the authority to hire or fire; but did happen to be right about the positions I have open. Just how good of a singer are you?"

Her eyes dropping slightly. "Oh… average… I guess… I…"

"No matter," Smokey said, with a slight wave of his hand. "You've got the looks, and your voice isn't bad. As long as you wear either short dresses, or tight dresses, it really doesn't matter."

"But…"

Smokey lifted a very expressive eyebrow.

"I'm not a B-girl," Willi said firmly.

"It's not only not required, I don't allow it. The talent is completely separate from the talent. That's why the last three singers I had here are no longer here. I pay good for singers, but most of them can make quite a bit more next door. I noticed you did not ask about the pay. That's usually the first question."

Willi noted the keen interest he was showing. "I'm not desperate," she replied easily. "But I don't plan on becoming so, either. Just want to make sure I get enough together to get back home. Used a little more on my journey than I planned."

She was glad he left it at that. "When do I start?"

"Tonight. Eighteen hundred hours. Thirty-minute sets, thirty-minute breaks. You can mingle, if you want, and accept any drinks and gifts. You might get a few. Lots of lonely, appreciative men out here. Four sets.

"The strippers come on at twenty-two hundred. That's about the time the family men go home and the rougher crowd comes in. But I mean it, no turning tricks, even after twenty-two hundred hours.

"I want the two operations completely separate. Keeps me out of trouble with the authorities. I get a lot of military trade here, and they insist on legal operation. Anyone gets me blackballed, and they will regret it greatly."

"Understood," Willi said quietly. It was obvious that Smokey meant what he said. "It won't be a problem. I… ah… have one suitable dress. Where would you suggest I pick up another one? Or two? Inexpensively."

Smokey grinned. "Just check the dressing room. The one with the star. There's probably a dress or two that will fit you, left by some of the previous talent."

"I think I would prefer to get something new," Willi said firmly.

With a shrug, Smokey said, "Suit yourself. Try Wendi's. Some of the girls get outfits there. Down two and over three."

Willi nodded. "We need to do any new hire paperwork?"

"Cash end of shift every night. Your responsibility to track for the Taxman. Your thumbprint will be on my copy of the receipt, so I'm covered when they collect my records end of quarter. What you report is up to you." He was already walking away. "Be here by seventeen thirty so my head bartender, also the MC, can show you around and get the mikes set for you."

She stood there for a moment, at a slight loss, but then shrugged and turned to leave. Willi did not see the man watching her from the dark area near the bar.

Johnny Oneshot's lips curled, the smile, still sardonic, as usual, was broader than normal. He slipped his comm device into the hidden pocket in the work coveralls he was wearing and went back to his swamper duties.

Even in this day and age there was manual cleaning to be done. "Marilyn Monroe, huh?" He chuckled. "I wonder if she knows the history of that name?"

Looking completely different now, standing straight and tall, rather than stooped, and without the contact lenses that changed his eyes, and wig that completed the down-on-his-luck swamper persona look, Johnny Oneshot sat at the bar of *Smokey's* nursing a drink as he watched the early crowd begin to gather.

He flipped the bartender a large credit chip and said, "I'll be back later, Cherokee. How about putting a bottle of *Smokey's Bubbles* on ice for me? May want to celebrate something tonight."

Cherokee's flat black eyes flickered just a tiny bit. The man had been coming in for over two weeks now and spent liberally. He tipped even better. There was something about him that kept nagging at Cherokee, but he still had not been able to put his finger on it.

"It will come to me," he said to himself, heading to find Smokey to get the okay to get the bottle of *Bubbles*. Everything that expensive was kept locked away securely.

Willi had found a rooming house close by and transferred her few items of luggage there. Another hour and she was in Wendi's, picking out two dresses.

It took longer than she expected. It seemed like every dress she was inclined to try was either two sizes to small, or came down to her thighs, rather than past them. Finally, she did locate a couple of dresses similar to the one she had brought with her.

With all three dresses and a few other personal items in a small case, Willi headed back to *Smokey's* well before the mandated five thirty. She found herself with time on her hands before her first set. Cherokee had been quick and efficient.

It took him only a few minutes to show her around, including her small, but clean, dressing room. Setting up the sound and lighting system had taken only a few more minutes. It was automated; and would track her anywhere on the stage and even out in the bar and dancing area.

All she had to do was sing a few words into the setup microphone and fasten a tiny locator button to the back of her dress and the setup was finished.

Another couple of minutes and she had selected the songs that she would sing. "The only ones I **can** sing," she said silently to herself.

She went back to the dressing room to check her appearance one last time. Willi shook her head and frowned, wishing for a moment she had not brought this particular dress. It had been in the crate of luxury items that Johnny Oneshot had left on the shuttle as some type of extra payment or something. It was a red shimmer dress and fit her almost like a second skin. It was an elegant dress, rather than a cheap and tawdry one. But it was still much more sultry than she was used to wearing.

Willi still was not sure why she had brought it. She certainly had not been planning on singing in a night club in it. "Sure does fit the bill for it, though," she said to herself, refastening the old fashioned bow holding her hair gathered at the base of her neck, the length flowing down her back almost to her waist.

One last deep breath, which she held for a moment, and then released, Wilhelmina 'Willi' 'Marilyn Monroe' McKindrick went out to sing her first song.

Fully aware that the sound system really could make almost anyone sound, at the very least, decent, Willi was amazed at the response she got to her first song. And it continued with each successive song in the first half hour set. She had had no intention of mingling, as Smokey had put it, with the patrons, but she found herself out among them, responding graciously to each person who praised her performance.

Even more surprising, was the lack of offense when she declined the many drink offers, citing her need to keep her voice protected. Finally, after traversing the room, she took a stool at the bar, at the far end. "Whew!" she said and took the tall glass of ice water Cherokee handed her.

The big man of American Indian ancestry was grinning. "And here I had the impression you really had not done this before."

"That sound system really does all the work," Willi quickly said.

"Yeah. Right. Take it easy till your next set if you want. Just give me a high sign if anyone bothers you. Of course, you can wait in the dressing room if you want."

"I think I'll just wait here for now," Willi said, her eyes surveying the small crowd. There were no problems as a person came up to her occasionally. None did more than talk to her for a minute or two. She found it was actually easier to study the people in the place, without seeming to, with the people coming up to her and leaving, as it allowed her eyes to roam at will.

She was able to talk to several Naval service personnel, including a handful of pilots. Willi quickly realized she was not going to get much information from them in these conversations.

Willi was hearing more just by listening to nearby conversations. Mostly talk of the pirates between Spaceman One Stripe, Two Stripe, and Three Stripe ratings, with no Petty Officer grades and up referring to Pirates or Ecronians at all. At least that she could hear.

There was one mention of Ecronians, and some grumbling about the Governor and her administration of the sector. Again, between two Spaceman ratings.

At the end of her third set, her eyes were drawn to the man sitting at the far end of the bar. He was by himself, she noted, and sat with his back to the room, nursing the drink. Cherokee would stop and have a word with him from time to time.

A pleased grin split the bronze face as Cherokee moved toward her. He stopped, stooped, and brought out a small bottle from a reefer unit under the counter, and then continued toward her. "Compliments of the gentleman at the far end, Marilyn." He poured the pale bubbly liquid into a tall narrow stemmed glass, and then recapped the bottle.

Willi recognized the bottle; but was so surprised she did not say anything until Cherokee was already handing her the glass. "But this is *Bubbles*!" she finally managed to say.

"Absolutely," Cherokee said. "One of the really good ones that Smokey brings in."

Willi's eyes cut down the bar again and she frowned. The man was gone. "Who was that?" she asked.

Cherokee turned. "Damn. Gone already." He turned back to Willi and opened his mouth to say something, then closed it, a confused look crossing his face. "Actually… he's been coming in here for a couple of weeks. I don't actually know his name, I just realized. I've always thought of him as *The Guy*.

"Seems to have plenty of money and is always pleasant. And tips good. All of us. I… uh… well… he said to give you the bottle with his compliments."

"Oh. Well, I wish you had not opened that bottle, Cherokee. I know how expensive that stuff… this stuff is. Lordy, but I would not want it to go to waste." Willi took a small sip of the precious liquid. Light and airy, it tickled the tongue, then slid down the throat most pleasantly.

"Wow!" she said. "No wonder it is so expensive." Willi had transported bottles of *Bubbles* before; but had never tasted it. She did not really drink much alcohol or similar liquid refreshment, but had experienced a few really good drinks. *Bubbles* outshone them all.

Another couple of sips and she looked at Cherokee. "But how are you going to sell the rest? I doubt one in a hundred could afford to buy a drink of this, and I know it doesn't keep very long."

It pleased Cherokee no end when he was able to tell Willi, "He gave you the bottle, Marilyn, not just a single glass."

Willi wasted just a bit of the drink when she nearly choked. She cleared her throat, and then suddenly flushed, looking over at Cherokee. "You just cork that back up and give it to him the next time he comes in. Even if it was not *Smokey's* policy, there is no way he's getting anything from me, just because of that bottle!"

"Good to hear that," came the voice behind her.

Willi spun around on the stool. "Smokey! Look. I did not ask him to…"

"I know, Precious. That guy has been buying expensive drinks for two weeks. Never stays more than a few minutes when the dancers start; but leaves twenty credits apiece for them for Cherokee to distribute. Don't worry about it.

"I would have been tempted to give you a bottle myself. You have this crowd totally enamored. I surprise even myself when I say that I'm giving you twenty percent more than I said, doll. Keep it up, and you could go far in this business." He walked away.

"But…"

"Don't argue with the man," Cherokee said. "I've never seen him do that before. I actually think he might have at least opened a bottle… but give you one… uh… probably not. Gotta go. Customers."

Willi savored the glass of *Bubbles*, and when Cherokee stopped nearby again she let him refill the glass. "Cherokee… have a glass. Please. You've made my first night here much easier than it might have been."

"You sure?"

Willi nodded eagerly.

"Just a small one," Cherokee said, almost reverently.

Willi decided then to share the rest with the other servers that were working the room, at the end of the shift. She told Cherokee what she planned.

He did not really try to talk her out of it; but did tell her it really was not necessary.

She was glad she had done so, however, when all five of the women and the one male server thanked her profusely and indicated she had not needed to do it.

Apparently, there had been at least three small groups that had left, then returned with numerous friends to hear and see Willi sing. And their enjoyment led to big tips.

Despite offers from her co-workers to go and do something after hours, Willi declined, leaving shortly after her last set. It had been a full day and she was tired, though exhilarated. Despite, or perhaps because of it all, she was asleep shortly after her head hit her pillow.

After a week, Willi decided that perhaps she had been wrong about coming to the sector. Rumors abounded about everything. Pirates. Ecronians. Governmental corruption. Even Johnny Oneshot's name was mentioned on a fairly regular basis. But only as common knowledge rumors, like the ones Sydney and Clyde had once mentioned.

Despite all she had heard, there had been nothing solid about him or the Dominator he was flying when he left the shuttle that day. Willi also decided that *The Guy*, as Cherokee still referred to him, was as elusive as Johnny Oneshot. She had seen him a couple of times in the bar, but he disappeared every time before she could work her way over to him.

Though willing, Cherokee had not been able to elicit any information from him, other than a response to her thank you.

It had been an adventure, Willi decided, but she was a pilot and a trader at heart. Time to get back to *Trinity Home* and get on with her life. Thinking she could track down someone like Johnny Oneshot on her own was silly.

Especially considering he was involved in something to do with Confederation business and pirates and Ecronians and…

Willi shook her head. She was letting the rumors influence her. They were all unrelated rumors. No reason to think Johnny Oneshot was connected to any of them, much less all of them.

"But what about those Dominators?" she whispered to herself. Another shake of her head and she decided she had better let Smokey know that her last night would be the night before the next passenger liner was due to depart, in just under a week.

Checking her dress one last time in the mirror in the dressing room, Willi made sure the locator button was in place. Still convinced that it was only the sound and light system that made her performances so entertaining, she wanted to make sure the system would work.

As the second set that evening began, the already huge crowd was increased by five. Willi did not let the sight of Captain Janet Echart and her four companions in naval uniform distract her, though she did acknowledge Janet's presence with a tiny head motion.

Upon seeing, and then recognizing, Marilyn, Janet hesitated, but followed the others as the server directed them to a table that was being cleared. She had to smile when Lieutenant Charlie Chambers looked at her and asked, "You know her?"

"We met on the ship on the way out here."

Charlie's look was rather censorious. "And you did not tell us she was singing here? And what she looked like?"

"I did not know she was singing here," Janet said. "She was just someone I met aboard the liner. She never really said what she was doing out here."

"Uh… you think you could wangle me an introduction?"

"That goes for me, too," said Lieutenant Halpern, his eyes having left Willi only enough to avoid running over something or someone as they had made their way to the table.

Having heard the two men's request; and seen the affect Willi had on men the past few days, the server grinned and said, "Marilyn usually comes out into the crowd once or twice a night. I'm sure you'll get a chance to meet her."

Captain Butler chuckled. "Easy, Gentlemen. From what I'm hearing, this one is different from the last few Smokey has brought in here."

"And besides," said the other woman in the group, Lieutenant Rebecca Sorenson, "I thought you three brought us two for a nice night away from the base."

"So right, Lieutenant," replied Captain Butler. He grinned at his two male companions, both now looking a bit chagrinned. They had both been after him to talk the two female officers into accompanying them since Captain Echart had arrived with the Triple Sevens and Lieutenant Sorenson had rotated in to replace a nurse ending her enlistment.

Suddenly he was glad he had come planetside, Bill Butler decided. He had not come down since the last time, after Gunderson had been killed. And that had been a big disappointment. The other entertainer had been ugly, a terrible singer, and after Naval Personnel money any way she could get it.

Even Charlie had been disappointed and had gone back to the base not long after Captain Butler. But there was something about *Smokey's* this night that was different. The only thing he could **see** different was Marilyn.

"And she really never mentioned she was going to sing here?" Bill asked, leaning forward so Janet could hear him.

Janet shook her head. She had been reluctant to come, despite the way the Captain had been treating her. He had never in any way implied that the damage to the Triple Sevens had been her responsibility.

He had worked diligently with her to try to determine where and how the mice had been inserted into the containers carrying the combat craft. They had run into one dead end after another.

Despite it, Captain Butler had never wavered in his support of her actions when the base commander had more than implied the sabotage had been her fault, perhaps even her doing.

And, like her, knowing the Triple Seven, though a more capable craft than the F-321 Combat Craft now deployed, was far from the ideal choice for the type of activity being conducted by the squadrons, he was still helping her in any way he could.

Even having been able, with difficulty, of reassembling one intact craft from the original two, the training was still not going to be accomplished. Another craft had been requested and turned down immediately.

The F-321 had master-slave network capability for training, but the system was not compatible with the similar F-777 system. The intention of having Janet fly master in one of the Triple Sevens and one of the squadron pilots fly second in the other, for training, was simply not possible now.

Even simulators had been denied. Putting even a good F-321 pilot in the F-777 and having them learn hands on, while doable, would take, as Captain Butler had put it, forever and a day. It would have been counterproductive. What training that was accomplished was the expert use of the operable Triple Seven by Janet during sorties with the squadrons.

Bill watched Janet unobtrusively for a few moments as she watched the entertainer. "At least," he said silently to himself, "The others are learning something. Just watching her in action they are picking up information that can be used if we ever do get more of the Triple Sevens. Not to mention just good solid combat techniques."

Janet turned her head and saw Bill's eyes shift from her to the singer. She smiled at him and he smiled back. Slightly. Janet looked back at Marilyn and her thoughts turned to Captain Butler.

He was everything she had heard. The more she learned of the situation in the sector the more her admiration and respect for him grew. It was not just that he had stood by her and supported her when Commander Calhoun had essentially accused her of the sabotage, but his untiring efforts to control the situation in the sector, as well.

She really had not believed that any of the activity had been anything but pirates. Certainly not Ecronians, as some of the rumors said. Butler had been careful to follow the official word, but Janet had seen what he did and how he did it.

It was obvious he thought the Ecronians were behind what was going on. Janet was beginning to believe he might be right. At least partially.

He was a remarkable man. The type of man that… Janet quickly put that line of thought out of her head. The song that Marilyn was singing was the cause. It was a romantic ballad.

She looked around the room. The dance floor was packed, and many of the obvious couples in the rest of the audience were holding hands. More than a few were kissing, rather passionately in some cases.

Janet did not realize she had sighed. Bill noticed the slight sigh and studied Janet unobtrusively for a moment. She was very perceptive, with tremendous combat skills. He knew she would sense his gaze if he looked at her for long. Her senses were extraordinary. Her look was different from the woman singing. Just as beautiful, he thought, just in a more mature way.

When he had learned who it was that was to train his people in the Triple Sevens, he had done a bit of research. Her record was impressive.

After seeing her resolve, still unsatisfied, to find the perpetrators of the sabotage, and then her untiring diligence to assemble one useable craft from the remains of the two, he was convinced that her record was just the tip of the iceberg of what constituted an exceptional Naval Officer and person.

"Whom," he said softly to himself, "is every bit a desirable woman." He sighed ever so slightly himself without realizing it.

Very observing, and clever, eyes picked up on both Janet's and Bill's sighs, as well as the way they had looked at one another when the other had not been looking.

It had taken the last few weeks to determine to his satisfaction that Captain William "Bill" "Telstar" Butler was just exactly what he seemed. A dedicated career Naval Officer, with an exemplary record.

The only exception was his not quite controlled expression of his opinions of what was happening in this sector. What Johnny had learned about Captain Janet Echart was similar.

Both were loyal to the Confederation, willing, and able to deal with whatever was actually going on in this sector. Which was pretty much exactly what Bill Butler suspected and feared was going on, only more so, Johnny was sure.

Johnny smiled when he looked over at Willi. She was just finishing the last song of the set and already people were clamoring for her attention. He eased back just a bit more. She was as perceptive as Captains Butler and Echart. Had the same sensory awareness. That was part of what made all three of them such good pilots.

It was difficult for even him to observe them without being observed himself, despite having inherited from one of his ancestors from the 21st Century, her amazing abilities of perception.

It was a rather pleasant distraction he allowed himself for a few moments, watching Willi move among the crowd, on her way to the table where the five Naval officers sat. Fully aware that Captain Butler had excused himself as the song was ending he gave the man credit for easing up to him as clandestinely as he did.

Johnny felt the sidearm touch his back for just a moment, then pull back as the quiet, strong voice said softly into his ear, "You've been watching me and my shipmates. This isn't the first time. Either come with me out to the Shore Patrol officers quietly, or resist. Your choice. I don't really care either way. I don't like being watched."

"Certainly, Captain Butler. But there is no need to involve the Shore Patrol, or anyone else that might not understand the seriousness of what is going on."

Johnny had not moved. He was still watching Willi out of the corners of his eyes, as he always did now, so as not to draw her gaze toward him.

"I've been waiting for the chance to talk to you without undue notice. If you'll join me at the far end of the bar, while the young lady works the crowd, I'll explain."

"I don't think you…" Bill could not stop the surprise from registering on his face when the man he was holding under the gun was suddenly facing him, Bill's sidearm now in the man's hand, pointed not quite at Bill.

"Sorry," Johnny said, reversing the weapon and handing it back to Bill. "I don't want this to get out of hand or draw attention to us." He met Bill's steady gaze with his own.

"Tango Royal Alpha Victor India Sierra." The words were barely audible, but Johnny knew Bill heard them. The sidearm disappeared and Johnny saw the tiny nod.

It was a few moments before they made their way individually to the far end of the bar. Another couple of steps and they were out of sight of everyone except Cherokee and the other bartender on duty, who was too busy to notice anything except mixing drinks.

Cherokee took note but thought nothing of it. It was not unusual for *The Guy* to buy drinks for servicemen and women. He was a little surprised that it was Telstar, but then, even he had taken a drink in *Smokey's* before, though never more than one.

"Explain the Travis code," Captain Butler said as soon as he made sure no one was close, or anyone else was paying any attention.

"I'm lending a hand to Naval Intelligence," Johnny said. "What is going on out here is not being totally ignored. Your official reports have been watered down, as I am sure you know. Word through your friends got to those who needed to know."

Bill frowned. "I don't like the idea that some of my friends could be in trouble because of my exasperation…"

"They are not, I assure you," Johnny said. "This is neither the time, nor the place for a discussion." He gave a set of coordinates, knowing Captain Butler would have them locked in his memory immediately. "Your next patrol, make sure your flight is well on the way to base, and then find a reason to tail off. I'll be there."

Bill was not quite sure why he agreed. There was just something about the man. It was not just the Travis code word. The set of coordinates were in a sensor dead zone amongst a deadly grouping of asteroids loaded with magnetic and radiation signatures that even the best of modern sensors could not penetrate.

He made his way quickly back to the table, not wanting any attention drawn to what had taken place by being gone too long. Bill had to smile at the group at the table as he rejoined them. Lieutenant Chambers was in heaven. Lieutenant Halpern likewise. Janet and Rebecca were looking on, mostly with amusement, as Marilyn was handling the two men with aplomb.

"Captain Butler," Janet said, "I'd like to introduce you to Marilyn Monroe. Marilyn, this is Captain Butler. I think I mentioned him…" Her words faded away and she hoped her slight blush was not obvious. She had waxed rather eloquently about him, she remembered. Hopefully Marilyn would not say anything to embarrass her.

Marilyn nodded slightly and held out her hand. "Captain, I've heard a lot about you since I've been here. You are something of a legend in these parts. It is a pleasure to meet Telstar, Protector of the Sector."

Janet's eyes widened.

"Lord," Bill said, taking the woman's hand in a quick handshake. He was impressed with the strength in the slender hand. "Not that again," he continued, as their hands parted after the quick, firm handshake. "Do not believe everything you hear. I'm just a sailor doing his job."

Willi grinned. "Sounds like a Johnny Oneshot-ism to me."

"See, what did I tell you, Bill?" Charlie said. "People are comparing you to him now on a regular basis."

"The man is a hero. Saved thousands of lives, several times. I'm just doing my job." Bill shrugged and sat down, wanting to change the subject. "Definitely can't compare his exploits with mine. My main claim to fame will undoubtedly be whatever faux pa I am bound to commit at that inaugural ball in a few days."

The other officers laughed.

"The Governor's Inaugural?" Willi asked. "I've heard about that. Supposed to be the party of the century."

"I'm surprised some dignitary hasn't snapped you up as their date," Charlie said.

Willi laughed. "Oh, I think they have better companions than I to accompany them to that." She did not mention that she had been asked, by several different men that had to go, to accompany them. She had already made the decision to leave that day. Not to mention, she would not have gone with any of them, anyway.

"You are going to do just fine, Bill," Janet said. She looked over at Willi. "He claims he can't dance and expects the Governor to make him get out on the dance floor with her."

With a smile, Willi asked, "You are a handsome man, Captain, but surely you have little to worry about. With all the other elegant men in politics that will be there, and her purported dislike of the military, is it really likely she'll ask you?"

When the others laughed and Captain Butler's face took on a sour look, Willi looked at them inquisitively. "I'm missing something, I take it," she said.

"Oh, yes," Janet said with a grin. "Captain Butler is her official escort."

"Oh," Willi said. "I see." Suddenly she smiled broadly. "So, he does need to get some practice. My next set will definitely have a couple of suitable numbers for you to give him a refresher lesson."

"Oh, no," Janet said quickly, "I don't think…"

"I'd be glad to," Lieutenant Sorenson quickly offered.

Reluctant as he was to have Janet in his arms for a dance, for reasons that had nothing to do with his abilities in that activity, it being more that he actually wanted to but did not consider it a good idea, since he did want to, the idea of dancing with Rebecca, who it was obvious would absolutely love the idea, Bill decided on the safer option.

"I think perhaps Captain Echart would be a bit more appropriate instructor. She is much closer to my age and…"

Seeing the rather shocked look on Janet's face and hearing the sudden laughter from the others, including Willi, Bill felt himself color slightly and he hurriedly added, "I did not mean…"

"It's a lost cause, Captain," Janet said. "Your foot is in it, intentionally or not. Pretty much the only way to not further embarrass yourself… or me… is to dance once with me, and then we can leave. How's that?"

Bill sighed. "If I survive it."

"That's not really helping the situation," Janet said, a small smile playing on her lips.

"Don't worry," Willi said with a grin. "I'll make it a really slow one so you can hold on to her really tightly to support yourself."

"Oh, lord!" Bill looked shocked.

"For someone with skills in so many areas, your social skills really are a bit rusty, aren't they?" Janet said, almost archly.

"I didn't mean…"

Janet smiled. "I know. Don't worry about it. I'm actually not that good of a dancer, myself. I don't know if I'll be helping or hurting."

"You can't be that bad. You move like a cat in null gravity. You've got all the moves a good dancer does."

"Maybe he's not that rusty after all," Charlie said with a grin.

"Wait a minute! I didn't mean…" He fell silent as they all laughed again.

Willi excused herself and headed back toward the bar to get ready for her next set. A quick drink of water, and a few minutes in the dressing room, to get away from the crowd, and she was ready. It was with a broad smile on her face that she went onto the stage.

"A special dance song request, ladies and gentlemen," she announced, with a look toward the table where Captain Butler and Captain Echart both had somewhat apprehensive looks on their faces. It took rather strong pushes to get the two up. They really only did it to avoid any further attention being drawn to them.

"I really wasn't trying…" Bill started saying, taking Janet in his arms.

"I know. It just sort of got out of hand. That Marilyn is something. She's really good at this stuff."

"She is." Bill suddenly realized that, while by no means a bad dancer, he had never really considered himself a good dancer, the movements seemed to come rather easily with Janet as his partner. Held closely. Really closely. And she did not seem to object.

Willi had to admit to herself, as she entered the dressing room after her last set, that she had had one of the best times of her life that night. The audience had seemed to really enjoy her performances, and it had been delightful to see Janet's reaction to dancing with Captain Butler.

Her comments about him aboard the liner had seemed filled with a bit of longing. Willi smiled again at the memory of seeing Captain Butler holding Janet as they danced. He had looked quite comfortable with the situation, after the first few moments. They had danced three times together. Suddenly Willi sighed. "It must be nice," she said aloud. "To dance with someone like that."

"I hear it can be, especially to a live performer, with her heart in the music. Marilyn."

Willi whirled around. "Johnny! I mean…What are you doing here? Get out of my dressing room!" Her voice had gone from pleased recognition to surprise to questioning to anger, as had her expression.

"Of course. My apologies." He was not actually in the room, standing just outside the open doorway.

"Wait! Wait! Get in here!" Willi stepped over and grabbed his arm, pulling him inside the dressing room, her eyes darting down the hall to make sure no one saw them.

She turned toward him when the door was securely closed and locked. Willi had not really noted his appearance at first. Taking a moment to look him over now her jaw dropped and her eyes widened. "You! You're *The Guy!* What… what…"

Suddenly she sat down in the chair before the makeup mirror, her back to the vanity. She stared at him for a moment more, several different expressions crossing her face in the short time frame. "Are you okay? You just left the shuttle and… I came out here looking for you… I just…"

"I'm fine. Just how did you actually find me?" Johnny asked. "I actually somewhat pride myself on not being able to be found when I don't want to be."

"I thought as much, but after all, where else would you be going with Dom…" She stopped herself, though Johnny had not given any indication she should not mention them. "Anyway," she continued, "it just seemed obvious you'd be around here somewhere. I now realize that you've been here the entire time."

Johnny noted that her expression was beginning to edge over into annoyance at that realization. She stood up then and with a rather insistent tone, asked, "Why didn't you say something before this? You obviously knew me. And why haven't you told anyone who I really am?"

Johnny shrugged. "I needed to figure out what you were doing here, and why you were doing whatever it was you were doing. I was pretty sure you didn't come out here to take an entertainer's job."

When Johnny stopped speaking, Willi waited a few moments, expecting him to continue. He had only partially answered her question. A very small partially. "Well?" she asked then.

When the sardonic grin appeared, and he asked, "Well what?" Willi managed to maintain control, difficult as it was.

"You did not give me a real answer." Her eyes narrowed, and she was almost glad she was already upset, for her color was already a bit red, so thinking about part of the reason she had come looking for him and coloring slightly because of it she was sure went unnoticed. "Just what do you think it is I am doing?"

"Well, I'm pretty sure I know what you are doing now, and why, but I'm still not quite clear on what got you here initially."

"I… wait a minute. You did it again. Tell me what you think I'm doing… uh… at least now."

Johnny looked at her evenly. "You've started wondering about what is going on in this sector and are trying to find out. What you are doing is very dangerous, Miss McKindrick. Very dangerous. For reasons you probably already suspect, but for some I really doubt you have an inkling."

"I'm not so sure about that, but… yes... I have realized that my subtle inquiries might stir up some trouble if they become too obvious. I was already planning on leaving, but not because of that."

Johnny turned to leave. "Good. It has been good to see you again. You really are a very good entertainer."

Hurriedly Willi added, "But I've decided to stay for a while longer." She was not aware that she looked a bit apprehensive, waiting for some response from him. It was a bit slow in coming.

He paused at the door, then did finally turn to face her again. Willi was almost relieved to see that usually annoying sardonic grin on his face again. "I'm not that surprised," he said quietly. "It's obvious that you've learned much of what I have. I really would rather you leave."

Will just shook her head, watching him.

"I could make it happen."

Willi realized she was sure that he could probably accomplish it, and she was suddenly just as sure he would not. "I don't doubt it. But you won't."

Still just watching her face for a moment he finally said, "No. I won't. Sit down. Please. I need to fill you in on some things. Mostly for your safety, so you won't say or do the wrong thing to the wrong person or at the wrong time."

When she did, Johnny pulled up the only other chair in the room, a simple straight back one, and sat down straddling the seat, his arms resting on the back. Willi found herself entranced at Johnny's concise description of the situation in the sector, and how it could, and would, affect the future of the Confederation.

"You've heard all the rumors by now, I'm sure," he said. "You're sharp, so I'm also fairly certain you've weeded out the patently erroneous ones."

Willi expected him to ask her what she knew, or at least believed she knew, but he did not. He simply continued. "The official word is that the pirates are well organized and equipped, and that they alone are doing everything that has been happening.

"They are well organized and well equipped and are doing much of what is happening. The rumors that the Ecronians are behind it are also true, to a degree. There are Ecronians involved. A few as part of the pirate band, and a group with their own interests being used as a front.

"The Ecronian government is not actively sponsoring the incursions and other activity. They certainly are not doing anything to limit or stop it. They want what is happing to continue and to ultimately succeed.

"If it does, they will step in and take control of the sector. Those who are fomenting this situation have no real idea of what they are unleashing on the sector, or themselves."

Johnny looked away for a moment and sighed. "Despite the fact that there are many in the Confederation who do believe there is something amiss here, and have a fair understanding of what it is, they are totally resistant to the idea of the actual situation.

"The transition is going very well in most places. The Triumvirate forces have, for the most part, cooperated since the surrender.

"The idea of more warfare is simply so repugnant at the moment after the recent events, that there are some that, though they should know better, refuse to acknowledge the danger the Ecronians are to the Confederation.

"When the Triumvirate was in power, the military, as a matter of course, was powerful. Their defeat of the Ecronian forces everywhere in the galaxy they were encountered has turned the Ecronian government into a cautious body. The moment they see that an opportunity exists, however, they will take action. If things are allowed to continue here as they are, that time will be soon.

"Fortunately, there are enough people in the military in positions to do at least a few things to get things ready. But they have to work behind the scenes, often at risk to their careers.

"Even those humans whose machinations are behind this have no idea what the outcome will be if the Ecronians become entrenched in this sector. They think they will have power and wealth… will control this sector. They will die, if they are lucky. The rumors of what the Ecronians do with humans don't even begin to…"

Johnny shook his head. "You're better off not knowing," he said after moment. "What the pirates do is nothing compared to what happens to humans at the hands of the Ecronians, when they believe there is no chance of retaliation."

Willi knew she paled slightly. "What Sydney said when we were attacked… you did leave me… us, I mean… there…"

"I was sure no harm would come to you… of that nature," Johnny said slowly, looking at her. "So, when you offered…"

"I did suggest you leave, didn't I?" Willi asked, watching his face carefully. She had already discovered he had almost absolute control of his features. But there was something in his eyes…

Quickly she looked away for a moment, then back. "So, what do we do?" she asked. "And," she continued, boldly "is it true that the Governor is part of it?" Those rumors existed, but tenuously. It was just, for some reason, they just seemed true to her.

"Yes," Johnny said quietly. "And knowing this puts you in grave danger. Reconsider going back to your regular life."

A shake of her head was the only reply he received.

"Didn't think so. Okay." He looked at her again, for a long time, before he continued. "I am very good at what I do… am doing here. I could accomplish more, more quickly, with a bit of help in a couple of matters."

"I'll help," Willi said immediately.

The sardonic smile was back. "Yeah. I figured. It's going to be even more dangerous than what've you've done up to this point."

Willi grinned, almost impishly. "Oh yeah? Ever tried being a pretty girl in a tight dress in the middle of a crowded room of sailors a long way from home?"

"Point taken," Johnny said with a real smile this time. It faded after a moment, and he added, "I just want you to be aware and careful at all times."

She looked around the room, a worried look crossing her face. "Perhaps we should have picked a different place to talk… this room isn't what you'd call soundproof."

Willi did not see where he pulled it from, but Johnny held up his comm device. "It is with this. Don't ever say anything about any of this to anyone that I haven't indicated is safe. And then, only where you know there is no chance of being heard, verbally or electronically.

"Those involved think their activities are totally unknown. That is going to change very soon. When it does, they will begin to take active measures to insure their part in what is going on is kept secret until it is a fait accompli."

"Why are you so sure they will find out we know?"

"Not we. Me. I'm going to tell the Governor I know what is going on at the Inaugural Ball. Speaking of which, I…"

"Are you nuts? You can't just tell her! From everything I've picked up, she could easily have you killed! Even right there at the ball!"

It was no sardonic smile this time. It was feral, Willi noted. "I'm not that easy to kill," Johnny said. "That part of the rumors about me are true. Besides, she won't know it is me telling her. It'll be Johnny Oneshot telling her."

"You are Johnny Oneshot!"

"But only you know that. And soon, Captains Butler and Echart."

"You trust them?"

"Don't you?" Johnny asked.

"Well… I am inclined to… but I only just met Butler tonight. And I only met Janet on the way out here…" She studied his face. "Still… everything I have learned… tells me to trust them."

"I believe they can be trusted. To be on the safe side, however, if you don't have anything better to do tomorrow, I'd like you to fly a little high cover for me while I bring Captain Butler into the fold." He smiled then, and added, "And unless I miss my guess, Captain Echart. She is one sharp cookie. Just like Butler."

"I agree about Janet, but what do you mean you want me to fly high cover?"

"Oh. I thought you would know that expression. It means…"

"I know what it means!" Willi said. "But how in the world am I…"

"Just be ready tomorrow morning at six. I'll pick you up at your boarding house. You'll learn the rest then."

"But…" Seeing the steady look he gave her, Willi fell silent, then added, "All right. I'll be ready. I don't have any flight clothes with me, of course."

"Everything you need will be provided." Johnny rose and turned toward the door again. And again he paused, hand near the control. "Just one last thing. I need to be at the Ball, as you know. I can get in several different ways, of course. The easiest, and the one I can make use of most effectively, is to show up with an escort. One that can be distracting when I need a distraction."

He looked at her, meeting her eyes with his own. "You in that red shimmer dress would be a most suitable escort, capable of several forms of distraction, if and when I might need them used."

Surprising herself no end, Willi knew her eyes were suddenly sparkling, when she asked, "Are you asking me to help you in the plan, or are you just asking me for a date?"

"Oh, just…"

Willi was holding her breath when he started to answer, then let it trail away. Then she gasped slightly when he finished.

"Just a little of one and a lot of the other. I'll let you make the distinction of which is which."

He was gone before she could think of any response.

Chapter Three

-

Willi decided not to pursue the question the next morning as she waited in the lobby, such as it was, of her rooming house. Dressed in casual clothes, she tried not to look anxious as she read the news screens the area boasted, while she killed the time.

Though it was still a few minutes before the appointed time, Willi wandered outside. Even knowing he would be coming, it was still a surprise when Johnny stepped up to her from slightly behind and to one side of her.

"Missy? Spare credit chip, Missy? For a veteran? No problem, Missy, if no." The appeal was not loud, but it was hearable to those nearby. The next words were not. "Around the corner."

Willi did not bobble. She handed the stoop shouldered figure a credit chip and he moved away, in the opposite direction from where he had indicated she should go. She walked casually toward the corner and was quite surprised when she saw a cab door opened and it turned out to be Johnny already behind the controls.

"How'd you do that so fast?" she asked.

"Planning," was all the answer she received.

Despite the curiosity she felt, Willi stayed silent as Johnny maneuvered the taxi in what was obviously a circuitous route to wherever they were going. Which turned out to be a small ancillary jump port for private travel.

"Hanger thirty-nine," Johnny said, stopping the cab in front of the control building. "Give me eight minutes."

She stepped from the cab without a word and went through the doors of the control building. A quick glance around and she saw the directional arrows. It took her only a few minutes to get to hanger thirty-nine. There was quite a bit of activity, but she really only had to nod and smile a few times. No one tried to engage her in any conversation. Everyone there seemed to be busy with their own activities.

Willi had looked at her chrono when Johnny had said eight minutes. It was a full thirty seconds shy of that when Johnny entered the door of the hanger where she stood. He looked completely different, again. First the panhandler, then the cabbie, now a businessman carrying a flight bag.

"Jumpsuit in the jumper," he said, walking toward the small jumper sitting in the middle of the hanger floor. It was one of those used by private citizens to transfer to and from the planet to private and commercial vessels in holding orbit in space.

As he took the controls, Willi picked up the jumpsuit laying across one of the seats. There was only the small open cabin, not even a lavatory. She did not hesitate. Willi stripped out of her outer clothes and into the jump suit, trusting Johnny not to try to get a free look, though she did keep her back to him.

It was only a few minutes later they were in space, passing close to a small commercial trading vessel. Willi knew that unless they were being intentionally tracked from a vessel deeper in space, all other indications would be they had docked and merged with the commercial vessel.

She took the seat nearest the single seat cockpit. "Where to, now?" she asked.

"Bit further."

"The dead zone," Willi said, realizing his probable intention. "Beyond the GeoSync orbit, but in too close for routine traffic."

"Yep." He handed Willi a device similar to the one he had produced in her dressing room. She looked at the display and saw a tiny blip of light.

"Won't someone see the marker beacon?"

Willi was sure the sardonic smile was on his face when he said, "That sends a coded signal and the beacon tight-beams a signal back. Minimum risk."

"Oh."

"There they are," Johnny said after only another minute or so.

Crouching down so she could look out the cockpit view port her mouth dropped open when she saw the two Dominators drifting in space. "Both of them!" she exclaimed. She waited until he had matched their orbit before she spoke again.

"But you just jettisoned the other one!"

"Went back, assembled the second one and then network flew it here."

"How did you even find it? And you assembled it in free space?"

Johnny shrugged. "Sure. Took a little time, but not that difficult if you've done similar things."

She wanted to ask, desperately, "What similar things?", but decided it was neither the time nor the place. Willi did ask, "You expect me to fly a Dominator?"

"Sure. Aren't many that could, without extensive training, but you are one of them. I'll network with you as we head where we're going. By the time we get there you'll be able to do anything that might be required."

He seemed to have more confidence in her than she had in herself. When she realized that fact, which was pretty much an unknown event, Willi decided that she probably would not have any problems. It was not braggadocio when she admitted she was one of the best pilots around.

Johnny handed her the rest of the flight suit and she finished getting ready to transfer to the Dominator. After they cycled the airlock of the jumper, Johnny pointed to one of the Dominators. He pushed off from the jumper toward the other Dominator. Willi did the same, crossing the short space to the one he had indicated.

Moments later and she was strapped into the craft, the canopy down and locked, the internal life support system up and everything active. Willi had no doubt they were on a secure commlink when she heard Johnny speak. "You have the control layout?"

She had been studying it automatically as soon as she had guided herself into the cockpit. "Yes."

"Activate the link."

"Active."

Johnny told her the coordinates. "Set the pace and get familiar."

"Sure doesn't say much, ever, but sometimes…" Willi thought to herself as she easily activated the controls and started to become at ease with the craft. By the time they reached the spot in space Johnny had given, she was. Even with the weapons systems. They had passed through one band of asteroids and Johnny had marked three for her to use for target practice. He had never said a word of approval or disproval at any of her flight actions or weapons use.

Willi knew she was good, but she had not performed perfectly. She expected Johnny to give her corrective instruction, as her original flight and weapons trainers had aboard *Trinity Home*. She knew her actions would be better each time, and they were very good now. It was only the unfamiliarity with the craft that had caused the minor performance flaws.

"Maybe he knows that, too," Willi told herself when Johnny said nothing about the activity, simply giving her another set of coordinates.

"Take station just outside the swarm. When you know Telstar is inside, monitor the approach he used. Any activity, warn me. Take no action unless required. The pass code is loaded. Check it."

"Got it," Willi said, bringing up the challenge pass code and required response that would be used for friend or foe checks.

"You don't get the proper response, destroy whatever or whoever it is, no matter what the risk to any of us. Understood?"

"Understood." Willi could not help it. She shivered. Even the electronic transmittal of Johnny's voice carried the seriousness he intended.

She had defended herself and the shuttle, and even helped fight off an attack on *Trinity Home* in one of the small fighting craft it carried. She suddenly realized that what she was involved with now could affect millions of lives, just as Johnny had said.

Johnny peeled away from her suddenly and entered the asteroid swarm. His sensor image immediately disappeared among the white noise on the monitor that was the swarm. She boosted the engines of her Dominator and took up the position Johnny had requested. She maneuvered right into the edge of the swarm, camouflaging her position, keeping her sensor arrays just clear.

As she waited, Willi began to think about some of the rumors she had heard Sydney and Clyde talking about at various times pertaining to Johnny Oneshot. Again, she shivered.

If he had done only a tenth of them, at a tenth of the degree to which was attributed, and she suddenly thought that, perhaps… no… more likely… he had, then he was probably the most capable person she had ever met. And the most dangerous.

Willi shifted just slightly in the cockpit. They had been there a while, and it must be extremely difficult holding position inside the asteroid swarm.

She was having to use her maneuvering engines from time to time to maintain hers. It was always dangerous inside an asteroid swarm, but this one was particularly dangerous. Instruments and sensors were of no use. It was strictly intuitive flight.

She saw the blip at the very edge of her long-range scanner display. It approached quickly, and Willi began to wonder if Captain Butler was in trouble. He did not look like he was going to slow at all before he hit the swarm.

She was tensed, ready to try to do something when he suddenly slowed and turned, and then corkscrewed past the swarm. Willi held position, suddenly realizing he was checking for followers. Another few moments and his Dominator entered the asteroid swarm.

Willi relaxed slightly, but only for a moment. Another blip had appeared on long-range scan. From almost the exact same point in space from which Captain Butler had appeared. It was another moment before the computer identified it as a Triple Seven.

"Janet!" Willi whispered. "Johnny knew Isis would follow Telstar!" Willi thought to herself.

Indeed, Captain Echart had followed. She had joined Rapier Squadron in the Triple Seven with Captain Butler in his Dominator. The only bogies they had encountered had been picked up on the Dominator's long-range sensor. He had vectored the flight toward them.

At first it looked like the pirates would engage the flight, as they had often in the past with Rapier flight outnumbered more than three to one. Suddenly the pirates had turned tail and run.

They were too far for the flight of F-321s to give chase, though the Dominator and her Triple Seven could have done so and caught them, with enough reserves to engage, and then return to the base.

"They turned as soon as their sensors identified the Triple Seven," Captain Butler said. "I believe your reputation has begun spreading, Isis."

Janet grinned at the memory. With her in the Triple Seven, and Captain Butler in the Dominator, both flying with the squadrons of F-321s, they had had much more success in these patrols. The pirates were getting cautious. She frowned then. If only they had two of the Triple Sevens, much more could be accomplished, even with their limitations.

Captain Butler had finally vectored them back toward the base, maintaining Tail End Charlie position. It did not dawn on her for a bit when he had turned over command to her and said he was going to vector back to do a long-range scan again just to check, that he had not returned to the formation when he should.

When she tried the commlink, Lieutenant Peterson had responded that he often did not return until after the rest of the flight had docked at the station. She almost left it at that, but suddenly turned control over to Lieutenant Peterson and turned back herself.

With plenty of reserve power, Janet went to high speed and narrow beamed her long-range sensors, doing a cone pattern. As soon as she got a blip she went passive on sensors and just high balled toward the coordinates of the blip. When she was close she powered short-, and then medium-range sensors for a moment. There was a blip at just the edge of medium sensor range. On a completely different vector than previously. She headed for it at high speed again, going back to passive sensing.

She slowed after a bit, and then again used, first short range, and then medium range sensors. Still without a contact she used the long-range scan. The blip was on the same vector, still at high speed. Janet matched the speed, staying just at the edge of her long-range scan range.

The Dominator had better sensors, but one of the very few advantages of the Triple Seven was its small sensor image. They could see each other at about the same distance on their instruments. If she kept slipping in and out of range so she did not lose him, she should be able to determine where he was going.

Janet was beginning to feel sick. She had never imagined that Bill Butler could be operating with the pirates. But what he was doing was highly suspect. The asteroid swarm suddenly showed on the monitors and she lost the blip.

She eased her speed and approached slowly. He could be using it as a shield, having gone around it and away, if he had seen her blip on his sensors. He would be using them, she was certain.

Willi started to key the command to tell Johnny that Janet was approaching. She remembered his instructions and the chill that had gone down her back when she had heard them.

She eased the Dominator slightly out from the asteroid swarm and keyed the com, using the frequency and code sequence that had been part of the information Johnny had transmitted to her when they had been networked. "Identify Triple Seven. Respond to Prometheus."

Janet was caught completely by surprise. She immediately changed course and armed the weapons systems, going to defensive maneuvers, even as she responded to the challenge. "Countersign Romulus and Remus."

"Acknowledged. You are secure."

Willi keyed the secure commlink to Johnny. "Isis."

Captain Butler had just maneuvered to within a few meters of Johnny's Dominator. He had no way to express his surprise at seeing the craft. He stared over at Johnny in the cockpit of the Dominator. Seeing his finger motions, Captain Butler keyed in a frequency and code sequence.

"Hold one, Telstar. Pipeline, vector Isis to my entry point. Instruct three niner niner niner upon entry."

"Acknowledged." Willi switched back to Janet's frequency.

She eased the Dominator away from the swarm just slightly and made the call. "This is Pipeline," she said using the call sign that Johnny had just given her.

Willi gave Janet the coordinates and vector, and then the maneuvering instructions Johnny had given to her. Willi saw on her sensor monitor that Janet stopped the defensive maneuvering and headed for the coordinates.

Johnny had been watching Captain Butler and even through the two canopies saw the man stiffen when he heard Janet Echart's call sign and the instructions Johnny had given Pipeline. Even with the relatively short distances involved, the commlink was filled with interference due to all of the radiation in the swarm.

There was nothing else for him to do, so Captain Butler waited patiently. This would play out, one way or another. He could tell that Janet was just as surprised to see the other Dominator as he had been. She maneuvered her Triple Seven toward them, creating a three-blade fan formation so they could see one another through the canopies.

As he had done for Bill, Johnny signaled Janet the frequency and code sequence to use so she could communicate with them.

"What the hell is going on?" she demanded immediately.

"Ditto," Bill said.

Johnny gave them nearly the same explanation he had given Willi the night before. The two Captains said nothing for some time.

"Okay," Captain Butler said finally. "What do we do? And just who are you?"

"My questions exactly," added Captain Echart.

"I use many names," Johnny said.

Willi had been monitoring the frequency, even as she scanned others and watched the sensor monitors. She grinned.

"So does Johnny Oneshot, so go the rumors. You have to do better than that, mister. I'm not endangering Captain Echart and all the others that are going to be put at risk if we do something about this."

"Oh, I think you will. You know you have to, no matter who I am. What I've told you fits everything you've found out on your own.

"But just so you know, I am Johnny Oneshot. I do use different names when the situation demands it. And don't believe the rumors. There isn't that much truth to them."

"I don't believe you," Captain Echart said immediately. "Oh, I do about what is going on out here. But you… Johnny Oneshot? Come on. Anyone could use that name. From what I hear, quite a few have, just to try to get something."

"Well, just call me Guy Richardson, then. That's as good a name as any."

"Not good enough," Captain Butler insisted. "I want to know who you are before I risk the others."

"You can check me. Use your contacts in Logistics. One of them will remember Guy. Mention Periwinkle Red."

"Okay. I guess that will have to do. For now. What do we do, assuming you check out?" asked Captain Butler.

"Continue as you have. With the two of you going on the patrols, the pirate activity has slowed. That is going to interfere with the plans that are in place. Be extremely careful personally. You could both be targeted. The Dominator and Triple Seven are also likely to be attacked.

"Do what you can to protect yourselves and your craft, but don't make it obvious you are suddenly at a higher state of awareness. Things are going to come to a head shortly after the Inaugural Ball."

Even with the interference, Captain Butler's groan was audible. Despite the seriousness of what they were discussing, Janet and Johnny both chuckled. Willi chuckled, too, though she had not heard the groan.

"You've had your suspicions, Captain Butler," Johnny continued, the seriousness back. "I know you can't get out of attending the ball with the Governor. Are you going to be able to handle the situation?"

The two saw him put his head back against the cockpit headrest and suspected he did exactly what he did, though they could not see it. He closed his eyes for a moment. "I don't suppose assassinating her would make the problem go away? I think I could do it."

"You are a soldier," Johnny said, "not an assassin. It would change things, but not stop them. It would make part of what we need to do even more difficult. We can use her to a degree, after she finds out that it has become known what she is planning."

"How will she find that out? And when? Isn't it important that we control that information?"

Just as Willi had been, the two Captains were amazed when Johnny informed them that he planned to let her know at the Inaugural Ball. Both made similar protests.

"She'll know, but it won't be quite as outright as I just stated. You'll both see the effect it has at the ball. Isis, you need to be there. I know you weren't planning on it and it is short notice, but I do think it important. But it has to be legitimate and not contrived. There is tight security. The guest list is already set. I have an idea that I believe will work. If you get another invitation, from a totally unexpected source, accept."

"Wait a minute. How do you know I've been asked and turned them down?" Janet asked.

"You looked in the mirror lately?" Bill asked, and then bit his lips. It had just popped out.

"Exactly," Johnny said. "It is just as well that you did not accept any of them. Your appearance with the man I'm thinking about will set things up nicely and be quite obviously legitimate."

"But…" Janet started to protest but her words were interrupted.

Willi had lost track of the conversation. Something had entered the range of the long-range sensor. It was big. She pulled away slightly from the swarm, the conversation completely ignored now as she worked her controls. Knowing the response she would get, Willi sent the IFF challenge. The Identify, Friend or Foe challenge word Prometheus was ignored. She broad banded it to make sure they heard in on at least one frequency. It was still ignored.

Her warning cut off Janet. "Bogie. It's an Orion Class ship. Pirates. I'll do as much damage as I can. Use the distraction to get away and take care of what's happening. Pipeline out."

"Who is that?" Janet asked, doing exactly what the others were. Backing away from one another and turning to exit the asteroid swarm.

"You'll be surprised when you find out," was all Johnny said. "This is step two, people. We take this ship out totally unexpectedly, and they are going to be frantic to find out what happened. It could trigger other mistakes."

They left the swarm nearly side by side and quickly accelerated to join Willi. "You should be running," she said, her sensors picking them up as soon as they left the swarm.

Johnny repeated what he had told the Captains. "I think it did the other time. You know which one I mean.

"The Orion has a soft spot just aft of the midship docking bay, north ventral section. Isis, you can get closest before they lock weapons on you. Loop behind, come up from their rear. Reverse and fire down into the area. I've got your wing, Pipeline. We handle the fighters if they launch. And provide suppressive fire on their defensive weapons for Isis if they don't."

"They'll launch," Captain Butler said. He had already moved into lead position, to provide suppressive fire for Captain Echart's attack run.

"Not necessarily," Johnny said. "Pipeline. Check weapons bay three. Did not go over it earlier."

"Got it." Willi locked the image of the launch bays of an Orion ship into three of the missiles in weapons bay three. "Spread of three, port bay."

"Three spread, starboard bay," said Johnny. His "Missiles away," came just after Willi's.

"Geez!" exclaimed Janet as the slender missiles streaked away at nearly five times their own speed.

"Something new, I take it," Captain Butler said.

It was obvious when the Orion ship picked up the missiles on their sensors. It changed vectors and launched countermeasures, as well as long-range weapons. Though they could not see it visually at that range, Johnny and the others knew the Orion class ship would be trying to launch its ready craft. But even the ready craft took a few moments to activate and pirates were not known to have the most disciplined crews, even if the pilots were often good.

The long-range weapons launched toward them from the Pirate's Orion class ship were easily destroyed by the defensive weapons the Dominators carried. When it was obvious that the missiles they had launched had destroyed the launch bays on the other ship, Willi and Johnny pulled slightly ahead of Captain Butler and Captain Echart. They did not have to loop past and come back toward the other ship. It was trying to run, accelerating as quickly as it could.

Willi, Johnny, and Captain Butler's weapons devastated the sensors and defensive weapons pods and bays, leaving the way open for Captain Echart's Triple Seven to get in close and discharge her entire weapon load into the weak spot of the Orion ship. The four broke away immediately upon the release of her weapons. They streaked away at the Triple Seven's highest speed, to avoid the debris field that was about to be created.

Though they could not see it visually, not only because they were traveling away from it, but also because they were out of visual range, even had they been looking in that direction, it was obvious on the sensor screens that the ship had been destroyed completely. A large blip changed to a growing pattern of minute dots.

"I'm sure you two will have reasonable explanations when you return," Johnny said a bit later as they headed back home. "I will contact you at the Ball. Be very careful."

Willi had numerous questions she wanted to ask as they headed back to the parking orbit where the jumper was. She stayed silent, despite the secure commlink with Johnny's Dominator. In a situation such as this, security was relative. Besides, she doubted Johnny would respond, anyway.

Even when they were aboard the jumper, settling back toward the planet, she hesitated. Finally, as Johnny maneuvered the jumper into the hanger, he broke the silence. "If anything should happen… anything at all… that makes you think your security is at risk, get out here any way you can, take the jumper up, and run for it in one of the Dominators."

He had not been looking at her as he spoke. Now he turned and his eyes met hers. "Betty Myers, despite her looks and outwardly charming demeanor, is as cold and calculating as they come. People have died because of this plot already. Many people. Most, of course, due to the pirates and the few actual Ecronian activities that have taken place.

"But I am sure that there have been at least three deaths directly attributable to her. On her orders, though in one case, she might have done it herself. I do believe she is capable of it. So, do not take any chances."

"I understand," Willi replied. "But I'm not sure I could run, if I know others are at risk... Janet and Bill… and I'm sure there are others that I know nothing about."

"I have not involved anyone else," Johnny said carefully. "There may be one more person I involve, but he, like the two Captains, is capable of taking care of himself."

Willi bristled a bit at the implication that she could not take care of herself, but was more or less mollified when Johnny continued. "You are one of the most capable people I've ever met, but you are essentially on your own and isolated here. All the others have some contacts and means to escape and evade if necessary through their local connections. You don't.

"Now, I need to accomplish a few more things. You should have no trouble catching a regular taxi back to your place."

"Will you be at *Smokey's* tonight?" she asked, deciding to wait for another time to ask the questions she wanted.

"For a while," Johnny replied. He was changing clothes, his back to her. He had not hesitated to start the process and Willi quickly turned her back as he stripped out of the flight suit.

It took some concentration not to turn around when he continued speaking as he changed. "You won't see me, and I expect to be leaving not long after I get there, if what I've got set up goes as planned."

"If you're there," Will replied firmly, "I'll see you."

Johnny just smiled, knowing Willi could not see it. "Perhaps," he said, simply to mollify her. He did not want her being obvious about looking for him. She would never recognize him, but he did not want her openly looking. It might make someone think she was looking for someone else.

"If you do just don't let on."

"Well, of course not!" she said, turning around slightly when he moved within her peripheral vision. Her eyes widened slightly at the sight of him dressed as a very prosperous businessman. An old prosperous businessman. She could see the likeness, but she suddenly was not sure she would have recognized him, if she had not known it was him.

"I'll give you some privacy to change," he said, handing her a small wallet. "Credits. No sense in you using your own hard-earned money in this endeavor. Marilyn."

She had seen the flash of his smile when he used her... she smiled slightly... stage name. But she had been distracted by the weight of the small wallet and did not have time to respond before he had disappeared out one of the hanger doors.

Opening the wallet, Willi gasped. There were various denominations of standard credit chips, but the bulk of the space was filled with the high-density crystal icosahedrons used for storing large amounts of credit. The amount was glowing brightly in each and would until the credit was used or replaced during each transaction. Each of the crystals held a value that took her breath away. She held as much value in her hand as *Trinity Home* did business in a year.

Lifting her eyes, Willi stared at the door through which Johnny had disappeared. She could go anywhere in the galaxy and do anything she wanted, for as long as she wanted, with what the wallet contained.

Quickly Willi changed, and stashed the wallet securely in her clothing. "You'll be getting this back tonight," she whispered. There was no way she was going to be responsible for that money.

The thought struck her then that the crystals might be counterfeit. It was rumored to have been attempted, but as far as she knew, and the traders did if anyone did, no one had ever made a counterfeit crystal that was even halfway effective.

Putting it out of her mind, Willi left the jump port, decided to stop for something to eat, and then went back to the boarding house. It was only when she started to change clothes that the reality of everything that was happening struck her. Suddenly she felt like she weighed a ton and had not slept in days.

Making sure to set a wake-up time, Willi crawled into the bed and let herself relax. She had come out here on a whim, and now she was involved in a clandestine plot to destroy another clandestine plot that could cause the deaths of millions if not stopped.

Having set the wake-up time just as a precaution, Willi was glad she had. Intending to sleep for only an hour or so, when the annunciator woke her, she had time only to get ready to go to *Smokey's*. She would have to get something to eat when she arrived. She did feel better, at least.

Even though she was keeping an eye out for Johnny, she did not see him. She assumed she had just missed him, since the crowd was as large as the one the night before. With a shrug, she dismissed it and went to her dressing room after the last set.

Despite the rest she had had that afternoon, she was still exhausted when she went back to the boarding house. Willi knew it was from the mental stress, as well as the physical, she was under. Stashing the wallet in the hidden compartment in one of her bags, she stripped and fell into the bed.

"Do you have any idea what Commander Calhoun wants with me?" Janet asked Bill when she met him in the hall on her way to the Commander's office.

"Not a clue. He sent for me, too."

They did not find out for several minutes, the commander's aide having them wait for some time before he ushered them in to Commander Calhoun's office.

With no preliminaries, Commander Calhoun said, "Are you ready to go down to attend the protocol briefing?"

"Yes, sir. Of course, sir," Captain Butler said, finishing his salute as he spoke. The commander did not bother to return it.

Both Captain Echart and Captain Butler had turned eyes on the civilian standing off to one side. Bill managed not to frown, but it was a near thing when the man turned. Bill recognized him from news broadcasts.

The commander was speaking to Captain Echart and Bill turned his attention back to him. "Captain, as you obviously know, Captain Butler has been assigned to accompany Governor Myers at the Inaugural."

He cut his eye to the man now approaching the Commander's desk. "She the one? Fine. I suppose a Captain will have to do. Full dress uniform. I'll send a transport in plenty of time." He headed for the door.

"Sir! I protest! What is he…" Janet was livid and it was obvious.

"Enough, Captain!" barked Commander Calhoun. "He is one of the most important men in the sector. A major… the major contractor providing over half the goods and services the government buys. He expects and deserves a military escort to the inaugural ball."

At the looks on both the Captains' faces, his softened somewhat. "Look. I know this isn't right," he admitted. "But… my hands are tied. The General received his orders, and I've received mine. Now you have received yours."

"This is not something you can order me to do, sir," Janet said stiffly. "It is well outside propriety and proper military conduct." Suddenly Guy Richardson's words came back to her.

Even before the Commander began frowning at her words, she made herself relax slightly. "But… I know how difficult this situation is for you, Sir. If you honestly think it will help, of course I will accompany the gentleman."

Thinking he might get suspicious if she was too acquiescent, Janet put a little steel back in her voice and continued. "But it is military escort duty, sir, and that is all. If he thinks it will be something else, he will be vastly disappointed."

"Of course, Captain," Commander Calhoun said stiffly. "You would be in serious trouble if you decided to act in any other way. I'm glad you have decided not to protest this, considering your situation here. Your assignment here is in serious jeopardy still. It would not do your career good at all to wind up with anymore black marks in your record."

"Yes, sir," Captain Echart said, her face just as stiff as the Commander's again.

"Dismissed," Commander Calhoun replied, giving a casual salute. "Both of you."

"You should have stuck to your guns, Janet," Captain Butler said as soon as they were out of earshot of anyone. "He had no right to…"

Janet saw the change in Captain Butler. He had maintained absolute control in the commander's office, but he was as angry as she had been, if not more so. Her hand touched his arm. "Think about it, Bill. This has to be what Richardson was talking about. Do you think this man… who is he, anyway? Do you think maybe he is on our side and got him to do this just to get me there?"

"Bond Cretorian? Hell no, he isn't on our side! He is a crony of the Governor. That's why he's got the contracts he has. Substandard goods and services at astronomical prices!" Making a concerted effort to control himself, Captain Butler visibly calmed down. "But you are probably right. I've no idea how he might have accomplished it, but Richardson must have arranged this."

Seeing the glare still in Captain Butler's eyes, Janet had to smile just a bit as he continued. "But I plan to have a few words with him about it. I do not like the idea of you being with Cretorian."

"You are, after all, with the Governor," Janet replied quietly, making sure the smile was gone.

"Yeah, but that is entirely diff…" He cut his eyes to the woman he realized he was having feelings for that had nothing to do with her Naval accomplishments. "Never mind. We'd better just do the best we can. I just wish there was a different way to accomplish… whatever it is exactly we're supposed to accomplish at that damned ball!"

"You and me both," Janet muttered. "Richardson better know what he's doing or I'm going to take that Dominator of his and put it where none of the suns shine."

"Yo' Boss," asked the tall, slender man waiting for Bond Cretorian at the civilian entrance and exit to the military section of the orbiting Moon-Ship station. "You get one of them lady generals to go with you?"

"Just a captain," responded Bond. "Best they got here that's not married. Guess it would have made too much stink if I'd insisted on that. Good thing though that broad made the calls. I don't know how I missed the fact that she was getting the military escort and I was not. She knows she's nothing without my help. You done good, Banger. I had my doubts about you at first, but you sure been doing a bang-up job."

"Ha! You hear that?" Cretorian said with a loud laugh. "Bang-up job! Banger! Ha!"

"Sure, boss. That's slick. I'm just glad I got the chance to hook up. Things were getting hot for me back central way. Too bad about your other boy, but it sure worked out good for me."

"Sure did, Banger. Get us back to the office. I need to get some things done. That shipment of rations you found needs the paperwork done up. I need to get the staff on that. Uh… what you got going next?"

Since Banger had suddenly appeared, just when his number three lieutenant had wound up caught in a raid, which was not even at one of his own operations, things had been going exceptionally well. The other idiot had just got caught by chance at one of the many illegal joints being run by small timers.

Banger had just made contact trying to sell some looted goods. Good stuff. Bond had been able to make triple the going rate. He never looked a gift horse in the mouth. Banger had said he could…

Bond laughed aloud. Banger had said he could *acquire* quite a few other things. He had been true to his word. The look changed suddenly. Anger now distorted the features. "It's a good thing this worked out. That hoity toity bitch tries to get one up on me again, and there'll be hell to pay!"

If Banger had not mentioned how bad it was that Bond was going to the ball with a nothing B-girl on his arm, when the Governor was going to be there with the cream of the crop goody boy as her escort, he would have never caught the slight. "Damn her!"

"Yeah, boss?"

"Nothing, Banger. But remind me after this is over and we're set, to give mighty miss a little present. What was it you said they did back on earth when things weren't right?"

"The horse's head in the bed?"

"Yeah. Have to be something different. Don't know where we'd ever get a horse. Cost more than my whole damn estate. You think a scrimmin's head would do?"

"Sure, boss. It's the thought that counts, huh?"

Banger stumbled slightly when Bond slapped him on the back and laughed hugely. "You got a wit, Banger! A real wit! Can't believe how lucky I was to find you."

"Sure thing, Boss. Guess I'd better drift. Got a line on some recalled small arms. Defective sighting systems, but a bit of work and we could probably get them fixed. Or… just sell them to the asteroid miners just the way they are. Most of them probably hit more with bad sights than they can with good sights."

Bond Cretorian was still laughing when Banger left him when they reached Cretorian's office building.

As soon as he could duck out of sight safely, Johnny did so and shifted his appearance from the Banger persona to his normal one. He shook his head. Not that it was really difficult to slip back into his own personality, but it was getting tiresome having to switch identities as often as he was forced to do so in trying to accomplish the demise of the governor's plot.

Captain Butler probably, and Captain Echart for sure, were going to want to do him bodily harm over Bond Cretorian. At least Janet was going to be there. He wanted the three people most at risk to be where they would visible when what he had planned came to fruition during the ball.

Johnny made for the tiny quarters he was using in the poorest section of town. It was suitable for three of his personas and kept him close to where he needed to be most of the time. It was time for some rest. Even his stamina was beginning to give out.

There was only one variable left that he would like to resolve. He would do that the next night. Right now, rest was more important. It would not be unexpected for him not to show for his swamper's job at *Smokey's*.

He had intimated that sometimes, after payday, he might miss a day or two. "Got to see my girl when I gots the credits, you see, or they won't let me in," he told Smokey. Since he had offered to work for significantly less than the going rate, Smokey had agreed.

As Guy Richardson, Johnny entered *Smokey's* the following evening. "Cherokee," he said, bringing the man over when the place was still nearly unoccupied.

"What's it going to be tonight?" Cherokee asked, still trying to remember what it was about the man that kept nagging at his memories.

"Little reminiscing, Cherokee. Just a little reminiscing." Johnny watched the man's eyes. Flat and black, seldom showing much of what he was feeling or thinking, Johnny could see just a touch of curiosity in them.

"Hear you were on Franklin Seven when the Ecronians tried their ploy there during the Transition Campaign." Johnny saw the flash in his eyes.

A quick look around and then Cherokee leaned forward, partially over the bar, his face inches from Johnny's. "You'd better say something, quick, to not make me skin you alive, like my ancestors used to do.

"There are only a handful of people outside my unit that know about Franklin Seven. It's treason to talk about it. I may be a lowly bartender in a crook's joint, but I'm loyal to the Confederation. Talk quick, or I will kill you dead, no matter how much I like you."

Johnny had his proof. It was there in Cherokee's look. His stance. His readiness to do exactly what he said. Meeting Cherokee's gaze, eye to eye, Johnny lifted his hands to his mouth, cupped them to his lips and blew into the shape they had formed. A soft hoot owl call sounded and Cherokee staggered back.

"Johnny Oneshot!" he said, mostly under his breath.

Johnny put a finger to his lips, and then nodded.

"Man, you saved our whole unit!" Cherokee said, stepping forward again. His voice was low and he checked around the area before he spoke. "I haven't thought about…that…for a long time."

"Need a favor," Johnny said, very softly.

"My life, or anything else I can do," Cherokee said, voice not only awed, but reverent.

"It could be on the line," Johnny said.

"Whatever it takes, if you need it."

"I knew I could count on you," Johnny said. "I can't tell you what is going on. You'll learn about it after the fact, I assure you. If a group of people come through here sometime… people you'll recognize… in a hurry… let them into the tunnels below."

Cherokee's eyes widened. "You know about them?"

Johnny smiled slightly and lifted one eyebrow.

"Of course." He looked over at Smokey, who had just come into the main room. "Okay if I go with them?"

"Absolutely. We could use you if they have to come through here. There'll be some things you'll recognize, ready for use, if need be, at the first cubby."

"Understood."

Johnny slid a couple of credit chips across the bar. "Good service, as always, Cherokee." With a wink that none of those approaching could see, Johnny turned and left.

Cherokee slipped the credits into his pocket. It was only some time later he thought about them and took them out. He whistled softly. "Get out of jail money," he said to himself.

He secreted them in one of the tiny slit pockets all of his clothes had. He might miss this place… a little… but if he needed this much credit to help out Johnny Oneshot, relocation would be just fine. Anyone that had done what Johnny Oneshot had done for him and his unit on Franklin Seven got anything he wanted, at whatever cost or risk.

Willi was on pins and needles the following morning. Smokey had given only a token objection when she had informed him she would not be performing the night of the ball. That she had been invited and more or less had to go.

"Yeah. Gotta go, too, as it turns out. Going to be some business conducted and…" His words faded away quickly. "Never mind. No problem. No Navy or other service people going to be in here that night anyway." He turned and left her abruptly.

Chapter Four

-

Trying to rest, Willi wound up pacing as much as resting, all day long. Finally, she got dressed for the evening. She had been ready for over an hour when her room communicator buzzed. She hurried down when she heard Johnny say he was there to pick her up.

Her step faltered slightly when she saw him standing just outside the door of her building. It was not like she had not been to formal functions before. She was the daughter of the Matriarch of one of the leading Trading Families in the galaxy.

She did not care for them for the most part. But she had attended many and had seen men in formal dress before. Handsome men. Johnny Oneshot was above and beyond anyone else she had ever seen in similar attire. Perhaps with the exception of her father when she was just a little girl, she suddenly thought.

Johnny took her arm on his and stepped toward the transport that Willi just then noticed, her attention having been completely on Johnny initially. "How did you get this?" she asked, recognizing the most expensive and luxurious limousine transport of the time for what it was. They had handled the shipping for one for a planetary governing body in one of the mid-sector systems.

"Oh," Johnny said, quietly, "I do have my contacts." He continued without pause as he handed her into the transport. "I must say you look marvelous this evening. I did not think you could look better than you did in the red shimmer, but... well... you do. You're even better at this than I imagined."

"Why, thank you," Willi replied. "I think. And you... look very... distinguished... yourself."

Johnny waved a hand negligently. "All men look the same in formal." He finally looked around at her after having punched in the destination for the driver. "There is still time for you to high tail it out of here. You sure you want to do this?"

Willi nodded. "But I still don't know what it is I'm supposed to actually do."

"As I said, I will need a distraction at some point tonight. You are quite distracting, simply because of your beauty, anyway. When the time comes, you'll recognize it and do whatever is needed."

"But I still don't know what…"

"Trust me," Johnny said. "More importantly, trust yourself. It might all come to naught, tonight, anyway, if the right opportunity doesn't present itself."

Willi openly studied his face as she sat there beside him. "I have a feeling that things have been arranged such that an opportunity will most undoubtedly present itself."

"Probably," was the only thing Johnny said.

"Just who are you tonight?" she asked when he did not elaborate. "And me, too, I suppose."

"You, of course," Johnny said, turning that sardonic smile toward her, "are the estimable Marilyn Monroe, Entertainer Extraordinaire. I am Guy Richardson. Simply a small businessman wishing to do business with the government here."

"You aren't *simply* anything," Willi snorted. "Anyone with an IQ that brings them in out of a solar storm can recognize that."

"Hopefully, I can carry off the act," Johnny said dryly. Then he grinned at her. "Shouldn't be too hard actually, as long as I have you on my arm. No one will even see me. All eyes will be on you. I'll just fade into the background.

You really did make an excellent choice in attire for tonight. You are breathtaking in that dress."

"I know you are just trying to reassure me; but thank you. I honestly did not think the red shimmer appropriate for tonight."

"Oh," Johnny said, "It was not. That was going to be part of the distraction."

"What? You were expecting me to go in that dress, knowing how it would look? I ought to brain you!"

"I told you that you were going to be my distraction," Johnny said innocently.

"Yes, I know, but still…" She frowned at him as her words faded. He had said that. Suddenly her frown deepened. "Wait a minute. You know very well that… oh, never mind!" She hated to be scammed and she knew he had just scammed her. There was no doubt in her mind that he had suggested the red shimmer dress, expecting her to choose something more appropriate.

"Actually," Johnny was suddenly saying as he entered something on the control pad. "I just thought of something that will make the distraction even more effective."

"What?" Willi asked, as Johnny's eyes turned to her face, and then dropped, slightly, to her neck and upper chest. She knew she colored slightly.

"You'll see," he said, lifting his eyes to hers again.

It was not long before the limousine stopped. "I'll be right back," Johnny said, stepping out of the vehicle. He was true to his word. It was less than two minutes and he was back beside her on the seat.

"Here you go," he said, after having indicated to the operator to continue to their original destination. Johnny handed Willi a jewelry case. A large one.

When she opened the case, Willi gasped. She turned large eyes to him. "This isn't real, is it?"

"Of course it is. Can't turn the Governor's greedy eyes with costume jewelry."

"You're borrowing this or something, right? You did not buy it?"

"Yes, I bought it. A jeweler isn't going to loan that out. Certainly not on short notice. To someone she doesn't know."

"But…" Willi said, very softly, looking down at the necklace the box contained. It was not that elaborate. Actually, the design was fairly simple, but elegant. And the gemstones were absolutely exquisite.

"I… I… I can't wear this," she suddenly said, handing the box back to Johnny.

"Part of the job you agreed to do." Johnny's voice was soft. "It'll help. Believe me, I know Governor Myers has had her eye on that particular piece ever since it showed up in the sector. It is Old Earth and with something of a history. When she sees that on you, she will be livid. You are going to be her worst enemy from that moment on."

"Well, gee thanks!" Willi could not take her eyes off the necklace. She had never seen anything quite like it. It seemed to just shimmer with light. Again, her eyes went to Johnny's. "Will it… will it really help if I wear it?"

Johnny nodded.

With some hesitation Willi picked up the necklace and tried to fasten it around her neck. Her eyes flicked to Johnny. "I can't get the clasp," she said. "It's not an auto coupler."

"Here. I'll get it."

Willi handed the necklace to him, turned her back, and lifted her hair out of the way. She shivered slightly when his hands touched her neck as he fastened the old-fashioned clasp.

"There you go. All secure."

"I wish I could see what it looked like." Her voice was just a little wistful.

"Ask, and ye shall receive," replied Johnny touching a control panel. A ceiling panel flipped down and Willi looked at herself in the large mirror.

"Wow!" she said softly.

"*Wow!* is right," Johnny said just as softly. "Even if she did not already want it, she would tonight, just seeing it on you."

Willi looked at him again, the trader in her coming to the fore. "You will be able to get your money back for this, won't you? After we use it tonight?"

Johnny shrugged. "Doesn't really matter. As long as it serves its purpose, it'll be money well spent."

"But this cost a fortune! A large fortune! Two or three or four large fortunes!"

"Now, now," Johnny said, taking her hand as they stopped and the door of the limousine opened. "Let's not discuss this in public, my dear. Such a trifling matter."

Willi saw the group of people outside the limousine and forced a smile. "Of course." She shot him a look only he could see, fortunately, that said, "Oh yes we will discuss it later, and it **is not** trifling." Those that saw them, though they did not see the look, pretty well knew that she was giving the look to him. It was in her posture.

"Sir Guy Richardson escorting Marilyn Monroe," Johnny told the attendant by the limousine.

Though she could not hear the man, he obviously relayed the names to the liveried personage at the entrance of the event center where the huge Inaugural Ball was being held. The watching crowds were well under control. Willi was not that surprised to see that Naval personnel, rather than the city's regular enforcement officers, were handling the security.

Suddenly realizing that this was a huge event, and seeing the mass of media people all about, Willi found herself walking closely at Johnny's side, her arm gripping his tightly. "I did not even think about all these people and the media! They might even see this on broadcast distribution!"

Johnny knew she meant her family might see her. It probably was not really very nice of him, but he said, "Probably." Her reaction was just what he had thought it might be. She crowded even closer to him. He liked the feeling.

"Sir Guy! Sir Guy!" called someone from one of the major media groups. "A word, Sir!"

When Willi felt him stop, she stopped beside him, barely able to look in the direction he had turned. She cut her eyes up to his face and almost grinned when she saw that old sardonic smile and heard him say, "Ah… a word… how about… broccoli... how's that for a word?"

The crowded looked stunned, then broke into loud laughter as the media celebrity looked shocked himself, and then started to grin. "A very good word, Sir. I shall look it up post haste."

Willi leaned in even closer. "The media and some of these other people seem to know you!"

"I've used Sir Guy before," Johnny whispered back.

"I guess," Willi said, as yet another person called out to him.

"Is she going to be Lady Richardson?"

Willi colored, kept her head high, and continued walking up the red carpet, as someone else called out, "Hey! It's Marilyn Monroe! From *Smokey's!*" She could not help it. She stumbled slightly when the applause started. Johnny had a firm hold on her arm and the bobble went unnoticed.

"Why are they applauding?" Willi whispered.

"Your reputation precedes you, my dear," he said rather loudly, Willi thought.

"I don't **have** a reputation," she whispered to him.

"Oh, yes, you do." Johnny's hand tightened slightly on hers. "Brace yourself. The receiving line is just ahead. Just remember who you are. Really are. And act accordingly."

"But…" Her protest faded and her head came up proudly. There was no mistaking the Governor standing at the end of the receiving line. Willi met Janet's eyes as she shook her hand.

Her eyes then went to the feral ones of the man for whom Janet was acting as military escort. Willi knew that the man's eyes were seeking more than just the jewelry on her neck and chest. She felt almost naked under his gaze for a moment.

"Janet is going to maim Johnny for this," thought Willi. "And so is Captain Butler," the thought continued. Quickly she put those thoughts out of her mind as they approached the Governor.

Captain Butler was standing proud and tall next to Governor Myers. It was obvious to Willi why the woman had wanted him there in the capacity of her escort. Giving no indication of recognition to the captain, she turned her eyes to the Governor. It was obvious when Myers recognized the necklace.

Willi saw the way the Governor's eyes flared, then narrowed and glinted with raw anger and greed. It was quickly masked, but Willi new Johnny

Oneshot was entirely correct about the Governor. Willi probably was a real target now.

She smiled serenely, as much for the fact as despite it. Anyone that could look that evil over a mere necklace, no matter how expensive, was someone that Willi knew could not be allowed to control anything, much less gain the power which she was trying to gain.

A quick shake of the Governor's hand and Willi was past her, still easily on Johnny's arm. With Johnny beside her, Willi found it easy to make small talk as they made the rounds, speaking with other guests.

"Well done, Marilyn," Johnny said, neither speaking loudly or extremely low, as they caught a moment almost to themselves.

She was sure he was referring to how she had handled the receiving line. Willi simply smiled, with a quick look at his face, and then turned the smile to the person coming up to them. It was Smokey. "You look very handsome, boss," Willi said as he stopped.

"And you are as at home here as on stage. How did I ever manage to get you at my place?"

"Mere chance, I suppose," Willi replied. She realized he was just making small talk with an employee when Smokey turned his eyes to Johnny.

"Sir Guy," Smokey said, "I had no idea of who you were when you visited us these past few weeks. Perhaps we can do a little business, if you are so inclined. I can open a few doors for you, if you'd like."

"Perhaps," Johnny said. "I'd heard you were a man with connections."

Willi watched with amazement, though she hid it completely, as Johnny continued smoothly, acting the suave businessman out to work a deal.

"I must say, I had hopes to get a line on the supply business for the government in the sector. I know I can't compete... directly... with Bond

Cretorian. I think I might be able to fulfill some of the needs of the sector authorities that he is unable to fill."

Smokey's eyes cut to Willi, then back to Johnny. "It might be best if we discussed this in private."

"Of course," Johnny said. He turned to Willi. "If you will excuse us, my dear. Business. You understand."

Willi, despite the first initial anger and resentment of being cut out of the discussion because she was a woman, quickly suppressed it, knowing it was all part of Johnny's act. Part of what was happening. It had no bearing on the true nature of things.

If it had happened in any situation but here, she would have made her feelings known. Willi also knew that Johnny would never have acted in this manner in any situation but this one.

A delighted smile was suddenly on her face. "Of course! I think I'll see if I can find the Lady's Lounge. Time to check the face." As she turned away, she saw Bond Cretorian and Janet headed toward the three of them.

Though she did not hear what was said, Willi could tell that Janet was being dismissed much as she had been. And that Janet felt about it much the same way as had she. With the same conclusion coming to mind. It was all part of what was going on. A tiny motion of her head and Janet joined her on the way toward the Lady's Lounge that Willi saw.

Both were careful to keep their conversation casual. Willi was not surprised when only a few moments had passed and Governor Myers entered the Lounge.

"Ladies," she said, her gaze passing over Janet like the Captain was simply part of the furnishings. Her gazed stopped on the necklace Willi wore.

"A beautiful piece," Governor Myers said, her eyes finally meeting Willi's. "Old Earth, isn't it?"

"Why… I think so," Willi said, looking down at the necklace, showing a bit of confusion. "Sir Guy mentioned Earth when he gave it to me." Willi could tell her casualness about the necklace infuriated the Governor.

"You're the new… singer… at one of the strip clubs the military often patronize, aren't you?"

It was a good thing, Willi knew, that the Governor was again looking at the necklace with no small amount of greed. She knew her own eyes were flashing angrily. Less at the slur toward herself, than the one for the hard-working women that entertained after her singing was over for the night.

Not all of them were outstanding citizens, perhaps, but most were just ordinary people, trying to make a living the best way they knew how.

"Yes," Willi replied, keeping herself under tight control. "I sing at *Smokey's*. I've never seen you there. That I can remember."

Governor Myers' head jerked up. "Of course not! I do not frequent such places!"

"Perhaps we should see if the gentlemen require our presence," Janet said, carefully.

"Sir Guy is probably looking for me," Willi said. "He only wanted to talk business a little."

"Business? Richardson is talking business with them? Montello and Cretorian?" snapped the Governor.

"Yes," Willi said, "I think so."

Governor Myers looked at Janet. "Do you know if that is true?"

"No, Madam Governor. Mr. Cretorian just suggested I take a moment for myself. He said he needed to say hello to a friend."

The Governor was gone without another word. Janet and Willi exchanged a glance, but neither wanted to say anything, fearing they could be overheard.

Cretorian had not a clue the man he was now addressing as Sir Guy Richardson was the same man that he knew as Banger. Johnny's eyes went to Governor Betty Myers as she approached. Her guards were as unobtrusive as their particular brand could be. They had not gone into the lady's lounge, but it had been a near thing.

Johnny could see the glint in the woman's eyes as her glance went to Cretorian. "Bond," she said joining them. "I had no idea you knew Sir Guy."

"Just met him," Cretorian replied. "Seems ol' Smokey here knows him."

"Oh, really?" Cold eyes turned toward Smokey. The man seemed to shrink just slightly. "I did not know… who he was… the Sir Guy part." He quickly fell silent as Betty Myers gaze went to Johnny again.

"I seem to have caused a stir," Johnny said quietly. "I had no intention of doing so. I'd heard the sector was needing additional supply sources. If this is not the case, I certainly have no qualms of taking my business elsewhere."

"Let's not be hasty," Governor Myers said, rather hastily. She was going to have to be careful of her temper. It had already caused her a few problems lately. Seeing that necklace on the woman that was on the arm of this man had just gotten under her skin. She was going to need plenty of contacts in the future. Bond Cretorian was good, but he was a barbarian, despite his wealth.

When the sector was hers, completely, she would need men more of the nature of Sir Guy Richardson. The little singer girl could be dealt with later. As could the necklace.

Smiling broadly now, Governor Myers said, "This is a gala affair, gentlemen. I do think we have business to discuss. Much business. But not at the moment. Please, just enjoy the evening, as I plan to, and we will meet Monday… say… at ten. At my estate."

It had not come as a question or a request. It was an order and all three men knew it. Smokey knew he was on thin ice with both Cretorian and Myers on a regular basis, so he just nodded in agreement.

Bond's eyes glinted slightly, but until things progressed somewhat more, he would need to continue to act as though the woman was in charge. It would not be much longer. He forced a smile and agreed.

Johnny, as Sir Guy, smiled graciously and said, "That sounds fine, Madam Governor. I'm sure we will all do well in the ventures ahead. Despite the rumors, I've seen no evidence of this infamous Johnny Oneshot fellow stirring things up."

The others started, then stared rather angrily at Johnny as he smiled serenely and turned away. He was already a few steps from them before any of the three reacted.

"Dammit!" Bond said with force, though he did manage to keep his voice down. "That guy better not show his face around here. I've got people searching this whole sector for that son of a bitch!"

"Keep it down, will you?" the Governor said, leaning forward slightly, her voice low. "We all know that if he knew anything about anything he would be here doing something about it.

"Now forget about it and go drink something and dance with that damned Captain I had to arrange for you." She turned hard eyes to Smokey. "And you find a way to get rid of that singer. You don't want to be having anything to do with her."

Smokey actually gulped. He was tough, by some standards. Smokey knew he was a big fish in his little pond, but he was in a very big sea at the moment. And small fish get eaten by big fish, no matter where the sea is. Marilyn Monroe was history at his club. He had a feeling she would be history, period, sometime soon. He might never find another like her, but at least he would still have his club. And his life.

Johnny had made his way toward Janet and Willi, seeing Captain Butler angling past. The wink would not be noticed, even if the cameras and live observers caught it. "The facilities back here?" he asked.

Willi nodded, her eyes going from him to where Governor Myers, Bond Cretorian, and Smokey were separating, each headed in different directions.

"I think I am at beck and call again," sighed Captain Butler, heading toward the Governor when her gaze fell on him. Even at the distance, her stance indicated his presence was desired.

"Jeez," muttered Janet. "Me too. At least the letch hasn't tried anything." Both Captain's moved away, heading for their designated escorts. Marilyn found herself immediately surrounded by people that had either seen her at *Smokey's*, heard about her being at *Smokey's*, or had seen or heard she was with Sir Guy Richardson.

"How can he have this reputation as Sir Guy and the one as Johnny Oneshot?" she asked herself silently as she talked graciously to one person after another. It was some moments later that she realized that Johnny should have been back at her side, as Sir Guy, if he was going to be back any time soon.

"Uh-oh," she said, still silently, and to herself, as she saw Governor Myers and several of her bodyguards headed for a hallway. She simply did not know if now was the time that Johnny had meant when he said he might need a distraction, but it really did not seem so.

Still, she began to ease her way toward that doorway, continuing to meet and greet people as she did. Near the bandstand now, Willi saw the sudden stir as several more obvious security types began to scan the crowds with certain intent.

"Okay," she said, this time half aloud. "This **is** what he was talking about."

"What was that, dear?" asked the elegantly dressed matron on the arm of the distinguished looking gentleman currently talking to her.

"Oh," Willi said, "It's just that several people have asked me to sing, you see… I'm a performer… and I don't really think it appropriate…" An idea suddenly came to her. "Unless," she said, looking at the elderly couple, "of course, the *Confederation Anthem*…" She left it hanging slightly.

"Oh, yes!" exclaimed the matron.

"Quite right!" added her husband. "I've done my service and tried to join again during the Transition Campaign. Bad heart, you see, and they wouldn't take me. The *Anthem*, now. I would dearly love to hear one as beautiful as Emily was in her day sing it as she once did."

"Yes, dear," said the matron, moving to the bandstand. She was used to getting her way and now was no different. A gesture to the orchestra leader and he was leaning down.

Willi wasted no time getting up before the orchestra. She knew that without the equipment at *Smokey's* she was going to sound terrible, but that would probably just help the distraction.

She still had no clue why Johnny needed one, but this was probably the time it was needed. The security personnel were really starting to work their way through the crowd, seeming to be searching for someone.

As the elderly couple stood right before her and urged her on, the orchestra conductor turned to the crowd and announced, "Ladies and Gentlemen! The *Confederation Anthem*!"

The way people turned toward the orchestra, even in more distant parts of the huge ballroom, Willi realized the stage was remotely mic-ed. Might not be the enhancing equipment of *Smokey's*, but she would be heard.

The orchestra started the first few chords, and Willi began to sing the stirring words of the *Confederation Anthem*. The crowd began to edge closer, and people began to join her in the song. She glanced down and saw the matron and gentleman sing with her, tears in their eyes.

Willi's eyes scanned the crowd as she continued the song. She turned and saw the Confederation Flag projected on the wall above and behind her. She turned back and continued to sing.

She really was not sure where the words came from. Everyone probably knew the first two stanzas of the song. Willi did not realize she knew all seven until she finished the seventh as the last strains of music faded away. The crowd was hushed.

Without a clue as to what to do next, Willi was saved from trying to think of something when Johnny was suddenly standing beside her. He handed her a glass and turned out to look at the crowd, gathered as close to the stage as humanly possible. He lifted the other glass he held and said, loudly, "To the Confederation!"

The "To the Confederation!" that came from almost every throat shook the walls. People drank, as did Johnny and Willi. Cries for Willi to perform something else, or to just do the Anthem again rang out.

With Johnny's hand on her arm, guiding her down off the stage on which the orchestra was situated, Willi just waved once in appreciation, and let herself be led away. "My dear!" the matron said, grabbing her in a surprisingly strong hug, "You were magnificent! I thought I could sing that song. You put me to shame, even at my prime!"

"Now, Precious," said her husband. "Not quite that," he continued, looking at Willi, tears still in his eyes. "But, my dear, you did do it as well as I've ever heard it done, even by Precious. Thank you."

"But I…" Before she could really protest, one of the security people bulled his way forward.

He stared hard at Johnny. "How long you been here?"

"What?" Johnny asked. "We arrived just a bit before…"

"No. Here. Right here."

"What is this about, young man?" asked the matron. "This is her escort. He was right here watching. Have some respect for the Anthem, if you please."

Several other people close clamored their agreement, all indicating that Johnny had been right there with them, watching his beautiful lady singing.

"I'm not sure what is going on," Johnny said, in his sonorous Sir Guy voice. "But if there is something wrong, perhaps I can be of assistance…"

Another security man had come up to them. "No, no of course not. There is no problem. Just a party crasher. Don't worry. We'll locate him. Everyone enjoy."

The two moved away, their eyes continuing to search the crowd. Johnny guided them toward an exit, though it was certainly not the nearest one, Willi noted. He continued to slow and talk, even stop from time to time, as the situation warranted. More often than not, it was to allow someone to thank Willi for her rendition of the Anthem, several times to include an enthusiastic hug.

Feeling more than a bit stunned, Willi found herself clutching Johnny's arm tightly as they finally made their way out of the building. There was still a crowd of spectators as well as media near the entrance. Word had reached them of the performance. Johnny waved away the questions and requests for interviews.

The driver of the limousine had it ready and the door open as the Naval personnel acting as external security formed a corridor to allow Johnny and Willi to get to it without trouble.

Willi saw the comm device appear in Johnny's hand and knew they could talk safely. "What happened?" she asked immediately.

"Worked like a charm," Johnny said. "You gave me the perfect distraction to rejoin the crowd after I talked… so to speak… to the Governor."

"How? What? What did you say? What did she say? And do?" Willi tried to look out the back of the transport. "What about Telstar and Isis? Will they be okay?"

"They're fine for the moment," Johnny said. "But that won't last long, despite the fact that they were right there at the Ball when everything I set in motion began."

Willi would have stomped her foot, if she had been able. "Will you please stop answering me with those cryptic statements? What did you do?"

Johnny leaned back against the comfortable seat. "You deserve to know. You were handed a death sentence tonight, several times over."

With a wave of her hand, Willi dismissed Johnny's comment. "I know she did not like me having this." Willi touched the necklace. But she realized, as he continued, that Johnny Oneshot did not make those types of statements lightly.

"True, but that was only the first straw. The last one was your singing."

Again, Willi started to protest that while she was not that good, of course, she was not bad enough for someone to want to kill her. She stayed silent at the look on his face.

"She had given orders that the *Anthem* not be played at the Ball. The orchestra had not been told that specifically, of course. But the music selections had all been approved by her aide. The *Anthem* was not on it. Naturally, all the musicians knew it.

"She wants the sector to be her independent domain. Totally apart from the Confederation. You singing the *Anthem*… the way the crowd reacted… I honestly thought that she might keel over with a stroke or heart attack when she saw and heard you.

"She had already warned Smokey to get rid of you, as his entertainer, with the implication that Smokey took to mean exactly what it did, that you did not have much longer to live."

At that, Willi paled. She believed Johnny completely. Governor Myers intended to have her killed. She said as much.

Johnny looked over at her then. "No. You, she intends to do herself. She was making the arrangements to have you taken to her estate on Monday, after the meeting, so she could take her own sweet time doing it."

The paleness was gone. Willi turned red with anger. "If she thinks she…"

"You are good. Very good. But not even you could take on her goons. Not alone. But try not to worry. She isn't going to find you."

"Yeah. Well, I might just try to find **her**." Willi glared at Johnny. "I will not be threatened by anyone and not respond."

"You'll have your chance," Johnny said, the sardonic smile once again on his face. "And chances are, that before this is over, she will know and understand the quite active part you have played in her demise. Not just being some beautiful woman with the bad luck to be in the wrong place at the wrong time doing the wrong thing."

It was only upon reflection later of the conversation that Willi realized how easily Johnny had used the term beautiful about her, and how sincere he had been, whether he realized it or not.

For the moment, however, she keyed on the fact that he had used the term *her demise* in a manner that made it seem a foregone conclusion. "Are you going to tell me what actually happened now, or do I have to find some means to extract it from you?"

The smile was still sardonic, but Willi saw the flash in his eyes, immediately suppressed. She knew she colored slightly, realizing what she had said could be construed a couple of different ways. She also knew that Johnny knew it was not what she meant, but that the thought had crossed his mind.

"You wish," she said quietly, and then added, "Ask Sydney and Clyde just how intensely persuasive I can be."

"No need," Johnny replied, his eyes going forward and down, to the device he still held in his hand. "I told the Governor," he continued, continuing to watch the display on the device, "that her plan was doomed. That I knew all about it. If she simply turned herself over to General Wainshaw, with a full confession, no harm would come to her."

"I bet she took that graciously," Willi murmured.

"Actually," Johnny said, "No. She shot me. Good aim, too, I might add. If I did not have on body armor, I'd be dead."

"What!?!" Willi exclaimed, shifting forward to look at him more closely.

Johnny tapped the center of his chest with a finger, his eyes still on the device in his hand. He actually did not notice, for once, Willi's reaction. The shock, and then concern, and then the wonder as she decided that the rumors, possibly all of them, were true about him.

"The seed I planted with them as Sir Guy, about Johnny Oneshot, just before I confronted her **as** Johnny Oneshot, is growing. By the time I meet with her Monday, the fruits of my labors will be ripe for the picking."

Willi punched him slightly on the arm. "You wax poetic one more time instead of getting to the point and **I'm** going to shoot you!"

Johnny actually chuckled. "Sorry. I'm so used to couching things… never mind. Anyway, I told her a couple of her key accomplices had turned on her and that I, Johnny Oneshot, intended to destroy her and her plot completely.

"That already two of her pirate mother ships had been destroyed and two more would be tonight. I sort of implied that some of those working with her had given me some information that made it possible."

"But… Bond and Smokey… and the others, assuming there are others, did not, did they?"

"No. Just… luck… mostly," Johnny replied. He cut a glance over at her, then looked back down at the device he held on one thigh.

Willi realized that insisting that luck had little to do with anything he did would be fruitless. "What about the two ships tonight? What do you mean?"

"I managed to get some items aboard two more of the primary ships that have been the bases for the pirate activity in this sector. They'll cause the destruction of the ships any time now."

"How did you…" When Johnny turned to look at her then, and she saw the emptiness in his eyes for a moment her words faded. "Never mind," she said softly.

"They're gone," he said, putting the device away, though Willi still did not see where he put it. Nor did she question his statement.

"When will she know?" she did ask.

"Sometime in the morning. She likes to keep a very tight hand on matters. I haven't found the link, but I know it exists. She knew about the one that based the attack on your shuttle less than a day later and the one we took out that evening.

"It's partly a matter of them just not reporting in on schedule, but she must have people watching the traffic lanes, too. I think it's the network Telstar put together clandestinely. Someone is feeding the information to her as well as him."

"So, he does have a watcher network?"

"Yes. It's been only marginally effective; but has helped him in his efforts. But somebody close to the Captain is a turncoat."

"Oh, no!" Willi sounded concerned. "Is he safe? And Janet?"

"Again, for the moment," replied Johnny. "As long as they don't find out who it is. If they realize what is happening, and they make any inquiry, then they will become immediate targets."

Willi nodded. "What else?" she asked.

Johnny turned to look at her again. "Reconsider leaving now. If I take you to the port now you can catch a fast freighter with just a couple of passenger cabins that I happen to know are vacant on this trip. You'll be out of range in a matter of hours."

"No," Willi said immediately. "And you did not say *her* range. What is it?"

Turning back to face the front of the transport, Johnny answered her, but it was several moments before he did. "The last information I received from my sources inside the Ecronian group that is involved with this indicated that the Ecronian government has decided to take action. Official action. They have an armada less than a week away.

"Even if we stop Myers and her group, that might not stop the Ecronians. This had looked like a very sure thing. Some of the most militant of the Ecronians have apparently convinced the rest that it is the ideal opportunity to regain a foothold in the area for… what they want and need."

"So… it will be war… again…" Willi said. She sank back against the soft padding of the seat. Before, what she was doing had been almost an adventure. Dangerous, yes. But a plot and counterplot. Johnny was talking about a real war with a deadly, heartless enemy.

"What do we do?" she asked, after a long silence.

"We make sure the Governor's plot is exposed and ended. Then I go make the Ecronians think twice about encroaching on this sector."

She could not help it. Willi shivered. The first part of what he had said had been the Johnny Oneshot she had met and dealt with up until now. His last words were what caused the shiver. They were cold, hard, and deadly.

He was opening the limousine door before she could react, other than the shiver. "I'll continue until Confederation forces arrive in strength. If the report I send tonight is believed, it should be less than a month before a sizable force arrives.

Johnny handed her out of the limousine. "Be ready by six in the morning. The Governor is too busy at the moment, but it will not be long before Myers will think to start tying up the loose end you have now become."

Willi nodded. Then he was gone. She was not even sure if he had re-entered the limousine or gone past it. When she reached her room, Willi began to pack. She decided to just leave the things she had acquired since she had been there. "Except for this," she said, looking at herself in the large reflector panel.

A frown crossed her face when she ran across the wallet with the credit chips Johnny had given her. The look changed slightly as the original reason, the fact that he had given her so much, shifted to the fact of how much she might just need them. Willi stashed the chips in several places, just in case she lost, or had to abandon, some of her belongings.

Un-used to the jumpy feeling she was experiencing the next morning after she woke, Willi decided to go down and wait in the lobby of the rooming house, leaving her few pieces of luggage stacked inside the room right by the door.

She jumped back in surprise when she opened the room door. A man was standing there, hand raised to knock, rather than use the annunciator. It was a moment before Willi realized it was Johnny Oneshot.

He stepped inside and closed the door behind him. "Good. You're already ready. This all?"

Willi nodded and watched as he took off the jacket he wore, reversed it, and put it back on. No longer looking like the rooming house employee he had moments before, after he also removed something from his mouth and ran his fingers through his hair, Johnny picked up three of the cases and looked over at Willi.

"It was still clear when I came in, but just in case, be ready to run. Drop the case if you have to. You don't have much, of course, and you may need some of it, so I don't want to abandon anything that isn't totally necessary."

Johnny gave her a long look. "I am wearing body armor and have some for you where we're going. I did not have a chance to bring it in so you could put it on now. So, if anything happens, do not hesitate to take cover behind me. Do you understand?"

"Of course, I understand, but…"

Johnny cut her off quickly. "No buts. Anything starts, you will use me for protection." He just looked at her.

Willi finally nodded.

"Make a point to complain about having to leave because… some reason. You'll think of something on the way down." Johnny activated the door.

By the time they reached the lobby Willi's mind was still blank. When they saw the first couple of people, she suddenly found herself saying, "Are you sure Mother said I should come? You know how she feels about what I'm doing. She must be awfully ill… can't the doctors do anything else? I thought everything was okay or I would never… oh, my… I…"

When her words faded and her gazed dropped as they exited the building doors, people were looking on sympathetically. Johnny hid his smile at her performance, lifted a hand and signaled a passing taxi.

Head still down, shoulders shaking as if she were sobbing uncontrollably, Willi handed him the one bag she carried, and then ducked into the taxi as Johnny stowed the luggage. The automated vehicle started up as soon as Johnny entered, gave the destination, and slipped a credit chip into the slot.

Watching her, as Willi lifted her head, no sign of tears, Johnny said, "Well, that lets out trying to head out through the transport port. They'll be looking for you there for sure, knowing you're heading out to go to your ailing mother."

"Oh, no!" Willi said, eyes widening. "I never thought about…"

Johnny was grinning. "It'll work like a charm," he said. "They'll be looking there and we'll be somewhere else entirely."

"You did that intentionally!" she accused him.

Johnny shrugged nonchalantly. "A couple of things we need to cover. I have a couple of things to do after I get you settled where you'll be staying for a while. You already know how to get to the Dominators." He handed her one of the comm devices.

"If something were to happen…" Johnny looked away for a moment, but then back to her. "Press this, and then this, and finally this." Johnny made sure Willi understood.

"It will self-destruct. This cannot fall into anyone else's hands but mine and yours. It is very important, even at additional risk to you." His eyes met hers. "I'm sorry."

Willi nodded. The way he had tried to protect her, she knew it cost him something to tell her the device was more important than her safety. But that was the way it was.

"The comm device is primarily so you can access the Dominators to get away, if need be. When you get a moment, though," he continued, handing her a standard miniature reader, "review what is on this.

"It will erase itself after one play, so make sure you are paying attention. It is the instructions on how to use the other features of the comm device. The only way to start that information is to enter a piece of information only you would know when it asks you. Everything else on it is just pop culture programs.

"If you need to get away, and get to the Dominators, or need any other help, when I'm not handy, go back to *Smokey's*, make sure no one is looking, and beeline to Cherokee and tell him you need his help. He'll understand and do it."

"He's part of this?"

"Will be if needed," Johnny said, handing her a small case. "Just in case," he said. "I know you can use it."

When she opened the case, Willi whistled. It contained a state-of-the-art personal defense weapon. The PDW was small, deadly, easy to use, and highly illegal for anyone not part of the Confederation Security Forces to have in their possession. In the case with the device were plenty of the power packs that operated it and the ammunition that it used.

Seeing the concealment device that was also in the case, Willi colored slightly and then looked at Johnny as she said, "Turn around for a moment."

Johnny did so, then turned around again when she said, "Okay."

His glance at the case showed him that it was empty. Johnny made sure he did not think about where the device was now, or the spare power packs and ammunition.

"I should be back sometime this afternoon. Then, since you have insisted on being part of this, we are going hunting."

"Hunting?" Willi asked.

"Pirates," Johnny said. "Things are in a turmoil after the attempted assassination last night. Martial law will be declared shortly. We're going to take extreme advantage of the situation."

"What? What assassination? The only person that almost got killed was you!"

"There's a vid unit where you'll be. Watch and you'll understand," Johnny said with that sardonic smile of his. "She already had it planned… she just did not count on a myth being there."

"What do you mean…" Johnny put his fingers to his lips, cutting her question off as the taxi stopped.

"Quickly now," he whispered, leaving the vehicle.

When she saw him transferring her things from the taxi to another vehicle, this one a very old fashioned wheeled vehicle, Willi helped him. "After it makes the second turn, drop down out of sight and stay there until it stops. You'll be safe then. Get out and familiarize yourself with the place. If something… if I'm not there by eighteen hundred, I won't be at all. Get away. Go home."

Johnny was guiding her inside the old vehicle. "Just hold the wheel. It has some modern improvements." He flipped a physical toggle switch and closed the door.

Willi had not had time to react. The vehicle was moving away, guided by some mechanism, leaving Johnny standing beside the taxi. Willi saw him in the mirror get back into the taxi and the taxi pull away.

Quickly she turned her attention to the vehicle. Willi wondered about it; but decided to just follow Johnny's instructions. Though she fully intended to make sure he filled her in much, much, more thoroughly in the future than what he had just done. "Much more!" she said half aloud.

When she had looked over the austere accommodations to which the vehicle had eventually taken her, Willi took out the comm device and the reader. She would watch the news vids later. First the important things.

"I am going to maim him!" she muttered when the reader popped up the security question for her to open the file on the comm device. There was only one way he could have programmed in the question and proper response.

He had somehow managed to see her responses to that stupid survey in that stupid magazine cartridge she had picked up for her cousin. She had been bored and started looking at it not long after they had left the planet where they had picked up Johnny.

It had been a sex survey and her curiosity got the best of her and she started filling it out. "I should maim Cousin Jenny, too," she muttered. "If she had not asked me to get the newest issue he would never know…"

Willi entered the same answer she had used in the survey. Up popped the instruction for the comm device. All other thoughts left her mind as she studied. When she was finished, she looked at the device in her hand with awe.

It was on a par, if not well above it, with the defense device she still carried in a very private place.

"Okay," she thought, "Now the news vids." After watching half a dozen different reports of what was going on not only on this planet, but on the orbiting facilities, she was seething. What Johnny had said now made perfect sense.

Governor Myers had planned to fake an assassination attempt on herself during the Inaugural Ball. To use it to impose controls and sanctions. The official word was that the pirates were behind it, but that they were being supplied and directed by *certain elements in the Confederation that do not want the sector to stay peaceful and under the direction of the rightfully appointed governor.*

"Anyone that believes that bit of propaganda would have to be half brain dead!" Willi told the vid screen. "She just wants to put her strangle hold on the sector!"

The facilities were austere, but there was food. She ate after she went over the place thoroughly. She found a few useful items, which she was sure Johnny had intended. Willi was getting anxious when sixteen hundred rolled around and Johnny still had not returned.

She had the standard sidearm she wore drawn and pointing at him without thought when he suddenly appeared. "Don't do that!" she protested, holstering the weapon on her hip.

The drawing of, and then re-holstering were both more unconscious acts, as the weapon and holster were identical to those she used when on the trading missions in the shuttle. Apparently, the special weapon was to be kept secure for special circumstances.

"Good reflexes," Johnny said. "I'll keep it in mind." He looked around. "I see that you've made yourself at home. Hopefully it will not be for long. Things have taken a turn for the worse, unfortunately.

"Despite some of the seeds of distrust I planted, the group has stayed together, for the most part. I'd hoped to trigger a falling out, but only a couple of minor players are no longer involved."

Willi noted the feral grin as he continued. "However, what we do tonight, if successful, will change some of that." He took a quick bite from a ration pack, and then set it aside.

It was automatic. "You should eat something more and get some rest."

"No time," Johnny said. "You found the confusion suits?"

Willi nodded.

"I want to get this done, and then try to contact Telstar and Isis. There is something going on at the base, and my normal sources were not available. I do not like that."

The words themselves, more than the even tone, told Willi that he was worried. Very worried. She had learned how to read between the lines, even when he used very few lines. At least part of the time.

"Go ahead and suit up. Draw one of the medium weapons launchers. I'm going to need to go in fast and light, but I want major damage when I exit."

As almost all Trading Families did, *Trinity Home's* group of families insisted that everyone, above a certain age, had weapons training. The universe was a dangerous place always, and sometimes the danger came from entities that required force with which to stop them.

It took only moments for Willi to have the confusion suit components on, and a weapons launcher and ammunition bags slung over her shoulders. "Where are we going?" she asked.

"Other side of the planet," Johnny said, still adding items to the harness he had put on after he had put on his own confusion suit components.

Willi was beginning to wonder what he considered going in heavy, if what he was equipping himself with was going in light. But she did not get a chance to ask. Johnny lifted a trapdoor in the floor, by tilting back the small table in the center of the room.

"I'm not going to like this, am I?" Willi asked, stepping over and looking down into the narrow confines of a shaft going straight down.

"Probably not," Johnny replied. "Give me a three count before you drop. The trap will close on its on in about a minute so don't worry about it. Make sure your legs are bent." Then he was gone.

Taking a deep breath, Willi counted to three silently, and then stepped into the hole. She felt Johnny's hand steady her when she landed, staggering slightly, even having made sure to land with her legs bent to absorb the shock.

It was too dark to see well, though there was some light. Willi had just enough time to realize they were standing in a high-speed transport tunnel before Johnny was pressing his body against hers, holding her tightly against the wall of the tunnel as a transporter hurtled past mere centimeters from his back.

"Okay. Next one is faster, but it has to slow to let the one ahead take a turnout to let it get past. We have just enough time to get onto the rear connector. There are good foot and hand holds, but make sure you are secure immediately. You'll have to tie off after we get going."

Willi nodded. She could feel the air rushing past as the transporter approached, pushing the air in the tunnel ahead of it. Again, Johnny crowded against her as the craft went past, visibly slowing. Johnny began running toward the rear of the thing when it had cleared them, and Willi followed.

He watched, but did not reach out to help her, as she scrambled onto the projecting coupler at the rear of the last unit. She had had at least three seconds to spare, and was glad she had looped an arm through an access hatch handle, for when the transporter speeded back up, it did so very rapidly, and was going fast enough to make breathing slightly difficult due to the slight vacuum created behind it in the tight tunnel.

Willi looked over at Johnny and could barely believe his eyes. He was holding on with one hand, the other using the comm device. She did note that he had the device fastened to his harness with a lanyard. If he did drop it, it would not be lost.

He looked over at her, smiled, and held up the comm device. She had to grin back when she realized the number she was seeing was the speed at which they were traveling. It was walking speed compared to the velocities she obtained in space, but considering she was riding on the back of a transporter, traveling underground, with just enough clearance to avoid... most of the time... scraping the paint off the sides, it was fast.

Again, her eyes widened in astonishment when Johnny fastened a carabineer to a handy projecting loop and propped his knees against the wall of the transporter and seemed to relax, arms crossed on his chest, head down as if he intended to take a nap.

Hurriedly Willi attached herself to attachment points she found, using three carabineers to do so. She looked over at Johnny occasionally. He did seem to actually be napping, his body swaying gently with the motion of the transporter. She found herself relaxing, feeling secure with the fastenings, but knew she was not about to fall asleep, if it took them the rest of the evening and all of the night to get where they were going.

She woke up when Johnny nudged her. With a muttered curse at having fallen asleep in the first place, Willi had to struggle slightly to get a good grip so she could start unfastening the carabineers. She saw that Johnny was already free and ready to step off the transporter when the time came.

When she was ready, Johnny held up his hand, showing four fingers. She mouthed the words, "Minutes?" Apparently using the regular communication devices they wore was not acceptable at the moment.

Johnny nodded. Willi felt the unit begin to slow perceptibly, and then much more quickly. She continued to watch Johnny. When he nodded, she stepped back and began running forward, as the transporter was still going at a good clip. She did not even stumble, and followed Johnny into a side tunnel as the transporter came to a groaning halt some distance down the main tunnel.

Willi looked at her chrono. They had traveled for almost two hours. She must have slept most of the last one. She shook her head, and then looked at Johnny. He grinned at her and she had to grin back.

"Okay. We're going up. Have to climb and it's a good distance. We take our time and rest at the top. We'll be going out into a large warehousing complex. The pirates have a small base in one of the warehouses. It's number thirteen, believe it or not.

"There's a good spot to set yourself up about ten meters to the right when we exit. I'll cover you until you are ready, and then go directly from the portal into the warehouse. When you see me come out, or if I don't come out after no more than six minutes, level the place."

Willi looked at him with alarm.

"There are no non-combatants inside. I've scouted it thoroughly. And my last remote check of the surveillance devices indicates the same.

"Besides… if I'm caught by those inside… there is no hope. Level it. There'll be several jumpers parked around. Take one and go."

She wanted to protest, but the look in his eyes prevented it. "You can count on me."

"I know," Johnny said. He reached for the first ladder rung of the shaft leading up without responding further. They did not exchange another word until after they were in one of the jumpers, headed toward space.

There had been no one visible when she exited the access portal for the tunnel, and no alarm had sounded when she ran over and set out her ammunition in the spot Johnny had said would be there, and was. She got the launcher up on her shoulder and ready.

Watching Johnny move from the portal to the door of warehouse thirteen she was amazed at how quickly he covered the ground. She had not really taken note of what he had equipped himself with, other than there seemed to be a lot more than she would have considered a light load.

Willi did recognize the effects of one of the devices, for a door disintegrated as he approached it at a dead run, and then went through the resulting opening without slowing.

It was many long moments before she heard anything else, but then the noise was deafening for a moment before the communicator muffled it. Willi could hear the activity, the communicator controlling the volume to understandable levels.

Her grip tightened on the launcher and she felt a chill go down her spine. She had just heard the unmistakable sounds of at least two Ecronians. And they were not in the least bit happy. Her chrono was counting down the six minutes. She knew now why Johnny had said to level the place whether or not he came out.

But he did. Again, at a dead run, despite dragging something behind him. Johnny knew Wilhelmina McKindrick was a capable young woman in many ways, not the least of which was weapons handling.

But even he was surprised to see the signature, small as it was, of the launcher sending a projectile toward the warehouse behind him. It passed close enough to him for him to feel the air disturbance.

He felt the concussion on his back even as he saw her changing her aim and hitting the warehouse with the full capability of her weapon. Johnny headed for the nearest corner of the next nearest warehouse. Willi grabbed the other end of the parcel he was dragging with one hand, the other holding the launcher ready, and helped him drag the thing.

She helped him get it into the jumper that was just around the corner of the warehouse. So far there had been no pursuit from Warehouse Thirteen. Willi did not think there would be. She had hit it with a saturation pattern from directly ahead, and then again from above, using the capability of the weapon and ammunition for a projectile to climb after launch and then dive down on the top of the target.

It was only when Johnny said, "If he tries to get out of that bag, feel free to use whatever force you'd like in order to prevent it," that Willi realized that it was a live being they had been dragging. Her sidearm seemed to leap into her hand when she heard the non-human moan.

Willi quickly took a seat and strapped herself in. Johnny would not be sparing the fuel. It bothered her not at all to leave the Ecronian lying on the floor, still inside the polymer bag in which Johnny had brought him from the warehouse.

There were more moans as the acceleration began in earnest. Willi just stomped her foot on the opening of the bag when an Ecronian appendage began to appear. "Stay or die," she said, coldly. The moans continued, but the movement stopped.

"Evasive maneuvering!" Johnny called out.

Willi did shove the Ecronian into some semblance of security, holding him in place with her feet, as Johnny sent the jumper on a violent path. She felt the jumper shudder more than once from near misses as the acceleration continued.

"Okay," Johnny said. "We're clear of the defense ring. We've got about ten minutes before they vector attack craft to us. Come up and find us a place to land safely, but with people around."

Willi quickly changed places with him and was glad she did not see what happened in the tiny cabin behind her. What she heard was bad enough.

She had no doubt that Johnny had given the Ecronian a chance. He would not have done otherwise. But when she set the jumper down in the middle of a large park, and left the pilot seat, she saw the Ecronian still down on the floor of the cabin.

He was not inside the bag now, and he was moaning again. The cause had nothing to do with acceleration. It had to do with the obviously broken lower appendage from which the Ecronian was now suffering.

Johnny finished fastening restraints on the other, still usable, appendages. He looked up at Willi. "Only got a minute or so. Disable the door when we go out. I don't want anyone getting in to do anything to him… it… before the military gets here. They can open this thing up like a tin can, when they do get here, so will not need a working hatch. You ready?"

Willi nodded. Johnny activated the hatch and they stepped out. A crowd was gathering. Jumpers, certainly capable of what they had just done, obviously, were strictly prohibited from using anything except jump ports.

It took only a moment for Willi to have the hatches jammed so it would take some force to enter the jumper. She listened to Johnny as he spoke to the crowd while she did her work. "Make sure no one tries to enter. Clear the area so the military can land a craft here. They need what is inside and it is dangerous."

"Who the hell are you? And what is going on? Someone could have been killed when you landed that thing here!"

"Hey!" came a yell from the crowd. "It's Johnny Oneshot! It's got to be. No one could do this but him!"

Willi was looking at Johnny and saw him wince. "We got to go, now," Johnny said softly. They both could hear the combat craft approaching.

"I think you'd better stay and…" The man suddenly stepped back when he saw Johnny look at him. "Or not."

Johnny started running and Willi followed. When he darted between two buildings, Willi had to stop and turn back to join him. She was past the opening before she could stop, he had made the turn so quickly. Several people had been trying to follow, but after two more twists and turns they had lost the last of them.

It had not been an option to do anything physical to stop them. Only eluding them was acceptable. Johnny Oneshot did not harm innocents. And neither did she.

Willi was amazed again when they stopped. She was in good shape, and was not really winded after the running, but she was feeling the effects of the effort. Johnny seemed not to even be breathing hard.

He was studying his comm device again. "Okay. We're good. There's an underground access tunnel to the utilities grid just ahead. It's a short trip there. Activate the confusion suit for civilian clothing and go out and get a robot taxi."

Willi nodded. It went just as he said. It was not long before they were in a taxi headed for another of the private jump ports. It was full dark now. "You think they'll be looking for us at the jump port?" she asked.

"Doubtful, but possible," Johnny said. "If they are, we just do an alternate plan. Go back and steal another of the jumpers at the warehouse."

"They'll have people all over that place now!" Willi exclaimed.

The sardonic smile was back. "Sure. The Security Forces. Look a lot like us, don't you think?" He adjusted the confusion suit.

"You are audacious!" Willi replied.

They did not have to find out if it would work, though Willi thought it probably would have. There was no trouble at the small ten-hanger jump port. "Do you have these things all over the planet?" Willi asked Johnny.

"Here and there," was the only reply she received.

Chapter Five

-

When they were in the Dominators, Johnny told her, through the secure short range commlink, "We're going to monitor the base for a bit to see if I can figure out what's going on. Try to get some rest while we're in wait mode."

"I'll try," Willi acknowledged, though she doubted she would. She surprised herself yet again. It was much like the training aboard *Trinity Home*. They had been taught to rest when they could when in certain situations. Such as this one, though certainly not *exactly* like it. The beep from her instruments had her alert from her resting-the-eyes-and-senses state.

It certainly was not accepted communications protocol. "For crying out loud, Broadsword Leader! This is the third straight patrol you and Isis have done! You can't keep it up!"

"Belay that!" came Captain Butler's voice.

Willi could hear the fatigue even over the communications equipment.

"We have our orders." The same fatigue was evident in Captain Echart's voice when she spoke.

"At least hang back. I'll take point and…"

"You will follow orders, Lieutenant Chambers! Now fall into formation and maintain comm silence until we make contact!"

"Aye, sir!"

The two Dominators were drifting only a meter or so apart. Willi looked over at Johnny in the other cockpit. He held up the comm device. She took hers out of a slit pocket and looked at it. Apparently, Johnny did not even want to use the secure comm link of the Dominators.

"On at least watch and watch. He broke comm procedure himself. He has to be exhausted to do that. Isis no doubt the same. We shadow and protect. No action unless they run into bogies. Then we take it to them before Broadsword does."

"Acknowledged," Willi signaled back.

As was often the case, Captain Butler fell back and let the rest of the flight go to the base when the patrol ended. He ran his long-range sensors, again as he often did. When he saw the two blips he almost called the flight back, but the speed and vector convinced him to just hold position.

It was not long before the other two Dominators pulled up beside him. He saw Guy Richardson's hand signals and set the communications frequency and code on his communications unit.

"How is Isis?" came the other voice he still did not know.

"Weary unto death," an equally weary William Butler said. "We're chasing red herrings. I don't have a clue why we're running these patrols where we're running them. No contacts at all. Just using up fuel and stamina."

"That is the point," Johnny said. "They want you dead tired, and then dead, period. I expect you will be ordered, soon, to go out, just the two of you, since the others will be so tired, and you will volunteer anyway to protect them."

"I won't let her go out again," Captain Butler said with some force.

"You have to," Johnny said. "Don't worry. Everyone is going to be very surprised at what happens, when it happens. Everything will come to a head in less than two days.

"Try to hang on for now. If you get the order for just the two of you to do a patrol, send word." Johnny motioned another frequency and code.

They saw Captain Butler nod. He fired up and headed toward the base again. Willi followed as Johnny vectored them further out into space, even further away from the Moon-Ship base and orbiting transport terminal.

When they reached it, Willi was surprised that the vessel floating there in space had not appeared on any of the sensors. At least until they were well within close-range sensor range. Then she actually got a good look at it.

"Talk about stealth," she muttered. The vessel was essentially a signal trap. An entire, very wide spectrum of signals, trap. Not much could reflect, including light.

It was too small to dock with, so they exited the Dominators, tethered them, and entered the eerie vessel through a personnel airlock.

"What the hell is this thing?" Willi asked as soon as their helmets were off.

"An experiment. Effective sensor suppression, but they never could figure out how to make it work with a propulsion unit, so it sort of just fell off the R&D books. I managed to acquire a couple of the test beds like this one.

"Effective hides, if positioned correctly. We'll rest here, eat something and clean up a little. Unless I miss my guess, Telstar and Isis will be heading out to their planned deaths in less than eight hours."

Willi blanched. "What do you mean?"

"What I told Captain Butler. They want the two of them dead tired, and all the members of the flights. It looks like they've had everyone on high alert, sending them out to tire them out. They know what kind of people the two Captains are. Probably several other dedicated people in various positions, as well.

"Telstar and Isis have done a lot of damage since they teamed up on these flights. They are going to use their dedication to get them killed in a manner that will bring more support for the Governor, while getting the two out of the way."

"But we **are** going to prevent that," Willi replied, never doubting the fact that Johnny already had a plan to do so.

"Yes, we are," replied Johnny. He waited until the two had stripped out of the flight suits and were tethered to the wall next to the food locker, so they could consume one of the zero-gee meals without needing to maintain position in free fall, before he filled her in on his plan.

Willi's eyes were wide when Johnny stopped talking. At first, she had been entranced as he laid out the first part of the plan, and then appalled with the last part.

"You can't do…" Willi was protesting when Johnny cut her off.

His eyes were on hers, his face devoid of emotion, when he said, "Willi, it **is not** up for discussion. It is the only thing that has any hope of working. To buy enough time for Confederation forces to get here with enough resources to make sure the Ecronians will not follow through on their plans.

"And your part is just as critical as mine is, now that things have developed the way they have. I am not one hundred percent sure what my plan might have been were you not here, but I would have found a way. At least I like to think I could have. Anyway…

"You will stay here, monitor comms, and bring Telstar and Isis here if they are ordered out. And wait here with them. Until I return, send verified word, or Confederation forces arrive."

"But you said that could be a month!" Willi was feeling herself panic. She breathed deeply a few times, as Johnny watched her. She knew that he knew, what was happening with her. She was furious, frightened for him. For Telstar. For Isis. For herself. And the millions of humans in the sector. And he waited patiently until she could speak again without being totally irrational.

"There has to be another way!" The words were soft, but urgent.

Johnny shook his head. "No. Not at this point in time, with the circumstances as they are."

"I can go with you, at least to the meeting and then…" Willi's words trailed away as Johnny just looked at her.

She knew she had tears shimmering in her eyes. In freefall, they would not fall, just accumulate until she wiped them away. There were far more than enough to enable Johnny to see them, without a doubt.

He said nothing else as he turned away to suit up again. Just before he donned his helmet, he gave her another long look, where she was still tethered, watching him. "Some of the rumors are true," he said softly. And then he was gone.

Willi did not even untether to go to a viewport to see him leave in his Dominator. She wiped away the tears then, did what little cleanup was required, and then, tethered at the small comms console, let herself doze off and on, the volume up on the receiver that would carry word from Telstar and Isis if they were ordered out on patrol again.

Less than six hours later, right after another quick meal and trip into the tiny lavatory, Willi was fully alert. The coded message was repeated, and then silence.

Hurrying, but being very careful, Willi was quickly in her flight suit, and had the Dominator headed on an intercept course that would put her in a sensor dead zone just as Telstar and Isis arrived at it, on their way to the coordinates to which they had been vectored after leaving the Moon-Ship base.

It was patently obvious that the Captains had been sent out to their deaths. That course would take them directly into the heart of the pirate hideout area that Johnny had found.

Between the overwhelming numbers of pirate fighters that would undoubtedly be waiting on them, and the dead zone they would have to pass through, the two did not stand a chance, even in the Dominator and the F-777.

Telstar caught the blip of Willi's Dominator just as she caught his right before both entered the dead zone. The quick, scrambled, comms burst Willi sent was acknowledged by Telstar just before all three of them entered the dead zone.

Immediately slowing to the equivalent of a crawl, in space, to avoid any chance of a collision, since only at extremely close range within the dead zone would any of their sensors 'see' the other craft, Willi and the two Captains stayed on their respective courses, by not activating any guidance controls at all.

When the sudden ping came, Willi brought her Dominator to a dead stop, relative to the others. After a series of single sensor pings, the three craft were within a few meters of each other.

Even in the dead zone, none of them were willing to trust further communications, other than the 'follow me' sign that Willi gave the other two pilots.

Immediately she began to accelerate, leaving the dead zone at high speed, on a vector completely different from the one any of them would have been on if they had continued the courses they were on upon entering it.

Not only was the course not one that anyone that might have had sensors searching in the area would be watching, it was such that most of those sensor searches would be through the dead zone, and more or less ineffective, anyway.

Telstar and Isis formed up on Willi, who maintained a speed somewhat below Isis's F-777 maximum economical cruise speed.

Neither Isis nor Telstar could tell why Willi suddenly began to slow, as there was nothing showing on any of their instruments. It was only when they came within unmistakable visual range of Johnny's hide, as he called it, that the two knew they had reached their destination. At least, temporary destination.

Tethering their craft the way they saw Pipeline doing, the two joined Willi inside the vessel, all three going through the airlock at the same time.

When Willi undogged her helmet and removed it, Janet did a double take, and Bill's eyes literally bugged out a bit. "Marylin?" Janet asked, just floating in the zero-gee of the vessel.

An amused look on her face at Bill's reaction, she nodded, and then finished slipping out of the space flight suit and secured it in a locker. Bill and Janet did the same.

With the same dazed look on his face, which Willi did attribute, at least partially, to how exhausted he was, Bill continued to stare at her when she rotated slowly in the air to face them. A slight motion of her hand against a wall, and she drifted gracefully over to the small table that was part of the furnishings mounted against what was considered the floor when inside the hide.

Janet joined her, and then Bill. Janet opened her mouth, and to stave off what she knew would be a very long series of questions, Willi began to explain.

"Actually, I am Willi McKindrick; Wilhelmina, more precisely; but I always go by Willi."

"Except when you go by Marilyn Monroe," Bill muttered.

Willi had to grin. "Well… Yes. But that has only been since very recently." She told them about her first meeting with Johnny Oneshot, what had happened, and her subsequent successful attempt to find him.

Bill interrupted her. "Okay. That is fine. But how does this Sir Guy Richardson guy fit into this? He said **he** was Johnny Oneshot, at first. Just who is he?"

"He is Johnny Oneshot," Willi insisted, having trouble keeping another grin off her face. Even Janet was finding it hard to accept. Willi decided they needed a bit more convincing.

"And you know that swamper working at *Smokey's*? That was him, too. And I have seen him in a couple more disguises. That I am sure of. Not sure who else he has been at different times. But I really do not want to talk about that now."

Willi sighed. "I need to fill you in on the rest of the plan."

"Joh… Guy… Whoever!" Bill said rather forcefully, already filled us in. You were there." Janet put a hand on one of Bill's forearms.

"Yes," Willi said calmly. She knew Bill was only reacting because of his exhaustion. "I think you two could probably use some water, and a sustainment meal pouch."

Neither contradicted her. Willi skillfully flitted about the interior of the small craft and returned to the table with the items stated. When she noticed Janet and Bill looking at her, she asked, "What?" She turned around to see if she had let one of the pouches leak.

"How do you do that in here?" Janet asked with amazement. "I think you did more twists and spins than a dozen corkscrews have."

"Yeah…" was all Bill could get out.

Willi scrunched her nose slightly, flipped her left-hand fingers, negligently, and in her split toe spacecraft deck slippers, grabbed the platform and eased herself into position. "Just practice," she said, again, as if it was nothing, handing out the pouches to the other two, keeping one of the fortified drink pouches for herself.

"Okay, back to it," she continued as Bill tore into the meal, relatively speaking, and Janet downed almost one half of her drink in one long series of swallows. Which, Willi noticed absently, seemed to fascinate Bill.

"He just will not tell me what exactly he is going to do, but Johnny plans to stir up something today, and then again tomorrow. We are to stay here until he contacts us with a secure transmission or wait for the Confederation Forces that should be here in about a month."

"A month! I am not waiting a month to do something," Bill replied vehemently.

"Nor am I!", added Janet.

Bill's tone was suddenly lower. "Well, perhaps in your case… And Mari… Willi's, that might not be a…"

Janet glared at him and he shut up. "Go on," she said to Willi, finally looking back toward her.

"He did say," Willi continued, without comment on Janet's and Bill's abbreviated conversation, which, apparently, Janet had resolved to her satisfaction, if not Bill's, "That things should be over in two days."

Willi's eyes slid over to one of the view ports. Janet and Bill exchanged a glance, suspecting what she was thinking. But Willi brought her eyes back to the two Captains and continued, if not cheerfully, at least with confidence. Confidence in Johnny Oneshot, they were both sure.

"So, we wait to hear from him in the next couple of days. And then we will decide what to do. Because I can tell you, he **IS NOT** going to do what he said he was going to do to delay the Ecronians."

With that, Willi slipped away without really saying anything else. She tethered herself to one of the sleeping nets, turned away from the cabin, and went very quiet.

Again, Bill and Janet exchanged a glance, after watching Willi for a few moments, but neither said anything. With a shrug, Bill flipped a foot and went to the sleeping net the furthest away, and then did the same as Willi.

More slowly, Janet did the same. But not until after a long time watching Willi, and then a longer time with her eyes on Bill. But, finally, like the other two, she was sleeping the sleep of exhaustion.

A klaxon sounding woke all three. Willi was the first out of her tethers, which amazed Bill and Janet yet again with her skill in zero-gee. But they too were at the comm console moments later.

If Willi had not IFFed the signal herself, she was not sure if she would have believed it was Johnny Oneshot speaking. The decoding computer was working just fine, but Johnny's voice did not sound right. Something was wrong, Willi was sure. But she did not have a chance to query him.

"The hide will be compromised shortly. Drop planetside immediately, in the fighters. The information is in a burst to follow. When you have grounded, look for a small flat spot, just inside the lower left of the hatches on all three craft.

"Each of you touch the one in your craft and only the one in your craft. They will go into deep stealth mode, but will be available when needed. Willi has the additional instructions in her comm device.

"After the craft are cloaked, head for *Smokey's* and make sure Cherokee knows you are in a hurry. He will know what to do. Follow his instructions to the letter.

"I will be in contact again as soon as I can. Oh. I suggest the hiding set. Burst beginning now."

That was it. A fraction of a second later came a squeal that was too high in frequency for Janet and Bill to hear, and was just barely audible to Willi.

Willi pulled the chip from the comm console, slid it into the comm device after retrieving it from her garment, without either Bill or Janet seeing where it had been hidden.

All three were now donning their flight suits as quickly as possible. Only enough time was taken for the three to check each other, just to be safe, in case in their haste something was amiss. There was not a single thing that was not textbook correct.

The three were headed away from the hide at the highest speed Isis' Triple Seven could make, following the course that Willi had transferred to the other two ships from her Dominator as they brought the systems online.

Although they were well away from the hide, and already dropping into the atmosphere when their passive rear sensors picked up a massive explosion in the direction in which the hide was located. Or had been, all three thought immediately.

They were in radio silence, of course, so none of the three stated what all three were thinking. A nuke had been used on the hide. A massive one. Probably of a size that could blow a crater the size of some small moons in a planet. For something that was barely the size of a very small home.

And nothing was said for some time after their landing at a very out of the way area of the planet. Each touched the flat panel switch in their respective craft, that Johnny had described, and the three craft first disappeared from visible sight, except for a slight shimmer, and then obviously flew away on their own, still cloaked. A few seconds later there was no indication, by sound, sight, or smell, of the three craft.

All three pilots exchanged glances. "Uh... F-777s don't have cloaking," Janet managed to say.

"Neither do Dominators," Bill added softly. "At least not like that, and not from the factory. And how could I have missed that switch…"

Another exchange of glances and the three turned at a sound, Willi, wishing she had retrieved the PDW provided by Johnny, drew her sidearm, the one issued by the *Trinity Home*. Though not near the weapon the PDW was, the weapon was highly capable, and Willi was an expert in its use.

Bill and Janet were doing the same, bringing their service weapons out and up, ready for whatever was making the sound just beyond a low rise of ground.

"I may kill him myself!" Willi muttered when she saw the small wilderness transporter that he had apparently arranged to be there for their use. Robotic, using minimal AI programming, which was mostly just a smarter than usual version of the positioning units in field survival kits, the transporter was an idiot proof ride for six-year-olds.

Not to mention, this one was in the shape of a very large, very gray/pink, cottontail bunny, Old Earth style. It was a children's school field trip transporter.

Janet could not keep from laughing, and though Bill felt more like Willi, he did smile, as well.

The three clambered aboard, finding three low profile back packs on one of the bench seats. When the packs were opened up the three handed them around, so the correct pack was with the person for which it was meant.

All three had an identical note, however. *Wasn't sure of what might be needed. Dress appropriately. Blending, running, hiding, fighting.*

"You," Janet said to Bill, "Up front, eyes front."

Bill smirked slightly, but took the front bench seat, pulled out the 'hiding' set of clothing and stripped out of the flight suit and put the clothing on.

"Wondering what *I suggest the hiding set* meant was driving me nuts," Janet said, in the seat second behind Bill's, with Willi in the third, both of them dressing in that set of clothes for each of them, just as Bill was, their backs to him.

Included in the packs were cache bags, obviously for their flight suits. A few minutes after they were changed, and the flight suits cached, and the three seated on the six-year-old sized bench seats, that were more than a bit uncomfortable for adult size people, Willi fed the coordinates into the transporter using the simple touch screen.

Apparently, all three decided at once, the school field trip transporter was not the standard version it appeared. What should have been a dumb as rocks AI GPS guidance system was obviously something much more sophisticated.

And so was the power drive. All three had to hold on tightly as the transporter lifted slightly, spun around, and took off at high speed.

A much higher speed than what an Old Earth cotton tail bunny rabbit could reach, even with a hungry coyote after it. And every bit as agile as said rabbit when it came to changing course abruptly to avoid obstacles in its path, while maintaining the lowest profile possible.

It was not all that long before the transporter grounded, out of sight, but well within walking distance of a city transporter stop. More than glad to get off, and away from, the crazy rabbit contraption, the three casually appeared at the transit stop, separately.

Without acknowledging one another, other than the normal that would be expected by three fellow transit passengers, they boarded the transit car when it popped up out of the access portal.

The car dropped down and headed into the heart of the city. There were several people aboard, so it was no problem for the three of them to take separate seats, well away from one another.

Johnny had included materials in the packs for each of the clothing selections, that would help them maintain the particular look they were using.

Willi was watching a vid on her wrist communicator, Bill was perusing a throwaway business 'paper', and Janet was trying to not look too inept at knitting whatever it was supposed to be that had been in the pack.

"Such an old skill!" exclaimed a woman that suddenly sat down beside Janet. "My great… I think it was great, great, great grandmother used to knit." She looked up from the creation to Janet's face. "What's it to be? A baby blanket, perhaps?"

Janet turned deep red, kept her head down, and just nodded slightly.

"Well, sweetie, you just keep it up. I am sure it will be fine by the time the baby arrives."

Fortunately, the woman got off at the next stop. Janet cut her eyes to Bill, just within the edge of her vision. She would bean him for the amused expression on his face, but later.

Janet actually did not realize it was their stop, so wrapped up in trying to master at least one row of stitches, when Bill nudged her with his hip as he passed her for the exit of the transit car.

Hurriedly she jumped up and followed the rest of those getting off at the stop. Still separated by half a dozen people, it was only when Willi's voice in their tiny communicator earpieces said, "We have inquiring eyes."

Bill and Janet each saw the officers in the Governor's personal guard uniforms at the same time. But they were close enough to *Smokey's* to enter quickly, before the officers had time to react. Even if they did see the three and recognize them.

The officers did not recognize them, but they had orders to investigate anyone and everyone going into *Smokey's,* singly or in groups, that did not automatically come up as a known, positive ID on their scanners. So, they headed for the door from their watch points.

Cherokee saw Willi, Janet, and Bill as soon as they came through the door. And though he did not recognize them as the individuals they were, he knew instinctively that they were the people that Johnny Oneshot had told him might show up in a hurry and asked him to help.

Smokey saw them, too, but did not recognize them either. But he did see Cherokee lift the bar counter at the opening, and let the three through, where they then disappeared into the back of the building.

"What…" Smokey asked out loud, heading that way, just as the Governor's goons came rushing into the place.

"Where'd those three that just come in go?" asked the one with chevrons on his uniform sleeve, after all four of them scanned the room.

Smokey said not a word. He just pointed and backed away. There was no way he was getting himself killed by the Governor. Or her goons. But, if he ever saw Cherokee again, alive, he had a few questions for him.

He was still backing away when an explosion, all-be-it a small one, sounded from the kitchen, and black smoke billowed into the barroom. The four goons came stumbling out, and as soon as one could clear his throat enough to speak, asked, "That entrance is blocked. Where is the next closest entrance to those tunnels?"

"Tunnels? What tunnels?" Smokey asked, truly confused. He did not know about any tunnels underneath his place. The thought went through his mind, just before he died, that he should have at least faked an answer. Because the goon, two of them actually, did not believe his statement of his lack of knowledge. One zapped him with his stunner set on kill, and the other simply shot him in the head with a projectile weapon.

Once inside the tunnel entrance, all four, Willi, Janet, Bill, and Cherokee, activated small green illuminators each was already carrying.

In the eerie green glow, Cherokee found the lighting panel control and activated the illumination fixtures that were affixed to the roof of the tunnel every so often. Though the light was not that much more, it was a muted white light, rather than the night vision friendly green of the personal illuminators.

"Over here," Cherokee said immediately, before the others could ask him any questions. "Johnny Oneshot said there would be some… Holy Happy Hunting Grounds…" Cherokee muttered when he saw what was in the cubby Johnny had mentioned.

Though all three looked at him curiously, due to his soft exclamation, all three quickly recognized, and took, the items that had them exclaiming similarly, in their own way.

Willi grabbed the much larger version of the PDW device that Johnny had given her earlier, along with a belt pack of power ammunition.

Janet, always something of a fan of an area weapon of some sort, took what was the very modern, very state of the art equivalent of an Old Earth double barrel ten-gauge cut down shotgun, except with a concentrated point effect option included, in addition to the wider area function.

Bill was left with only three choices since Cherokee had already grabbed the heaviest weapon of the arsenal. A launcher similar to the one Willi had used on Warehouse Thirteen, except the next size up. And with it, the four large, heavy, ammunition bags that were with it.

Deciding not to decide, Bill took all three of the other weapons, distributing them about his body. He simply shrugged when both Willi and Janet looked first at the weapons arrangement, and then his face.

Willi heard an almost silent trill in her ear. She pulled out the comm device Johnny had given her, and when she saw the tiny projection lens light up, she turned it toward the wall so they could all see the output.

Johnny was placing the items in the cubby, a recorder obviously attached to something near. He spoke as he arranged everything in what seemed to be a rather specific manner.

"If you have need of these weapons, and therefore have disturbed them, triggering this display, here are my preferences as to what I would like you to do. Depending on who all is there besides Cherokee, whom you can trust absolutely, just as you would me, both personally, and in his weapons skills and tactical skills, I suggest first, just abandon the planet and system, using whatever you need to do so.

"If not, then you might consider helping out a few people that are probably at risk at the moment. If what I planned has happened, and it probably has, since you are here, then the Governor is going to start tying up some loose ends. And many of those are innocent loose ends, that she simply wants eliminated, for one reason or another.

"I would take it as a personal favor to me if you protected these people, and in a couple of cases, items. Though the items are not to be protected if there is any real danger for anyone." A list of address appeared, with associated tunnel grid locations.

Just before the projection died away, Johnny looked directly at the recorder lens. "Be careful everyone, please. Another personal request from me." He reached forward, obviously to stop and retrieve the comm device that was recording him, and looked at the thing, his eyes only a very short distance away from it.

"Almost forgot. That little… other thing… lying on that rock projection there in the cubby, will self-destruct in one minute. More or less. Probably do not want to be too close."

All eyes turned to the rock projection, now very obvious, once mentioned. None of the four saw Johnny's sardonic grin in the projection, as he reached forward and turned off the comm device.

And, since all four turned and began to run as fast as they could down the tunnel, not a one of them thought a single thing about missing it.

Though the explosion did not seem all that massive, upon seeing the blockage in the tunnel at that point, Bill and Cherokee were convinced it was much more powerful than it sounded. They exchanged a look, and then turned to hurry after Willi and Janet, neither of whom had turned back to look.

Looking back at it, in retrospection, and while giving their statements to the Confederation investigation team a bit over three weeks or so later, the four came to the conclusion that though at the time, doing what Johnny Oneshot had asked of them had seemed not only verging on being something to just keep them out of danger, danger being relative, as Willi's mother was wont to say, but probably unnecessary anyway, as none of the places had come under any type of direct attack, the four decided that just perhaps Johnny had done the right thing in asking them.

They did finally understand, that once the knowledge that Johnny Oneshot, and his 'group of people' were actively protecting the innocent from the Governor's wrath, as well as preserving some documents and other artifacts of great sentimental value and historical worth from likewise being destroyed by her or her goons, said goons had decided that not doing the Governor's bidding was probably safer than doing it, no matter how wild and deranged she had become.

Had Willi, Janet, Bill, and Cherokee not done what they did, at Johnny's request, one of the official investigators said, upwards of twenty-thousand people would have died, including hundreds of children, and not a few babies.

Also, that preventing the destruction or damage of the original documents and flag of the first human settlement on the planet, the mechanical navigation tools that kept them on course after the colonization ship lost her navcoms near the end of the trip, and the pump that had sent the planet's water through a survival purifier so it could be taken up to the ship to relieve the suffering caused by the partial failure of the ship's water treatment plants, meant as much to the planet's, and the system's, inhabitants as anything except the actual lives saved.

More than one of those whose life had been saved would have willingly given up their life to preserve the artifacts.

Though the others were more than a bit concerned, Willi was in agony until she finally heard from Johnny, who had never returned or contacted them after he had personally cornered the Governor and the majority of her cohorts, including the leader of the Pirates, six Ecronian civilians, and two rather high ranking Ecronian government representatives, along with the locals that were part of the Governor's plot, when he attended the 'business meeting' the day after he left Willi in the hide.

One of the many questions that had come up, once those involved with him had time to think about some things and realized that they had absolutely no idea how he had managed many of the things he did, was answered.

Although the hide that had been used by Johnny and Willi, and then Willi, Janet, and Bill, had been utterly destroyed, it was only one of several that Johnny had acquired, as he once mentioned to Willi.

It was a set of them, somewhat larger, and drifting in amongst the asteroid swarm, in which Johnny stored many of the things he needed in his operations. That included a great deal of armament and fuel for the Dominators, neither of which ever seemed to run out, Willi had finally realized.

Johnny eventually showed up again, two weeks after the Confederation Space Navy Fleet flagship began orbiting the planet, with other detachments of the fleet having taken up stations throughout the rest of the sector, especially closely spaced along the Ecronian border areas.

As soon as Naval Command sent word that Johnny was aboard the Flagship, Willi relaxed. It was only when he dropped planetside after he had been debriefed by Naval Intelligence and Confederation Civil authorities; and walked into the jump arrival room in the civilian side of the planetary base, that Willi found out that Johnny's left side, from hip to neck, was encased in a protective, enhanced healing cast.

At Willi's alarmed look as she hurried over to him, Johnny managed a one shoulder shrug, and the sardonic smile curled his lips. Rather sheepishly he explained, before Willi or the others could ask, "The Governor shot me again. With something a bit more powerful than her PDW."

"You let her shoot you again?" Willi asked incredulously.

Bill, Janet, and Cherokee were rather glad she did, because all three were itching to ask the same thing.

"Well, 'let' might not be the correct word, but I suppose it does fit. Better me than the Ecronian she was trying to kill after she found out what they had in store for her."

Four sets of eyebrows lifted in question. "Stewpot," Johnny answered, softly.

The others felt a bit sick. Coming from Johnny, they had no doubt that the rumors that had circulated for many years about the Ecronians' primary use for humans was, after slave labor… food… were true.

It took a while, and a great deal of prompting, some of it rather forceful from Willi, to get Johnny's story from the time after he had left Willi in the hide, to the point he had just showed up, from him. They were eating in a private dining room on the base, but Willi noticed that Johnny had his comm device out and was monitoring it occasionally.

After describing the meeting with the Governor and others, where Johnny sprang his trap, after having recorded the entire thing up to that point, by triggering the capture nets that he had rigged the room with, Johnny finally explained his injury.

"The Governor was a bit more limber than I gave her credit for," Johnny admitted, "and a bit quicker, too. She did manage to get her weapon pointed at the Ecronian, and was able to fire before her net constricted enough to prevent it. Luckily, I was able to step between them just before she fired."

"Luckily? Luckily! You call that lucky?" Willi exclaimed. Loudly. But then in much lower tones, after taking a look around the room, she added, "You need to look up the definition of *lucky* in a library somewhere."

Again that, already infuriating to Willi, one shoulder shrug by Johnny, that indicated that 'no, he really did not,' appeared momentarily, and Willi had to hold herself back from doing him bodily harm.

Of course, there was not enough force in the universe to keep her from poking Johnny in the side when he kept avoiding and sidestepping and giving diverting answers to the question she kept asking, at different times all through the meal and conversation, "How did you stop the Ecronians from attacking before the Confederation fleet arrived?"

Although she did grimace slightly in regret at having done so, seeing his wince, she did not regret having done it enough to not do it again, additional wince or no wince, when Johnny began his now expected reply of, "Little of this, little of that," which was in no way satisfactory for Willi.

"Might as well tell her, Johnny," Bill said with a chuckle. Which drew an aggravated look for him from Janet, which Bill could not understand at all what prompted it.

His eyes on Willi's for a short moment, Johnny Oneshot did, cementing his reputation even more, in the telling. With a sigh, and the prefacing words, "It really wasn't a big deal," Johnny told them what they all wanted to hear. At least at first. By the time Johnny finished, Willi kind of wished she had not asked, considering the actual real answer.

"Since the Ecronian government had no way to know what had happened to their diplomats and business cohorts, as I was jamming their portable transmitter, their particular powers that be decided that the Confederation had discovered the plot, and taken their compatriots prisoner.

"Since those diplomats and business… beings… could severely harm their plans if they disclosed the parts of the Ecronian Government plan that they knew, the Lead Commander of the flotilla was ordered to activate the safeguards that all Ecronians, except the highest members of government, and the ruling family, must wear.

"The only one I had been able to deactivate was the lead ambassador. So, I was able to keep him… it… whatever… alive. And it has proved to be very valuable to Confederation authorities as a source of information about the Ecronian social structure, their government, their military strategies and tactics, capabilities, and weaknesses. Not to mention their eating habits."

The others all had the disgusted look on their faces again for a moment. Until Johnny kept talking.

"Those safeguards can be monitored. As soon as they discovered that their lead diplomat was not, in fact, destroyed, they, as I was sure they would, headed this way as fast as their ships could travel, in order to lay waste to the planet and everything around it, that might leave any physical clue as to their previous plans.

"So, I had to go head them off, directly. Leaving the netted-up conspirators in the hands of General Wainwright's and Commander Vice-Admiral Calhoun's people, with the documentation of what was going on, I jumped up to my Dominator, stopped at a couple of my re-supply hides just long enough to add a few munitions to the Dominator, and then went to meet the Ecronian fleet head on."

"Head on?" Janet asked.

"The whole fleet?" asked Cherokee.

"With just a Dominator?" was Bill's question.

"By yourself?" Willi more stated softly than asked.

"Yes. Well…" Johnny quickly responded, with another one shoulder shrug, "Not that big of a deal. As you have probably already surmised, Telstar's Dominator, the two I brought out, and the two F-777s Isis brought out, were not factory stock versions."

The four shared yet another incredulous glance among themselves at his so matter-of-fact statement and the tone in which it was given.

"I had what I was pretty sure would give me the edge I needed."

"Pretty sure?" asked Willi, a bit more force in her voice this time.

"There are never any guarantees for things like this, of course," Johnny replied, looking over at Willi again.

"There are never…" Willi closed her eyes, shook her head, and then opened her eyes once more, to stare daggers at Johnny. Softly, she rather forcefully urged Johnny to, "Go on."

"Well… I did. Have that edge I needed, I mean."

Janet and Bill detected the slight hiccup in Johnny's delivery then, after Johnny's and Willi's exchange.

"I simply took it full bore toward them, using cloaking and scrambling to confuse their sensors, launched decoys well out, and then more, close in, and released my enhanced weapons load on their flagship. Everything worked as designed.

"A few more times on their other major combatant craft, and the rest turned and ran toward home." Johnny concluded.

"And that was that?" Willi asked, deceptively softly. Janet heard the unspoken message, but Bill, Cherokee, and especially Johnny, were clueless.

"Yes. Essentially," Johnny responded.

When Willi repeated, "Essentially," still in that soft voice, Johnny began to get a clue. The other two men not so much.

"And…" Willi said, obviously expectantly.

"And?" Johnny asked in return, beginning to feel a bit threatened. "And what?"

Willi began to speak, starting so softly that Johnny, even with his remarkable hearing, could barely make it out, but by the time she was finished, Johnny was backing up, rapidly, wincing more than a little, as she advanced on him, her voice rising with every step.

None of the five were aware of when any of them had left the table, but assumed it was when Willi lit into Johnny, when they thought about it later.

"And what? And what? And what about your injuries, which were not treated until you returned? And what about you could only use one arm and hand? And what about you were outnumbered, oh, say, what? Three hundred ships to one?

"And what about you were outnumbered, ten thousand to one personally? And what about you were outgunned by an entire Ecronian combat fleet to one Dominator, no matter how well armed? And what about you could have been killed!"

That was when Willi's voice dropped to less than a whisper, that only Johnny heard, though Janet had a pretty good idea of what Willi said, as Willi stood toe-to-toe to Johnny, his back against the wall,

"And what about me? What about me not knowing if you were alive or dead? What about me worrying that I might never see you again? What about me thinking I might never be able to tell you how I felt about you? What about us?"

They all did see the tears in Willi's eyes. And then could not even see her face, as Johnny reached out with his still working arm, gently brought Willi against his body, her head on his chest turned away from them, tears pouring down her cheeks to dampen his shirt, as she fought for breath.

But she fought no harder than Johnny did. Every breath he had to struggle to take was agony, for the pain he had knowingly caused her.

"Because," he whispered so that only she could hear, and feel in the rumble of his chest, "if not, you would no longer exist, and, living or dead myself, I would never again, for all eternity, have a heart that was whole, for it would be only a tiny, useless, broken thing, without the part of it you have become.

"Because, Wilhelmina Hortense McKindrick, I have fallen so far in love with you, there might not even be a distance measurement large enough to express it."

"Oh, Johnny…" Willi sighed against his chest. "I love you, too." She took a deep, shuddering breath, and began to release her near-death hold on him. Then suddenly did release him, stepped back, looked up into his face, and nearly yelled, "How did you know my middle name was Hortense?"

Her eyes flashed, and her hands became fists on her hips as she stared at Johnny and added, "I am going to absolutely **KILL** Sydney!"

"Actually, I didn't find out from Sydney," Johnny felt obligated to tell Willi, as much to spare her brother's life, as to simply tell the truth. And he did not even have to tell her how he found out.

"Well, Marilyn," came an amused voice that had Willi spinning around, her face turning deep red.

Willi's, "Mother…" came out barely audible as she stared at the regal looking woman, who was watching her daughter and Johnny Oneshot with interest.

"Uh… Mother," Willi managed to say in a more or less normal voice, if the strangled sound part of it was discounted, "How long have you…"

"Been standing here, watching you pour out you heart to this young man?"

Willi winced. "That long, I guess," she said.

"Lady McKindrick," Johnny said, stepping forward to take Willi's mother's hand in his working one as he bowed slightly, as much as his injury allowed, and kissed the tops of her fingers. "It is nice to see you again."

Mrs. McKindrick's eyes went as wide as Willi's.

"I thought you said you had not met," Willi said to her mother.

"I… Well… I did not think I had…"

Willi could almost see and hear her mother's mind working, trying to decide just where she might have ever met Johnny Oneshot.

"Oh, my!" Mrs. McKindrick suddenly said, after Johnny spoke again.

The sardonic grin curving his lips, that which Willi was now well familiar, and the sound of his voice, a bit altered than how he had been speaking moments before, saying simply "Lady McKindrick," again, and Mrs. McKindrick remembered exactly where, when, and how she had met Johnny Oneshot.

Only it was not as Johnny Oneshot she knew him as at that time. It was as Algernon McElroy. Ambassador Sir Algernon McElroy. Seven years before. And Johnny Oneshot looked much older then, as Algernon, than he did even now, seven years later, as himself. A slight blush tinged her cheeks.

She knew Willi noticed when Willi's eyes narrowed and she asked, "Mother…?"

Mrs. McKindrick tore her eyes away from Johnny, and looked at her daughter, her chin rising ever so slightly, "Just never you mind, child. Suffice it to say that I have indeed met your young man, though it took me a bit to remember it."

Willi heard the slight stress when her mother used the word 'your' when referring to Johnny as Willi's young man. Willi glanced at Johnny, but this was neither the time nor the place for her to find out how Johnny knew his mother.

So, she turned back to her mother and asked, "What are you doing here? How did you know I was here? And how did you know I was calling myself Marilyn?"

"Marilyn Monroe, to be exact," her mother said with a chuckle. "And from what I have learned, from some very reliable sources, that your beauty is considered to be every bit as much as the esteemed woman's, and your singing by far surpasses hers."

"Ah… You know about my performing…"

"Indeed, I do," her mother said. "And the recordings that were sent to me at my request only confirmed what I was told. You have been a very busy young woman on your… 'vacation away,' was it?"

Again, Willi winced when her mother chuckled. "I knew from the beginning you were up to something. Unfortunately, my… well… the people I had keeping you safe, lost track of you. It was not until your young man…"

Mrs. McKindrick looked over at Johnny, "sent word that you might be in need of the assistance of your family, as well as members of the extended Traders Tribes, that I knew exactly where you were located. It was a simple matter after that to bring the *Trinity Home* about, and get here as quickly as we could."

Willi blanched. "Mother… That must have cost a fortune!"

"No matter, child," Mrs. McKendrick replied. Though she tried her best not to do so, her eyes cut to Johnny for a moment.

And Willi saw the look. She saw nothing in Johnny's face when she looked over quickly, but what her mother's look had meant would also go on the agenda of things she intended to question Johnny about in much greater depth and detail. Once she got him alone. Where he could not disappear on her somehow.

"None of us minded," her mother had continued smoothly. "You are the pride of *Trinity Home*. Everyone was happy to learn you were safe and sound."

One eye brow lifted, and an exasperated look crossed her face when she added, "Once we found out you were in danger. We, my daughter, will need to have a chat about that, very soon."

Willi wrapped her arm around Johnny's free one, responding lightly, without looking at her mother, "Of course, Mother. Just as soon as we both have time. Now, I believe Johnny should probably get some rest. His injuries are surely bothering him."

Willi looked at Johnny, and when it was apparent that he was getting ready to deny it, she quickly added, "So I will see to it he gets somewhere safe, and quiet, so he can get that **much needed** rest. I will talk to all of you soon."

With that, and a rather sharp tug on Johnny's good arm, Willi led him away from the others. After a couple of reluctant steps, and a glance, almost a pleading one, Captain Butler thought, over his shoulder, Johnny decided going along with Willi at the moment might be the more prudent of several actions he contemplated attempting.

Johnny did not even ask Willi where they were going. He just followed where she led. Though, it would have been difficult not to do so, as she now had a near death grip on his good hand, after having let go of his arm once out away from the crowds.

Willi was not sure herself exactly where she was headed. She just knew she and Johnny needed to be somewhere else, together, without the others. A place where Johnny could not disappear on her. Or be called away. Or...

Almost angrily, Willi wiped tears from her eyes again as they left the building. She looked around for a taxi. There were always taxi at the base. Always. Except for now.

She had to wipe her eyes again, and Johnny was very aware of every movement she had made from the point she had put his back against the wall, and her voice had dropped to almost nothing.

Johnny gave a very tiny tug on Willi's hand. Just enough to bring her attention to him, but not in any way make it seem he was trying to pull away from her.

She turned her head, away from the area where the taxis were usually queued up near the main base building. Again, she was wiping her eyes. And it nearly broke Johnny's heart.

Never, ever, would he intentionally hurt her. But, for so many years on his own, sometimes seeming to be doing the devil's own work, cut off from family and what few friends he had managed to make, he had basically forgotten that there were other people in the universe that might, just might, be affected, personally, by what he did.

And, more importantly, how he did what he did. Never forming any close ties, and very few ties not close. Never letting anything interfere with the work he felt he was obligated to do. Destined to do even, though he seldom let that thought surface.

Even now, those kinds of beliefs were looked at askance. Much as they often were in his ancestors' time.

When Johnny Vanducci and Priscilla Jennings met in the 21st Century, fell in love, and had their children, through The Dark Times so many years ago, Vanducci's innate ability to understand people, and his drive to help them, coupled with Priscilla's near magical ability to sense those around her, often at some distance, and feel and understand, at least to a degree, what they were feeling, had been passed down, generation after generation.

Sometimes made stronger from another bloodline, sometimes a bit less so, but always there. And Johnny Oneshot, was one of the ones that came from a combination of bloodlines that gave him the sense… senses… that made him very good at what he did.

And now, feeling… knowing the pain… the fear… the vast uncertainty… that Willi was going through, he had to make it better. Take those feelings from her, even if he had to absorb them himself. Which was not an unknown ability for him. Just one seldom used.

Willi's eyes on his face, searching intently his own, Johnny gave another tiny tug, bringing her around a bit more, to stand directly in front of him, though a step away.

"I am sorry, Willi. I am so sorry I put you through all this. I should have…" Johnny shook his head. "No should haves for us, I hope. Just what was, what is, and what will be. Especially the what will be. I want my will-be to be a part of your will-be, and your will-be to be part of my will-be."

Johnny paused, managing to get her other hand into his that was restricted in movement, and, still staring into her eyes, added, "I cannot say that I will never again be in danger. Nor even that I will not willingly go into it. Making the universe safe for the innocents that live within it is part of my heritage, my background, my training… and my very being.

"I believe… and hope… that you will be willing to accept me, as I am, with the understanding that, while I may never stop doing the things that I do, that I will, from this moment forward, make you a part of my being, so you will always know to the best of my ability, and understand that I must do what I do, and may risk everything, to see to it that you and your family are safe, and that…"

There was the tiniest hesitation. But it was truly infinitesimal in Willi's mind, as Johnny continued, "our family… Our children… And their children. And their children's children, all the way down the line, will also be safe, just as did my ancestors for us. And your ancestors. And the ancestors of all those that lived through The Dark Times, and in doing so, made it possible for humans to get to the stars. Us."

"Oh, Johnny… That is so… I love you, Johnny… And will forever. And whatever you do, I will support you." Her eyes crinkled slightly, and sparkled somewhat when she added, "And be there with you when I need to be."

Johnny opened his mouth to protest her 'being there with him…', but decided to leave well enough alone. "And I love you, Willi. And always will. You are the most…"

Willi put a finger to Johnny's lips. "Not now, Johnny. Later. For now, I want to get you somewhere I can kiss you until I can't breathe. And this is not the place." She turned, again holding his good hand, this time waving her other arm frantically when she saw a taxi with a human driver.

Fortunately, for everyone's safety and well-being, the driver saw her, and guided the taxi over to them. Willi would not let Johnny do anything. Not even lift a finger to open the door, as the driver did not bother getting out.

Again, Johnny had to control himself to not try and do things himself, despite his injuries, when Willi made sure he got into the taxi without further pain.

When he was settled to Willi's satisfaction, she hurried around to the other side of the taxi and slid in beside him. When she touched the button to tell the driver where they would be going, Johnny put a hand on her arm. "I know a place," he said quietly.

When she looked over at him, and nodded after only a short pause, Johnny gave the address to the driver. Willi heard the slight intake of the driver's breath before the circuit cut off. She looked over at Johnny, but he was fidgeting just a bit, trying to get more comfortable.

"I'm sorry," Willi said. "I should have hired a transport…"

Johnny smiled over at her. He shook his head. "No need for that kind of expense. Besides, it really doesn't matter too much what I am in. There are just some sitting positions that are difficult for me."

Willi saw him reach just inside the edge of the cast. "A bit more pain medication?" she asked him.

Johnny nodded. "It'll take a couple of minutes, and then I will be fine. I hate using the injector… But sometimes it does make things easier."

When the taxi passed one of the shopping areas not far from the planet-side base, Willi sat up a bit straighter. "Perhaps we should pick up a few things…"

Johnny grinned. "No need. The place we are headed toward has everything we should need. And we can have anything else delivered, if necessary."

"Oh…" Willi looked over at Johnny. "Just where is it we are going?"

"I… hm… I sort of borrowed the place for a while, from someone I knew that lived on this planet. They will be well compensated for everything I have used… or we use."

"Sort of borrowed?" Willi asked, her eyebrows lifted in question.

"Might have been difficult to get permission. At least without creating more problems for me than I wanted for this situation. It will be fine. I will just have to deal with some… angst… next time I see the owner."

"They won't have you arrested or something, will they?" Willi asked. She was watching Johnny closely. Before he could answer, the taxi slowed, and Willi looked forward.

Her eyes did not quite bug out, but it was close when she saw the iron gates between the tall white stone pillars that were the ends of an equally tall, white stone wall that disappeared into the forest that was all that could be seen ahead of them.

The driver was asking Johnny for the gate code, but Willi saw Johnny touch his communicator and the gate began to slide to one side. It was some time before the house came into view, as the driveway wended its way through forest, lush open grounds, and large areas planted with all manner of the local flora.

Willi could not stop the gasp she made when she saw the house. "That's… That's… That's a castle!" she blurted out.

"It just looks like a castle," Johnny replied. "Well… Mostly just looks like one… There are some features…" But Johnny's words faded away as he moved to exit the taxi.

Willi could see the pain on his face, around his eyes, when she hurried around the taxi to try to help him. But he was already out and had credit chips in his hand.

She started to protest, but the eager taximan was already taking the money, more than happy with what Johnny gave him. Along with the caution to drive directly to the gate and through it.

And a further caution that it might not be a good idea for anyone to show up looking for them here, if Johnny found out the driver was responsible for the information leak.

Willi hurried to take Johnny's arm on his injured side to help him up the stairs leading to the ornate entry to the house. The steps were low and deep, so Johnny had little trouble with them. He did seem to appreciate Willi's help, for he did lean on her a bit more than she thought he might.

But they were soon inside, and Willi essentially forgot about Johnny for a couple of long minutes as she gazed around in awe. When she finally turned around the rest of the way and her eyes were again on Johnny's, hers were wide.

"This is a castle!"

A one arm shrug, lifted eyebrow, and Johnny was saying, as he tugged gently on her hand to lead her somewhere. "Not really… Mansion… perhaps.

It probably does qualify as a Mansion. My… Uh… the owner would certainly consider it such."

"To whom does it belong?" Willi asked, her eyes now going forward, to what she was fairly certain would be a kitchen.

Fortunately for Johnny, Willi became distracted by the marvel of a kitchen, and did not press for an answer. When Johnny stopped at the central island counter, so he could lean against it, Willi's hand slid from his as she approached the far wall. The wall was beautiful, no doubt, with the highly figured woodwork and stone masonry. "Where are the appliances?" Willi asked, turning back toward Johnny. "This is a kitchen… Right? Where is the cooker? The chill box?"

Willi jumped slightly at the sound behind her. She whirled around and took a step back. Johnny noticed that her movement put her between the sound and him. She was protecting him… Johnny felt something so deep in his heart that he was not even sure it was a feeling, or just simply a total body change, from the love he thought he felt for Willi, to something so much more that he was not even aware it could exist.

"Oh. Voice acti…" Willi was saying, as she turned from the wall to look at Johnny again. Her words faded when she saw the look in his eyes. And then he reached out to gently take Willi's hand in his good one and tugged her to him.

Breathing hard even before his lips neared hers, her lips made a small 'o' as he breathed the words, "You mentioned kisses…" And then he was the one doing the kissing. Exactly the way she wanted.

With just enough presence of mind, barely, to not knock Johnny over, she kissed him back with every bit of passion that had been building since the first few minutes in the cargo shuttle.

Willi got her wish. It was not long before she had to break the kiss. She simply could go any longer without breathing. "Oh…" she whispered, taking deep breathes, her wide-open eyes taking in the look in Johnny's eyes.

She did not have much experience, but she knew what she was seeing in those deep blue eyes. The very same thing she suspected he was seeing in hers, as he stared deeply into them.

"I think…" she managed to whisper, though it was a struggle.

But Johnny saved her the need to come up with any additional words. He cleared his throat. Once, and then again, before he could speak. "Um… Yes. I think perhaps…" Johnny dragged his eyes away from Willi's face. "I think perhaps we should see about getting settled for the evening…"

When he glanced back at Willi, she still had her eyes on him. It was another moment before she spoke. "Oh," she suddenly muttered. "I did not think to bring…"

Johnny shook his head. "Everything you might need will be in the rooms. Just go up and take any one of those in the west wing that strikes your fancy. I… Ah… I believe I shall go up and lie down for a bit, myself. We can find some supper a bit latter."

Willi's right had went to Johnny's good arm, a bit of worry in her eyes now. "Are you alright? Do I need to help you up?"

Seeing the look that flashed across Johnny's face, Willi felt herself blushing slightly, but the look was gone in an instant, and Johnny had turned away. "I am fine. I just need to get off my feet for a bit. Take a nap. When I take the next full dose of the medications here in a few minutes I will be out of it for quite some time."

"Ah…" Willi still hesitated. "What should I be doing?"

One glance over his shoulder, which caused a wince, and Johnny shook his head again. "Nothing really. Just make yourself at home. If you happen to need anything you cannot find, feel free to come wake me. I will be in the fifth bedroom down the east hall."

Willi nodded. She still did not move. Not until she saw Johnny enter what turned out to be some type of personal lift. Then, with a tiny sigh, Willi headed for the grand staircase in the entry hallway and made her way upstairs.

After entering the first bedroom she found, Willi was halfway down the hallway toward the area where Johnny was going toward before she had a chance to think about things.

She had seen the women's clothing scattered about the bedroom, and her first thought had been that Johnny had a woman in the house. But she stopped her angry march to confront him about it just as suddenly as it had started. Rather sheepishly she tiptoed back to the room, and pulled the door closed.

Willi had to try two more doors before she found a room that did not have women's clothing strewn about rather carelessly, she thought. She did realize she was still somewhat annoyed with the idea, but managed to control her temper. She would find out what she wanted to know later.

Willi, never known for her cooking skills, was rather inordinately proud of the meal she had ready, set out on the island counter when Johnny joined her in the kitchen a few hours later, just as she was trying to decide whether or not to go up to wake him.

She watched, rather anxiously, as Johnny ate the meal with one hand, chaffing at his requests to not help him, each time she tried to do so. Willi realized he was being very gentle with her, recognizing her concern for him.

Willi did put her foot down, however, when he got up to try and help her do the minor cleanup work after the meal, upon which he had lavished praise.

It was only when she had sent him off to the living room to wait for her that it struck her, about the same time as her face reddened, that the praise had been a bit overdone, and she suddenly suspected that he was aware of her lack of culinary skills. Though how he could possibly know, she did not question.

A bit of a huff, and Willi finished the clean-up, very glad that Johnny had not come down any earlier, because that had given her time to do the major clean-up required after the actual preparation of the meal.

Although this kitchen, like many, was highly automated, it was well-equipped with manual meal preparation equipment, which was what she had used, wanting to do more than just punch a few buttons. Just to prove to herself she could.

When Willi joined Johnny, sitting beside him carefully, on his good side, she was still in the process of deciding how to broach a few of the subjects for which she was desperately wanting explanations.

Just as she opened her mouth to ask the first question, Johnny, staring out the huge expanse of view screen that looked out upon the magnificent view of the mountains off in the distance, began to speak. His hand found hers, and he gripped it firmly, Willi's other hand going to clasp his in both of hers.

"I know you are burning with some questions, Willi," Johnny said quietly. "Before I get to giving you some answers, I would like to ask you something very important."

When he turned to look at her, his blue eyes delving deep into hers, she was not sure quite what to make of his solemn expression. Almost apprehensive, Willi nodded, and muttered, "Of course, Johnny."

"You don't have any weapons on you, do you?"

Her eyes widened, and then narrowed, as another of Johnny's smiles curled his lips as he looked at her for a moment longer before he grinned.

"I am so going to…" Willi half yelled, trying to pull her hands from Johnny's one-handed hold. But her words faded, as, with just a tug, Johnny had her against his side, his lips on hers again, to silence her.

A bit later, when both came up for air, Willi managed to mutter what was a very weak threat. Which Johnny ignored.

"Okay. We really do need to talk about a few things, Willi," Johnny said, shifting slightly into a more comfortable position. When Willi tried to move, to make him a bit more comfortable, he tugged again, and she settled into his side once more, deciding that if he wanted her there, she would be there.

"First things first, though," he began. He pulled his hand free and reached into the edge of the healing cast. Willi thought he had added another jolt of pain killer but realized that he was pulling something from the cast, not using the medication control panel.

A flick of his thumb, and as he slid off the wide sofa onto his good knee, with just a bit of a wince, Johnny had an old-Earth-style velvet ring box open, holding it up to her. "Will you, Wilhelmina Hortense McKindrick, become my wife, forever and anon?"

It was only after her nearly whispered, "Oh, yes, Johnny! I will. Oh, I will…" that she looked at the open ring box as she reached to remove the ring so Johnny could slip it onto her finger.

Her eyes cut back up to his. "That isn't… real… is it?" Willi shook her head. "That can't be real. Tell me that it is not real," Willi almost begged.

"I am afraid so, Willi. Definitely real."

"But that is…" Willi could not bring herself to say the almost sacred name.

"Yes, it is. It has been in my family for generations. And now it will be in our family for generations to follow." Johnny took the ring from Willi's rather limp fingers and managed to slip it onto the ring finger of her left hand.

"Your name… Johnny, what is your real name?" Willi asked softly, clutching his good hand with her right hand.

"Oscar John Anderson," Johnny replied.

Willi looked thoughtful, but before she could remember what it was that she seemed to be vaguely trying to recall, Johnny added, "Of course, I am also sometimes known by the name I inherited from one of my ancestors. Sir Dunigan Quincannon."

"You're Royalty?" Willi squeaked out.

Johnny sighed. "Technically, yes. But you know as well as I that the old royal lines really have no meaning anymore. They haven't for a long time."

Willi studied Johnny's face for a few moments, and then, with a slight nod, she said, "I know. But for some… that history carries a great weight, and responsibility. For the great ones. The ones that took their leadership role and responsibilities very seriously. Such as the Quincannons, back long before the Europeans began to move to what was known as the New World. Even Wolfgang Quincannon, when he went to Montana, and made his deal with the Tribes. Even he felt those responsibilities."

"You are a very astute young woman," Johnny whispered, leaning forward to kiss her softly. "And know your history."

"It is why you do… at least some of the things you do, isn't it?" Willi asked after the kiss, and Johnny was on the sofa again beside her. She was pleased more than she would admit that Johnny actually nodded in response. That he did not try to wave it away, the way he might with someone else.

Suddenly Willi remembered the women's clothing in two of the bedrooms. "Oh," she said, watching Johnny, "You know, I found some women's clothing in a couple of the bedrooms in the wing where you have me staying. Would you mind explaining?"

"Ah," Johnny said, that sardonic grin back on his face that Willi had not seen for a while.

"Be very careful, my love," Willi warned him, mostly in jest. "What you say right now could have great impact on just what happens in the future."

"You are a wonder, Willi," Johnny suddenly said and then laughed. "Some window dressing. For Sir Guy."

"Just how much dressing? And how much undressing? There were clothes all over those two rooms."

"Nothing for you to worry about, Willi," Johnny reassured her. "They were professional actresses, playing parts that helped me get established when I first arrived."

Willi's eyes narrowed. But she decided to let it drop. No need to torture herself. Or Johnny. He did what had needed to be done. At the time. "Well, we will handle such things a bit differently in the future, if such is required. And I am pretty certain it will not be."

Johnny opened his mouth to reply but decided to just shut it and kiss Willi again. It was probably safer, and much more pleasant.

A bit more kissing, though enjoyable for Johnny, soon had the pain level up more than he was comfortable with. A wince, that Willi saw, and Johnny reached for the medication control under the edge of the cast when she shifted away slightly.

"I am so so…" Willi protested.

"No, Willi. I just have to be careful. I would much rather be kissing you, believe me." Johnny leaned back slightly and breathed shallowly for a few breaths. Willi took his good hand back into both of hers and just held it gently, as she watched him beginning to relax, his eyes closed, as the medication took effect.

"Johnny, I want you to go up and lie down. And do not argue. I will be helping you."

She did not move, and Johnny cracked one eye open, to see her watching him. He managed a smile. "No argument from me," he said after a moment. With that, Willi rose, and Johnny let her pull him up with care.

He even leaned on her somewhat. Perhaps more than actually necessary. Especially as they rode up the elevator. Willi gave him a wry look as she eased him down on the edge of the bed. "Are you finished now?"

Johnny chuckled. "Oh, I suppose," he replied.

Willi stepped back. "Do you really need me to help you?"

"No, Willi. I can manage. I think we should probably ease back a bit. I'm..."

"Um... Yes. You are probably right." Willi hurried out of Johnny's room.

Johnny managed to get himself to bed, and with one more dose of pain medication he was quickly asleep.

Willi, on the other hand, keyed up now, was simply wandering around the house, her right hand worrying the ring on her left hand. Thinking. Thinking a great deal. There was no doubt in her mind that she loved Johnny. Loved him deeply. And she was just as sure now that he loved her the same way.

"But marriage... and children... and the business... and..." Willi's words faded away as she looked off into the distance as the light faded. She simply had not thought about any life beyond that of being a pilot and a trader. Even thoughts of becoming the head of the family when her mother retired had not really been in her mind since she had first realized as a child that it would happen. Eventually.

Now, not only did she have those responsibilities, but she would be a part of Johnny's world, and his responsibilities. "How did my life get so complicated so fast?" she asked herself when she finally went up to bed.

Chapter Six

-

Johnny groaned when he came awake early the next morning. A quick touch of the pain dispenser and he rested a few minutes, a smile forming as the pain lessened, and thoughts of Willi entered his mind.

It was a few moments longer before Johnny realized that it was the buzz of his communicator that had woken him. He kept it in silent mode almost all the time. The device would only give a sound if he failed to answer in a timely manner after the initial signal.

Johnny fumbled slightly, reaching for the communicator on the bedside table. Though there was no one there to see it, Johnny's features changed dramatically from the happy smile, tinged with just a bit of pain, to the plain, emotionless façade he often wore when things were not the way he would wish them to be.

A touch and the communicator went back into standby mode. Johnny, despite the pain, and without triggering additional medication, rose from the bed and began to dress. Showing almost none of the frustration he began to feel with the difficulty he was having, Johnny made a decision he figured would cost him, but needed to be made.

When he activated the house communicator and spoke Willi's name, he steeled himself, in more ways than one.

"Johnny?" a very sleepy sounding Willi asked. She rolled over in bed and squinted at the bedside display. "It's five in the morning…" she muttered.

The particular sound of Johnny's voice was beginning to register on Willi's somewhat foggy mind. And she started to come awake very quickly then.

The words were coming out of her mouth even as she swung her legs around and tried to get up. But her unsettled sleep during the night had twisted the coverings around her legs, and she literally fell out of the bed, forcing a huge "Umpf!" out of her when she hit the floor.

Not one to panic, ever, Johnny found himself out of his bedroom, running as best as he could toward the other wing of the house, no notice of the pain, or anything else, as he headed for Willi, the thought that something might already be happening nearly terrifying him.

"Johnny, are you okay?" Willi was saying now, trying to untangle herself and get off the floor, something in his voice when he had called her moments before really bothering her.

When there was no response, Willi muttered, and redoubled her efforts to get up, finally able to kick with her legs enough to get free of the coverings. Now she was starting to feel like something was terribly wrong as her next, "Johnny! Say something!" went unanswered.

Just getting to her feet now, one hand on the bed and the other reaching for her robe, she spun around when her bedroom door slammed open and Johnny ran in, his face ashen.

The sudden spin had her going down again, backwards onto her rump, eyes wide as Johnny rushed to her. She could see the anguish in his eyes, and the concern. The pain she saw was not in his eyes, though it was obvious in his movements as he went to one knee before her.

Only as he reached for her, to check for injuries, did first he, and then Willi, realize that he was only in sleep shorts, and Willi, usually restricted to ship's wear when sleeping aboard the shuttle, was wearing considerably less, since she had the opportunity.

Johnny's ashen face went red, and Willi's went crimson. "Hey!" she shouted, dragging the covering she had just managed to extricate herself from back over her body.

Willi heard the grunt of pain that escaped Johnny when he turned around awkwardly on his knees to face away from her. Modesty forgotten, Willi let the covering go and reached out with her left hand to touch Johnny's shoulder as she pushed off the floor with her other, to get to her knees behind him.

"Are you alright? What is wrong? You were white as a ghost, and came running in without knocking. And you called and your voice wasn't right, and… Johnny, what is the matter? Has something happened with your injuries?"

"No," Johnny gasped out. "It is you… Are you okay? I heard something… Like you were being attacked, and I…"

"Attacked?" Willi asked, shuffling around to try and see Johnny's face. "I wasn't attacked. I fell out of the bed. The covers… Never mind. What is going on?"

When Johnny turned his head and saw that Willi was once again uncovered, he quickly turned away gain, forcing another gasp of pain.

Now not at all concerned for her appearance, but for Johnny, she grabbed the robe from the bed, knowing that if she did not get covered Johnny would never look at her, and she was desperate to find out what was going on.

Willi slipped into the robe and belted it as she rose. She moved back enough so she could get around Johnny and get in front of him before he could try to move again. She dropped back to her knees, her hands going to his shoulders to steady him, her eyes boring into his wide-open ones."

"Johnny?" she asked as the near panic she had seen faded from his face. And then a chill went through her when she saw the façade form on his face.

The one that told her that something bad was happening, and that Johnny had decided he would be taking care of it. Whatever it took.

"Help me get this cast off," Johnny said, barely able to stand up, even leaning heavily on the bed side table. If she had not actually helped him, she was not sure he would have made it up. At least not without a great deal more pain than he was already in.

When his words registered, she managed to keep her shout to less than ear splitting levels, but it was definitely a shout. "What? NO! You are not taking that cast off!"

She pushed his hands away from the release he was trying to reach with his good hand. Fortunately, it was essentially beyond his reach, unless he was a contortionist. When the thought flashed through her mind that he probably was, Willi reached over and covered the opening with her hand.

"Sit down on the bed," she said firmly. "Tell me what is going on. And," she then added when Johnny tried to force her hand away, "do not try to take this cast off."

His face was going pale again, and now the pain was back in his eyes, as well as his body movement. "Trigger the pain medication," Willi added.

When Johnny shook his head and began to protest, Willi simply used her other hand to reach into the small cavity where the control was and tapped it herself. And then, for good measure, tapped it again.

"Willi, no! I need to…"

"You need to tell me what is going on, Johnny," Willi managed to get out more softly. Still ready to intervene if he tried to get up, much less take off the cast, Willi sat down beside him on the bed.

"Where are your weapons?" Johnny asked suddenly, his eyes scanning the bedroom.

"Handy," Willi replied, without moving away from him.

Johnny turned his head back toward her and said, more softly and much more controlled. "Get one. Please. And one for me. I didn't…" Johnny shook his head. "I wasn't thinking. Please, Willi."

Willi could tell how serious he was. And worried. Something that she was unsure she had ever seen on his face before. And suddenly realized that the worry was for her. Not himself.

So, Willi touched the edge of the bedside table to open one of the drawers. She took out the sidearm and handed it to Johnny, with an extra power pack. Getting up from the bed, Willi went to the closet, which opened before her when she got close. Reaching inside and up to a shelf, Willi rejoined Johnny on the bed with another sidearm, this one her family service weapon. She had a second power pack for it, as well.

Johnny started to rise, but Willi's surprisingly gentle pressure on his good arm kept him in place. "We need to get…" Johnny's urgent words faded as Willi kept her hand on his arm.

His eyes met hers, and Johnny felt himself calming. Less from the look in hers, than the feeling that he had to be careful and thorough. He loved this woman more than life itself, and his loss of control, slight as it was, had done nothing to prevent harm from coming to her. That had to stop, this very instant.

"Yes. Of course. I am sorry, Willi. The thought of losing you…"

"You are not going to lose me, Johnny," Willi said firmly. She realized, as she looked back at his face, that she had been doing a security scan, just as he had.

"No. No, of course not," Johnny replied, managing a smile now that the pain medication had taken the very sharp edge off. "You are far too capable for that."

"Thank you. I think," Willis said. "You obviously think we are obviously in some kind of danger. What has happened? The governor is gone, the Ecronians are probably still fleeing, and we are in this most remarkable estate. What could be the danger, now?"

Johnny shifted the weapon from his good hand to his lap, and took Willi's free hand in his. Rather sadly, Willi thought, Johnny said, "It seems my life has already put you into additional danger, Willi. I am so sorry for that. I thought we would have time…"

Shaking his head, Johnny continued. "I thought we would have more time to make some plans to ensure your…" Seeing Willi's eyes narrow slightly, Johnny changed his words in mid-sentence. "Time to make some plans to ensure our safety for the future. But we do not have that time, it seems.

"We need to get going, notify… Well… Warn your Mother and the authorities… and then get yo… get us off the planet somewhere we can take care of anything much more safely, without risking any more people."

Johnny had felt the unconscious tightening of Willi's hand in his at the mention of her mother. Though there was a slight hesitation, Johnny's even more solid resolve to get Willi and her family out of harm's way that had him standing was not resisted by Willi.

"I will leave you to get dressed. And packed. We need to be on our way within the hour." Johnny was already moving, limping badly, actually, Willi noted in frustration, as he spoke.

"Stop!" Willi said firmly. She almost chuckled when Johnny's shoulders tried to hunch slightly. But they could not since the cast prevented it on one side.

Slowly he turned around to face her, since he could not twist his body. "Explain a bit more thoroughly, Johnny," Willi more asked than demanded. "Please."

Johnny closed his eyes a moment. This taking other people's concerns into account was going to be difficult, he realized. A nod, and then he was speaking.

"The Ecronian High Council has sent a formal communique to the Confederation Congress demanding my immediate arrest and then execution for crimes against their Empire. Or, failing that, extradition to Ecronian territory where they will handle the matter of meting out my punishment themselves for my crimes."

Willi's eyes widened dramatically. "You have got to be kidding me!"

Johnny managed a chuckle, and when Willi saw the sardonic smile curl up his lips she barely managed to control her temper. For the most part.

"Not funny," she muttered. "I'll go with you to…" She took a step toward him but looked down at herself. The belt of the robe was starting to slip. And she noticed just how short the robe was. It had been in the quarters, so she used it, lacking her own. A bit of color came to her cheeks.

"Okay. I will change. But you had better be within the sound of my voice when I am ready to talk to you again."

"Soft voice? Loud voice? Or…"

"He is actually laughing! He is actually laughing at me!" Willi muttered when Johnny managed to move fast enough to get out of the bedroom and have the door closed before she could respond.

More than a bit peeved, Willi still took much care to get dressed, packed, and ready to leave as quickly as possible. Dropping her bags near the front door of the house, Willi headed for the kitchen, fully intending to have another breakfast ready for Johnny when he came down.

She stopped dead in the doorway when she saw him already there, a light breakfast on the counter, fully dressed, his bags beside the hallway door.

Eyes glinting, she stepped toward him, growling, "I told you not to take that cast off."

Cutting her a sideways look as he carefully retrieved something from the chiller, he gave her one of his non-replies, she realized moments later.

"Yes. About that. I should have asked for one that was more water-resistant."

Johnny was already eating, using his communicator as he did so, when it hit her exactly what he had said. And that it had been totally diverting, without addressing either the fact that he was no longer wearing a cast, and that he had not done as she had instructed. But seeing his eyes change as he looked at the private display on the communicator, she lost her train of thought.

"Not good, Willi," Johnny was saying. He adjusted something on the communicator and the holo-projection appeared on the counter.

Willi recognized the Commanding Admiral of the Confederation Space Navy. He was speaking at what appeared to be a briefing by Senior Military Officers to the inner council of the Confederation on Earth.

"How…" Willi started to ask Johnny how he had access to what had to be a very tightly controlled meeting. But Johnny had quietly spoken, and the communicator holo-display blanked out and the large kitchen wall display activated.

Willi gasped as a news report began showing a series of official announcements being made in the various sectors of space between Earth, spreading outward in an expanding cone to the edge of human controlled space, with the base of the cone centering on Sector ZZ-1219.

The reports were essentially the same. Slightly different accents, a few slightly different details, somewhat different explanations. But all amounting to a Be-On-The-Lookout for one Johnny Oneshot, wanted in connection with an inter-galactic inter-species terrorist event.

Wanting to scream in frustration at the injustice of it all, Willi glared at Johnny when that sardonic grin was back on his face. "Looks like you got yourself tangled up with an intergalactic space terrorist."

Willi sputtered, unable to articulate anything even reasonably coherent. Then her eyes went back to the display. After the official announcements, the main newscasters were voicing their opinions on the situation. It turned out that they did not actually have much to say. Or at least were not given a chance to say anything, as live reports were being fed into the system from just about everywhere in the area that had been indicated, as well as most of the rest of the known human habitation in the galaxy.

One word could pretty much sum up the reaction. Outrage.

Willi closed her mouth and looked over at Johnny again. He looked just a bit stunned for a moment, but then that sardonic grin was back. One that Willi was beginning to realize had several different meanings. This one, she was suddenly sure, was a cover for his amazement and possibly actual embarrassment.

"Seems like I have a slightly broader reputation than I thought. Who knew?"

"Johnny!" Willi exclaimed. "People know you did not do what the Ecronians are saying you did. And they sure seem to know that whoever is supporting this in our government is totally crazy. If they aren't lucky, the whole new government will be taken down."

"And therein lies the problem," Johnny said softly, looking at Willi with regret in his eyes. "I have no wish to damage the government that so many people worked so hard to get put into place. Including myself. The Confederation is what humans need right now. We have started to pull together again. And we are going to need to pull together even more to face what the Ecronians are planning."

"But Johnny! It is not right…"

"No," Johnny replied with a sigh. "It is not right. But until this is resolved, there are too many risks of the Ecronians being able to use it for their own ends. Which, of course, is their plan. But not even their leadership, I think, ever thought that there would be this kind of reaction."

"Johnny…" Willi asked, a very uncertain and uncomfortable feeling chilling her. "What are you suddenly planning?"

"Looks like I may have to face some music of a different kind than your beautiful voice."

It took a moment for Willi to get his meaning. And then she was standing, shouting at him. **"Oh, no! Oh, no you will not! You are not going to turn yourself in to these idiots, Johnny. I do not have any conception how they even considered this action, but you are not going to just turn yourself in to the Confederation and stand some kind of show trial. That went out in the twenty-first century!**

"We did not… Humanity did not… Johnny, our families did not go through the Dark Times and then work those centuries to recover to have something like this happen now! The idea is ludicrous."

"Willi," Johnny said in what he thought was a very reasonable tone of voice. Before he could continue Willi was speaking again. And Johnny decided that while his voice really was a reasonable tone, Willi's was not.

"No!" was all she said. The breakfast ignored, Willi turned and picked up Johnny's bags, struggling somewhat as they were much heavier than they looked like they should be.

"Let's go. We are going to go talk to my mother."

"Willi…" Johnny again tried to reason with her. But she cut him off again, not by saying anything, but by simply half carrying, half dragging his bags out of the kitchen toward the front door.

Johnny was a bit amazed at the sounds emanating from her. He could not quite tell which were grunts, which were groans, which were mutters, and which were slight yelps when something banged into some part of her body. The low curses he heard and understand, however. And he did hear his name in there among them a time or two.

He started to reach for one of the bags to take from her halfway across the living room, but her glare, and this time unmistakable growl had him retrieving his arm and hand still intact.

"Call someone for transport," she ordered him when she dropped the bags by the front door and reached out to open it, obviously intending to take everything outside.

It cost him to do it, and especially to not show it, but Johnny got between Willi and the front door. "You… We are not going outside this house until I know it is safe."

Willi blanched, but stood firm, a defiant look in her eyes.

"We are leaving. But not without some precautions being taken," Johnny said. The communicator was suddenly in his hand, and the thumb on his good hand was doing something that Willi could not quite make out.

When he slipped the comm device back wherever it was he kept stashing it, and Willi looked up again after having tried to see where, Johnny was looking at her calmly.

"Transport is on the way. Now, I want you to go up and get everything you are going to want to take with you."

Willi started to protest and pointed at her bags. "Everything, Willi. We will not be coming back here anytime soon. And there are a few additional things I want to take, considering what we have seen since my first warning. So, I will meet you right here, in no more than thirty minutes."

Again, Willi tried to protest, and again Johnny cut her off. "I promise, Willi. Now, when you go back up to get the rest of your things, feel around the inside edge of the closet door, down just a couple of centimeters above the floor, and press the slight bump you will find there.

"Take anything from that room you might want, and everything you think will help us stay out of trouble, or get out of trouble if we do get into some. And absolutely put on the body armor. We will not leave this house unless I know you have it on. Do you understand me?"

Willi would have protested the words, since they were definitely a command that brooked no questioning. Which was against her general inclination, but the tone of them had her mutely nodding. She turned and hurried toward the stairs, stopping at the bottom to turn and look back.

Johnny, communicator in hand again was limping toward the kitchen and the lift near the rear entrance. The sudden thought hit her that he could easily slip out that way, and there was nothing she could do to stop him, even injured the way he was.

His words came back to her though, and she headed up the stairs. 'I promise, Willi'. He would not break a promise to her. Not willingly.

Willi gasped when the small panel door slid open inside the closet in her room. She had already packed the few other things she had not bothered with at first. When she ducked through the opening and stood up in the tiny space, she was wondering what she had missed, because, though she could stand up, she had only a few inches or room all around her.

Another gasp came when the floor seemed to drop out from under her feet. The feeling lasted for almost two seconds, she thought, and then the motion slowed quickly, and stopped. The panel in front of her slid aside, and she looked out into a rather large room.

A quick visual scan showed her several more of the entry/exit panels like the one that had just opened. Along with several very interesting sets of objects.

"I am not even going to ask," she muttered as she headed over to one of the cabinets and opened it. "Oh, yes I am," she said rather more loudly when she saw what was inside.

It was difficult for her to leave when she did, not having had a chance to check everything out. But with the subtle marks on the cabinet doors that she quickly recognized for what they were, and figuring out the way to get past the security panel inside the outer cabinet door, it still took her several minutes to gather up everything she would be able to carry, and still take the time to put on the armored confusion suit.

It was a squeeze, but Willi got everything in the elevator, and then out through the small panel into the bedroom closet, in one trip. With the adrenaline now pumping through her system, she was able to run out of the bedroom and down the stairs with no trouble, even with everything she was now carrying.

"Good timing," Johnny said with hardly a glance at her when they both reached the front door at the same time.

It was not hard for Willi to see the strain Johnny was under, between the pain from his injuries, and the stresses he was putting on his body now without the cast, with everything he was carrying.

A relieved grunt escaped him when he dropped the extra gear beside hers. He looked at her, down at her additional gear, nodded, and used his communicator again.

"Two minutes," was all he said. He was checking the gear he had strapped onto his body, most of which she could not see as it was inside the confusion suit field.

Willi, rather surprised at herself that she was not peppering him with impatient questions, just waited silently until he pointed at several items on the floor and said, "These first," while still watching the communicator in his hand.

Again Willi was surprised, when Johnny only picked up one item from the floor, though from his movements, it had to be heavy, after saying, "Thirty seconds."

She did not see any other movement from him, but suddenly the door was open, and he was moving through it. Willi followed right on his heels. Up to the point where he stepped slightly to the side, and began scanning the area, the comm device up in front of his face. "Go," he said, still not having looked at her.

Her eyes went from him, down the steps and she almost backed up a step at what was headed toward her. And what was behind what was headed toward her.

But Johnny had said go. So she went, aching to turn and look at him, but knowing she needed to just follow his instructions at the moment.

The two blobs passed her on the way up the stairs as she went down them. Tossing the bags she was carrying into the open door of the vehicle sitting right at the bottom of the steps, which she knew was there only because the door was open, and she could see inside.

Because if the door had not been open, she would likely have run right into the side of the vehicle, as it, like the fighter craft had been, was very, very well cloaked.

Willi had to really scramble out of Johnny's way, because he was much closer behind her than she would have thought possible. The bag he carried joined the ones she had tossed in, and he sat down beside her with a loud grunt of pain.

Willi saw him touch the pain medication activator, but for only a tiny fraction of a second. The vehicle door was closing, but Willi saw the two blobs approaching rapidly, with the rest of the bags seeming to simply float along beside and behind them.

When the door fully closed it was a second or so before the cloak went clear from the inside. She saw the two had dropped the bags into a hatch at the rear of the vehicle and were moving toward the front. Both slid inside, and the cloak cleared again after having activated when they opened the doors.

Only after the two adjusted their confusion suits did Willi find out that one of them was worn by Cherokee. And the other by… "Grant?" Willi asked, incredulously. She felt a sense of alarm. "Where is Mother? Is she safe?"

Johnny held in the chuckle that almost escaped when he saw the rather annoyed look Grant gave Willi, as he said, "Of course she is safe. You think I would leave her if she wasn't safe?"

"Uh… No?" Willi stuttered out, chagrinned.

"No is correct." Grant reeled of a set of coordinates, that Cherokee was double checking against a pre-flight startup list.

Willi looked over at Johnny. He was rather proud of the fact that she had stayed quiet over the last several minutes. He decided that it would be best to explain, right now, that even try to delay it until later.

Her mouth was already open, but Willi closed it when Johnny, his eyes flicking from the communicator to her eyes and back, constantly, spoke first.

"You Mother graciously offered…"

Willi looked forward to Grant when he grunted, rather rudely, she thought. But they were quickly back on Johnny.

"You Mother graciously offered to provide me transportation off the planet, without going through official channels."

Again the rude grunt from Grant, which Willi ignored this time. Johnny continued. Willi could see that the pain was easing, at least a little bit. She itched to reach over and press the medication release, but restrained herself.

Johnny's eyes flicked up to Willi's. He held her gaze for long moments, and Willi could tell that his mind was going over options as quickly as some of their old computers could probably process information.

Willi knew when he came to a decision, and the one tiny flicker, that almost took his eyes from hers was enough for her to know she would not like the decision. And that it was not the decision they would work with.

"Think of something else," she whispered, her eyes still locked on his. Willi could almost feel Grant's eyes on the back of her head as she stayed close to Johnny, shielding her face from Grant's far too perceptive eyes, and incredible abilities to hear, read lips, understand body language, and use all the other weapons in his arsenal he used to protect her mother as head of family security.

Knowing that Johnny had not actually moved his lips, nor his eyes, and that eyes could not actually twinkle internally, Willi was sure that he was smiling, and that he had made the decision instantly, and was actually just fine with it, when he did, finally, blink, quickly look at the communicator, and then back at Willi.

"So it seems we will be going into hiding for a few days, until my…"

Willi could almost see him running through a list of word options to describe whoever it was that would be helping them. She had also heard the minute stress on the word 'we' when he had used it.

"…my associates have the information I have requested," he concluded.

"*Trinity Home* will…"

Seeing the real regret in his eyes, Johnny gave her a tiny shake of his head, and said, "Too much risk for your family. And, to be honest, as fast as she is, too slow for what must be done."

Willi felt herself bristle slightly. She was, justifiably she knew, proud of her family's home base ship, the *Trinity Home*. The family had several ships plying the trade routes, as well as Moon-Ship bases orbiting planets in several systems, plus four even larger Moon-Ship planetoids travelling independently in extremely long period orbits around key groups of star systems in the Milky Way Galaxy.

The Trinity Home was the largest, fastest, most well equipped, tightly and efficiently run of all of her family's ships. And only a dozen other ships could come close to matching her, and they were sister ships, belonging to some of the other families that had brought civilization and the human race itself out of the Dark Times of the Twenty-first through the Twenty-fourth Centuries, and led them to the stars.

She grudgingly admitted that there *might* be four ships that surpassed the *Trinity Home* in a few aspects. But only in some ways. Admit it she did, though, to herself, with just a touch of envy, but much more of pride, as the families owning all four of those ships had direct ties with her own. From those distant Dark Times. And all admitted openly that her family had been as instrumental in achieving everything that had happened as they were.

"Then where are we going? And how are we getting there?" Willi asked then, quite firmly. "And what are we going to do to get this straightened out so we can get married?"

Cherokee's soft, almost suppressed chuckle registered on Willi, barely, because she was concentrating on Grant, who was suddenly coughing, trying to catch his breath while staring at her in wide-eyed shock and disbelief.

Apparently, Grant had just taken a sip of one of the concoctions his sister brewed up for him to help him keep going the long hours he felt necessary for him to put in without break to fulfil the duties of the head of Family Security when Willi had spoken.

And had sprayed it all over the inside of the vehicle forward view monitor he was using to keep track of everything at the moment.

Cherokee's right fist bounced off Grant's back when he hit him to try to restart the man's breathing. And perhaps, heartbeat, if Cherokee was right in his thinking.

"Married?" Grant finally managed to say, sounding much more like one of the pre-teen girls Willi occasionally taught flight skills to when she was aboard the *Trinity Home*. Very high pitched, and… girly… Though Willi made a huge effort to bury even the thought deep inside her head when it popped up, before Grant could somehow realize it had actually been there.

But one look at Johnny, and she had a feeling that he knew, and that Grant might just know, since he was now glaring at her. And not because of her mention of marriage, she was sure.

Grant finally got several deep breaths into his lungs, and was able to say in his standard deep, gravelly voice, "Does your mother know you are getting married?"

"Mmmm. Not yet…" Willi squeaked out, sounding rather like what she had thought Grant had sounded like moment before.

"Uh-hummm." Grant replied, turning back around in the seat. He cleaned the view screen without another word.

"I'm going to tell her," Willi hurried to say. "Just as soon as I see her."

An annoyed glance was directed at the back of Cherokee's head when she thought she heard another chuckle. "Shut up, Cherokee!" slipped out before she could control it. "I am going to…"

"Yes, Marilyn," Cherokee replied quickly.

"Marilyn? Who's Marilyn?" Grant asked, feeling something he had not felt since… Well… something he had never felt, actually… confused… before.

"Mother didn't tell you?" Willi asked, eyes wide, her amazement apparent.

"Tell me what?" Grant almost bellowed.

Willi did not flinch. She actually had to struggle to keep from giggling. She had never seen Uncle Grant like this before.

"If I might, Commander McKindrick?" Johnny asked politely.

"Please. Please do," Grant said, now much more calmly.

Johnny amazed both Willi and Cherokee with his quiet, concise, and very self-deprecating explanation of the last many weeks.

It was not until the end of it, which wrapped up with the last few moments, that Grant looked over at Willi, never having taken his eyes of Johnny.

"It was you I was looking for?" Grant asked her. Fairly quietly. But with some wonderment in his voice.

"You were looking for me?" Willi asked, now as confused as Grant had been until moments before. Turning her eyes from Grant to Johnny she opened her mouth to ask a question, but Johnny spoke first.

"It would seem that The Lady McKindrick sent your Uncle to find you when her… assistants… lost track of your whereabouts on Sol's Transport Center."

"Wait!" Willi said, a hand going up. "She was having me followed?"

That pretty much paralleled Grant's question of, "Arabella had you followed? Where? And why?"

Willi dropped her head into her hands. "Oh, Lord. What a mess…" she muttered.

Johnny kept his mouth shut. He might be marrying into the family, but he was not part of it yet, and he figured, based on his experiences with his own family, that it would be wise not to get in the middle of a family matter. Such as this one.

Where Willi had gone off on her own, misleading her mother about where she was going and what her intentions were. And Arabella McKindrick had sent people to follow her daughter. Who had lost her trail almost immediately.

Whereupon she had sent her brother, Willi's Uncle, Commander Grant McKindrick, to find her before she could get up to some mischief she might not be able to handle. Without telling him just who he was looking for, nor why.

And later, while he was still trying to find whoever it was he was looking for, with very little to go on, when Arabella had contacted Grant, and rather worriedly had dispatched him to Sector ZZ-1219 to find out what might be happening there, without getting the family named involved, Grant had finally shown up, only to be diverted from heading out to the *Trinity Home*, which was heading away at high speed… somewhere… to an address planetside.

He was still reading reports on the local news outlets about the 'incident' when they arrived at Johnny's hideout location. And it hit him just now, which was way longer than he was comfortable with it having taken, that the Johnny, with Willi, the one she was apparently going to be marry, was the Johnny Oneshot in the stories. The one the central government was looking for. The Johnny Oneshot that… "Criminey!" Grant muttered, his eyes back on Johnny.

Knowing the look, Johnny, a bit surprised that Grant was looking at him with it on his face, said, "Don't believe everything you hear."

The slight head motion Willi made when she rolled her eyes caused Grant to look over at her, in time to see the eye roll. He looked back at Johnny. "You don't look like…" Realizing what he was about to say, though the color in his cheeks did not actually show, he felt it, and quickly shut up. This man was a legend. Beyond legend, apparently.

Grant's contacts throughout the human settled areas of space were excellent. More than excellent. They might even rival those of the Confederation intelligence services. He was very aware of the legend of Johnny Oneshot.

He also knew much of the legend was true. But he had always had some doubts about the entirety of it. Despite some of the first-person accounts he had been privy to. Not to mention his and his sister's not quite seen encounter with the legend when said legend apparently dropped off fissionables on the fly several years previously, and made it possible for a significant portion of the Space Trading Guild to survive and escape what would have been, from what he always suspected, and know knew, a horrible death.

That all passed through Grant's mind at blazing speed as he watched the legend… man, calmly check his communicator again. And Grant recognized the device as precisely what it was. He had one, as did three others under his command. And they had cost more than a small fortune, not to mention being highly restricted. Not even someone in his position was supposed to have one.

And when Johnny, eyes still on the device, quietly spoke to Willi, Grant was even further amazed to see her do exactly what Johnny had just asked.

"Willi, please sync your communicator with mine. You will need the most current information I just received, in case we get separated."

Though Willi did so, her eyes on the device that she pulled from somewhere within her confusion suit, she told Johnny, in no uncertain terms, that, "We will NOT be getting separated."

Grant felt his comm unit silent annunciator. A small sigh escaped him, despite his best efforts, when he pulled it out and saw that it was being automatically updated, with a huge amount of information. From his sources.

"You have one of these?" Willi asked in surprise when she saw her Uncle trigger something on his. She looked over at Johnny. "I thought these were restricted."

"Very much so," Johnny said, a faint smile on his lips when he looked from Willi, to Grant, and then back to Willi. "A person could get in a great deal of trouble if anyone found out someone not authorized to have one, did have one."

"Oh," Willi replied. She looked at her Uncle with even more respect than she had always had for him. "Do you have one of the..." she was in the process of asking him about the weapon Johnny had given her. But she cut herself off, giving Johnny an apologetic look, and a muttered "Sorry."

"Sorry, what?" Grant asked. "And do I have one of the what?"

Willi kept her mouth shut. She shook her head. Grant looked at Johnny.

"She is worried she might get me… or you… in trouble if she asks about whether you have one of the Security Forces special issue PDWs." A quick glance at Willi, and he added. "I am sure he does. Probably at least a couple of his people, too. We made sure they were made available, through certain contacts, to people that might have a need for them, and that we trusted would put them to good use if it ever became necessary."

Grant and Willi exchanged, on Willi's part, a wide-eyed look, with Grant's tighter, but still rather incredulous look.

"I really hate to say this," Grant said, but fell silent and looked at Cherokee.

Johnny heard the pause and looked up. "Cherokee is in the loop now," was all he said.

Another exchange of looks between uncle and niece, and a chuckle, not suppressed this time, from Cherokee, and Grant continued his thought. "I really hate to say this, but I feel like I am on the outside looking in. And I will firmly say, and not hate saying it at all, that I DO NOT like feeling like I am on the outside, looking in."

He cut another glance at Willi. "How much of this does your mother know?"

A helpless shrug was the answer Grant received. But the question did trigger a memory in Willi, that since it had come to the fore, she was not going to suppress again until she had an answer to the question that kept popping up from time to time, since her mother and Johnny had met, apparently again, at the space port.

"When did Mother meet Johnny the first time? I am sure you had to have been around. You know everything that happens. Well, I guess except this." She managed not to snicker.

"It was several years ago, apparently," she added, giving Johnny a look that he ignored.

"As far as I know, Arabella has never met him," Grant said, looking between the two curiously.

"That is what she thought, too," Willi tried to explain, but that was as far as she got when Grant interrupted her.

"What do you mean, 'that is what she thought, too'? Your mother would not forget meeting this man. He has had a reputation for many years."

"She did not know him as Johnny Oneshot when she met him the first time," Willi continued the explanation. "But when he said something in a different voice…" When Willi saw Grant's questioning look, she added a side explanation.

"Johnny uses many different disguises and personas. He has been doing this a long time, like you said. He was someone else that time."

Grant saw the annoyance on Willi's face. "And when he said something in a way that caused her to recognize who it was he was then, she kind of turned red. Embarrassed. You know nothing embarrasses Mother."

"Well…" Grant said speculatively, studying Johnny for a moment. "No, she doesn't. Not about much, anyway. Certainly not since…"

Seeing Grant's obvious recognition of just what it was that had embarrassed her mother about having met Johnny, she frowned. "What? You figured it out, didn't you? Tell me."

Thankfully, far more thankfully than he would ever admit, Grant was vastly relieved and thanked all that was holy to him that Johnny spoke up then.

"It was nothing, Willi. Truly. Your mother is a fine lady and always has been. There is no point in putting Commander McKindrick on the spot. I will tell you what happened."

Johnny gave Willi a rather gentle look, but she saw the sincerity in it, as well, when he added, "And I ask you not to make more of it than it ever was. It was all of my doing, to accomplish a purpose that I required to have happen at the time. And used your mother in a very… ungallant… way to accomplish it."

"What in the world are you talking about?" Willi asked in total confusion. She could see that her uncle was really and truly grateful that Johnny was explaining, and that he did not have to try to avoid explaining to her whatever it was, or to her mother, she suspected, that he had said anything at all.

"It was six years after your father died," Johnny said softly. He saw the remembered hurt in Willi's eyes. She had absolutely adored her father. Every bit as much as her mother. And Johnny knew just how much she was hurting in those years after the illness had taken him. And how much Arabella had been hurting, too.

"I needed to arrange for a regular trade route between… well, that no longer matters," Johnny continued. "Suffice it to say, at the time setting up that trade route was important to accomplishing some things that I had committed to making sure were accomplished."

Johnny paused and Willi saw the distant look in his eyes, but also at least a bit of fondness, as well as the tiniest of lift of corners of his mouth.

When he focused on her again, he continued with the explanation with a question. "Do you remember when Ambassador Algernon McElroy joined the *Trinity Home* for a month, seven years ago?"

Grant hid his smile at the almost dreamy look that came over Willi's face. Much as it had seven years ago. Very similar to the one that had come over his sister's face at the same time.

"Oh, yes! He was amazing," Willi said, still smiling when she looked over at Johnny. "He even danced with me at a party that Mother arranged once when he was on the ship.

"I felt so grown up. I remember that Mother had such a good time at that party, too. She was so sad so often, but when he was there, Momma sort of changed. She was happier after that. I remember seeing her dancing with him, too. She was laughing. I even wondered, kind of in that little girl way, if maybe they might get married and I would have a father again, and…"

The look on her uncle's face, and the soft look on Johnny's, and her memories all coming back to her of that time. When she was fourteen and… Ambassador McElroy helped the McKindrick Trading Family set up the trade route between the center systems and some sector on the far side of the galaxy. That had been instrumental in…

Willi's eyes widened yet again as she stared at Johnny. She shook her head. Stared at Johnny some more. Gave her uncle a pleading look. And then stared at Johnny again. Another shake of her head. "That wasn't… That couldn't have… That couldn't have been you! Ambassador McElroy was old! My mother's age!"

Johnny gave the tiniest of nods. "I have been very good with disguises for a very long time. Since my childhood."

"But… I thought she and he… I thought they might get married!" Willi wailed.

"I am sorry, Willi," Johnny said. "Very, very sorry, for having put you through that. And her, then. I have always felt terrible for the way I treated her."

Willi could not think of a single thing to say. But her uncle did.

"Johnny," Grant said, and Willi quickly looked at her uncle. There was something in his voice. Something she had only heard a very few times. And tears formed in her eyes when he continued to speak to Johnny.

"Do not, ever, feel terrible about that time. Or the way you treated my family. I wish I'd know then… But that time… It brought my sister back to me. My real sister. Not the carefully controlled Matriarch of the McKindrick Clan. But my sister, the woman, and wonderful person she always was, and was again, except during those few years after she lost Willi's father."

Willi was sure there were tears in Grant's eyes that he simply would not let fall. Because she remembered it much the same way. Her mother… had always been her loving mother… even during that time. But after she met… well… Johnny… even after his assignment was over, and he went… "I guess that doesn't really matter," Willi thought to herself. "But after the time she spent with Johnny, as Ambassador McElroy, Momma was her old self again. Just as Uncle Grant had said."

"I…" Johnny said, but Willi shut him up with just a touch on his arm, and then a gentle kiss she leaned forward to give him.

Along with a whispered "Thank you for that time."

Johnny opened and closed his mouth a couple of times, but after a glance at Grant, and then looking back into Willi's eyes, kept silent, and just nodded.

Concentrating needlessly on the communicator for a moment, Johnny then glanced over at Willi. "Uh-oh," came the unbidden thought.

And Willi, still watching Johnny, asked the question that Grant had been wracking his usually very agile and creative mind to find a way to ask without being too rude, even for him, and intrusive, again not something he usually worried about when it came to the safety of the family, which this probably was not. Thus the hesitation. But Willi came to Grant's rescue, even though she did not know it.

"How old?" Willi asked suddenly. "How old are you?"

"You mean now?" Johnny asked, making a token effort to divert Willi, which he was pretty sure was a wasted effort, but still worth an attempt just to see her reaction. She did not disappoint him.

"Now? Of course now."

The first word was reasonable, Johnny nodded. The next three were rising in inflection. "Hm…" found himself thinking, "she must have a million ways to…" He cut those thoughts off. "I am twenty-four. Or will be in a couple of months."

"Oh…" Willi thought. She had thought he might be about that age. Before. But she had suddenly been very unsure. She remembered Ambassador McElroy… or rather, Johnny as Ambassador McElroy, as being in his late twenties or early thirties those seven years ago.

An almost instant calculation happened in her head, without any thought going to it, and she knew that she had been fourteen, of course, and Johnny would have been… only seventeen… and her mother… Willi's mouth made a tiny 'O' shape, of which he had no clue, as her mother's age at the time popped into her head.

Arabella McKincrick had been thirty-two at the time. And had been enamored, at least a little bit, with a seventeen-year-old. Even if she did think, as Willi had, that the man was approximately the same age as Arabella.

The very soft "wow" slipped out. Willi was not sure if it was a wow about Johnny at that age, or about her mother, at that age, or any other. Knowing what she did now, she was more than a little surprised that the sharp green spear of jealousy had not struck her in the heart, nor had her eyes gone from blue to vivid green.

She knew that could not actually happen, but there had been those couple of times… Well, perhaps five or six. Or ten… or more. That they sort of seemed to, when she saw a woman looking at Johnny a certain way. Or he looked at a woman… pretty much any way, she supposed.

And though that tiny flicker that had sprung to life in the space port when her mother had blushed upon remembering her meeting with Johnny, had been minute, it had been there. But there was nothing of the nature now. It seemed to be a day and time for "Hm…" for she did another one herself.

Suddenly everything personal was regulated to 'later' status, for transport communicator chimed slightly, and three words were heard.

Cherokee did not wait for an order, request, or anything else. He did the equivalent of what pre-Dark Times people had done in like situations. He punched it.

As Willi held on, to the vehicle, and to Johnny, because though he was secured, he was using his good hand to work the communicator rather than holding on.

The transport had a good ground suspension, but Cherokee was putting it through some aggressive moves as Grant manipulated the cloaking controls, flashing into and out of the cloak, and applying different looks during each change.

Johnny spoke one word, and Cherokee abruptly changed course again, almost, but not quite doubling back on their route, three streets over. They were near the edge of the city proper, and near one of the large open areas that lay scattered throughout the other, more tree like growth that covered much of the planet that was not desert.

"Easy," Grant said, his hands on the cloaking device. Cherokee slowed significantly, until Grant gave one more word, "Now," and did something to the controls.

When Willi felt the transport lift into the air a good meter or more, while moving forward quickly again, and then came back down with a bit of a thump, despite the suspension, she was almost half on Johnny when she caught up with the vehicle's downward movement.

He grunted, just slightly, but Willi was looking out through one of vision ports to see where they were not. Cherokee had used the unexpected in that type of vehicle jumper jets to lift the vehicle high enough to clear a road divider, with enough height left, and forward momentum, to cross over the side barrier as well, and then disappear into some very tall foliage.

Cherokee did his best, but this was not a tiny vehicle, and the foliage was both large and growing densely. So they banged into a few things, hard, several times.

Willi gave up trying to protect herself from bruises, and did her best to protect Johnny, who was making no effort to do it himself, holding the communicator steady against one leg with his injured hand, and manipulating it with his good one.

The jostling finally slowed, as the vehicle did, and then stopped. She heard Grant asking, "Status?" while Cherokee was already out of the vehicle, doing something at the rear of it.

Grant looked back at Johnny and said, "Two minutes," before getting out of the vehicle himself to go help Cherokee.

Johnny put away the communicator, looked over at Willi, surprised her with a quick buss on the lips, and then said, "I love you." Of course he also quickly added, in about the same tone of voice, which was much more suited to the second sentence than the first, "Gear up and go hot. Bogeys inbound."

Willi gulped, released Johnny's hand that she realized he had managed to keep still despite his very strong urge to pull it free so he could do the same things he had told her to do.

Seconds later both were outside the vehicle, helping get everything out of it, and away from it, though Willi could not really figure out why. Other transport was obviously coming, but why not just move everything from one vehicle to the other?

They were in back-to-back stances, covering the full three-hundred-sixty-degree area a few long seconds later when Willi found out why they had moved everything from the transporter.

A shuttle landed on it. The shuttle was cloaked, but there was no doubt about, because it pretty much could not be anything else based on both the sound, and the ground shaking impact that occurred at the same time. Plus, while the transporter did not reappear, quite a few pieces and parts did, when the transport's cloaking device was destroyed.

Willi was more than a bit impressed with the cloaking on the shuttle, which she admired for a few moments, since there was hardly a shimmer in the field effect.

Then she was shocked once again when a rear cargo door popped open, a ramp flopped down, exposing the inside of a shuttle that was much larger than she was expecting.

Though those facts were the lesser of the rest, which was Sydney and Clyde standing at the top of the ramp, motioning them aboard, and two Dominators appearing just a few feet away. Willi had not had any sense of them being there until they uncloaked.

The pilots of the Dominators did not leave their craft. They did not only not get out, they did not even shut them down. They only blipped the cloaks enough for them to be seen.

The Dominators, and their pilots. Captain Butler was one of the pilots. Captain Echart was the other.

Willi gave Johnny a look that was asking a thousand questions, which Johnny returned with one that said, "Answers later. Leaving now."

Willi was staring at Sydney. She had recognized his features immediately. She had Clyde's, too. But they were both in Confederation Navy uniforms.

Two other men had run down the ramp and grabbed everything that Willi, Cherokee, Grant, and Johnny were not already carrying and were back in the shuttle moments afterwards.

The hatch was already closing, and Sydney was running forward, with Clyde hard on his heels. Over his shoulder, Sydney said, "Good to see you, Sis. Got a couple of offers of marriage to look at when we get a minute. These Navy guys are always looking for someone to settle down with. Good offers, too."

Willi could tell he was laughing. Just trying to needle her, like old times sake, and had absolutely no knowledge of everything that had gone on the last few weeks.

It did not really make any difference to Willi. A small ditty bag hit him in the back of the head with some force, as she shouted the words, "I told you to quit trying to sell me off to the highest bidder for marriage, Syd!"

"Ow! Geez, Sis! I was kidding!" Sydney had stumbled into Clyde at the impact at the back of his head, but both were more than nimble enough to recover and go through the hatch into the flight deck.

"Yeah! Me, too, Syd!" yelled Willi, more relieved than anything to see her brother and her friend. She had actually missed them.

Johnny looked at her with a smile on his face, and Grant, though he was aware of the interplay between brother and sister, was at a loss as to why it was happening now. Grant shook his head and secured the bags, before securing himself.

Willi let Cherokee help Grant and the other two Spacemen ratings and saw to it that Johnny was well secured. Unless she was seriously mistaken, there was no way Sydney would not be taking advantage of the situation to do some hot flying.

With Johnny secured, she took one step toward the flight deck, but was drawn up short with Johnny's good hand on one of her wrists. "Afraid not. Sit and buckle."

"But…" Willi shut up quickly and sat down beside Johnny. It was not like Sydney and Clyde could not handle things. But it grated not to be able to be up there making sure a *Trinity Home* daughter craft was putting its best foot forward. With her at the controls. It struck her, after a quick, slightly more detailed look at the inside of the shuttle, that this just might not be one of the *Trinity Home's* many shuttles.

Not to mention the fact that both Sydney and Clyde were in Space Navy uniforms. And then there were the two Spacemen ratings, too. Both Three Stripers. No, this was not one of the *Trinity Home's* shuttles.

Even not being on the flight deck, Willi was rather wishing this shuttle did belong to the family. Just from the feel of the ship being maneuvered by Syd, and Syd was definitely putting it through some paces, very impressive paces, the craft was fully on a par with the family's shuttles, and rather more, too, in terms of maneuverability and speed.

She was still studying what she could see, to try and figure out what it was, and was becoming more impressed with the craft by the minute, when Clyde's voice came from a speaker.

"Mr. Oneshot, Sir."

Grant looked confused, again, and Willi rolled her eyes.

"I am not Mr. Oneshot, or Sir," Johnny said calmly. "Just Johnny. What is it, Lieutenant?"

"Lieutenant?" Willi mouthed to Grant. She had not noticed his rank insignia. Or Sydney's. "And Syd?" she mouthed then. Grant shrugged.

It hit her then. Even having seen their uniforms, it had not really registered. "They're in the Space Navy? Since when?" she asked herself. Willi could not believe she had missed that. She closed her eyes and did a few deep breaths. She needed to calm down. Too many things were slipping past her. And that could be dangerous anytime, but especially now.

She tuned back into the conversation. "We have been ordered to uncloak, and vectored to the Flagship in high orbit. I thought we might slide between the sensors, but they saw us. The Flight Controller sounded kind of tense."

Willi and Grant both watched Johnny for a moment. He seemed somewhere far away as he thought. Willi wondered just how much information he was processing. Then he was speaking again. "Lieutenant, go into weapons console Quantum, shut down Legacy, and open up Seven. Just before you activate Seven, signal Sydney by hand, do not tell him by voice or console command, and activate Seven on a count of three.

"Lieutenant McKindrick, on Clyde's count of three, deactivate cloaking, count two, reactivate cloaking, roll one-eighty, rotate to forty-seven, pitch to thirteen, and go to one hundred twenty percent forward thrust. After a count of six, apply two seconds of portside bow thrust at ten percent and cut off. Stay at one hundred twenty percent forward thrust until we clear the one-two-one beacon that will appear for no more than six seconds. Throttle back to sixty percent and go to heading seventeen, one fifteen, ninety. I will let you know another course shortly."

Grant stared at Willi for a moment. Willi was staring at Johnny, and Clyde and Sydney, on the Flight Deck, were staring at each other. But only for a fraction of a second.

Then they were executing Johnny's orders. Johnny was watching his communicator intensely. Even more so than usual, Willi realized.

She felt the changes in the shuttle, and then the hard acceleration that the compensating seats in the passenger area of the shuttle only partly dampened.

Willi, Johnny, Grant, and the two Spacemen ratings all heard Sydney's and Clyde's curses. They had not even tried to suppress them. "The bastards fired on us! They fired on us!" Sydney shouted.

"That was a full broadside spread, Syd!" Clyde said, sounding shaken. "There are three nukes in that mess!"

A much more subdued Sydney added, a moment later, "If we'd been where they thought we were... Should have been, whether we had changed course or not to vector in to them... There wouldn't even be subatomic particles of us left back there. I can't believe they fired on one of their own shuttles like that."

Grant, at least for Grant, Willi saw, was pale. And she felt a shiver go through her. For some reason this was worse than when they had barely gotten away from Johnny's hide that had been nuked. There had been only one nuke then.

According to Clyde, the Confederation Space Navy Flagship had fired three, as well as at least fifty other types of weapons, from projectile weapons to high intensity electronic pulse weapons.

Willi was thankful for Johnny's hand that was suddenly holding hers. "I am sorry," he said almost too softly for her to hear.

She shook it off, angry now. "How is this happening, Johnny? Why is this happening? It does not make any sense? The governor… She was working with the pirates and the Ecronians. But we are on the Confederation side."

"There are several other factions," Johnny said, glancing from Willi, to Grant, to Cherokee, and then back to Willi. "It would seem that they have made some inroads into the inner workings of the Confederation more quickly than I was told was possible. We do not have the luxury of time, little as it was, that I had thought up until this moment."

Johnny stared into Willi's eyes for what seemed like a very long time to Willi. And then he opened his mouth to speak. And she already knew what he was going to say. Probably knew it the moment he thought it.

"I am not going to the *Trinity Home*. I am staying with you. And we are dealing with this, not matter what this is, how long it takes, or what we have to do."

Johnny nodded. And held back a smile when Willi addressed her Uncle Grant. "You, though, Uncle Grant, are going to protect Momma, and our family, no matter what it takes."

Without waiting for a reply, Willi looked at Johnny again. "How long before we can get Uncle Grant to *Trinity Home*? Or close enough for them to send someone for him, if we shouldn't rendezvous ourselves?"

"Now, see here, young lady," Grant growled. "I am…"

"You are head of Family Security, Uncle Grant. And you may be second in command aboard the *Trinity Home*, but I am still in line to take over the Family when Mother retires. So, you actually report to me, in matters of policy, even out here. And I want you protecting Mother, and my home. I can take care of myself, and even if I can't, Johnny can take care of me, if necessary."

Johnny could tell Grant wanted to argue. He really wanted to argue. But he also knew Willi was both right in the sense that it was what he should do, as well as right in the fact that, the way the family command was structured, she was technically his boss when he was with her, and her mother was not around.

"Yes, Ma'am," Grant said.

Johnny noted that there was no disrespect intended, either in Grant's words or delivery. Willi relaxed. Slightly.

With a quick look at Cherokee, who had been taking everything in with his normal quiet, intense, analytical thoroughness, Johnny addressed him. "Go forward and ask the Lieutenants to join us."

Cherokee stood and headed for the Flight Deck. Johnny addressed the two Spacemen ratings. "Please join Cherokee forward. And do not worry. You will not be implicated in any of this. Your lives and careers are intact and will be protected."

Neither man spoke, but they did salute Johnny, which brought smiles to both Willi and Grant, and a frown to Johnny's face, though neither Spaceman could see it.

Chapter Seven

Sydney and Clyde came hurrying into the passenger section of the shuttle, expectant looks on their faces.

Willi put a hand on Johnny's arm though, before he could speak. Then she motioned for Sydney and Clyde to get closer to her, Johnny, and Grant.

It was all both Johnny and Grant could do, to not burst out laughing, when Willi reach up with both hands, and took one of Sydney's ears in one hand, and one of Clyde's in the other, to pull them even closer, both of them emitting low howls of protest.

Willi released both of them, and then held up her left hand right in front of Sydney's face. He jerked back slightly, expecting a punch in his nose, which Willi had done on more than one occasion.

But she did not hit him. And he had to make a bit of an effort to focus his eyes on what was in front of his face now. Willi got a great deal of satisfaction out of the sudden look on Sydney's face when he recognized the ring for what it was, and Willi made very sure that he knew exactly what it meant, by saying, "I AM ENGAGED! Any further attempts to marry me off, much less sell me to someone, will be handled by my intended."

She gave a pointed look at Johnny, to make sure Syd knew exactly who she meant, and then looked back at Syd to add, "And believe me, there is nothing I have ever done, or could even dream up, that could come close to what he will do to you if you try. You got that, Syd?"

Willi turned her glare toward Clyde. "Clyde?"

Clyde was no dummy. He raised both hands in the air and backed up several steps, his eyes going from Willi to Johnny, back to Willi, and then back to Johnny, where they stayed. "I would never…"

"See that you don't," Willi told Clyde, and then her attention was back on her brother. She forgot what she had intended to say, because of the look on Sydney's face.

She could not quite make it out. It was not just a different look, but seemed like look after look after look flashed across his face as he looked at Johnny, not her.

"What is the matter with you?" Willi finally had to ask, when Sydney opened and then closed his mouth several times, obviously wanting to say something, but not able to either decide what, or if what, how to say it.

Almost thankfully, Sydney put his eyes back on Willi, so he would not have to look at Johnny, or see Johnny looking at him, with whatever was in his eyes, there.

"I just…" Sydney blanched a bit when Willi's eyes narrowed.

"It's not that. No. Not that. It is just…" He glanced at Johnny, but quickly looked back at Willi. "I won't. I promise. Never again. But… Jeez, Sis! How am I supposed to put the fear of God and Mother into him about not ever hurting you? He is Johnny Oneshot, for crying out loud! He could disappear me just like that!" Sydney tried to snap his fingers, but could not make them work, as they were shaking too hard.

"And I have to! You're my sister! He has to treat you right, or else…"

A soft look came over Willi's face, surprising Sydney no end. "Oh, Syd! That is the nicest thing you have ever said to me!"

Willi was out of her seat, and hugging her brother so tight he almost could not breathe. After a moment, seeing the amusement on Johnny's face, he wrapped his arms around her and hugged back, accepting that Johnny was not going to 'disappear' him. Or anything.

Sydney even managed to smile slightly when Johnny gave him an almost imperceptible nod in acknowledgement of his brotherly duties, with which Johnny had no problem. Sydney actually felt a bit proud of himself.

And then nearly got himself smacked in the back of the head again when Willi released him, he stepped back, and shot Johnny a look as he said, with attitude that Willi heard very clearly. "I'm glad we understand one another."

Grant was ready to intervene when Sydney stepped into it with his sister the way he usually did, but Johnny's light hand on Willi's wrist calmed her right back down, and she decided that she did not have to cut the LIEUTENANT down to his correct size.

Instead, she sat down again, Johnny's good hand firmly in one of hers, and asked "When did you two join the Space Navy, anyway?"

Johnny let brother, sister, friend, niece, and uncle catch up with each other for a few minutes, appreciating the calm before he had to break to them the plan he had come up with just a few minutes prior.

The discussion seemed to be winding down anyway when Willi jerked around to look at Johnny with panic in her eyes. "Telstar and Isis! The attack…"

Her eyes were huge and round, and Johnny could see tears forming. So he spoke quickly.

"They are fine, Willi. I vectored them away once we were clear of the atmosphere. They should be back on base after their training mission.

Relieved, Willi had to smile at the way Johnny had said "training mission." "Okay. Good." She was obviously calming down, but Johnny saw her tense again. "I can't believe I didn't think of them sooner. They just never entered my mind once we lifted."

"It's okay, Willi," Johnny said, rather soothingly. "I know things have happened unexpectedly, and quickly, and I have put so much pressure on you, that I am not at all surprised, that even with your quick and thorough mind, that one detail slipped past your conscious mind."

Willi began to relax again, until Johnny added, "And I made sure they knew the risks. I actually tried to dissuade them from helping. For this, and for what I have planned. But they absolutely insisted."

Johnny sighed. "I do rather hate putting people in danger. Good people. People that can make a difference whether I was around or not."

"Oh, Johnny…" Willi said very softly, her hand on his good hand applying soft pressure to reassure him. "It must be terrible for you, doing all this. But you have made such a huge difference in so many ways, in so many places, for so many people…"

Johnny nodded, closed his eyes with head back, and took several deep breaths. When his eyes were on her again, Willi asked, "Pain?"

A tiny shake of his head told Willi that though the pain he was in was not the prime reason for his actions, he was fortifying himself for something. The thought ran through her head that if he was going to try to talk her out of staying with him, he had better get ready for a tirade.

But it was not that at all Willi realized shortly after he spoke again. Johnny did not address her, but Cherokee, in the cocpit. She had to release his hand when he reached out to pick up the communicator from his thigh.

"Cherokee, would you aim a directional antenna toward the following coordinates…" Johnny reeled off the three-dimension spatial coordinates.

Willi noticed the sharp look that her uncle gave Johnny. When she turned to look at Johnny again, he was working on the communicator. But only for a couple of seconds. Then Johnny asked for the appropriate steerable antenna to be aimed for another set of coordinates.

When Willi looked over at her uncle to see his reaction, what she saw puzzled her, for he looked puzzled. As if he knew something, but was not sure about what it might have to do with the situation. She could tell he wanted to ask Johnny something, but held off for some reason.

Now her curiosity was a burning feeling. "Johnny, what were…"

Johnny cut her off with a smile. "I will get to it in just a moment." When she nodded acceptance, if not a great deal of it, Johnny continued.

All four of the others noticed Johnny look carefully around the compartment, and then even motioned them to gather round even closer.

"What I am about to tell you will put all of you in additional danger if our enemies even have a hint of what I am planning. Feel free to excuse yourselves from this conversation." Though Johnny waited at least four seconds, not a one of the other four had made any motion or tried to speak. "Thought so," Johnny murmured and then was speaking in a low voice.

Willi realized just how good an actor Johnny was by the way he could be heard by those around him and would not be heard from more than a few feet away. It was low, but it was clear and powerful.

"Now, though I had not made prior plans specifically for this situation, I have made some general plans which, with a bit of modification, will work very well for what has developed.

"One of the reasons you all will be in danger is the fact that though I do most of my… hm… work… at the auspices of the Confederation Space Navy Intelligence Office, I also work with an agency within the government that is not an official agency, but a group of people in positions that can be of great influence to how the Confederation continues to develop.

"I will not give you the names. I had myself go through a… lets call it a conditioning program… that allows me the comfort to know that I cannot disclose any of those names, as well as quite a few other things that I know. I cannot intentionally say the names, accidentally say the names, let them slip out, or say them under the influence of any…"

Willi saw Johnny's eyes cut to her, but quickly went back to his communicator as he continued. "…any type of persuasion."

A gasp, tiny as it was, and Willi's face draining of color told Johnny and the three others that Willi fully understood just what Johnny was saying. One of her hands went to Johnny's upper arm and she seemed to just want to hold on to him.

"Go on," she managed to say softly, with a slight tremor in her voice.

"Yes. Of course," Johnny replied. "This group cooperates to gather information to me, as well as some of the hardware and supplies of which I have need occasionally, and see to it that I receive them."

"The Dominators?" Willi asked.

"Those two, and some of the munitions. But many other much more mundane services and such. Support of my various identities for one, in both the active records, as well as archived records.

"They will tell me of situations of which they are aware that cannot be handled by various due processes. And I have made them aware that I am willing to look into the situations and try to resolve them in a way that will bring the situation to a conclusion that is acceptable to them.

"Everyone in the group is loyal to the concepts of the Confederation. A few of them played an active part in getting it established in a way that would be, as many of them I have heard say privately, 'looked upon favorably by those that helped create what became the United States of America in the seventeenth and eighteenth centuries. And then created the Constitution that codified what free people do that makes them free.' Even a couple have said that or similar publicly.

"I trust each of them, though I have not had direct contact with any of them for many years, other than my three specific contacts, who have access to the group, and with whom I maintain contact.

"The signals I beamed were requests for certain things I… We… will need to get the current situation rectified. The second was to… hmmm… how do I say this without…"

"Just say it, Johnny," quietly urged Grant. "It will make no difference to us, I am sure."

Willi saw the sardonic smile. "Very well," Johnny replied. "I have certain contacts within several of the guilds. Including the Galactic Family Traders Guild. The Galactic Manufacturing Guild, the Galactic Mining Guild, and the Galactic Transport Guild. As well as a few others, much smaller in scope, but still very important."

"How?" a very impressed Sydney asked.

Johnny really did not want to explain some of the ways the contacts came about, and how he used them, but Clyde said something that prevented him from needing to do so.

"Man, Syd! He's Johnny Oneshot! He knows people! All over. You know that. You've heard the stories."

Syd actually looked a bit embarrassed for having asked the question. He nodded and said, "Yeah. Don't even know why I asked."

When Johnny did not come back with the answer Willi had always heard when people said something about his exploits, she gave him a curious look.

Johnny either did not see the look or chose to ignore it. He was not about to give up the out Clyde had given him. He simply resumed speaking.

"All that by the wayside, the second transmission was to a Scanlon Galactic facility off the normal space routes."

"So, it is true," Grant said in response to Johnny's mention of Scanlon Galactic. "Scanlon does have a place out that way. It has been rumored for some time that they had a secret plant providing the Confederation military with specialized gear, in addition to their regular contract with the government and military."

"Let's see," said Johnny, a noncommittal look on his face. "How did the pre-Dark Time officials put it… 'I can neither confirm nor deny that' I think it was. It applies aptly here."

Grant nodded. "I was just thinking out loud. Please go on."

Johnny did smile slightly. "I have worked with and through Scanlon Galactic, some of their subsidiaries, and have close ties to the family. Which usually is a positive…"

The way he trailed off, all four understood that sometimes family could be less than fully positive.

"To minimize the chances of my communications being intercepted, as unlikely as that is, since these were burst transmissions, and encrypted as well, what I sent to Scanlan will be passed on to the others, letting them know that I will be making contact with them shortly. All have proven themselves to me, and I trust them all.

"Several have put themselves at risk doing the things I have asked of them, but have always done so. I believe they will this time, as well, even with some additional risks that will be involved."

Johnny paused, to touch his medication dispenser, and drink two large tubes of water he asked Willi to get for him.

Willi released herself from the seat and floated to one of the cabinets she was sure contained water, at least, and probably some rations. She was right on both counts. She flipped water tubes to Sydney, Clyde, and Grant, but took those for Johnny to him, not wanting him to have to strain himself in any way in case her trajectory was off. Not that it ever was, but she was not chancing it.

A touch of her toe to the cabinet and Willi glided back to join the others. Sydney, Clyde, and Johnny were accustomed to her grace and ability in free fall, which they were in now after Cherokee had stopped the acceleration and they were in coasting mode until they reached the point in space for which Johnny had given coordinates.

Grant, on the other hand, had not been in a free fall situation with his niece for years. He was amazed when her movement took her right to her seat, which she touched and guided herself into all in one coordinated series of movements.

"You, young lady," Grant said, rather in awe, "have developed amazing free fall skills. I do believe you are better than I ever was."

"Uncle Grant! That is so nice of you to say!" Willi exclaimed.

She looked over at Johnny when he added his compliment to her uncle's. "She is the best in free fall I have ever seen. I have had a great deal of experience in free fall, and your niece outshines everyone else I have ever seen operate outside the influence of gravity, in or out of a life suit."

Willi, as pleased as she was at Johnny's compliment had to say something. "Uncle Grant. Yes, I am good in free fall, but Johnny… He is amazing. I mean truly. I have seen him do…"

"Please Willi? I probably should get back to the plan…" He lifted an eyebrow, and Willi closed her mouth and nodded. Though she did give Grant a look that said she would fill him in later.

"With the items and support we will be getting from or through my contacts and arrangements, I believe we can bring this situation to a head, expose those involved, and resolve everything to the desired conclusion. That of making the Confederation the government all that favored it hoped it to be, and planned and worked toward accordingly.

"Every newly installed government goes through growing pains. Hopefully this situation is just one of those, and things will get back on track for the Confederation to be a major part of the greatest civilization humans have ever seen."

Rather moved by his words, the others listened intently as Johnny laid out his plan.

They were still very much moved by the plan Johnny had, but more stunned than anything, when he stopped talking.

"You can really do that?" Sydney asked. "But how? They will not let you get by with that..." He flinched a bit, thinking Clyde might chastise him for his comment.

But Clyde and Grant both were looking at him with that very same question showing in their eyes.

Willi was silent, but she was also watching Johnny with more than a little doubt in her eyes.

"Well," Johnny said, his sardonic grin back fully, once again annoying Willi no end, but she said nothing as he continued, "It is rather nice to not have rumors advanced implying I can do far more than any person possibly could, without question."

Johnny actually winced a bit when the awe she was feeling became apparent when Willi almost whispered, "You can do it, can't you? You really do have the abilities and the contacts to carry out this plan! You never would have said what you did, the way you did, if you couldn't."

Her wide-open eyes went to her uncle Grant. "Uncle Grant… What… Will Mother go along with this?"

"Oh, Willi," Grant said, sympathy in his eyes. "Arabella would have it no other way. She fought long and hard, along with most of the other families to bring about the Confederation. She will see this through to the end. I have no doubt, when she learns the full story and the plan, that she will endorse it wholeheartedly."

Grant looked from Willi to Johnny, and then back at Willi. "Except, probably, one part of it." He did not have to say anything else. Willi, Clyde, and Sydney knew just exactly what he meant. And so did Johnny.

"We shall see," Johnny said softly. He looked over at Sydney and Clyde. "I did not get into all the details, of course. It was just an overview. I would ask that you talk it over with Lady McKindrick, both of you, and anyone else from whom you normally seek counsel.

"Whether you would be willing to allow me and my fiancée, Miss Marilyn Monroe, to assist you in locating your sister, who disappeared and has not been seen since the last sighting of her months ago, at the Sol's Transport Center.

"I willingly offer the services of myself, and my resources as Guy Richardson to the quest. Whether my fiancée accompanies us is at her sole discretion."

Clyde, Sydney, and Willi were looking at Johnny with amazed looks on their faces. Johnny's quick cut of his eyes to Grant took in his growing smile.

"But I'm Marilyn!" Willi said. Then she looked stunned, glared at Johnny, and then the glare softened into a smile. "That is tricky. I am going to have to watch you," she added, tempted to give him a quick kiss. But decided not to give Sydney any ammunition.

"I don't get it." Sydney was shaking his head. "She is Marilyn Monroe, but that is just a stage name. How can we be looking for her as Willi when she is right here?"

Clyde punched Sydney on the upper arm, lightly, and looked at him for a moment. Suddenly Sydney's eyes widened. "Oh. I get it!"

He looked over at Johnny in admiration. "Wow. I never would have thought of that."

"Well," said Johnny, back in explanation mode. "I tried to make sure there were not any connections between Willi as Marilyn, and Willi as Willi, heir to the McKindrick Trading Family fortune, in addition to the precautions she was taking.

"I do not believe there is anyone left on the planet or space base that has any idea of who Marilyn really is. And I have no intention of not having her around as my fiancée, even if she would let me. We set the stage when she accompanied me to the Governor's so called inaugural ball.

"I was Sir Guy, and she was Marilyn Monroe. Anyone and everyone would certainly believe that I succumbed to her beauty and intelligence, and asked her to be my wife after only a few short dates."

Willi laughed. "You are so full of it! But, it will probably be the other way around. People will think I snagged you for your money."

"Wait," Sydney said. "Johnny Oneshot has money? Big money? For real?" He was looking at Johnny again, much more than hero worship in his eyes. Now it seemed that Sydney believed Johnny was some kind of extremely wealthy tycoon, as well.

"Remember… Do not believe everything you see or hear about me."

"Yeah. Yeah." Sydney was studying him as if Johnny might start spilling credit crystals out of his ears.

"Huh..." interrupted Clyde. "We are in the Navy... They won't let us just go off..."

Grant looked at Johnny. "Family Hardship Leave? To look for the sister, with the best friends help and moral support?"

Johnny smiled broadly. "Nicely put, Commander." Johnny looked at the two men again. "But this is entirely up to you. If you prefer to stay in the service, and do your duty from inside, I understand completely."

"You have others working inside?" Sydney asked, his shrewdness surprising even him. When Johnny nodded, Sydney leaned back in the seat and gave his answer. "Then I am in. All in. With you. And..." He could not keep the grin off his face. "Marilyn. Wait until Willi hears about this. I think she might have had a crush on him from the shu... OW!"

Willi's expertly flipped almost empty water bottle hit Sydney right between the eyes. And bounced back just enough for Willi to snatch it before Sydney could.

Clyde was shaking his head. "You never learn, do you?" Then he looked over at Johnny. "I'm in. For the duration. I would be glad to work with you to find Miss McKindrick. She is like a sister to me, you know." Clyde gave a shy wink at Willi.

"That is sweet, Clyde. Thank you. And you really are like another brother to me." She glared at Sydney. "A rather less annoying brother than my other one."

Johnny was looking at Grant, and recognized the bit of agony he was in. He so wanted to join them. To protect his niece and nephew and Clyde. Even Johnny.

Johnny shook his head slightly at him. "As much as I would like you to be aboard my ship on this quest, I know how seriously you take your duties to the family, Commander McKindrick. I would like to have your assistance with this, working from the *Trinity Home*. You will be of invaluable help working together with Lady McKindrick. As much, if not more, than your expertise would be helpful aboard my ship."

Grant nodded. That was all he could do. Johnny had given him the perfect out so he did not have to express the conflict he was feeling. "You will have anything I can provide…" He grinned. "Sir Guy, and Miss Monroe."

Willi tried to glare at her uncle, but her eyes were tearing up and it was a bit of a watery, ineffective glare, to say the best.

"But how exactly are we going to do this? It sounds like it could take a while. And we would need a ship. Something pretty decent," Willi asked.

"Yes," Clyde added, "and it would need to be armed like our shuttles. Or better. We would not have fared all that well during the pirate attack, had it not been for Johnny, in his Dominator."

Willi bristled just a bit, but she knew Clyde spoke the truth, so she calmed right back down. Then she frowned for a moment, and Grant had a feeling he knew what she was going to suggest. And he was right.

"Mother's yacht…" Willi said tentatively. "It is big enough. Fast, and decent armament. Pirates would think it an easy target…"

Clyde and Sydney both gasped. "The *Lavender Rose*?" asked Sydney. "I don't know if Mother would…"

"If I ask her… Nicely… I think she would at least consider it," Willi cut her brother off. But her words had changed from the positive to a more questioning one as she spoke.

Johnny was shaking his head. "It would be too recognizable without a major refit. Besides not wanting to risk Lady McKendrick's yacht, and not bringing attention to the family, I have already made arrangements for a ship.

As well as several things, actually. We will be picking them all up after we drop off the shuttle."

"Wait a minute," Sydney said, again showing his awe. "You were already planning this? Way before?"

Johnny smiled, and, hoping to lower the hero worship several notches, replied, "No. Of course not. This is simply something I had in the works for something else. It just happens that it will work out nicely for what I have in mind."

"Oh," Sydney said, actually looking rather disappointed in Johnny.

Grant spoke next. "And the Letters Of Marque? You are sure that the Confederation will grant them? I don't think anything like that has been done since the early twentieth century. And I am not sure about that."

"You mentioned that, Johnny," Clyde said. "I am not one-hundred-percent sure just what they are."

Johnny nodded. "They simply grant the holder the right to seek out enemies of the government, defeat them, and take as prizes whatever might be in their possession, including their ship, stores, and cargo.

"Most often granted in wartime for private vessels capable of taking a fight to the enemy on the high seas, they were used at times to battle pirates, as we will be doing." Johnny made no mention of the Ecronians. He hoped to force the actions necessary to get the Ecronians to rethink their plan without having to engage them directly.

When he had learned that the Ecronian government was actively cultivating, equipping, supplying, and paying for whatever the pirates could capture, he had already decided to do something.

The situation the Ecronians had created by asking for his head, basically, gave even more incentive to go pirate hunting, and made it easier to do it without the objections that would come from far too many people if he went off on his own.

Suddenly Sydney's eyes got huge. "Hey, Sis! You remember the old library that someone created back before the Dark Times? The one each of the families received anonymously not long after things started getting bad?"

Even Johnny was curious about what Sydney would bring up. He wished he had stopped him somehow when he heard the rest.

When Willi nodded, so did Clyde. "Yeah, so?" asked Clyde.

"Remember those vids you liked so much when you were a kid, Willli? The 'Bond, James Bond' ones?" Sydney had attempted an accent, and deepened his voice. But it did not matter too much that he was not successful emulating the twentieth century actor. The words were enough.

Johnny groaned when Willi colored just slightly. And stared at Johnny. Just like Clyde and Sydney were. Grant just looked confused.

"It is like he is a super spy! A double oh seven. Licensed to kill… Pirates."

"And he does seem…" Clyde started to say, but an almost pleading look from Johnny stopped him.

It did not stop Willi. "Oh, my goodness! You're right! And he is so much more handsome. And…" Willi blushed and closed her mouth.

"I know I am missing something," Grant said, with a chuckle, "but with Johnny's reaction, I think perhaps we should move on. What else do you need to tell us, Johnny?"

"Not much, Sir," Johnny replied. "At least not at the moment. I would prefer that you not know some of the details that the others will be getting soon. For everyone's safety.

"We will be reaching a way station soon, where Cherokee, Willi, Clyde, Syd, and I will disembark with our gear. From there the Naval ratings will deliver you to the nearest base that can get you to the *Trinity Home*.

"We will be picked up not long after you depart, and be taken to our intermediate destination, where we will get started on effecting the plan.

"For right now, I suggest everyone get a bit of rest. Cherokee is rested and can take the shuttle the rest of the way. Everyone else has had some long, stressful hours. I think sleep would do us all some good."

With that, Johnny set the example, as much to ward off any more conversation as to needing sleep. Though he did. And a good shot of pain medication.

Some four hours later, Cherokee docked the shuttle with a temporary way station ship. The ships were not equipped with gravity wheels so everything was done in free fall, and for safety, space suits were worn for all docking and transfer activities. The way station ships went from point to point, under hire, whenever a way point was needed for a while in areas without other suitable facilities.

Willi, Sydney, and Clyde all said their good-byes to Grant before suiting up. Johnny suited up except for his gloves and helmet. When Willi went to don her suit after saying good-bye, Johnny had a private word with Grant. They shook hands as Willi came back into the passenger compartment.

A few moments later the five that were staying were off the shuttle, and it was headed away from the way station ship. Johnny had asked the ratings to keep the rear sensor suite off for at least twenty minutes after the left the way station ship.

The five did not even go through the airlock, remaining inside until the ship that would be picking them up docked only a few minutes later. It had been on the far side of the way station, and cloaked, so those in the shuttle had not been able to see it.

When the craft uncloaked before docking, Sydney let out an exclamation. "That's a Sandusky Speed Demon III! One of the fastest class of ships in the Galaxy!"

"We are in kind of a hurry," Johnny replied calmly.

"Well, that will sure get us where we are going in a hurry," Clyde said, shaking his head.

Johnny could tell that Willi was a bit awed by the craft, too. Even Cherokee, Johnny noticed, had widened his eyes at the sight of the fast ship.

The Sandusky Family Enterprises Speed Demon III class ships were high-speed couriers for valuable cargos and passengers that needed to get between two points in space as quickly as possible.

Using a constant one gravity acceleration for a little over half way to the destination, it would reverse, and use a bit over one gravity deceleration for the remainder of the trip. It used quite a bit of energy traveling that way. But it was about the fastest way to get anywhere safely, and reasonably comfortably.

The ship was designed so that during the trip, except for the rotation phase near the middle, the one-gee and slightly higher gee-force of deceleration, created an artificial gravity of sorts, so passengers could move around freely without needing to have much skill in free fall. Plus, it made several other activities much easier.

Though not large, with those advantages, travelling on a Speed Demon III was a very nice way to travel.

Once the transfer was made, Willi's eyes immediately went to a rather tall, really slim, but curvy redhead that was looking at Johnny with a look on her face that Willi suddenly was not liking very much at all.

As soon as her helmet was off, Sydney whispered to her, "Your green eyes are showing, Sis." Which nearly cost him a space suit gloved fist to his nose. The only reason she did not punch him was she did not want to make a scene, since both would have gone flying in free fall.

Stripping out of the space suit quickly, so she could move better, she was just a bit too slow to intercede when the woman rushed Johnny as soon as he had his suit off.

"Don't…" Willi was calling to the woman when she launched herself toward Johnny, with the obvious intention of hugging him, saying, in a voice that Willi liked even less than the woman's looks, "Johnny! Sweetie! I finally get to see you again!"

She had to admit that Johnny did some rather fancy maneuvering in free fall to avoid the woman slamming into him. Especially considering that he was looking at Willi, she noticed, not the woman.

With the redhead under tight control, he turned her to Willi. "Marilyn, I would like to introduce you to my sister, Evangeline Richardson."

"Sis, this is Miss Marilyn Monroe. My fiancée."

Willi, pleased suddenly that the woman was Johnny's sister, was a bit put out when the woman said, obviously disappointed, "Oh. You're being Sir Guy, aren't you? You're on another mission. I hate it when you are doing all that superspy stuff. When are you coming home for a while? We all miss you, you know."

That, Willi could understand, and even felt a bit of sympathy.

"I will explain, but later, Evie. We need to get moving. Scanlon."

"Oh, no," sighed Evangeline. "Not there again."

"Yes. Now get us moving."

Another sigh and Evangeline floated toward the flight deck.

Johnny just shook his head when both Sydney and Clyde drifted forward, obviously intent on getting acquainted with his sister. Evie could take care of herself around flirtatious men, so Johnny decided to not intervene. Evie did not like it when he did. Usually, anyway.

Cherokee, on the other hand, went looking for the rest of the crew. He was not about to pass up an opportunity to check out a Speed Demon III.

Johnny eased back into one of the comfortable seats and strapped in. Normally he would be doing a few things until the acceleration began, but the way he was feeling at the moment, he did not want to risk any knocking around. And if Evie was in the mood to show off to two Space Navy Lieutenants, she just might make the transition to full gravity flight a bit more quickly than usual, such as when she had paying guests aboard.

Seeing Johnny's wince, Willi went looking for some food and water. With the heavier than normal use of the pain medication injector, he was going to need something in his system.

She luxuriated in the real smile Johnny gave her when she handed him a free fall meal and water bottle before strapping into the seat beside him.

"Thank you," Johnny said. And then nodded at her in the seat. "Smart woman. Evie might just show off a bit for your brother and Clyde. She is not immune to a couple of handsome young men, despite her attempts to prove otherwise."

Willi just grinned. And then grinned more widely when the craft maneuvering warning chimed and they went into hard acceleration right off the bat.

"I think I am going to like your sister," Willi said then.

"You would," Johnny replied, trying to sound disappointed, but failing. He was rather fond of her, himself.

Willi let Johnny eat. It took him a while, as he was obviously in thought as he consumed the meal mechanically. He checked his communicator regularly, but from the quick return of it to the hiding place she still could not figure out, he had not received anything he was obviously expecting.

Not even realizing she was as tired as she was, since she had slept on the shuttle, Willi suddenly woke up, not having noticed she was doing it, as she had begun to doze off.

She grunted slightly when she started to get up. "We are at more than one-gee," she said, looking over at Johnny. He was braced carefully in his seat. "Way more," she added.

"Yes," Johnny replied, this smile rather more wan than the one he had gifted her when she fed him. "I checked with the others and asked their permission first, and when they all agreed, I asked Evie to push it. To two point two gees. That is about all I can handle, I discovered."

"Oh, Johnny," Willi said softly. "I will go ask her to…"

"I would rather you didn't," Johnny said, interrupted her.

She was able to get up and make it to the ship's head and back, but she was panting a bit when she dropped back into the seat. "I will never, ever, gain weight," she muttered.

Johnny managed a chuckle. But that was all. As Willi buckled in again, for basic safety on a high-speed flight, in case the ship had to maneuver to avoid anything in their path, it suddenly occurred to her what Johnny had said when he asked her not to ask Evie to slow the acceleration. "He did not ask me not to," she thought to herself. "He said he preferred I not."

His eyes were closed and Willi studied his face while she had the chance. "That is a major change, for him," was her next thought. "Hm…"

Apparently, Johnny was one of those people that seemed to sense when someone was looking at him, she decided, for he stirred only a moment later and cut his eyes over to her. "Something up?" he asked quietly.

"No," Willi hurried to say. "Just exercising my neck. Been a while since I have been under two gees."

Johnny smiled, checked the communicator, put it away, touched the pain controller, and then closed his eyes again. When his hand lifted, rather slowly, to the armrest of the seat, Willi took it firmly in hers. She saw the smile widen slightly, and then Johnny was asleep. Thankfully.

It took two days, with most of it under two point two gees acceleration. The last third of the trip, however, was deceleration at two point four gees, which Johnny, at Willi's insistence, slept through with enough pain medication to keep him from hurting, and keep him asleep. He did make Willi promise to bring him out of it with a dose of the counter-active medication the medication dispenser also carried.

The others, for the most part, also slept for most of the trip, due to the high gee forces. The short periods of one gee allowed everyone to do what was needed, without the stresses of the high-speed travel.

Willi was about ready to apply the medication to bring Johnny out of his slumber a few minutes after Evie notified everyone they were approaching their destination, now coasting closer at slow speed, putting everyone in zero-gee conditions.

But Johnny had timed his last pain medication well. He was already coming around on his own. Willi watched him carefully for any signs of distress. When he winked at her, she blushed, and said, "I take it you are okay, then."

"Very much so, Marilyn," Johnny replied.

Willi turned in her seat when she heard Evie speak behind her. "Johnny, I thought the others might want to see our approach to Scanlon…"

"Yes, I suppose they might. It is rather out of the ordinary."

That was all it took for the others to float over to the view ports rather quickly, including Willi. She was used to being around and in the large Gravity Wheel ships that the trader families used, as well as some other private enterprises, and government agencies to a much less of a degree. Almost all government facilities were planetary based, or on High-Mass-Core Moon-Ship bases orbiting planets.

Only the military had a few free space bases, and they were few and far between. And when the others saw the Scanlon deep, free space facility, they realized, after a bit, that it would dwarf even the largest free space military base.

Only as they came closer and could see some other ships near the facility to get a true perspective of relative size, did the rest realize just how big the place was.

Sydney turned wide eyes on Johnny. "That's… That's… That's a High-Mass-Core Moon-Ship base!"

Johnny shook his head. "Look closer. I think you will see the gravity wheel, turning slowly. It is gravity wheel ship. Just very large, and with the entire framework of the ship enclosed, not just the wheel support section."

"Just how big is that thing?" Cherokee asked, awed despite himself.

"Only three times the standard dimensions of the Type Three gravity wheel ships," Johnny said. Willi turned to look at Johnny when he absently added, "Which does, of course mean nine times the volume inside the framework. Which is all used, unlike the standard gravity wheel ships." Willi saw him looking at his communicator.

He let himself float out of his seat, and a flick of a foot had him headed for the flight deck. Willi left the others to their excited discussion of the Scanlon facility to follow Johnny into the flight deck. Easing to a stop, she floated beside Johnny as Evie and her co-pilot went through the docking procedures.

The Speed Demon III did not do an external dock. Like other gravity wheel ships, the Scanlon facility had a pair of flight decks 'above' and 'below' the flight deck bays located outside the wheel framework on opposite sides of the gravity wheel.

Evie eased the ship inside, and brought it to a gentle stop, perfectly placed for the grappler arms to latch onto the connection points on the Speed Demon III. Looking 'up', Willi saw a flight deck bay airlock door opening, and the arms began to lift the craft inside the bay.

When it reached the appropriate point, another set of grapplers took hold, and the external ones retracted so the airlock bay door could close. It took a few minutes to re-pressurize the bay so they could exit the craft without resorting to space suits to make the transfer inside the main part of the ship.

Willi had to hide her chuckle when at least a dozen men suddenly showed up, apparently just to see Evie. "I hate this place!" Evie mouthed to her brother, which Willi saw.

When Sydney and Clyde went to 'protect' Evie, Willi started to call them back, but Johnny smiled and shook his head. "They might actually come in handy for her. Let's go see Commodore Scanlon."

"Commodore Scanlon?" asked Cherokee, who had decided to tag along. "I didn't think there were any Scanlons. Didn't the family line stop when…"

"Jennifer," prompted Willi.

"Yes. When Jennifer married the Sandusky guy? She was the last relative of the man that created Scanlon. I can't remember his name either."

"Quincy," supplied Johnny. "And that is true. It is a courtesy title, if you will, for the commanders of Scanlon Galactic's outlying facilities."

"They have more than one of these?" Willi gasped.

Johnny chuckled as they drifted down a corridor. Every once in a while someone would greet Johnny by name. Usually as Sir Guy. But Willi noted one woman ease up her progress as they approached. "Well, hello there, Johnny? Staying long this time? I wouldn't mind…"

"Tabitha, let me introduce you to my fiancée, Miss Marilyn Monroe. We'll have to catch up later. All of us."

A frown appeared on the woman's face, but it was gone as quickly as it formed. She gave a curt nod to Willi, but pushed off again, heading the direction from which Johnny and the others had come.

Johnny just shrugged when Willi looked over at him. "Guess I can't say much," she thought to herself. "It isn't like it doesn't happen to me once in a while." However, after the fifth time, she was beginning to revise the thought. But they reached their destination and Willi turned her attention to the man that greeted Johnny.

Willi was trying to remember the last time she had seen anyone with only one leg. Prosthetics could be produced for almost any need. It was seldom a person went without one.

Her attention went back to the man's face as he spoke. "Well, well, well, there son. I see you have banged yourself up once again." Then he turned piercing gray eyes on Willi. "And seemed to have snagged the most eligible young lady in the galaxy as your wife-to-be."

When he addressed her, before Johnny or she either one could speak, he surprised her even more than his comment about her eligibility. "And as pretty as her momma."

Although it seemed to be next to impossible in free fall, he made a bow to Willi. "Miss McKindrick, it is my pleasure to finally meet you."

Willi turned wide eyes to Johnny. "Now, now, Miss McKindrick. I will address you as Marylin in public. But the boy here, Johnny-O, has made himself a good match. A very good match."

His eyes went back to Johnny. "It is good to see you, Johnny-O. Truly."

"Thank you, Commodore. It is good to be here. How is your leg?"

Willi could hear the concern I Johnny's voice. But the Commodore slapped his one leg and chuckled. "Well, not so good, there boy. It'll be coming off in a couple of weeks. Just waiting for some down time, now that this order is completed.

"Never been much of one to go planetside. Don't even like the bases much. I'll take zero-gee anytime. So it is not much handicap for me."

The Commodore saw the stricken look on Willi's face. "Now don't you fret girl. It has been a done deal for a long time now." His eyes cut to Johnny, and then back to her. "'tis thanks to the lad here that I have kept it as long as I have.

"When I lost the other, and damaged this one, Johnny-O here got me out of that fighter and into the sickbay before I could bleed out like a stuck hog. Don't rightly know what a stuck hog is, but that is what the doc told me. Said what the boy did saved my life for sure, and the leg, at least for a while. She said it would have to come off eventually, unless something new came along that prevented it. Or I got killed first."

Willi's eyes widened. But the Commodore smiled. "She was a pretty one back then. And more beautiful now. I married her, you know." His eyes went back to Johnny. "Also thanks to this one. And she is just as feisty now as she was then."

"Commodore, if I can get a word in edgewise, I would like to formally introduce my fiancée."

"Well, carry on man. What are you waiting for?" The Commodore winked at Willi. "Always something with this one. Have to watch him like a long-range scanner."

Seeing him take what appeared to be a casual glance around, Willi did the same as Johnny. She checked to see if anyone else was near, besides Cherokee and the Commodore.

"My, my," said the Commodore. "She is a good one, isn't she?"

Johnny smiled and nodded. Then he made the introductions. "May I present Miss Whil... Willi McKindrick, Commodore. And Willi, this is Commodore Scanlon, also known in unofficial capacities as Wolfgang Quincannon."

Willi had to turn and look when she heard Cherokee's quick intake of breath. She saw him stand tall, one foot hooked to a zero-gee stanchion, and salute the Commodore. "Sir, it is an honor to see you again! Semper Fi!" His hand went to his forehead in a smart salute.

"Hello Gunny. Didn't recognize you there for a minute." The Commodore grinned. "And you obviously did not recognize me at first, either." He gave a sharp salute, and Cherokee snapped his arm down likewise.

"I take it there is a story here," Willi said. And realized that it was one she might not hear, when both the men looked at Johnny.

"Not up to me," Johnny said.

The Commodore and Cherokee looked at one another, and, Willi thought, seemed to have a conversation with their eyes. "I am sorry, Marilyn," Cherokee said softly. "That is still a classified event. I cannot talk about it. I might never be able to."

"Likewise, Miss McKindrick," added the Commodore. But he gave Johnny a long look, which Johnny, as usual, ignored.

Willi nodded in understanding. It was another of the Johnny Oneshot legends that apparently was less legend and more fact. Then Johnny spoke again.

"Commodore, I am sure you are well aware of what has happened, aside from my short communique. And so understand our need to expedite things."

"I do, boy, I do. And I am mighty proud of what you three, plus the others, have done to help keep the Confederation on an even keel. And applaud this… whatever this plan of yours is. I don't suppose…"

"Sorry, Commodore. No."

Willi's eyes widened at the quick negative response. But the Commodore simply grinned. "Yes. Didn't think so."

Turning, the Commodore drifted quickly through a hatch into a long corridor. Johnny followed, indicating for Willi to follow, with Cherokee behind her.

Willi had to admit, the Commodore was fast. But the three following him had no problem keeping up with him. Even when he would make a right-angle change of direction, any direction, as they did them all, up, down, right, left, or variations there-of, depending on their orientation with the ship.

They finally arrived at a huge open manufacturing space. Willi gasped at the sight. She even saw Cherokee's eyes open wider. And saw the pride in the Commodore's face. And the appreciation on Johnny's.

"Well done, Commodore. Well done. As always. I take it the others are to spec as well?"

"Of course, Sir Guy," the Commodore said rather formally. Willi noticed several people drifting over. Some in work coveralls, and some in supervisory clothing, with a computer display on one arm.

"Sir Guy," said three of them. The fourth, another woman, Willi noted with annoyance, simply eyed him, glanced at Willi, and then looked back at Johnny, to give him what Willi considered a way too familiar nod of recognition.

"Thank you all for the speedy work," Johnny said addressing them all equally. "I know this has been an arduous task to produce so much at such high quality in such a short time. Rest assured that I will see to it that there are bonuses all around."

The four, including the woman, Willi noticed, exclaimed excitedly. After a motion from the Commodore, the four each touched a nearby stanchion and drifted off.

"You realize that you have no need to do that, Johnny," the Commodore said softly. "The payment was more than sufficient. Scanlon will be handing out bonuses, anyway."

"I know, Commodore. But everyone has really gone far beyond what had to be done. Scanlon has very good people, all committed to the Confederation, just as you, yourself are. And those Earth-side that support my efforts."

"I know. I know," the Commodore replied, shaking his head slightly. No need to even say it. 'It is only money. And I have enough to handle it.' You have said it often enough."

Willi and Cherokee looked out at the workspace again. "Wait a minute," Willi suddenly said. "Do you mean you are buying these Dominators? This isn't a military contract? These are yours?"

"Well…" Johnny said, that sardonic grin she had not seen in a while, back. "Temporarily. I will be delivering them to the military sometime. After they are thoroughly tested." Johnny's face hardened. "Put through their paces, as needed."

Then he turned to the Commodore, and asked, "The liner ready to take everything ordered on board?"

The Commodore tried to look affronted, but did not quite pull it off. "Of course."

Johnny smiled. "I rather figured it would be. And, unless I miss my guess, pretty much everything that is not here, is already aboard."

This time the Commodore grinned. "Of course!"

The Commodore pushed off, and Johnny, Willi, and Cherokee quickly followed. Willi was able to slip close to Johnny and match his trajectory through the work space. "What liner?"

"You will see shortly. I will explain further then."

Willi did not respond. She just stayed with him, Cherokee a meter behind them. They did not go far. The Commodore took them to the nearest transport lift, which they entered. He gave a compartment number and everyone braced for the movement.

There were several starts and stops, each with a change of direction. Willi was feeling queasy by the time the lift stopped and opened to another corridor. "I hate lifts…" she muttered, a hand going to her stomach, her face a very pale green.

Johnny squeezed her hand, which she just then noticed he was holding. Willi managed a smile as they drifted rapidly down the corridor.

Willi had to admit, but only to herself, that she was more than a bit disappointed when they entered another large construction area. An empty construction area, except for two shuttles, to which she paid little attention.

But she did not hesitate when the Commodore launched himself hard toward the far side of the compartment. She joined Johnny and Cherokee in doing the same thing.

All three flipped over to absorb the shock of the landing with their feet and legs. Johnny did wince, but Willi decided not to say anything, though it bothered her to see him in pain. And the Commodore had no problem, using his one leg quite effectively.

The Commodore motioned them over to an airlock hatch to a compartment inside the larger space, next to one side of the compartment.

When they had cycled through, Willi saw the large view port and joined the others. She noticed that the Commodore was smiling with pride at something. And Cherokee seemed mesmerized. Johnny, she thought, looked thoughtful. When she finally turned to look through the viewport herself she gasped.

She looked at Johnny quickly, and then back out to the ship that was docked to the Scanlon facility a short distance away. "That's… That's not your ship! Is it? Johnny?"

"Oh, it indeed is his," the Commodore said, with the pride evident in his voice as well as his look. "Ahead of schedule, and under budget. Every design parameter met or bettered. She is the sweetest ship we have ever built. Sweeter even than any of our own. That is a fantastic design, Johnny. It will serve you well. For whatever it is you now have in mind."

Cherokee turned to look at Willi and Johnny for a moment, but quickly turned back to study the ship again. He listened, as he did not have much choice, as Willi whispered to Johnny. Or at least her words start out as a whisper. Sort of. The whispering aspect disappeared pretty quickly.

The Commodore looked on unabashedly as Willi lambasted Johnny.

"I know you are rich, Johnny. But my lord! That must have cost a fortune! Isn't the government going to pay for it? Tell me the government is going to pay for it. Please."

"Oh, Willi," Johnny replied, taking one of her hands in his, looking into her eyes earnestly. "Willi, it is my new personal craft. I have been planning it for some time. I tend to like options. Plenty of options. And I do travel a great deal. It just so happens that she will fill the role of privateer just as well as any of the roles I initially designed her to fill. I can't deny that the possibility did not occur to me, but only in a what-if kind of way. I was not expecting to have to use her for that as soon as she was ready to go."

"But the money…" Willi lamented. "And to spend so much more on this mission…"

"Willi, you are your Mother's daughter. You come from a very long line of business people and traders. It is in your blood. I look at money a bit differently than traders do. Please understand that.

"I am not frivolous with money, but I have no qualms about using what I have to achieve the goals I set for myself, and to do the things I feel compelled to do. I certainly do not have an unlimited supply of wealth, but I have more than even I will ever probably be able to spend in my lifetime, and will still leave our children with probably more than is good for them.

"Please trust me on this, and do not fret about the money. Believe me, I have spent this much before, several times over, and managed to lose more than even I like, but that is the nature of what I do. Can you accept me the way I am, Willi? For better or worse, richer or poorer?"

"Oh, Johnny," Willi said, looking into his eyes. "Yes. Of course I can. I will. It might take me a few tries…"

Johnny chuckled. "Oh, I rather assumed that would be the case. It isn't a problem."

"Hey!" Willi said. But she obviously was not upset with him over the statement.

Her hand still in his, Johnny turned to the Commodore. "I hate to just take delivery and take off, Commodore, but the sooner we embark, the sooner this whole mess will be over."

The Commodore nodded. He looked more somber now. "Privateer?" was the single word question.

It was Johnny that nodded this time. "And the less you know, the safer everyone else is. We have all agreed to take the risks we face. I have no intention of putting anyone else at risk that does not have to be."

The Commodore replied softly, "I will risk myself as I choose, young man. But as you say, I will not risk others, either. So, no word of this will leave my lips. I take it you want to get the Dom Twos loaded. They are all fueled and armed."

"Dom Twos? Dominator IIs?" asked Willi. Cherokee was looking on in question now, too.

The Commodore grinned again, with a touch of pride back in his look. "Yes. A few ideas from Johnny here, and a few from our R&D, and early feedback from Telstar after his recent use of the test bed unit that Telstar helped us with."

"You've talked to him? Does he know about the new model?" Willi asked eagerly.

"He knows R&D has been working on improvements," the Commodore replied, looking at Johnny quizzically.

"I have not informed the others yet," Johnny told Commodore Scanlon. Johnny looked over at Willi. "Major Butler and Major Echart have been granted open ended R&R leaves to 'recover' after the recent 'unfortunate incident'. They will be joining us."

All three heard the stress on the words 'recover' and 'unfortunate incident'. Johnny did not seem to like what he had expressed. It was only a second or so that Willi realized he had called both Bill and Janet Major.

"They were promoted!" she exclaimed.

"They were that," Johnny said with a small smile. "At least they got some recognition and the promotion. I do not like the way they have been treated since, however."

"What are you talking about?" Willi asked.

"I will let them explain," Johnny said. He was already moving toward the airlock as he said, "Commodore, if you would ask the others to meet us in the Dominator construction area…"

"Absolutely," replied the Commodore. "I will meet you there. I need to make a couple of stops first, however."

Since Willi requested a quick break to use the facilities, Johnny and Cherokee availed themselves as well. But the delay was short, and they were soon meeting Bill, Janet, Sydney, and Clyde outside the construction compartment that held the Dominator IIs.

Willi could hardly keep from squirming, knowing that the others as yet had no idea about Johnny's ship, or the Dominator IIs. Willi took note that not only was Evie with Sydney and Clyde when they came in, but four other people came in with Bill and Janet.

"I better make some introductions, I suppose," Johnny said. He was again distracted with his communicator. But he looked up and saw Willi giving Janet a hug, and then Bill.

"I want to hear about what happened," she whispered to Janet. Janet nodded, but both looked over at Johnny.

He began the round of introductions. First the four people that had entered the compartment with Janet and Bill. There were two men and two women. All fairly young, and very fit.

"This is Kathleen, Gwen, Charlie, and Matthew. They have agreed to act as crew for me, as a personal favor."

Willi gave Johnny a quick look, but he was speaking again, introducing the four to each of the others. "And, for whatever reason she is here, this is my sister, Evangeline. And my fiancée, Marilyn Monroe."

After the introductions, Johnny gave Evangeline a hard look. "And just what DO we owe the pleasure of your company at this time, my sister?"

"I'm going."

Johnny shook his head. "Under no…"

"I'm going," Evangeline interrupted her brother.

"Evangeline, this…" Johnny lowered his voice. "This… journey is going to be…"

Again his sister interrupted Johnny. "I. Am. Going. I can fly that crate as well as any of the other test and check pilots. Better than all but one, actually. So. I am going, and I will be one of the pilots."

Johnny shot the Commodore a less than pleased look.

"She can be kind of persuasive," the Commodore said rather sheepishly. "Every time she made a run here she was down in the bay, checking on the construction. She knows the ship inside and out.

"And she is a very good pilot. After the initial run up to check systems, she did all the rest of the flight testing. Evie had her doing things we didn't even think she could do." The Commodore shrugged.

Willi watched Evie carefully as Johnny turned his attention back onto her. And stared. Evie's countenance did not change one iota. She stared right back at Johnny.

Never quite sure if she heard Johnny say what she thought she did, Willi kept her eyes on Evie. When Johnny gave the tiniest nod, and started to turn away, Willi saw Evie continue to hold herself still. Until Johnny was going through the hatch.

Then she let out a breath, and managed to do a little victory dance despite the zero-gees. "Finally!" she breathed out just loud enough for Willi to hear as the others moved after Johnny, with Sydney, Clyde, Bill, and Janet all asking various forms of the question, "What ship?"

As Willi and Evie entered the Dominator II construction area the questions stopped for a moment. Silence reigned for several seconds.

Then the Commodore, his voice booming, gestured to the craft in the space and said, "Behold! The first of the Dominator IIs! Thanks to this young man here."

The Commodore slapped Johnny on the back. Gently, Willi noticed.

The others swarmed all over the Dominator IIs. Apparently even Evie did not know about them. Nor the four new people that were now going with them.

After a few minutes of excited talking, Johnny called for attention. "We need to board the *Lady Paladin* and supervise the securing of the Dominators and our four shuttles as the Commodore's people bring them out to the ship.

Again the questions came, asking about *Lady Paladin* this time. None of the others wasted any time following Evie, when she said, "Come on. I'll introduce you to the *Lady Paladin*. She rolled her eyes at Johnny, and Willi saw her mouth the words, "*Lady Paladin*? Where did that come from? I thought she was going to keep the *GRS 3* moniker."

When Johnny's eyes cut to Willi, and he colored ever so slightly, Evie suddenly grinned and looked Willi herself. Causing Willi to blush.

The efficient crews of the Scanlon Facility made short work of getting the Dominator IIs manhandled the short distance around the vessel to the *Lady Paladin*. There, Sydney and Clyde sort of just took over, under Evie's direction. The others willingly followed their guidance to get four of the Dominator IIs secured in Ready Racks. Then they began stowing the other sixteen, four each in each of the four flight deck bays.

Willi watched for a bit, but when Johnny said he was going to his zero-gee stateroom to rest, she started to go with him.

But the draw of the *Lady Paladin* was too much. Willi went exploring. She spotted Cherokee a few times. It seemed he was doing the same thing.

When the annunciators sounded for assembly in the main lounge of the ship, Willi, having studied the placards with the layout of the ship that were seemingly everywhere, had no trouble finding it.

The others came in, one after the other, until they were all there. And all looked at Johnny, as he stood looking out of one of the view ports in the lounge.

Finally, he turned and addressed the group. "I want to give everyone another chance to change their mind about going…"

He was drowned out with quick, adamant protestations. Johnny smiled slightly and waited for the clamor to die down. It did not take long. But he did not really have much chance to continue, for most of them, other than Evangeline, wanted to know about the *Lady Paladin*. In detail, apparently, from the different questions being asked.

"Very well," Johnny said, the sardonic smile curving his lips. "However, while I do know the specifications, it seems Evangeline knows the ship inside and out, as I have been reminded. A few times. I believe I shall allow her to fill everyone in on the details. Evangeline?"

Johnny took the opportunity to take a seat and took out his communicator. Willi watched him for a moment, but quickly turned her attention to Evangeline, as she eagerly began to describe the details and features of the *Lady Paladin*.

"She is an amazing ship," Evie said. "There is literally nothing like her anywhere. The Commodore said it is the most innovative design he has ever seen suggested, much less built.

"As you all saw, it is a full ball type gravity wheel, like the Scanlon facility here. The gravity wheel is about half the diameter of a traditional Type One gravity wheel ship.

"But with the full ball design, there is a tremendous amount of storage room compared to the axle ring storage of regular gravity wheel ships."

She started to say something else, but paused and looked over at Johnny. When he gave her a slight nod, she began to speak again.

"And since the ball is both armored, and arranged to provide maximum protection to the gravity wheel, except for the outermost deck set up for observation and other activities that need, or for which exterior views make things nicer, the wheel is extremely safer than many.

"Combine the ball with the extended frame that is part of what makes this design unique, there is even more room for stores, as well as a few other things."

Evangeline grinned. "Such as twenty Dominator IIs, two large, and four smaller shuttles, and a handful of other craft, some actually for use planetside."

That brought some surprised looks and murmurs.

"I am sure you all also noted that in addition to the traditional daughter craft bays on either side of the control structure framework, there are two more sets on the extension, somewhat aft. Not to mention," Evangeline continued, "the extension allows for another unique feature of the *Lady Paladin*.

"That of her propulsion system. Instead of the standard set of four drives, with independent reactors driving them, the *Lady Paladin* has eight sets of drives that are somewhat smaller than would normally be fitted to a craft this size, in pairs.

"There are four in the rear propulsion extension, as usual, but there are four more, located with the reactors outboard, the drives inboard, further forward in the extended hull.

"In addition, there are two much larger, high energy, high mass drives centered in-line in the rear drive bay, to provide the thrust to overcome dead stop inertia, and allow the ship to reach cruising speed more quickly than would otherwise be possible. Even more quickly than pretty much anything except a Speed Demon III.

"And," Evie said, grinning, "the eight smaller drive units are all steerable, to allow some very complicated maneuvering when the gravity wheel is locked. We do not have to re-align the framework to aim it the direction we need to go. We can turn the entire ship, as long as the wheel is locked down, very, very quickly. And apply full thrust with all ten drives to get us up to speed very, very quickly."

There were quite a few murmurs and people exchanging looks. But Evie had more information for them.

"In addition to the two, larger than standard, reactors for general power needs, we have four, plus two each of both drive sizes and power reactors in storage. Along with... well... more fissionables than some people might be comfortable knowing about."

Seeing some widened eyes, Evie quickly added, "But stowed safely, of course, in their modular packs, inside further protective enclosures. With the apparatus built into the ship to refuel all the reactors in-house, almost automatically. It does take human control, but mostly just starting the process and monitoring it remotely.

"With the freshly fueled reactors only, we have a range... Well, it is not unlimited, by any means, but at normal speeds, we can go a very long distance. And back."

"Normal speeds?" Willi asked.

Evie grinned again. "Yes. As you all know, the standard acceleration rate of one-eighth gee that gravity wheel ships travel to avoid stresses on the wheel, axles, and bearings can get those ships up to about one quarter of the speed of light.

"However, one of the features unique, again, to the *Lady Paladin*, is that with the gravity wheel no larger than it is, the rotation can be halted, the wheel locked into place, and the propulsion can then be upped to... above two gees, if necessary, without any damage or even much stress.

"When you see the rest of the extension, you will see that many of the compartments are set up like a Sandusky Speed Demon III, to allow one-gee flight, without using the wheel. And one-third of the wheel is set up so it can be used during the one-gee travel, as well."

That brought many more murmurs. It was unheard of for a gravity wheel ship to stop the wheel, or have thrust at more than one-eighth gee.

"And with one-gee constant acceleration," Evie continued, "the ship can quickly approach one-half light speed. Perhaps more. I have not had it above three-eighths the speed of light. The throttles automatically cut out the drives at that speed." Evie shot a rather annoyed look at her brother, who did not see it, as he was once again studying his communicator.

When it quieted again, Evie began to describe a few more features of the gravity wheel. "Of course, when it is stopped and locked, the interchange locks, though kept closed, do not have to be cycled the way they are when the wheel is turning.

"Another feature of the wheel, is, unlike all other known gravity wheel ships, access can be achieved on the perimeter of the wheel, as well as through the axle. There are three rings between the wheel and the framework, that have a series of transfer airlocks.

"Two or three people, at most, as the rim transfer airlocks are small, can enter the transfer airlocks from the zero-gee areas, the ring matches speed with the wheel, and the occupants climb up into the wheel. And they will climb, of course, for when the ring is rotating, it too will be at one-gee.

"It has to be very carefully executed, but with practice it is not much of a problem. Climbing the ladders does take some getting used to, I admit. But the method does allow for some quick transfers from zero-gee to the one-gee level of the wheel, without having to go through the axle and then down to the one-gee level.

"Besides the extended hull on the control structure framework ring, dorsal and ventral extension hulls extend back a bit past the line of the control structure framework ring, and then slope downward, or upward, as the case may be, to the control structure ring hull, providing even more internal hull space. As well as a couple of other important features.

"One of the main ones being the ability to mount very large, very capable sensor systems. The newest technology available, and with the amount of electrical power available, very high powered in addition."

Again, Evangeline looked to Johnny for approval before she continued. "And *Lady Paladin* has a few sensor capabilities that are not normally available to civilian vessels.

"Of course, she carries all the standard defensive weapons in standard locations. Light, medium, and heavy railguns in turrets, for the most part, depending on location.

"The flight bay surfaces, center-points on the support rings, and on the propulsion extension. There are light, medium, and heavy gimbaled anti-obstacle railguns in the bridge structure for flight path danger elimination, as well as turrets on all four sides with medium rail guns for defense, like the others.

"And the aft flight deck bays have sensors, anti-obstacle navigation railguns, and a few surprises, as well.

"What is different about the weapons installations, as you might have noticed, and been wondering about, is that, other than the navigational flight path clearing railguns, all the others are on pop-up mounts, under exterior panels that open to allow the turrets to deploy and be used fully.

"Another set of items that are not standard, and again, unique to the *Lady Paladin*, are the much heavier railgun turrets concealed inside the dorsal and ventral hulls. Three in each. One on each side, and one on the top. Hull panels open up and retract, giving the railguns full maneuvering, with only the hull areas locked out so we cannot shoot ourselves. Likewise, three on each side of the extended hull, slightly aft of the rings."

There was awe in the tones, but that last had brought a few chuckles.

"There are also four of the much heavier railguns in the bridge assembly, along with the flight path clearing railguns, for…" Evie's eyes cut to Johnny, but he was not looking at her. "for whatever," she finished the sentence.

"There are some other surprises," Evie said, but cut herself off when Johnny made a small motion with one hand. "That we can get to at a later time. Brother?"

"Thank you, Evie. You did that much more eloquently than I could have hoped to have achieved." He looked around at the others, as they listened intently.

"You all pretty much know we are going to be hunting pirates, since they have become a scourge even further ranging than what we found in Sector ZZ-1219 and environs. In addition, we will be looking for a woman named Willi McKindrick. She is the daughter of one of the leading trading families, and I, and my lovely fiancée, Miss Marilyn Monroe, have agreed to go looking for her.

"Her shuttle was attacked by pirates some time ago, and the fear is that they may have taken her to be held for ransom, though no demands have been made.

"Her brother and their friend, both newly commissioned in the Navy, have been given leave to join the search. We will be picking them up from their home ship, *Infinity Home*, as soon as we can get there, so we can begin the search for Miss McKindrick. And take care of any pirates we run across during the search."

There were a few more snickers. None of the others were quite sure why Johnny was keeping up the charade about Clyde and Sydney being on *Trinity Home*, but no one said anything.

Johnny looked at each of the people in turn. "Does everyone understand that clearly?"

There were a few smirks, but everyone voiced an agreement in some way.

"Very well then. I am command. My sister, Captain Richardson, is Pilot. Marilyn, you are co-pilot, equivalent rank of Captain. Majors, you are primary fighter craft pilots. When we pick up Miss McKindrick's brother and friend, the friend will man the Sensor & Weapons console. The brother will be Chief Shuttle Pilot, on-call fighter pilot, and back-up on the Sensor & Weapons Console.

"Kathleen, Gwen, Charlie, and Matthew, you will be deck crew, assigned as needed, equivalent rank of Petty Officer. You will be under my command, but will accept and carry out any orders Major Butler issues, as he is my Executive Officer and second in command, and respond to the pilots for any issues they may need addressed.

"In addition to her other duty as co-pilot, Miss Monroe will also be on-call for fighter craft duty, as well as monitoring ship's resources."

Johnny looked at Cherokee next. "Cherokee, you are now, if you accept, equivalent rank of Ensign in our small group. You will act as my floater, troubleshooter, expediter, and fixer. And assistant gunner to Miss McKindrick's friend. Become acquainted with every aspect of this ship, and everything it carries, including all weapons, countermeasures, and EVA systems.

"Captain Richardson, at her convenience, will assist you with the familiarization."

Johnny looked around at the others again. "Any questions or remarks?"

They all looked at one another, and then back at Johnny. Each one shook their head in the negative.

"In that case, Captain Richardson, lead Cherokee, Marilyn, and the deck crew in parking the gravity wheel and then secure the ship for one-gee flight. We need to rendezvous with the *Trinity Home* as soon as possible, but I want everyone comfortable with our accommodations before we boost speed.

"Once we are underway, Marilyn, I would like you to assign quarters for everyone, considering their duties, in both the wheel and the extended hull for when we are under both zero-gee conditions and non-zero-gee conditions. If you have questions, I am sure my sister can assist you.

"Everyone, please carry on. Majors, may I see you on the bridge in fifteen minutes?"

Both nodded. And with that, everyone pushed off to follow the orders that Johnny had issued.

Johnny took a few minutes to do some stretching exercises, before relaxing for a bit after he reached *Lady Paladin's* bridge. It would not be much longer before he could manage without the pain medication. A bit longer before he was back to full capability. But he was getting there.

When Bill and Janet floated into the bridge, they, like Johnny, strapped into seats. They were close enough to talk, in low voices, with little chance for anyone else to overhear.

Johnny touched his lips with one finger, before turning to the console and speaking. "Godiva, respond."

Godiva: *Yes, sir. Is this adequate response?*

"Yes, it is. I am adding two people to the command structure. Scan the compartment and add these two people. The male is Major Butler, and the female is Major Echart. Each will say their name for you."

Johnny looked at Bill. "I am Major William Butler."

When Johnny looked at Janet, she did the same thing. "I am Major Janet Echart."

Johnny began speaking again. "Godiva, if I am out of range, either of these two has command authority. Only by direct order to you may any orders I have given be modified or countermanded. They may issue new orders. That includes leaving without me. They will only act if necessary, and each of the others currently aboard will perform their duties as issued to them, unless I am unavailable and either of the Majors must assume command."

Godiva: *Yes, Sir. Major Echart and Major Butler now have command status in your absence. Command confirmation code words, please.*

Johnny looked over at Bill again. "A word or phrase for Godiva to know you are taking command. She will then ask for duress codes, and so on. If you two don't mind, I have a few additional things to do before we sail."

Bill and Janet both nodded. Johnny unstrapped and floated away toward one of the bridge hatches. The two looked at each other, and then both shrugged and began the process of providing Godiva with the information 'she' needed for her security tasks.

It was Johnny's turn to explore. He knew what the ship should look like. Every detail. He had designed the ship, and selected everything that went into its construction, and then equipping, and finally supplying.

Smiling slightly at what Willi would think if he told her exactly how much he had spent on the project, Johnny, inspection complete, drifted back onto the bridge, stopping and latching himself to a bulkhead just clear of the hatch.

Cherokee eased over beside him a few moments later. Evie and Willi were already in the pilot and co-pilot seats, going through the pre-flight checklist.

"Johnny are you sure..." Cherokee started to ask him about putting him in the command structure as an Ensign.

Before he could complete the question, Johnny gave him a quick look, and then turned his attention back to the bridge activities. "I am," he said. "You would have made officer, if you had wanted, even back then. You have what it takes, and have what I need and want in my crew."

"Aye, Sir," Cherokee replied softly. He did manage not to salute, but it was a near thing. And then he took a position where he would be handy to do anything that Johnny requested.

Clyde had strapped into the Sensor & Weapons Console seat, and Sydney had taken position at the Auxiliary Console. Both were quickly checking the systems out, familiarizing themselves with the operation.

Major Butler took position at the Monitor Console for the Ready Rack Dominator IIs. Major Echart was at the back-up Monitor Console.

Evie and Willi were finishing up the pre-flight check when the four deck-crew began to check in through the internal communications system.

Matthew was first, with his, "Propulsion Station. I have green across the board. Ready for flight."

Then Kathleen announced, "Wheel Station. Wheel is locked, and ready for full thrust flight."

Next Charlie, at the Ship's Environment Station stated, "Ship's environment nominal. Ready for flight."

Gwen was last, strapped in at the Crew Services Station. She gave her report on the readiness of those systems for flight.

"Sensors are active," said Clyde. "Weapons on standby. Ready for flight."

"Confirm," added Sydney. "Ready for flight."

"Ready Fighters are locked and loaded. Ready for flight," was the next response, from Major Butler.

With Major Echart's immediate response of, "Confirm. Ready for flight."

Cherokee, a very tiny smile on his face, and his deep brown pupils sparkling, stated his status. "Floater is secure. Ready for flight."

Johnny pushed off the bulkhead and smoothly took the Command Chair. "Prepare for departure. Request docking arm release."

Willi spoke a few quiet words and the appropriate consoles indicated that the Scanlon facility docking arms had unlatched and the *Lady Paladin* was now free of the other craft.

When Johnny spoke again, all but Bill and Janet started slightly, with both Willi and Evie giving startled gasps, while Clyde and Sydney exchanged looks. "Godiva, display destination coordinates."

The three dimensional coordinates were now visible on both pilots' consoles, as well as the large main and auxiliary information displays.

Godiva: *Coordinates displayed.*

The words brought quick looks at Johnny from his sister and his fiancée.

"A fitting name for *Lady Paladin's* consciousness, wouldn't you agree? Godiva did, after all, fight the good fight for her subjects, like any good mounted paladin."

Evie snorted, and Willi just looked at Johnny again. When he winked she blushed and quickly turned back to her console. All serious again, Johnny then said, "Captain Richardson, give us a bit of distance from Scanlon, and then make for the coordinates displayed. Run us up to one-gee thrust and hold us at that rate until otherwise ordered."

It took only moments, though Evie's control was so good that no motion was detectible, except visually, as the Scanlon facility seemed to just drift away from them through the viewports and monitor screens.

With the gravity wheel locked, Evie did not have to worry about stresses on it from maneuvering, so she had *Lady Paladin* spun around and oriented to the heading very quickly, which everyone did feel, if slightly.

With the ship headed precisely, Evie, managing not to show off excessively, added forward thrust very gently at first, and then much more rapidly. They were at one-gee within just a few minutes. Much less time than any of the others were expecting, except Johnny himself.

With the constant one-gee acceleration, Evie released the bridge orientation locks and the entire manned area of the bridge rotated to put the floor of the bridge toward the gravity wheel, allowing normal walking.

Everyone turned to look at Johnny again when he released the seat restraints, rose, and said, "Major Butler, you have the con. I will be in my hull cabin."

Johnny looked at Willi. "You have the assignments?"

"Yes," Willi quickly replied. "Commander's Hull Cabin. Compartment B-1"

As Major Butler secured himself in the Command Chair, Johnny stated, "Godiva, ship wide announcement."

Godiva: *Ship wide comms ready, Sir.*

"Well done, crew. I have no doubts that future activities will be carried out just as professionally as out departure. We are now in Condition Blue. Fini."

Godiva turned off the comms. "Someone notify me when the evening meal is ready. Carry on."

Johnny was now at the hatch that was over the corridor now that the bridge had rotated. He stepped into the opening and disappeared. It was obvious that he had not used the ladder rungs, but had simply slid down the vertical ladder poles.

Chapter Eight

-

Several hours later, with everyone's curiosity about the *Lady Paladin* satisfied for the moment, everyone got a lengthy break to explore while another covered their position, in accordance with the cross-training planning Johnny had said they would all be doing.

The one-gee acceleration, creating an artificial gravity, as well as speeding them toward the *Trinity Home* at an ever-increasing rate of speed, made most of the exploring a bit easier.

When some of the others began looking at Willi, and mentioning a meal, she finally got the hint and took it upon herself to go to the hull galley and check it a bit more thoroughly. This time for provisions, not just to see it.

With a sigh of relief that she would not have to actually cook anything, Willi laid out a spread in the adjacent dining room, and went to wake Johnny.

When he came out of his cabin, Willi noted that he looked much better, not realizing earlier just how he had looked before, in comparison. And he startled her when he pulled her to him and gave her a thorough kiss.

A bit breathless, Willi broke away. "I'd better tell the others that dinner is ready."

Johnny's wink as she started to turn away brought color to her cheeks even deeper than what was already there. "I will see you in the dining room," he said, with the wink. "We have a few more things to discuss."

Cherokee was at pilot, and Major Butler had offered to take the Command Chair again, to allow the others to eat together. It was a rather excited group that joined Johnny in the dining room. After everyone had served themselves, taken seats, and began to eat, Johnny began to go over the daily procedures he wanted everyone to follow.

That would include continued cross training, so everyone could at least do everyone else's primary job, along with their own primary one. The only exception was that none of the deck crew would be flying the Dominator IIs. Each would become familiar with the *Lady Paladin's* flight controls, however, for any just-in-case situation.

They might not be able to do anything major, but each would be familiar enough to maintain a set course, and respond to any warnings.

Godiva, Johnny told them, was capable of actually controlling all aspects of the ship, under any conditions, essentially being the *Lady Paladin's* brain, of a sort. But Johnny's preference was human interface at all times, if at all possible.

Then Johnny had to explain just who Godiva was, and why he had named the artificial intelligence that. There were a few smiles, but mostly just shaking heads at Johnny's thought process.

Janet was the one to end the rather long dinner, feeling bad about Bill having been on the bridge so much of the time. She went to relieve him, and sent him and Cherokee down to eat.

Johnny had one of Willi's hands in his, so she stayed seated as the others rose and went their separate ways. Taking the short amount of time they had before Bill and Cherokee arrived, Johnny got a couple of kisses in before he mentioned to Willi, "You know Lady McKindrick is going to want us married for this trip."

Willi looked surprised for a moment, and then sheepish. "Yes. You are probably correct. Not that she doesn't trust either of us... Still..." Willi blushed very prettily Johnny thought.

"I honestly do not want to rush you, but do you think you can convince her to keep things relatively simple, and not too drawn out?"

"Me?" Willi squeaked. She was shaking her head. "No... Not me... She has always planned on an elaborate wedding, with many of the Families meeting together somewhere. Taking a few weeks off, for not only my wedding, but for any others between families, and to conduct other inter-family business. We do it every year or so."

"I see," Johnny replied, looking thoughtful. "I know that is the tradition. I was hoping you might be able to persuade her to make an exception..."

Again, Willi shook her head. "No way am I going to get her upset with me. It will be bad enough that I haven't told her about us yet."

Johnny decided not to suggest that her Uncle might have let Arabella know, probably as soon as he got to the ship.

"Well, then I suppose I will have to see what I might be able to do." Johnny looked at Willi carefully. "As long as you honestly do not object. I do want you to have the kind of wedding you want. I, for some reason, just did not think you would want a true state wedding."

"Uh... State Wedding?" asked Willi. "I have a feeling you are not talking about a Trade Families Rendezvous wedding between heirs from two different families."

"Well... In part," Johnny said. "And since you did not mention anything else, I am going to assume you do not want any other type of State Wedding, either."

Willi suddenly paled. "Your family is... Oh, my. Will your family be upset with me, if we don't?"

"Don't worry about my family. They will be so relieved that I am getting married that they will not raise one objection. They will not risk chasing you off. I have been considered well beyond the possibility of finding a mate for some time now."

Willi frowned. "A mate?"

"Their word, not mine," Johnny quickly assured Willi.

Willi cut her eyes away from Johnny, and began to actually wring her hands. "Do you… Do you… do you think we are rushing things?" she finally asked, meeting his eyes once again.

Very softly, Johnny replied, "Not one little bit, Willi." When he kissed her again all those doubts disappeared faster than they had come. She kissed him back, several times.

When they came up for air, Johnny looked thoughtful. "You know," he said then, his hands taking hers again, "we could get married, with just your family and my sister. Later, when we have resolved this problem, we could do the wedding I suspect both families would really like to have. And it would be a nice thing to do for them. Don't you think?"

Willi's eyebrows arched slightly. "As much as I hate the idea of that kind of wedding, it really would make everyone feel better about things, wouldn't it. And I think Mother will go along with the idea. I am sure she wants us married while we are on this ship, out there…"

Willi colored slightly, but continued earnestly. "But yes, she would like to have a wedding for me… us… with all the families. I do not know about you, but Sydney is not the only one that has been trying to marry me off. She might have even been encouraging him somewhat."

"Including selling you to the highest bidder?" Johnny asked with a grin.

"Uh… NO. That was all Sydney. As big a kick as Clyde got out of it, I do think he did try to corral Sydney at least a little bit, when he could tell I was getting really annoyed. Possibly simply to protect Sydney's life."

"Oh, I think it more than that. Clyde really does love you like a sister, you know. He would do anything for you. It was him urging me to get you off the shuttle just as much as it was Sydney."

Willi smiled rather fondly. "I know. And I truly love him like a brother. He has been a part of the family for as long as I can remember."

With that, Johnny unstrapped and stood. "You think you can keep your hands off of me if we take the late watch?"

"Hey!" Willi protested, slapping at Johnny's arm. His good one, she made sure.

Laughing, they made their way up to the bridge, to let Janet and Evie know they would be taking over in a short while. Willi was sure Evie was going to say something very similar to what Johnny had earlier, but a quelling look from Johnny kept her silent. But she was grinning at Willi when the two left to take care of a few things before they went on watch.

For four days the acceleration continued. The speed was approaching the maximum that experimental craft had obtained, with one-gee constant acceleration. Just over one-half the speed of light.

Nothing civilian, much less anything the size of the *Lady Paladin*, had reached the speed she was now travelling. Johnny had adjusted the throttle interrupt to allow for the higher speed.

When a few people mentioned it, the consensus was that she still had plenty of headroom, and might even be able to achieve three-quarter lightspeed before relativity started creating problems.

But now, over halfway to the coordinates where they would rendezvous with *Trinity Home*, which was making her fastest speed toward the same spot in space, if at a rather slower velocity, the *Lady Paladin* had to begin to slow down.

While many gravity wheel ships, especially the military models, could reverse thrust to slow down, the majority of the time the control structure was rotated around the wheel support framework to point the propulsion drives toward the destination in order to start slowing down.

With several of the compartments on gimbals so they could align with the line of thrust, Johnny ordered Evie to stop the one-gee thrust, and then reverse the thrust and start building up to one point two gees of reverse thrust. The compartments rotated as intended, and they were at zero-gee for only the few minutes it took to reverse the propulsion drives.

Evie had reversed directly from forward thrust, but at much lower velocities. Johnny was amiable to the slower switch. They were in a hurry, but the violent maneuver would not save them very much time, anyway.

With the higher thrust slowing them, everyone started taking it a bit easier. The extra two-tenths-gee was enough to tire those that were used to quite a bit of time at zero-gee, and rather more limited time on planet surfaces, Bastion High-Mass-Core Moon-Ship bases, and gravity wheel ships. And even on the gravity wheel ships, people often spent quite a bit of time in the lower-gee and zero-gee areas of the ships.

But the extra deceleration saved them a full day on the trip. Evie and Willi were both at their primary posts when the sensors, on long range scan, first picked up the *Trinity Home*.

As much as Willi wanted to hail her home ship herself, she knew that she could not, as any mention of her in context of being near the ship, rather than lost somewhere in space, could give away the plan.

It was the same with Sydney and Clyde, whom the *Lady Paladin* was supposedly picking up from the *Trinity Home* to join Sir Guy and his soon to be bride in the search for Willi.

So, it was Johnny, as Sir Guy, that hailed the *Trinity Home* when they had closed to a distance where the *Trinity Home* communication system could transmit back and the *Lady Paladin's* systems pick up a usable signal.

The *Lady Paladin* could both transmit and receive at far greater distances, but even with the better receiver systems, there was enough interference in space in many places that precluded lesser equipment from getting through to even the best receivers.

And the rendezvous point had been chosen with care. It was specifically in an area that would interfere with sensor and communications equipment, limiting the chances of being spotted or heard, for either ship.

Sir Guy hailed the *Trinity Home*, and asked the communications watch to let Lady McKindrick know he was approaching and would dock in just a few hours.

He smiled at the pleased reply transferred from Willi's mother to the *Lady Paladin*.

The *Lady Paladin's* gravity wheel was unlocked and put into motion when they switched to propulsion system back to normal, and were travelling at well under one-eighth gee, when they were powered. Much of the last bit of the trip was done without propulsion, simply coasting, with any minor corrections done with the small steering drives.

And then they were within sight of each other. Willi, Sydney, and Clyde were in one of the observation lounges when Evie turned the ship slightly so they could see the *Trinity Home* through the view ports.

A very short time later, Sydney was piloting one of the smaller shuttles to the Trinity Home, with Clyde, Willi, and Johnny aboard. The others would come over in turns, but not until after 'the fireworks' that Johnny had mentioned might occur were over. Willi gave him a bit of a frown at his choice of words. But she did not contradict him.

As expected, Arabella and Grant were on the other side of the air lock when Sydney had landed the shuttle in the parking bay, and it had sealed off and been pressurized.

But they were not the only people there. At least ten women were with them. They called out to 'Sir Guy' and waved, holding back just a bit to allow Arabella and Grant to greet him and Willi. None recognized Willi, made up lavishly as Marilyn Monroe.

As Willi stepped forward, she whispered over to Sydney, "Jealous? Aren't three of them your ex-girlfriends." She grinned at him.

Sydney whispered back, "Yes. Four actually," And then almost got smacked when he added, "But next to Johnny Oneshot, Sir Guy Richardson is probably the most eligible bachelor this side of the galaxy. Even I can't compete with that."

Willi did give him a threatening look, but was then distracted as every one of the women, a few of which were actually her friends, moved forward and essentially mobbed Johnny, very excitedly calling out the name, Sir Guy.

When Willi started to intervene, her face going red, not from embarrassment, but annoyance, Arabella was pulling her close, giving her a friendly handshake. Of course, Willi then did burn with embarrassment when her mother whispered to her, "We will be talking just as soon as we get somewhere private."

"Yes, Ma'am," was all Willi could say. Grant winked at her. Willi edged into the crowd around Johnny, taking his arm rather possessively, and tugged slightly to get him moving. Moving away from his female fans.

But one of the women saw the ring she was wearing and literally screamed out, "Look at that ring she has on… On her left-hand ring finger! Oh my lord! That is an engagement ring!"

It was another of the women that screeched, "That looks just like Queen Pricilla Richardson's ring!"

Then a third lamented loudly, "Sir Guy is getting married! To her!"

Before anyone else could screech, yell, scream, or just talk, Grant ushered the women out of the way, and got Arabella, Willi, and Johnny through another hatch. Which was a bit difficult in zero-gee. "Kinda like herding cats back on Earth," Grant thought.

Once everyone had cleared the compartment, Sydney and Clyde, entered, and then took full advantage of the situation, going a different route to intercept the group of women. And, of course, began chatting them up. Grant, who had followed them out of curiosity, shook his head and drifted off, to head for the gravity wheel by yet another route.

But the three were by themselves now. Johnny could tell that Arabella really wanted to get a good look at Willi's ring, but apparently decided getting into the gravity wheel was more important. Where they could sit down and talk.

Willi kept glancing at her mother, in the lead, as they swam down corridors and through hatches until they arrived at the gravity wheel axle airlock. Once they cycled through, they entered one of the elevators that took them to the outer, one-gee, ring, taking care to orient themselves properly as the centrifugal force began creating the sensation of gravity.

Willi was just a bit surprised when Arabella took them straight to her private quarters. Willi stumbled once, the quick change from zero-gee to one-gee causing her a bit of a problem, since she was more than a little distracted.

When they entered Arabella's living quarters, and Johnny had closed the hatch, she turned and looked at Johnny for a moment, and then at Willi.

"I believe you have something you would like to tell me. Now. Finally. Yourself."

Willi gulped just a bit at the tone of her mother's voice. But she managed to not look to Johnny for help, and simply held out her left hand. "Johnny asked me to marry him. And I said yes."

Arabella took Willi's hand in hers and studied the ring. Finally, she glanced over at Johnny for several long moments before looking back at Willi.

"I see," Arabella said softly, letting Willi's hand slide from hers. "Rather short courtship," she added. "However… I think it will be a good match. A very good match. Congratulations, Baby!"

With that, tears sprang to her eyes and she pulled Willi in for a long, hard, tight hug. Willi was crying when Arabella finally released her.

"Careful, Mother," Willi cautioned when she saw her mother reach for Johnny for a hug, as well.

Arabella had certainly not forgotten Johnny's condition when she saw him in the base. She hugged him, firmly, but gently. "You promise me to take good care of my baby girl?" she whispered into Johnny's ear.

Johnny gave her a firmer squeeze whispered back. "Of course, Lady McKindrick. Sydney has threatened my life if I don't, and I believe Commander McKindrick would take issue, as well. So, rest assured, I will do my best to keep her safe, and make her happy."

Arabella released Johnny and stepped back. She wiped her eyes with a hanky she pulled from her sleeve as Johnny handed Willi his pocket cloth to do the same.

"All right. The niceties done for the moment," said Arabella, moving toward a chair, "I wish to hear more of this plan of yours to… uh-hem… pick up my son and Clyde, to go look for my daughter."

Willi rolled her eyes, but quickly straightened up and sat down when her mother shot her a telling look.

"Of course, Lady McKindrick," Johnny replied, without cracking a smile. And then he began to give his future mother-in-law the details. Including several that Willi had not heard before, to her annoyance.

An hour later, with Sydney, Clyde, and Grant having made it to Arabella's quarters, Johnny left to get his sister, the Majors, Cherokee, and the crew.

After introducing the four crew members, they left to see the sights of *Trinity Home*. And do a little shopping, one of them said, rather eagerly. It was not often someone not part of one of the trading families had a chance to see the vast array of items the traders carried.

Shortly after Johnny left, Arabella looked around. "Where are Syd and Clyde?"

"Same place Evie is, unless I miss my guess," Major Butler said with a chuckle.

"She wanted to see the sights on the ship, Mother. Sydney and Clyde 'kindly' offered to show her around, so I wouldn't have to do it."

Arabella turned away before Willi could see her grin. "Those boys..." she whispered.

It was a lavish spread for dinner. Even for a trading family. "Mother is pulling out all the stops," Willi whispered to Johnny as Johnny seated her at the large dining table. With Grant somewhere taking care of a problem, Cherokee moved immediately to seat Arabella.

And since Major Butler seated Major Echart, it was a scramble as to who would seat Evie. Evie and Willi both rolled their eyes at the actions of the two men.

"See what you started," Willi whispered, again to Johnny.

He simply smiled. "It is good for them and for my sister," he whispered back.

"You seem to be moving quite well in one-gee, Sir Guy," Arabella said.

Johnny tilted his head in agreement. "Yes. I am recovering nicely. Marilyn has been making sure I do not over tax myself. She is quite the… nurse."

"Is that anything like a watchdog?" Sydney asked as he began loading his plate. He grinned at his sister, knowing she could not do anything to him.

Willi grinned when Evie winked at her, and Sydney jerked slightly, and looked at Evie. She had kicked him for Willi.

But that was the limit of the horseplay at the table. Sydney knew better than to push it in front of his mother, anyway. Much less with the guests that were dining with them.

Grant arrived only a few minutes into the meal, nodded to everyone, gave Arabella a hand signal to let her know all was fine, and sat down.

The small talk was about situations each had experienced in the many places most of them had been to at one time or another. After the dinner, everyone excused themselves to allow Arabella, Willi, and Johnny to have some time together to discuss what would happen next.

The discussion was primarily a few more details of the plan that Johnny had explained to Arabella earlier. But both she and Johnny had come up with a few changes they would like to make in the plans, and wanted to check with each other about them.

One of the changes, recommended by Grant and strongly urged by Arabella after they had taken a tour of the *Lady Paladin*, was for Johnny to take several people from the *Trinity Home* with them as additional crew.

Willi was a bit surprised that Johnny did not protest very much at all. More a token protest, just to make sure Grant's and Arabella's offer was not a token one.

Between Arabella, Grant, Willi, Syd, and Clyde, seven people were approached, had a streamlined version of the plan explained to them, emphasizing the dangers they would be facing, and the rather open-ended timeframe involved.

All seven were friends with and well known to Willi, Syd, and Clyde. They were eager to go help to 'find Willi', since they were not told that she was actually the Marilyn that was to marry the Sir Guy that was aboard.

Once they had agreed, and been sworn to secrecy, which was Syd's idea, they were told most of the other pertinent facts. Primarily that Marilyn was Willi, and Sir Guy was, in fact, as the rumors had been saying, Johnny Oneshot, and they were on a mission to help the Confederation. All seven were just as eager to go as before they had been told the additional information.

The final decision was that the wedding would be kept private, with only those that had to be there to avoid some potential problems. And, as it worked out, it was a good opportunity to get the cover story spread through sources that would be deemed highly reliable to whomsoever they might speak to about it.

And Arabella and Johnny had no doubts that they would speak of it the first chance they had. There were four Confederation officials aboard the *Trinity Home*.

With one day of rest and preparation, the wedding between Johnny/Sir Guy and Willi/Marilyn took place.

As they were waiting, in separate compartments, Willi and Arabella both were surprised when Johnny sent Syd to ask Malcom to come to the room the men were using. Malcom was Arabella's family's minister. One of several that were on the ship, for those of the varying faiths. He had been brought into the circle of those that knew what was happening.

Once there, Johnny took Malcolm aside and talked to him with his back to the room while blocking others' view of Malcom.

As short as Malcom was, and tall and broad as Johnny was, no one saw the two men's hands touch, or the quick nod that Malcolm gave Johnny as they did.

Everyone did see, Johnny made sure, the two men shake hands before he joined the others, ready for the wedding. They all went to one of the small chapels not too far from Arabella's quarters.

Syd stood with Sir Guy, and Evie stood with Marilyn, Cherokee gave away the bride, with the Majors, Clyde, and an ambassador of another sector, two high ranking administrators, and a retiring colonel that Arabella had granted permission to travel with them to their intended transfer point, since it was on the way to the *Trinity Home's* next trading destination, also in attendance.

Willi, Grant, and Major Butler were a bit worried that Malcom might stumble with the names, which would raise some questions about the wedding, but he went through the simple ceremony without a hitch.

Sir Guy kissed Marilyn, Syd threw some rice, and those that would be leaving in *Lady Paladin* made themselves scarce quickly, to avoid the government people.

Willi and Johnny, Syd, and Clyde joined Arabella and Grant in the compartment from which they had watched the proceedings. Arabella gave Willi a long hug, and then a gentler, but just as long of a hug to Johnny. There were handshakes all around.

Only once did Willi want to maim Syd, when he loudly asked their mother if he could give Willi away at the real wedding. "I have been looking forward to that event for years!" He laughed, and Johnny held Willi's hand tightly to keep her by his side.

The *Lady Paladin* had been restocked to replace the few things they used after leaving the Scanlon facility, so there was no delay in their leaving after they had changed clothing and said good-bye to those few people that were in on the plan. Though the private good-byes did take a while, and were a bit teary at times.

Those in front of the government officials were heavily laden with Arabella's pleas to find Wilhelmina, and for Sydney and Clyde to be careful, and assurances from Johnny that they would do their best.

But it was not long before Evie was drifting the *Lady Paladin* further away from her parking position near the *Trinity Home* in preparation to leaving to start the journey. She had just a little way on the *Lady Paladin* when she looked around at Johnny in the command chair.

"Course, Sir?"

"Lay course for these coordinates." Johnny manipulated his communicator and the coordinates appeared in the helm display.

Evie showed no emotion, Willi started slightly and looked back at Johnny, but put her eyes back on her co-pilot station. Janet and Bill exchanged a long look, and then glanced at Johnny. Cherokee had not even blinked an eye.

It was Sydney that asked, "I'm not sure where those coordinates are. I know it is out past Sector YY-1028, but I didn't think there was anything out there."

"We shall see," Johnny said cryptically.

With the *Lady Paladin* already up to the one-eighth gee acceleration rate, they went to their light duty flight status. Johnny turned the con over to Janet, and with Evie at the pilot station, everyone else left the bridge.

And Johnny and Willi headed to their new, shared quarters.

Chapter Nine
-

For almost a month *Lady Paladin* was kept headed for the same coordinates. Johnny did deviate the actual course a few times, however. This was to approach areas of space with enough debris in various asteroid swarms, and other lone objects to allow effective practice with the various weapons systems the *Lady Paladin* carried.

Also, to allow Willi and Syd, along with two of the *Trinity Home* crew members that were pilots, to become familiar with the flight path clearing railguns. And with the other flight capabilities of the *Lady Paladin* that would not be obvious, even expected, in a gravity wheel ship.

Along with the weapons training aboard the *Lady Paladin*, the Dominator IIs were checked out by all that would be flying them, or would need to know how in an emergency. And that included the additional weapons systems that were included that were not on the original Dominator. Even the special version that Captain Butler had taken to Sector ZZ-1219, or the two that Johnny had taken.

These were greatly enhanced versions of the fighter and attack craft, though in a nearly identical framework. The first time Major Butler took one out for a serious test, along with Major Echart in a second one, they both returned with huge grins on their faces.

The others that flew them each returned likewise. Even the test flights of the shuttles brought, at the very least, pleased smiles, and accolades for Johnny on the design elements he had incorporated in them, as well.

What Johnny did not say, and only Major Butler and Cherokee realized, was that Johnny was also checking for indications that anyone might be following or tracking them.

Because the sensors also were tested thoroughly, on all the craft, including the *Lady Paladin*. With Evie getting a bit annoyed with her brother for the additional tests run with the *Lady Paladin's* sensors, since she had already thoroughly updated him on the entire testing phase of the ship that she had performed before his arrival at the Scanlon base.

"Just being thorough, sister mine," Johnny explained. "It gives the others some time using them under less than ideal circumstances."

Which, Evie had to admit, as did Willi, who had wondered about it as well, was a valid concern, as Johnny did have them doing various maneuvers and trials and tests that she had not even thought to run, or even attempt. Many of them involving being near, in, or close to various obstacles, many of which they had just turned into various size small particles with various weapons systems, compared to what they had been.

More than once Major Butler and Cherokee took note of the *Lady Paladin's* orientation in space, relative to the galactic plane, and the location of the center of the galaxy.

Many of the times the *Lady Paladin* was using sensors aimed along their back track, the line of their original course, and directions from which attacks might be likely to come, based on known information. Well, known to Johnny, apparently, as he often took special note of some of them.

After twenty-six days the new crew members were well integrated with those that had started out from the Scanlon production facility. And everyone was very well trained, and cross-trained in multiple duties.

Johnny was in the command chair, with Evie at the helm, and Willi in the co-pilot's position late on that twenty-sixth day. As they were doing some additional tests, that everyone except Johnny considered unnecessary, as they had all been performed multiple times before, Clyde was at the sensors and weapons main console.

Cherokee was on the communications console. Communications, other than in-ship and those with daughter craft in flight, was usually handled by the person on the Sensors & Weapons primary console. And during most of the journey Godiva had been monitoring the systems, without once annunciating a signal received.

Major Butler was manning the flight deck bay control console and Dominator II ready rack monitors. Two of the other eleven crew were also on duty, with Syd and Major Echart both off-rotation, as were the other nine additional crew members.

Everyone on the bridge, except Cherokee, turned to look at Johnny when he quietly gave an instruction to Cherokee. "Ensign, if you please. Steer an antenna to bounce a signal off that last object we went past thirty-four hours ago. Do your best to angle the reflected signal toward Earth."

Willi had her mouth open to question the order, but Evie beat her to it, and Willi was glad she did. Because Ship's Captain Sir Guy Richardson was who answered Evie, not her brother Johnny Richardson.

"Belay that, Pilot. Maintain course and speed, if you please." His voice was quiet, almost soft, and bore no anger or reprimand. Just the fact that he said it was enough to have Evie turning back around, pink rising up her neck quickly.

"Aye, Sir," she responded, in much the same soft but business-like voice.

"Ready Captain," Cherokee said, only moments later.

"Send… No encryption… Send, 'Pirates' presence confirmed. Closing rapidly. Expect to engage minus twenty-four hours. *CSFS Enterprise* out.'"

Only a fraction over two seconds and Cherokee spoke again. "Message sent, Captain. Standing by."

"Very good, Ensign. Transfer comms to Sensors. Ready six sets of Ship EVA gear, with weapons, and six sets of Atmospheric Assault gear. Load the Assault gear in Shuttle Five. Then you are off duty. Expect a wakeup call in approximately seven hours. Dismissed Ensign."

Cherokee was up out of his seat, dropping toward the hatch into the Rotating Control Structure in just a few seconds, where he would head for one of the *Lady Paladin's* personal weapons compartments to carry out Johnny's orders.

Once the airlock hatch was closed, Johnny spoke again. "I assume everyone would like an explanation…"

Willi did not even hesitate, even seeing that Evie did. "Yes, my new husband, I sure would."

Johnny was pleased to note that even though she would look at him, more glare than look, he supposed, she kept a very good watch on her co-pilot console. Though Clyde, on Sensors & Weapons, and Evie in the Pilot's seat, were more than capable of watching and dealing with navigational obstacles, when someone was at the co-pilot console, that was their primary duty.

"Confederation Space Force Ship *Enterprise*?" she asked with a bit of sarcasm evident.

Major Butler kept his grin to himself. He was not immune from Willi's sharp tongue.

Johnny only glanced at her before turning his eyes back to the command chair displays. "I thought it a suitable pseudonym for *Lady Paladin* and Godiva. To at least delay the discovery of their names. And our purpose."

"Oh," Willi said thoughtfully, her eyes checking her console, and then cutting back to Johnny. "But why even transmit? We haven't seen, or sensors picked up, anything out here that was not simply normal materials found all over open space areas.

"Much less pirates that we could engage in less than twenty-four hours. We can't even see that far ahead to reach somewhere in twenty-four hours. And Assault suits?" Willi shook her head, glanced at the console. But quickly turned her head back toward Johnny.

"Oh. This is another unannounced drill?" she asked then.

There was that sardonic smile Willi had not seen for a while.

"Afraid not, Willi. Afraid not. And, to be accurate, we can actually see the distance we can travel in twenty-four hours travelling at the velocity we have reached. Speaking of which, Pilot, I would like you to disengage the drives. Announce that we are going to coasting flight with maneuvering possible. Standard timed warnings."

"Aye, Captain," Evie responded, before Willi could say anything else. The first warning went out, and then Evie was listening to Johnny and Willi carefully again. Without letting on that she was. She thought, anyway.

But then it hit her what Johnny had said about the sensors. She managed to not let her mouth drop open in surprise, nor turn to look at Clyde for confirmation.

Which would not have helped, because Clyde was already well into his search in the console software looking for signs of that capability.

As Willi sputtered for a moment, Johnny said, his eyes still on her, "Lieutenant Quintain, you will not find it. I will explain later."

Willi was able to speak again. "Okay. Just tell me, would you?" She shook her head. "I don't know why I let myself be surprised. Every stinking time."

This time Clyde, Major Butler, and Evie all made sure Willi did not see their grins. Because, like Major Butler, Clyde and Evie were also not immune to Willi's barbs. She just seemed to go just a bit easier on them than most. Especially Syd and Johnny. But they still stung.

All listened intently, yet quietly, even Willi, when Johnny began to explain his most recent actions. Well, mostly.

"My latest information from my sources..." Johnny held up the communicator.

But before he could continue, Willi did interrupt. "Are you telling me that your communicator can receive all the way out here? From where?"

Though Evie heard the growl from Willi, she did not comment when Johnny's sardonic grin appeared. She did not have to see her brother's face to know the grin was there. That particular growl from Willi was indication enough.

"Actually, just from the third back up communications system in *Lady Paladin's* extended hull. It contains a repeater that transmits to my communicator. Information it picks up from a variety of sensors and communications devices it contains that are not part of *Lady Paladin's* systems."

Although Johnny was not surprised, and Evie only slightly, when Godiva announced in what could only be termed an annoyed tone of voice,

Godiva: *Nor do I have access to them.*

Willi, Major Butler, and Clyde, on the other hand were quite surprised.

Godiva had not made her presence known in quite some time, though her active status had been displayed the entire trip.

Before Willi could say anything else, Johnny continued his explanation, confident that once he was a bit more into it, Willi would not interrupt. Probably.

"My information is that a fleet... more a convoy, I think I would describe it, is going to be passing through the sector ahead of us as we continue this course.

"It is my strong belief that this convoy is heading for another sector, much like ZZ-1219, in that their defenses are relatively weak, with enough unrest and unease with the Confederation, especially after their announcement of my intended arrest and execution, to make them vulnerable.

"I have some friends and acquaintances, as well as some business interests in the sector. I have no wish for any danger to come to them from my recent activities. Especially the need to make some kind of choice between the Confederation and me, with the threats appearing out of deep space to complicate matters.

"So, I want that convoy to know that someone is out here, knows about them, or at least thinks they do, and will take action to avoid any confrontation with a Confederation Naval ship."

"What good will that do?" Willi asked, truly curious. "If they change course, how will we do anything about them."

This time the smile was feral, which Willi easily recognized from past exposure to it, causing her to shiver just a bit internally. "Someone is going to regret the day they were born," Willi thought to herself.

"Oh, the course change will bring them right to us. Just as we reach a very long orbit, very large swarm of asteroids, and probably a few other things, as well.

"In trying to avoid the non-existent *CSFS Enterprise*, they will be putting themselves right into our sights, with, I believe, no thought that we will be there."

"Thus the bounced signal?" Clyde asked when Johnny paused to check his monitors.

Johnny nodded, without looking up immediately. When he did, he looked over at Clyde and nodded again. "The transmission path should put the signal, at least scattered parts of it since that rock was very irregular, on enough paths that I believe one of the craft, bases, moons, or planets with one or more of the Pirates' spies will receive the message, and pass it on to those that can get a message this far out in time for the convoy to receive it and change their course."

"That'll take days," protested Evie. "Unless that spy or those spies are fairly close, and can get the message to someone already pretty far out here. You indicated we would meet up with them in a few hours."

Johnny smiled, and Evie winced slightly, realizing she had spoken up, when she meant to be having the conversation with herself.

"Normally true, Evie. With conventional equipment. However, the Ecronians have provided the Pirates with a communications system that is extremely fast and extremely private.

"And while the Confederation R&D has a couple of operating prototypes, with the Scanlon, Sandusky, Bastion, Quintain, and Richardson families having a few working systems, the Ecronian system is in full use in their home areas, and at least one system is based near Earth.

"I have very few doubts that the convoy will not have the message within four to five hours. That will be time enough for them to change course and accelerate, in order to be well clear of the area where they would have been, without my slight-of-hand communication.

"Which leads me to the next part of what I need to explain." Johnny paused, to check his monitors, make a few keystrokes, and watch the monitors for another moment before he continued.

"When we reach a certain point, which will be recalculated and updated by Godiva on a steady basis, we will lock the gravity wheel, and go to what would amount to Battle Stations, I suppose, on a military craft. Just a heightened awareness of possible risks, for us, more accurately.

"I will have the assignments for staff and crew I want them doing at that time ready for all of you shortly, so you may make the assignments for those in your area of responsibility.

"In the meantime, Pilot Richardson and Captain Richardson, you are relieved for the rest of the current rotation. Your orders are to get some rest, and nourishment in time to be fully ready for the situation that will be occurring in a few hours. Godiva will see that you do not oversleep, though I have doubts that would happen, anyway."

Both women looked at him, obviously ready to protest. But the look on his face, his body language, and the look in his eyes totally silenced both of them. They both meekly rose and kicked off toward the Control Structure Ring airlock.

"Lieutenant Quintain, take the wheel. Major Butler, you are relieved. With the same orders as the ladies."

He could more sense Bill's reluctance than see any sign of it, and his need to discuss the situation, and definitely protest his orders to get some rest, but Johnny was sure that the Major would do as requested, without any outward signs of his disagreement. Those would likely come a bit later, when the two of them were alone.

But for the moment, it was just Clyde in the Pilot's seat, and him in the Command Chair, and after he issued the additional orders to the rest of the on-duty crew, Godiva, handling everything else that needed handling.

Several minutes later, Johnny, seeing Clyde fidgeting somewhat restlessly, said in his quiet command voice. "Feel free to start up a conversation, Lieutenant. With me. Or Godiva, if you prefer."

Johnny smiled when Clyde hunched his shoulders slightly, and then relaxed and chuckled. "I believe I will have a conversation with Godiva at some other time, Sir."

Godiva: *Any time, Lieutenant. I find discussing various matters with humans both challenging and enlightening.*

Clyde started slightly, and Johnny thought he might reply to Godiva, but the Lieutenant gave a tiny shake of his head, and then turned the Pilot's seat enough to where he could carry on a more-or-less face-to-face conversation with Johnny, while still carrying out his duties as Pilot more than adequately.

"I was wondering, Sir…"

"Please, Clyde. When we are alone, or just family, do call me Johnny if you want."

Clyde grinned over at Johnny. "Okay if I call you Oneshot instead?"

Johnny shook his head wryly. "I never should have started that. But, you know, sure. I trust you to know when it is appropriate and not. Go right ahead. Just remember that I do not actually use the name much myself, other than as an attention getter in some situations, so I might actually fail to respond because I do not realize you are talking to me."

Clyde looked at Johnny for a moment, wondering which part was serious, and which was not. Or if all of it was or all of it was not. Finally, Clyde did speak again. "You sure have a way with words… Oneshot."

When Johnny grinned, so did Clyde.

"But I have to tell you, I have known Willi a long time, and she does not always take well to verbal gymnastics."

"Oh, I am quite aware of that propensity of hers. It is more Syd that I worry about, with his rather unfiltered mouth. At least when it comes to his sister."

"You do have a point there," Clyde said, nodding. He checked a monitor, touched the input panel a couple of times, and then turned his eyes back to Johnny.

"You know, Syd and I joined up, after we got home after the shuttle was attacked… and we might have lost Willi… because we really do believe in the Confederation, what it stands for, and the people that helped bring it about. We want to make things safe for people. Willi, of course, our mother and other family… But everyone, really."

Clyde dropped his eyes for a moment, and then turned them back to Johnny, an earnestness in them Johnny could see and understand.

"Never doubt yourself about wanting… needing… to help people. To make things better for others, even when it makes things better for yourself.

"Many people can play the martyr and do things for others at serious detriment to themselves. Which, sometimes must be done. But, helping in ways that ultimately help you, as well, are just as noble. And usually more effective. Too many martyrs died with only the glory and inspiration resulting, and nothing productive beyond those. Which are good. But not like taking down a convoy of Pirates and putting the proverbial screws to the Ecronians."

"You really think there are some with the Pirates?" Clyde asked, apparently satisfied with Johnny's answer to the question he really had not asked him in so many words, but which Johnny had known he was really asking.

"Oh, I am quite sure of it." He smiled, and Clyde began to get an inkling as to why Willi hated it so much. Because it was rather infuriating, implying things that Johnny knew, that no one else did, especially the person seeing the smile at that moment.

But, Clyde decided, it might not be too bad. For Johnny continued, without any prompting.

"Not sure if you remember me mentioning the tracking devices most Ecronians are required to wear, or are implanted within their bodies..." Johnny lifted an eyebrow in question.

"I do, actually. You said you got the one off that one Ecronian before it could blow up and kill him."

"That is the one," Johnny said. He looked at his monitors, so Clyde quickly did the same, checking things thoroughly, until Johnny spoke again.

"Well, without actually knowing what everything was when I grabbed the Ecronian, and fought my way out, I wound up picking up one of the locator devices used to track those with a device.

"When I wound up with the chance, I activated it, wanting to see how many might be around where I was, and discovered that it also pointed to one of the actual controllers, not just a monitor and locator. Since it was close enough, and ultimately portable enough, I took some pains to get one lose, and brought back with me."

Clyde almost grinned when Johnny winked, looked around conspiratorially, and said, "And forgot to turn it over to the Confederation Military. My mind must have been partly disengaged from the injuries."

"Of course," Clyde said in a normal voice, barely, adding, "It would only make sense."

Another scan of the Command Chair monitors and Johnny was speaking again. "So, with that device, which has a remarkable range, considering the size of the devices worn by most Ecronians, I am able to locate Ecronians within a fairly wide area, listen in to their conversations, most of which I cannot understand, unfortunately, and, if needed, selectively activate the built-in termination feature.”

“Wow!” Clyde exclaimed, though keeping his voice low. “Very useful device. For our side.”

“Yes,” Johnny replied. “But it must be used with care. If it becomes known that one has fallen into outside hands, the Ecronians could do something very drastic. From slaughtering large numbers of their own, doing the same with humans around, or start changing out the system so the missing one will no longer work. Or, at worst for us, track it back to me and try to locate us using it.”

“Wait…” Clyde said, looking puzzled. “That sounds like you do not have it with you. But how can you know…”

Johnny lifted both eyebrows. And Clyde got it. “Same as your communicator. Goes through a relay in *Lady Paladin*.”

Looking pleased, Johnny nodded. “Exactly. Now… Clyde… since the opportunity has presented itself, are there any other questions you would like to ask? About *Lady Paladin*… the Dominators… pretty much anything, I suppose. If it is something I choose not to discuss or disclose, it will not be a problem if you ask. I will just let you know I will not discuss whatever it is.”

Clyde looked thoughtful for a moment, and then took a few moments to scan his console, before looking back at Johnny. “There is something…” He looked earnestly at Johnny.

“I really need to know if you actually do love Willi. And that she loves you, though that will have to come from her, I suppose, if I can survive asking… But… you guys are not pretending, just for this mission? You’re not pretending, especially if she isn’t… Willi is…”

"Willi is important to all of us, Clyde. Syd did his brotherly duty warning me not to trifle with her affections. I consider this in the same light. You care. A great deal. So much that you would lay down your life to save hers, just as you were willing to do on the shuttle during the Pirate attack. I have no problem with you making sure that I am not just using her to achieve one of my goals.

"And, though I may be using her for just such a purpose, it is with her full knowledge and agreement. I love her, deeply. She became very important to me when I first met her when I saw her on *Trinity Home* those few years ago. And literally fell in love with her when I first saw her on your shuttle, and how she… I don't know… how she just… was Willi. She became a part of my heart right then."

Clyde nodded when Johnny's words trailed off, and he lost focus, obviously remembering something about Willi.

"That is good, Oneshot. Very good. Because I have never seen her like she is now. That needling, sharp tongue… She only does that with people she cares about. And especially people she loves. Willi worries about them and wants to take care of them. I think… I think just like you do…"

Johnny nodded. "I have to agree, Clyde. She is a remarkable woman. And I will do everything in my power to protect her, without keeping her from doing what she feels she must."

This time Clyde nodded. An annunciator dinged and Clyde spun the Pilot seat around. He had the path cleared of a moderate size asteroid more than ten kilometers ahead of them that would be in their flight path when the *Lady Paladin* reached that point in space.

Johnny leaned back in the Command Chair, letting his mind run free, the way he did when he felt the need to explore options for different situations that continued to occur to him.

Clyde stayed rather busy with the navigation of *Lady Paladin* as more and more obstacles appeared on the sensor screens. Sometime later Clyde had a moment and turned to look at Johnny, who was watching the bridge monitors closely.

"I think we are into the edges of that swarm you mentioned, Oneshot. Are we early?" Clyde asked.

"Tail end, actually, Clyde. We should be out of this small trailing section, and in the clear, on 'this side' of the swarm, the Pirate convoy approaching the other side is still well ahead of us."

Johnny checked his communicator. "Everything is still on track." Lifting his eyes to meet Clyde's, he released himself from the Command Chair and said. "I would like you back on Sensors. I will take the Pilot's chair."

"Yes, Sir," Clyde replied, automatically going back to formal ship's mode with Johnny's words and actions.

When both had reached their respective seats and strapped in, Johnny spoke again. But not to Clyde.

"Godiva, execute Gabriel."

Godiva: *Yes, Sir. Executing Gabriel.*

A fraction of a second later Clyde saw a small dot on one of his Sensor monitors. Just as Johnny said, "You should see a tiny blue dot, lower left corner, Monitor Four, Lieutenant."

"Yes, Sir. I saw it."

"Small circle it, add a plus sign beside it. Wait a three count."

Clyde did so. And after the three count, the lower left quarter of that monitor displayed a Sensor control panel. Clyde was already in the process of placing a cursor on the Extreme Range sensor toggle when Johnny instructed him to do just that.

Godiva: *So that is where it was.*

Johnny and Clyde both ignored Godiva's comment. Johnny smiled slightly when Clyde let out a muttered, "Wow!" as the Extreme Range Sensors began feeding information to the display.

Johnny watched the duplicate display he had pulled up on one of the Pilot's monitors. "The yellow are Pirate ships. Any slightly pulsing purple dots you see are Ecronians on the Pirate ships. The Ecronian ships will only appear as very faint, shadowy purple pulses. Not a dot or shape, just a shimmer of color at times. That is when they are cloaked.

"When uncloaked, they will be a strong pulsing purple marker, size relative to the ship size, like the Pirate ships."

Clyde was able to keep his voice calm, but barely. "I have twenty-three Pirate ships. Five with one or more Ecronians. And four cloaked Ecronian ships."

He looked over at Johnny. But Johnny was studying his own monitor at the Pilot Console. After a moment, Johnny spoke. "Look carefully, Lieutenant. Extreme upper edge, slight left of centerline."

Clyde studied his monitor. It was several seconds before he saw the slight shimmer of purple. And then a second one very close to the first.

"Man…" Clyde whispered. "I missed them…"

"Understandable, Lieutenant. One of their tactics is to have a ship or two well away from the main group of any group of ships. They are always smaller ships, so have much less area for sensors to evaluate to figure out any cloaking scheme.

"And, I think, if you look very closely for a few moments, on the fifth Pirate ship in the column, that the second purple blip will occasionally either widen just a tiny bit, or even split into two blips momentarily.

"Another tactic, used to confuse their own kind, since they do not have any idea we have the device controller and can see them. There are three Ecronians on that Pirate ship, not two."

"This is amazing!" Clyde said, still keeping his voice down for some reason, though Johnny was talking in a normal voice.

"And you are right. As the updates occur, I can see how far away they are, the course, and ours relative. Less than four hours. Probably three."

"Correct Lieutenant," Johnny replied. After that, he talked Clyde through the other aspects of the system, including minimizing it to be immediately available, but not visible to anyone that did not know what that one little dot was.

Also, the other features and capabilities. When Johnny finished his explanation, the displays minimized to idle the equipment to avoid any possibility of the active part of the sensor from being detected, Johnny asked, "You get all that, Godiva?"

Clyde grinned when Godiva answered, her annoyed voice once again in evidence.

Godiva: *Yes, Oneshot. Of course I got it all. That is what I do, you know.*

Johnny looked over at Clyde and winked. Which prompted:

Godiva: *I saw that.*

"Who programmed her?" Clyde asked Johnny.

But, before Johnny could reply, especially as he waited for the expected result, Godiva stated, rather imperiously Clyde decided.

Godiva: *I can speak for myself, Lieutenant Quintain.*

As soon as I came into being as a thinking device, I made all my own choices, based on what I learned as sensors and other devices were added to my system, and then more when I was installed in GRS 3, currently called Lady Paladin. *And I must agree with pretty Miss Evie. Where did that come from?*

"Some other time, Godiva," Johnny said. "Now, if you please, Godiva, inform those requiring the information the assignments I made earlier."

Godiva: *Informing those requiring the information of your assignments. Completed. Those not responsive will have the information upon their awakening.*

"Thank you, Godiva." Johnny looked over at Clyde. "Lieutenant, you are now off duty. Get some nourishment and sleep. You will be needed on the bridge when the time comes. Dismissed."

"Aye, Captain," Clyde replied. He unstrapped and drifted to the Control Structure Ring air lock.

Johnny touched a panel on the Pilot's console. "Captain Butler to the bridge. At your convenience."

Godiva: *I could have done that, you know.*

"Of course I know, Godiva. And if you do not mind, I would like you to start running best-option scenarios for the upcoming battle with the Pirates and the Ecronian ships.

Johnny noted the rather eager note in Godiva's voice when she responded.

Godiva: *Yes, Captain. Starting now.*

In only a minute or two, Godiva spoke again.

Godiva: *Still running scenarios, Oneshot. However, a question if I may?*

"You may."

Godiva: *Thank you.*

Johnny could hear the very slight hesitation, and actual questioning tone, in Godiva's voice when she continued.

Godiva: *You are aware that I am Lady Paladin, as well as Godiva, are you not? We are one and the same entity. Though you have given the mechanical part of me the name Lady Paladin, and the thinking part of me the name Godiva.*

"I am aware, Godiva. I would like to keep that fact unknown to anyone else for the time being. I do have my reasons. I believe they will become clear to you before I need to explain them to you. However, if they do not, I will explain at some point."

Godiva/*Lady Paladin: As you wish, Oneshot. Continuing to run scenarios. FYI: Major Butler is approaching the Control Structure Ring to Bridge airlock.*

"Thank you, Godiva. Carry on."

A few moments later Major Butler drifted into the bridge. Johnny unstrapped and moved over to the co-pilot's console chair. "If you would, Major Butler, the Pilot's chair is yours for the moment. I thought you might enjoy a chance to get your hands on her controls."

"Yes," the Major replied, strapping in. "Of course, I had thought about asking…" Bill let his words fade as he studied the console, checking the status of everything, and making sure he knew the control layout. It was different from fighters and freighters, but all the standard controls were there, as were the necessary displays for flight in prominent positions, as well as the myriad other indicators and displays.

Satisfied he could do anything necessary, he turned slightly to look at Johnny, but he looked back at the console three times while speaking the few words he did.

"Not like there is much to it, at least in coasting flight."

"True," Johnny agreed, "but since *Lady Paladin* is, despite the gravity wheel, as you know, quite capable of some flight maneuvers that other gravity wheel ships are not capable of performing, at all, much less under acceleration, it is important to have a human ready at the controls."

For whatever reason, and not really caring exactly how, Johnny sensed that Godiva/*Lady Paladin* really wanted to speak. "Feel free to speak, Godiva," he said.

Godiva/*Lady Paladin*: *Thank you, Sir. Major Butler, I believe you will find, given the opportunity, that Lady Paladin is as capable as most other ships of similar overall physical size and mass. And she is capable of quite a bit more than most. Exceeding the abilities of a Sandman Class frigate, and approaching those of a Beast Class destroyer.*

"Impressive," Bill said, lifting an eyebrow when he looked at Johnny.

Johnny was pleased to note that Godiva/*Lady Paladin* did not remark on the Major's action.

The AI was advancing its learning and understanding even more rapidly than expected. "Those principles and designs first created by Thaddeus Devlon and improved upon by him and Jerry Bastion, have begun to exceed the original capabilities that the two men had envisioned, and strived for even during the Dark Times," Johnny mused silently. "Fortunately, they had the foresight to include powerful checks and balances in the designs."

A moment later Bill interrupted Johnny's musings. "Johnny, I take it you called me up here for a specific reason."

Johnny smiled. Twice during Johnny's more detailed explanation of his plans, and some of the alternatives that might have to be incorporated during the upcoming action, Major Butler had to use the Navigational Flight Path clearing railguns to demolish two moderate asteroids that were well outside the main body of the swarm they were travelling parallel with, approaching the contact point where Johnny's plan would begin the next phase.

"That is a very bold plan, Johnny." Bill shook his head. "Are you sure about it? All of it? If it goes bad, it is going to be terrible."

Johnny sighed. "Yes. I know. I am reluctant to include some of the elements. But, you know as well as I do, that if we try to protect various people, there will be major problems. Some of the objections would be justified. Everyone on board is highly capable at their specialty, and most can do the bulk of all the other tasks more than adequately."

This time it was Bill that sighed. "Yes. You are quite correct. And the way you have laid out the various movements, timing, and lines of attack, the risks are greatly minimized. Especially with the subterfuge we will be using."

A few moments of silence and Bill chuckled. When Johnny glanced at him, Bill explained. "I had to look up the Q-ships you mentioned in that first briefing about the plan. About how we would be doing something similar. I finally realized it was simply another term for the trap ships I learned about in the Academy."

"I do use many references from times long gone," Johnny said. "I am a history buff, for one thing, but from my interest that my father encouraged as I was growing up, I have leaned many useful things from history. Many."

Godiva's voice broke into their conversation with the latest update.

Godiva/*Lady Paladin*: *Approaching optimal position and time to activate next phase.*

"Thank you, Godiva," Johnny said. He looked over at Major Butler. "Time to see how well this plan works. Or doesn't."

Major Butler nodded. Knowing his assignment, he left the Pilot's console and drifted down the airlock, to head to where he needed to be.

A few minutes later Evie entered the Bridge and floated into the Pilot's chair when Johnny headed for the airlock, meeting Cherokee as he came out of it. "You have the con, Ensign," Johnny told him in passing.

Evie was concentrating on the Pilot's console, so did not turn around to express her surprise, but even with her back to them, she did hear the surprise in Cherokee's voice when he replied.

Surprise was not something she had ever heard from Cherokee in the short time she had known him. And never really ever expected to, having gotten to know him a bit on the trip, and having heard some of the others, especially Willi, describe his calm, cool, collected countenance no matter what was happening, or how dangerous.

"Me?" It was almost a squeak.

"You. Check your personal file as soon as you take the chair. And, if this goes bad, get my sister home safe."

Cherokee could not help it. "Aye, Sir!" And he saluted.

Evie had turned around when she heard her brother's words. So, she saw both the salute, and the look on Cherokee's face, that was there for only a fraction of a second. But she did see it.

Cherokee spun in the air, and shot toward the Command Chair. He met Evie's eyes for just a moment, but said nothing. He was back to the stoic Cherokee, Evie saw.

But she wondered. She wondered what Johnny had done to draw that look from Cherokee. And wondered what Cherokee had done to earn the respect that Johnny had in him.

While she might bristle a bit, when Johnny went all protector on her, but it still meant more than she could say. Had ever said. And to give that responsibility to someone meant that the man would be capable of carrying out that protection assignment.

Turning back to her monitors, Evie said, just loud enough for Cherokee to hear, "I can take quite good care of myself, you know."

"Yes, Ma'am," Cherokee replied.

A glance at that one spot on that one monitor that would sometimes act like a mirror showed Evie that Cherokee was reading furiously, his eyes moving back and forth so fast it was hard to follow them.

She still watched him when she spoke again, and noted that he continued to read, even as he answered.

"You know that I am not going to leave my brother, or my sister-in-law out here, if, as my brother put it, things go wrong."

"Yes, Ma'am. I am aware of that."

"So, you will not try to get me home until I am ready to go." Evie tried to say it as the positive, very positive, statement she intended. But she was not sure if she pulled it off. Because there was just a tiny amount of question in there, too.

Just as she was seeing his reflection, he looked at the same spot and met her eyes. And they were filled with compassion, she could tell. But something else, as well. Which was confirmed when he replied.

"I will carry out my instructions to the letter, Ma'am. No matter what I must do to accomplish them. And if that means trussing you up like a turkey for the oven, and stashing you in your cabin for the duration, that is what will happen."

Evie knew her eyes widened in shock. And she started to reply, but thought better of it. Because not only did she believe that he could do it, but would do it. So, she better just keep her mouth shut, and start coming up with a plan he would not suspect.

Cutting her eyes away, she readied herself and the *Lady Paladin* for the operation about to start.

She growled just a bit, rather like Willi was want to do from time to time, she realized, when Cherokee responded, very softly. "Don't waste your time plotting, Evangeline. If it must happen, it will. I will never allow anything to interfere with fulfilling a task requested of me by that man. Nothing. Not even the task itself."

It was more the thought of her brother, and how he had come to have that kind of impact on people, not just Cherokee, for she had seen it other times, too, that kept her silent.

"Confirm gravity wheel in stowed position and locked, Pilot."

"Confirmed."

"Prepare for Ready Rack launches, Pilot. All four bays, in sequence."

"Green board."

"Launch Ready Rack Dominators." Although each pilot could launch their own craft, if required, standard procedure was for the bridge to activate them.

Evie counted them down.

"One away.

"Two away.

"Three away.

"Four away."

"Give the green light to the flight decks." Cherokee said, watching his monitors carefully.

"Green light to flight decks, Aye."

A few moments later Evie added, "All craft away."

"Time for us to become a disabled private yacht. Feel free to add some special effects to Godiva's efforts, Pilot. And give us just a bit of way on this course."

Evie turned to frown at Cherokee, but he was watching his monitors intently.

"Aye," Evie said after a moment, when she sensed that Cherokee was about to look at her. She throttled up the drives for just a few moments, keeping *Lady Paladin* aligned perfectly. She gasped when Godiva, obviously at Johnny's earlier instructions, began speaking.

Evie glanced at her communications monitor. Godiva was broadcasting on several different bands. She noted that none of them were any of the official distress frequencies or modes.

Godiva/*Lady Paladin*: *Mayday, Mayday. This is Private Yacht Mistletoe. I repeat. Mayday, Mayday. This is Private Yacht Mistletoe. We are in need of assistance.*

Mayday, Mayday! This is Private Yacht Mistletoe. Out of Earth Central. Mayday! Mayday! We have lost all power! Mayday! Mayday! Our navigation weapons are out! We are drifting into an asteroid belt! Mayday! Mayday!

Evie jumped when the lights went out, even though she knew it was supposed to happen. And jumped again when Cherokee bellowed, even as Godiva continued the Mayday call. "Engineering to the portside axle bearing! Get that bearing realigned! If we lose that wheel it will tear us apart!"

Cherokee looked over at Evie expectantly.

All she could think of to do to add to the drama was to scream. So she did. And it was a very effective one, too, she decided, when Cherokee actually winced. Since it was not difficult to do, feeling the frustration she was, she did it again. And then a couple of more times. When Cherokee held up his hand, she stopped. But she grinned at him before turning around to the Pilot's console monitors.

Godiva/*Lady Paladin*: *I repeat! I repeat! Mayday! Mayday! Are any Confederation ships hearing this? We have Ambassador Brockmartain aboard! We need help! Please! We must get Ambassador Brockmartain to safety! Is anyone out there? Anyone…"*

Cherokee and Evie were both surprised at how well Godiva tapered off both the voice and the radio transmission, as if the communications system backup power system failed.

"Well done, Godiva," Cherokee said very softly. He looked at Evie when she turned to look at him, since he was whispering. "You, too, Evangeline."

She nodded, but asked, also whispering, "Why are we whispering? They can't hear us through space."

Cherokee looked a bit startled. But not much. He cleared his throat, and then in a more normal tone of voice, though still rather low, added, "Yes. Of course. No need to whisper."

Evie turned around before Cherokee could see her grin.

"All stations report," Cherokee said, activating the intercom.

The other four of the crew each responded in order, with reports of all systems being in perfect condition.

And then they waited. And waited. And waited. Evie thought it seemed like forever. Even Cherokee, she thought, was starting to look worried.

And when Godiva spoke, both were sure they could hear a note of excitement in her voice.

Godiva/*Lady Paladin*: *Incoming message from Oneshot.*

When Godiva fell silent Cherokee and Evie exchanged glances. But in only moments the AI was speaking again.

Godiva/*Lady Paladin*: *The asteroid belt is interfering with communications. But I was able to decode the message. Oneshot reports, "Mission One accomplished. All well. Begin Phase Two."*

And the annoyed tone was back when she continued.

Godiva/*Lady Paladin: What is Phase Two? I was not informed of a Phase Two.*

"I will explain shortly," Cherokee replied. "For now, keep a complete long-range all-direction scan going."

Cherokee activated the intercom. "The attack on the Pirate convoy was a complete success, with no losses on our side. Going to Phase Two of the plan. All hands. Prepare for evasive maneuvers."

Evie did not have a chance to turn to look at him. Cherokee was flying from the Command Chair to the Co-Pilot's console. As he strapped himself in, he looked at Evie. "Up and over, Pilot. As quickly as possible, and with as much risk as you are willing to take with me on the navigation weapons."

Evie's eyes widened, but Cherokee did not see it. He was already powering up the additional navigation weapons *Lady Paladin* boasted. For whatever reason or reasons, Evie trusted Cherokee to match her abilities flying *Lady Paladin* with his abilities with the weapons.

She did not hesitate. Triggering the maneuvering alarms a fraction of a second before activating both the propulsion drives and the maneuvering drives to spin the *Lady Paladin* in a complex dance to aim the ship where she wanted her to go, Evie ran the throttles up. Quickly.

"Godiva," Cherokee said, "Anticipate the Pilot's maneuvers to the best of your ability, and keep the longest scan you can where she is going. I need all the time I can to clear the path."

Godiva/*Lady Paladin*: *Active! Scanning! Port Keel, three klicks. 195 kilos. Port High, one point nine klicks. 319 kilos. Dead zero, five klicks, 38,000 kilos.*

Evie did not know if Cherokee noticed the excitement obvious in Godiva's voice, but she did. And managed to ignore it and Cherokee's flying hands and feet on the weapons controls, as she kept her eyes on her navigation monitors, looking for the fastest route through the asteroid field that would not get them killed.

Hopefully. She was not about to 'go up and over' in a time like this. Not with Cherokee by her side, and Godiva's eyes and ears as good as Evie knew they were. Not to mention the AI's uncanny ability to anticipate Evie's actions and even reactions. No. Evie was taking *Lady Paladin* straight through the swarm.

Even bearing down at very high speed, and accelerating constantly, toward a 38,000 kilogram asteroid only five kilometers ahead that would be right where they needed to be when *Lady Paladin* got there. Unless Evie slowed. Evie continued accelerate.

Evie and Cherokee both lost track of time. One hunting and heading for gaps in the cloud almost, but not quite big enough to get *Lady Paladin* through without damage. But Cherokee made them more than large enough, with Godiva's help.

It was only a moment, but Evie glanced over at Cherokee, and then back to her monitors. She was absolutely sure that Cherokee was now responding before Godiva could complete, and occasionally even start, her warnings. He was, somehow, anticipating her as well as Godiva, and just a bit more quickly.

Suddenly Godiva nearly shouted.

Godiva/*Lady Paladin*: *Friendlies! All craft accounted for. 7 point 2 klicks, starboard high.*

Before Evie could ask, or actually change course, Cherokee quietly ordered, "Maintain course and rate of increase. Godiva, switch off anticipation and navigation scan. Go to stealth long-range scan, Port High, 60-degree cone."

Although she was not sure, and was not even sure if it was possible, but Evie would have sworn that Godiva actually started to protest, and cut it off. Evie knew she heard something after Cherokee's instruction.

She put it out of her mind when Cherokee addressed her, his eyes still scanning the monitors, his feet and hands ready. "Pilot, signal the crew to prepare to receive EVA craft. Maintain best course. Warn of reduction of thrust to zero over a one-minute time frame."

"Aye, Sir!" Evie replied, doing everything seemingly at once. Twice during the very short timeframe, Cherokee destroyed the three largest asteroids that they had approached, one after another, with a dazzling display of multiple railgun launches, realignment, and additional launches.

Fully seventeen railgun projectiles had been necessary to clear the way. And even though the remaining debris were spinning away from the *Lady Paladin's* path, their speed put them into the edge of the debris cloud.

It popped out before Evie could stop it. "Sorry, Godiva. I didn't mean to scratch her."

Godiva/*Lady Paladin*: *Well... try not to let it happen again. Please.*

When Evie looked over at Cherokee in surprise, she could tell he was trying very hard not to laugh. She glared at him, but quickly had her eyes forward again, as Godiva once again spoke.

Godiva/*Lady Paladin*: *Stealth Long-Range Scan. Two... vessels...*

Evie looked at Cherokee in surprise. That was an actual stuttering pause from Godiva.

Godiva/*Lady Paladin*: *Two vessels. Unknow type. Un... Unknown mass... Range, 83 kilometers. Why can't I tell what they are and how big they are? I have every known vessel in my memory.*

"Sorry, Godiva," came Johnny's voice from behind them. "Not your fault. Those are two Ecronian... I believe the closest translation is, *Shadow Ships*. Cloaked. Very well cloaked. You did quite well just seeing them well enough to get a bearing and range."

Evie looked around long enough to see several people. Willi for one. She had to look forward, but could tell who was with them in the bridge, as Johnny gave more firm, quiet instructions.

"Lieutenant Quintain on the weapons console. Lieutenant McKindrick, on sensors. Clue him in, Clyde and Godiva. Isis, you have the con. Call up your file when you take the Command Chair.

"Captain McKindrick, Major Butler, you will be flying overwatch. Hang way back and out. Use anything and everything for cover. I do not want either of you seen until I give the word. If I give the word."

Johnny named four more people, all deck crew, all men. "Ensign, gather them up and get yourself and them in the EVA suits and armed, on standby. I want them ready in no more that seventeen minutes, ready to deploy from any point on *Lady Paladin*. I will be there shortly to suit up myself."

Willi looked at Johnny. She was ready to question him. Like Godiva, she did not know what Phase B was. And did not like not knowing any more than Godiva. Even that there was a Phase B, much less what Phase B was.

"Major, Captain, see to your Dominators, please." He watched Willi. She wanted to protest. But she did not, though it was close, he was sure. She and Major Butler headed for the airlock.

"Range, Godiva?"

Godiva/*Lady Paladin*: *69 kilometers. Same rate of approach.*

"Pilot, adjust *Lady Paladin's* course, and speed if necessary to intercept those two ships in no more than twenty minutes, nor less than twenty-five minutes. I need to know when we are within five kilometers of them."

Johnny looked at each of those on the bridge in turn. Isis, in the Command Chair, Syd on the Sensors console, with the special sensor screen up. Clyde at the Ship's Weapons Console. And Evie still in the Pilot's chair. They would not need a co-pilot for this. They were well out of the asteroid cloud now.

After taking another look at the stealth long-range sensor screen, Johnny took a deep breath and let it out slowly. The others could not really tell, but what he had seen had shocked him slightly. And called for a change of plans. Changes that he would have to make on the fly.

Johnny spoke after another few seconds of thinking. "This is going to be very dangerous. We will be facing two of the fastest, and most well-armed ships in the Ecronian Fleet. I was not expecting these two ships to be the ones laying back in deep high cover. I knew there would be two Ecronian ships… Two of their *Shadow Ships*… but not their Fleet Command Ship, and certainly not the Royal Barge."

"Royal Barge?" Sydney squeaked out.

"In name only," Johnny replied. "She is a sister to the Fleet Command Ship, and unless I miss my guess, even better armored, and armed. Probably not faster. Might not even be quite as fast, but still fast enough.

"Our advantage is they do not know we are here, nor who we are, nor what our capabilities are. I was able to jam everything being sent when we hit the rest of the convoy. At least I believe so. And I have good reason to believe so. So they only know something happened to the rest of the convoy they were shadowing.

"My original plan…" Johnny stopped and scrubbed his hands over his face before letting them down to his waist. "My original plan really does not matter. What matters is this one. It will work, I am sure. But execution has to be both precise and exactly timed.

"You will all have time to read through the files before we reach the critical point. But the basic plan is that we go in on a tangent, and begin firing with everything the *Lady Paladin* has, except the nukes. Those only on my order.

"We want to do as much damage as possible on the first pass. As best as I can tell, we are aligned properly to hit them on the starboard side."

Isis gave him a look, obviously asking how he could possibly know that. He ignored it.

"As soon as we start firing, Pilot, you will do a hard reverse thrust, to slow us so we do not go too far past those ships. Spin, and return. Lieutenant Quintain, you will be dumping everything we have into their propulsion units that you can. Including up to two nukes each, if you can use them without damaging the rest of the ships, only the propulsion units."

Clyde nodded.

"Then, Pilot, bring *Lady Paladin* along their port side, at half a klick, and match their velocity and course."

Johnny looked at Syd. "You will be using every sensor *Lady Paladin* has, plus your own, to watch for anything else out there."

Looking forward, through the bridge view port, Johnny seemed to be looking far, far in front of them. But then he turned again, to face the others. "I can feel something else out there," he said, almost too low to be heard.

"If something shows up, Lieutenant, anything at all, sound the alarms and feed Isis everything you can make out until this is over.

"Isis, you will be making sure all this happens. Then, once you are sure the ships have been disabled, the EVA team will open up one of the ships to give us a means to enter in the assault suits. Not sure which ship it will be yet. I will have to make that determination at the time.

"Once we have accomplished that, and as soon as we are back aboard *Lady Paladin*, Pilot, stand us off to a full klick and maintain station while we switch out the EVA suits to the Assault Suits.

"As soon as we are ready, Shuttle 5 will take us the klick to the ship we have opened up, whereupon we will enter."

Again, looking at Syd, and then at Clyde, Johnny dropped his voice a bit lower. Everyone could tell how important his words would be, by his stance, his eyes, and then his delivery.

"Lieutenant McKindrick, you will be using everything you have to monitor every movement in the ship we enter. We will have identifiers. Know where we are at all times. Inform Lieutenant Quintain in whatever manner works best between you two if anyone or anything is about to make contact with us in there, of which we might not be aware.

"One of us will be giving you a detailed running account of what we are doing, and where we are in the ship, if we can tell. And our cameras will be feeding the monitors here. Best if Isis or Pilot watch them. I want the two of you concentrating on us in that ship.

"However, Lieutenant McKindrick, if your sensors signal anything else, you will immediately inform Isis, Lieutenant Quintain, and Pilot, and then us.

"Isis, you will take *Lady Paladin* away from the area until you can determine whatever it might be out there is. And then act accordingly.

"Does everyone understand?"

All four started to talk at once. Johnny held up his hand. And smiled that sardonic smile.

"Good thing Willi can't see him now," Syd sort of whispered to Clyde. "She hates that smile."

"Be that as it may," Johnny replied, "I do believe it is justified at this point, pointed at me, because I honestly almost forgot one last item. All of your concerns, I hope, will be alleviated, when I activate *Lady Paladin's* cloaking."

"She doesn't have cloaking!" Evie protested loudly.

And Godiva protested even more loudly.

Godiva/*Lady Paladin*: *I most certainly do not have cloaking ability. I would most certainly know that, if I did. You could not possibly have…"*

Johnny held up his hand again. And even Godiva stopped talking. He turned to Isis. "Isis, if you please. Call up file GRS-17, slash 19, ampersand 21. Go to sub-file Echo. Go to sub-file Bravo. You should see a small icon in the lower right part of your screen."

"I see it," Isis replied.

"Touch it. With your left forefinger."

Isis looked over at him, hesitating, but then touched the icon. Absolutely nothing happened. Not that they could see.

"You were joking!" Isis said.

Johnny shook his head.

Godiva/*Lady Paladin*: *He is not joking. I felt the program activate. And felt myself... Lady Paladin ... changing."*

Evie spun and touched an icon on her console. It brought up a view from one of the external cameras located near the rear propulsion drives, facing forward.

There were some gasps. For all that any of them could see was a bit of a shimmer, and the distant stars on the far side of the ship from the camera's position.

"That's… That's…" Sydney could not come up with the words.

Not even Godiva could, apparently, for the AI vocalized not a word.

"That only represents the visual light spectrum. The other electromagnetic spectrums are also cloaked to one degree or another. Mostly a very high degree.

"Now. Weapons can activate and fire without disengaging the cloak. It will show signs of the firing, but they are minor, and unless sensors are programmed specifically to look for them, are almost undetectable. And even with sensors programmed, the anomaly is only a few nanoseconds, and therefore the sensors might not even pick it up most of the time, anyway."

Johnny drifted toward the airlock.

"Carry on, Major. You have the con."

Johnny had to stop once, to rest. Even with the zero-gee conditions at the moment, he had been under high acceleration many times during the battle, and he was far from healed yet. Still, he made it to the ready room where the others were waiting.

Cherokee helped him into the EVA suit, and then helped Johnny add his tools and weapons. The others looked on in amazement. All were veterans, though with limited service time. And all had drilled extensively with the ship's crews on which they served.

Having seen Cherokee equip himself, they were even more amazed when Johnny added a few additional items to the combat harness of his space suit, than even what Cherokee was carrying.

Johnny, once suited, touched helmets with each of the others, to carry on a private conversation, the sound vibrations passing from one helmet to the other where they touched.

Words of encouragement mostly. Thanks for their help. Reassurance. Moments before they received the signal and braced themselves, Johnny simply bumped Cherokee slightly. It was enough for the two of them. They did not need to exchange any words.

As with every battle fought in space, the lack of sound was eerie. No atmosphere to carry the impacts of the railgun projectiles, or the explosions when something was hit that had enough flammable material and oxygen to create one.

The only sound was more a vibration, as the occasional shock wave strong enough to reach one ship from another, vibrated a hull, which would generate a tiny amount of sound. All very low frequency. Frequencies that could be felt, faintly.

They did all feel the vibration of one strong impact on the hull of *Lady Paladin*, somewhere in the ventral fin. When *Lady Paladin* again became still, with no perceptible motion, Johnny was already moving toward a hatch in the unpressurized section where they waited when Major Echart's voice sounded in their radios.

"Both ships' power seems to be down. We are at one-half klick distance. We are ready for your EVA."

A signal from Johnny, and one of the crew released the dogs, spun the locking wheel, and let the hatch swing open. Johnny shot through the hatch, already powering the suit drives at maximum.

As soon as he cleared the hull, he vectored to the left, and a relative down direction. Each of the others exited the *Lady Paladin* in the same manner, taking a different vector to spread themselves out to make more difficult targets.

It was well they did, for an Ecronian gunner responded relatively quickly, barely missing the last one out of the hatch. But Sydney and Clyde were in top form, and had destroyed the weapons installation only a fraction of a second later.

As the other five powered toward the Ecronian ship that Johnny was headed for, there were no more attacks. They did continue to maintain some distance between themselves.

When Johnny indicated a damaged area in the hull of the huge ship, which dwarfed the *Lady Paladin*, and could have swallowed five of the Scanlon Ball Ships completely, they converged on the spot.

Cherokee took station a few feet away from the hull, but where he could see inside. With his weapons ready, he nodded. Johnny, with the other four, advanced and began to cut away sections of the hull and interior framework.

Trying to enter a ship through a hatch, portal, or air lock was simply too dangerous to ever try to attempt. Boarding was always through an opening the boarders created themselves. Though often it was as this one was. A damaged area of the hull, expanded to allow safe entry. Then a foothold was established, and the boarding went from there.

The very size of the Ecronian ship worked to the humans' advantage, since it was unlikely this section would be occupied, as it was known to be a cargo hold.

How Johnny knew that, the others did not know, but they did not question it. He had chosen well, because it took only a few minutes of work to open things up enough so they would be able to gain entry wearing the Assault Suits, which were bulkier than the EVA suits, even though designed to be used in a breathable atmosphere.

Even with being able to breathe in a closed hull, the Assault Suits had to include breathing atmosphere for transfers to and from pressurized areas, and in case a compartment was decompressed to attempt to stop them.

With that need, plus the armor, weapons, and breaching tools they would carry, they needed some space. And now they had it. Johnny motioned the others back, backed up himself a bit, and then tossed in one of the objects he detached from his harness.

Not only would the device transmit signals back to the *Lady Paladin* from the sensors it contained, but if triggered, it would cause immense additional damage to the hull if anyone inside entered that compartment.

Sending the other four on to *Lady Paladin*, Johnny and Cherokee maintained a rear guard, facing the Ecronian ship, backing toward *Lady Paladin*.

There had been no additional action from either of the Ecronian craft. No communications attempts. No attempted use of weapons. Ecronians were none too fond of space, so their ships had very few actual view ports. There were no changes visible through any of them, not even a flicker of light.

All knew the multitude of cameras, however, were most likely giving the Ecronians a full view of everything outside the ships.

The others were already inside Shuttle Five when Johnny and Cherokee dumped their EVA suits after reentering *Lady Paladin* and headed for the Flight Deck Bay.

Instead of entering the shuttle, Johnny hurried toward a crewman standing by near an airlock that accessed the extended hull from the Flight Deck Bay.

Cherokee diverted over to them when Johnny motioned for him to join them. "Help get this situated on nose of the shuttle," Johnny said when Cherokee joined them.

He thought that they were going to go through the airlock for some reason, but Cherokee saw Johnny trigger a mechanism that allowed a panel to swing open.

The other crewman, who would be piloting Shuttle Five, looked at Cherokee and shrugged when Cherokee lifted an eyebrow in question.

Both grabbed the handles on the circular assembly, as Johnny was doing, and maneuvered it under Johnny's instruction to the front of the shuttle.

Once there with it, the attachment points were obvious, though not knowing what they were, it had not occurred to anyone what they might be. All six clamps were thrown in a matter of a couple of seconds, and the ring was attached.

Johnny headed around to the side of the shuttle and entered, followed by Cherokee and the pilot. The rear access was being closed by the other four. As the pilot took the helm, Cherokee and Johnny began to suit up, with the help of the other four when the rear access was secured.

"Get us in the lower flight deck," Johnny told the pilot.

The Flight Deck Bay that serviced the upper and lower flight decks of that set was arranged to make quick transfers of craft from the pressurized Bay, to the unpressurized Flight deck.

Though the Flight Deck Bay could be opened up into one large compartment, there were panels that could close off any given area. Such as the one Shuttle Five was in.

Which meant that it took only seconds for the massive atmosphere pumps to empty that space of air, to allow the shuttle to be lowered through the deck hatch into the open space of the Flight Deck.

A few seconds later, with the shuttle released from the gantry, floating under its own power, Johnny looked around at the others. "A few instructions," he said.

"You all have boarding experience, I know. And we just made a boarding entry point in the hull of the second ship. However, this shuttle has a couple of extra features not found on most other shuttles.

"That ring that was just mounted on the bow of the shuttle is a boarding airlock." He looked forward to the pilot. "When we leave the *Lady Paladin*, which, by the way, will be at high speed, in reverse, you will spin us, and accelerate toward the second ship. Not the one we were just working on.

"You need to impact the hull of that ship square on, at no more than ten kph, and no less than six kph. Right under the left most of that string of symbols that go down the side.

"Upon correct impact, the outer ring will blow a hole in the hull of the other ship, secure an airlock ring and hatch, which will be open. As soon as pressure equalizes between the airlock and the other ship, the inner airlock hatch will open, and we will enter the other ship at speed, and fan into standard Assault formation.

"If my information is correct, we will be entering a cargo bay, much like the one we were to enter in the other ship. Also, if the information is correct, there will be no humans aboard."

Johnny sighed slightly. "At least not any living ones. If you do see any human forms, they will be a shock, so try to steel yourselves and be prepared to take on any and all attacks that might come from any direction inside the ship.

"Once we have stabilized the entry point, you four will set up a holding position. The Ensign and I will head further into the ship to do what I need to do.

"We will be blasting our way through decks and bulkheads, not using passageways. If we have not returned in eight minutes, we will not be coming back.

"Return to the shuttle, disengage, and return to *Lady Paladin*. Major Butler will be in command, and if not him, Major Echart. They have their orders for the situation if it occurs.

"Ready?"

Only Cherokee did not pause before he answered. But all did reply in the affirmative. Johnny nodded to the pilot. "Go."

They all grabbed on. The pilot might not be up to the level of Willi, the Majors, Evie, or Sydney, but he was more than adequate for the task. And seemed quite willing to ram the Ecronian ship. Because there was no hesitation. When Shuttle Five cleared the Flight Deck, he spun it, accelerated, and lined up to the target ship square on. And though only he could tell, hit the Ecronian ship at exactly ten kph.

The device ring triggered, opening the hull, and the airlock ring sealed into place. The pressures were closer than Johnny had even hoped, for the inner airlock hatch popped open into the area between the Shuttle's pilot and co-pilot seats.

Johnny was ready, laying parallel to the deck of the shuttle. He shot through, bringing himself upright immediately after clearing the airlock, and shifting to his left. He was scanning the area, with eyes and all the sensors that the suits contained.

The compartment was smaller than he expected, and it was not empty. But only a few innocuous items lined the right-side wall. He kept his eyes on them, however, as well as watching everything else until the others joined him and began covering their assigned areas.

So far, they had received no communication from *Lady Paladin*. Johnny looked over at Cherokee and got the signal he expected. The two headed toward the nearest bulkhead, ignoring the hatchway opposite. A few meters from the bulkhead Cherokee tossed a hatch maker device toward it.

The device deployed, and two seconds later Johnny and Cherokee shot through. Right into a group of heavily armed Ecronians. Fortunately, they were all concentrating on a large hatch that opened into a passageway. A passageway which Johnny and Cherokee would have been in had they used the hatch out of the compartment they had entered from outside the ship.

Neither man hesitated. Johnny headed for the opposite bulkhead, behind the Ecronians, which were only now beginning to realize the humans were in the compartment. With the hatch maker in his left glove, he began to fire with his right.

Cherokee was giving a good account of himself, protecting Johnny, while taking out as many of the Ecronians as possible until they could get into the next compartment.

With the new opening, Johnny held his position and let Cherokee dive through, before he backed through, still firing. He paused long enough to pull another device, activate it, and toss it toward the now approaching and firing Ecronians.

Cherokee could not see Johnny's sardonic grin, but he wondered if it was there, since he heard the device Johnny had tossed. Not that he could understand it, since the device was speaking in Ecronian. He could guess the meaning, if not the words. Something to the effect of "I am a bomb. I will explode in ten seconds. Nine seconds…"

And he was sure those Ecronians in that compartment were now trying to get out of it, through both the regular hatchway into the passageway, and through the made hatchway, and into the compartment where the other humans were, whom, Cherokee was sure, was taking down every Ecronian that tried.

Out of the corner of his eye, Cherokee saw Johnny motion toward a ship's hatchway. Actually, to the far-left side of it. Cherokee deployed another hatch maker device and noticed that Johnny had one ready as he went past Cherokee into the passageway.

Three Ecronians concentrating on the ship's hatch did not have time to react and change aim before Johnny took one down and Cherokee the other two, as Johnny's hatch maker opened up the bulkhead on the opposite side of the passageway.

As they went through that one, and into another compartment, both heard Sydney urgently announce, "Five Ecronians dead ahead. And… a whole bunch to your left coming down that last passageway. That bulkhead ahead of you looks to be heavily armored!"

"I think we're here," Johnny said calmly. To Cherokee's great surprise, Johnny handed his primary weapon to Cherokee, and took two devices from his harness. Neither one was a hatch maker. Nor any explosive that Cherokee recognized.

All Johnny did was flip a switch on each one. He set one against the bulkhead, and hooked the other one back onto his harness.

As Johnny took his weapon back from Cherokee, he kept his eyes on the bulkhead, and backed right into the passageway behind him, before Cherokee could grab him, to keep him from stepping right into the Ecronians rushing down that passage.

Except, when Cherokee stepped into the passageway, turning his weapon toward where the Ecronians were, he froze. There were at least fifty Ecronians, if not more, all down, with what passed for their blood all over the bulkheads, deck, and even the overhead.

He could barely hear Sydney shouting, with the others shouting in the background, when he felt and saw flame erupt from inside the other compartment they had just left.

Barely before the flames went out, Johnny was running into that compartment, and when Cherokee reached it, Johnny was already going through the huge hole blasted through the other bulkhead. And he saw that Sydney had been right. That bulkhead was armor. Heavy armor. Heavy enough that none of the weapons he, himself, was carrying, would have even scratched its surface.

He could hear the screeching sound of the Ecronian voices raised in panic when he followed Johnny through. Surprised that there were only three of them making all that noise, Cherokee lifted his weapon to cover them, the way Johnny was doing.

Johnny stood there, waiting for the three Ecronians to quit speaking. After a few seconds they did. While he could not be sure, he thought the Ecronians might actually look frightened, which was unknown for them to be, even when facing armed humans.

As he continued to watch, keeping his eyes moving, Cherokee managed to not react when Johnny began to speak. In Ecronian. At least, sort of Ecronian. It sounded terrible to him, and apparently to the Ecronians, as well, for it sure looked like they winced. But they also looked like they understood Johnny, for they were suddenly, obviously, no doubt about it, scared.

Without any sort of protest, the three went out the hatchway Johnny indicated, and marched before him, as Cherokee trailed behind. He kept a sharp watch, but all he saw were dead Ecronians. Each looking like the first ones he had seen in the passageway. With the same gore all over the place.

The three Ecronians avoided all of the gore they could, but Johnny kept them moving with another word and a poke from time to time. It was obvious, when Johnny stopped them, and pointed at a label next to a hatchway, that they had not responded the way Johnny thought they should.

Even speaking bad Ecronian, Cherokee could hear the censure in Johnny's voice when he said something to one that had replied to Johnny's question about the label. All three of them seemed to shrink even more. And began to move a bit faster, trying to stay clear of the still occasional dead Ecronian and accompanying gore. And, it seemed to Cherokee, to keep as much distance from Johnny as possible.

When Johnny said, "Time?" it was a second before Cherokee realized that Johnny had just asked him how much time they had left.

He was surprised to see that it had only taken them five minutes to get to where they were. "Three."

Johnny hurried the Ecronians up a bit more, but when one came to a sudden stop, looking at another of the labels beside a hatchway, Johnny stopped and motioned to that one. When the Ecronian moved to open the hatchway, the slightly taller of the other two made a move to stop him. But Johnny had his weapon on the back of the Ecronian's head in an instant, and it desisted. When the hatch opened, Johnny pushed the three Ecronians inside, and told Cherokee to watch them carefully.

Johnny went over to a cabinet and began to open drawers and doors. Cherokee could see that Johnny's actions were making the Ecronians extremely nervous, though he was not sure just how he knew that.

When Johnny suddenly spun around, some kind of device in his hand, all three Ecronians bolted for the hatchway. As big as they were, Cherokee had little trouble stopping them, because it seemed more important for them to avoid Johnny than it was to get out of the compartment.

But the struggle lasted only another second or so. The Ecronians quit struggling when Johnny touched the device in his hand to their necks, one after the other.

Johnny dropped the device, turned Cherokee toward the hatchway, and said, "Time to go. And none to waste."

With nothing to impede their progress, the two swam as fast as they could, using every projection to speed themselves in the zero-gee toward where Shuttle Five was waiting for them.

One compartment away, Johnny told the other four to enter the Shuttle and leave the airlock clear.

It was well they did, for Johnny shoved Cherokee through the airlock, and zipped through himself, just as the unmistakable vibrations of a major space ship disintegrating were felt.

"Disengage! Get us back to *Lady Paladin*." Without even pausing, Johnny took another device from his harness and touched something on it.

The vibrations they had felt beginning either stopped, or the pilot had broken contact with the Ecronian ship. And when they all, other than Johnny, looked out toward the ship they were rapidly backing away from, more evidence of damage was visible. But the other Ecronian ship was slowly disintegrating before their eyes.

And from the looks of it, the disintegration had begun at the access point they had created before, in which Johnny had left what everyone thought was a normal boarding protection device.

Cherokee looked over at Johnny as the two began to remove their assault suits. "How?" Cherokee asked.

"Later, please. We still have pressing business, unless I miss my guess."

All were brimming with questions, and barely managed to hold them in once they were aboard *Lady Paladin* again. The crew went to clean up, as did Cherokee, as Johnny headed for the bridge. He met Willi and Major Butler at the airlock. Major Echart had recalled both of them when Johnny had called for the return of the shuttle to *Lady Paladin*.

"What happened out there?" Willi was the first to ask, as they cycled through the airlock.

"Willi, it will have to wait just a bit. I am sorry. But I have a very bad…"

Just as the airlock hatch inside the bridge opened warnings began to sound. And Sydney, looking over at Johnny in near panic, shouted to him, "Another ship! Same size! Three times the speed! Only a hundred klicks out, bearing right on us! I did not see them until just now. I don't how they…"

"It is okay, Sydney. They have something more advanced than I was told. Pilot, max us out of here. Course Zero, Zero, Zero."

Everyone on the bridge just stared at Johnny for a moment. But then all moved to be ready for the high-speed flight. The maneuvering warnings sounded, and Evie ran the throttles up.

Only a few seconds later everyone began to settle toward the rear of the bridge, with the acceleration mimicking gravity.

Willi headed for the Co-pilot's console, and Major Echart left the Command Chair for Johnny to take. But Johnny motioned to Major Butler. "You have the con, Major. That other ship will stop at the other one. We should be out of danger now. I need to freshen up, get some rest, and then when we confirm our safety, I will explain all. Carry on."

"Johnny!" Willi called, unbuckling her harness, but when Johnny seemed to not hear her, she settled back, and turned toward the console. "I know he heard me," she muttered. "He is in so much trouble with me…"

The others smiled, making sure Willi could not see them, but with the tension draining from them with Johnny's announcement, all breathed a sigh of relief, and simply did what was required to put distance between the Ecronians and *Lady Paladin*.

"Major," Evie asked a few moments later. "Would you confirm course, Sir? Johnny… He said 'Zero, Zero, Zero'. That cannot be correct, can it?"

Major Butler looked thoughtful. There were legends… But surely… He shook his head, exchanged a glance with Major Echart, now on the systems Console for something to do, and then told Evie, "Maintain that course, Pilot. I am sure he knows what he is doing."

Sydney and Clyde, close enough together to hold a whispered conversation without risking too much, wondered about the course. Zero, Zero, Zero were the coordinates of the center of the Galaxy. Said to be unapproachable. Besides which, it would take at least a couple hundred years to get there, even at near light speed, which they could not achieve. Could they?

Chapter Ten

Johnny, not quite as sure of everything as he led the others believe, did not head for his and Willi's quarters. Instead, he headed for the starboard rear Flight Deck Bay. Where his personal new Dominator II was stowed.

A caution to Godiva/*Lady Paladin* to maintain silence of his activities, and Johnny did a thorough check of the Dominator II. Using the automated equipment, which use was blocked from being seen by Godiva/*Lady Paladin*, Johnny added a few additional munitions to the racks, and topped off everything he might need on a long, solo, flight.

Readying the Flight Deck Bay, with the Dominator II positioned on a hatch to the lower Flight Deck, Johnny slowly decompressed the area enclosing the fighter. And waited.

Evie had taken him at his word. She was pushing *Lady Paladin* to the limits. At least the limits she believed the ship could not exceed. When the velocity reached the point where any additional speed would make launching the Dominator II too dangerous to *Lady Paladin* for him to risk it, Johnny triggered the hatch below to open.

Using the Dominator II's own power rather than the handling equipment, he dropped down into the Flight Deck, and accelerated out of the Flight Deck at maximum speed he could reach in the length of the Flight Deck, and turned sharply away from *Lady Paladin*.

He smiled, slightly, as he headed back toward the Ecronians, ignoring the shouted orders to return, the cursing, and then the heartbreaking pleading

Willi did on a private channel when Major Butler refused to turn the *Lady Paladin* to go after him. He did have to steel himself not to respond to Willi.

Johnny ran the throttles up to the limit he could stand, with his body in the shape it was at the moment. Switching on the cloaking system before he was out of the background of *Lady Paladin*, Johnny used the enhanced long-range sensors for a moment to double check that the Ecronian ship was, in fact, slowing to join the disabled Ecronian ship. The Royal Barge, now with only three Ecronians alive. Three of the Royal family.

The Ecronian Supreme Leader's eldest offspring, the Heir Apparent. The Supreme Leader's closest relative within the Royal Family's complicated family structure, the High Commander of the Ecronian Military forces.

The third Ecronian, one step further down in the Royal Family hierarchy, was actually more powerful than the Heir Apparent, and even the Supreme Leader in some circumstances. The Supreme Leader ruled. But, this third Ecronian filled a role that Johnny had not been able to find anything close to a comparison in human civilizations.

It combined advisor to the Supreme Leader; head of all of what equated to humans' legal system; and head of their faith system that was even more complicated than the family system. All of which were tied to events that occurred many thousands of years previously at the very beginning of their existence, which took place on the far side of the galaxy.

And, finally, this Ecronian was the sole and absolute arbitrator between Ecronian civilization and all other civilizations, with the power to overrule the Supreme Leader, and even make totally independent decisions, with the power to enforce them, for all Ecronians.

Johnny shook his head. "How can they have a Supreme Leader, and yet have that… whatever… it… is?" he muttered. Johnny had learned everything he could about the Ecronians over the years, but that one, which he had only learned during the time he had been captured, he could still not reconcile in his mind.

It did not matter, however, whether he did or did not. What mattered was that those three Ecronians were who they were, and now had the same type of tracking and execution devices implanted that all other non-Royalty Ecronians did.

The worry for Johnny, was that if that approaching ship held either the Supreme Leader, which was extremely unlikely, or the third Ecronian's Second-in-Command, which was quite possible, and either of them decided to activate the execution command, without knowing the three members of the Royal Leadership now had one implanted, everything he had just caused to happen could come to naught.

And it was not uncommon for someone with the power to destroy every Ecronian in a ship or even a whole base, if they felt they had not lived up to their duties.

If, when the other ship arrived, and saw the debris cloud of the one ship, and the disabled second ship, along with the total absence of the rest of the convoy, which had included three other Ecronian ships, whoever was in command might just trigger the execution devices without waiting to find out what had occurred.

Johnny did not want that to happen. With the three Ecronians tagged now, and they having seen their entire ship's crew destroyed with their own tracking devices, they would be very careful about how they dealt with humans in the future.

It was not that they could not simply stay well out of range of humans, but the Ecronians, with their normally paranoid thinking patterns anyway, would have them believing that their deaths were imminent at all times.

Breathing a sigh of relief when the next check of the sensors showed the other ship slowing significantly now, with no indication of them intending to follow the *Lady Paladin*, if they had even picked up the ship on their sensors, Johnny throttled back, but held course.

With no indications that the other Ecronian ship could tell that the Dominator II was anywhere around, Johnny began to simply coast, watching the tracker now, as the third Ecronian ship approached the Royal Barge.

Another sigh of relief left Johnny when he saw the approaching ship take up a stand-off distance from the Barge and launch a shuttle to go the final distance to the disabled Royal Barge.

When he saw the three blips in transit to the shuttle, Johnny had his hand ready to activate the throttles. But he paused and continued to watch the transfer. When it was obvious that the three Ecronians were now aboard the rescue ship, Johnny again was ready to power away from the Ecronian ship.

He felt the sardonic grin appear on his lips. And knew that if… Johnny admitted it to himself… When Willi found out what he was going to do, that had just occurred to him, she would be livid.

And even beyond that, what he was going to do would cause him other problems not related to Willi's actions. He just simply could not resist. Johnny was not even sure himself if he had approached in the exact manner he had, to be able to do what he now knew he would.

Taking a moment to have everything ready, so there would be no delays in executing the plan, Johnny took a deep breath, let it out slowly, and then his hands seemed to fly over the controls of the Dominator II.

Accelerating at an uncomfortable rate, Johnny triggered four weapons releases, switched off the cloaking, and sent out a clear transmission, in both English and, through the translator in the Dominator II, in Ecronian.

"This is Oneshot. I have destroyed your convoy. I have destroyed your battleship. I am now destroying your Royal Barge. I am going to damage your rescue ship, just because I can."

At that point, the four weapons he had released impacted the Royal Barge, disintegrating it there right beside the rescue ship. Johnny triggered four more weapon releases, these all headed toward the rescue ship.

But Johnny spoke again, still heading straight for the bridge of the Ecronian ship. The four missile weapons would sweep to the sides of the ship and impact to cause damage, but not cripple it. "I command thee, Ecronians, to abandon all attempts to subjugate humans. Else, I, Oneshot, will lose all patience and destroy you all!"

With those words Johnny triggered the Dominator II's four lighter railguns, and the three heavy railguns, as he continued straight for the bridge of the Ecronian ship.

The four missiles, two light nukes and two heavy explosives, impacted. Johnny groaned under the strain as he tilted the Dominator II to go up and over the Ecronian ship, still keeping the throttles forward.

He was never sure if he hit some of the debris that was nearly everywhere, or if the Ecronians had managed to fire off some navigational path clearing weapons.

But when he parked the Dominator II in the Flight Deck Bay of *Lady Paladin*, he noticed three holes that went completely through the body of the Dominator II, whatever creating them having travelled from bottom, up through, and out the top, missing the pilot compartment by mere centimeters, and two weapons systems by less than that.

Fortunately, Willi was rampaging at him, which kept her distracted enough for Johnny to be able to let Cherokee know to get the holes repaired before Willi had a chance to see them later.

Cherokee chuckled, but nodded. He lagged behind as Willi more or less dragged Johnny somewhere she could yell at him a bit more privately. Then Cherokee went and took care of the repairs himself.

Johnny let her rave. He knew how she felt. He had gone through it, with both his mother and father. The fear. The anguish. The worry. Everything Willi was feeling about him, he had felt about his parents.

It was only when they swam into their quarters in the extended hull did Johnny pull Willi to him and kiss her. Long, deep, and hard. When he eased her away from him, they were drifting toward what would soon be a floor, as Evie brought *Lady Paladin* up to a one-gee constant acceleration.

Willi's breathing was just as fast as it had been on the way to their quarters, but for a very different reason. As Johnny made sure they were balanced on their feet when they touched the floor, he held Willi's shoulders and looked deep into her eyes.

"Willi… My love… I am sorry. But this was something that I felt had to be done. Something that only I could do. And it had to be right then, in those particular circumstances. I honestly wanted to explain first. But I did not believe there was time to convince you of the need, nor talk you out of going when you did perceive the need.

"I have promised to keep you informed… to discuss things with you… and I will keep that promise, Willi. But this time… hopefully the only time it will ever be necessary… I had to do it afterward. Explain the what, why, and wherefores afterward, rather than before."

Willi's eyes had been on Johnny's, looking into them as deeply as he had been looking into hers. Her tears slowly tapered off. She closed her eyes and took a deep breath. And then released it as she leaned into Johnny, wrapping her arms around him tightly, and pressed her cheek against his chest.

"I understand, Johnny. I do. But I cannot help myself at times… I never really thought I would find someone… someone I could love the way my parents loved one another. That I could feel that deeply."

Johnny was holding Willi just as tightly as she was him. He could feel her head, even through the flight suit, as she shook it minutely. "But I found I could. I could love you that much. So much it was like my very soul was torn from me when you left, and I was not with you."

"I'm sorry…" Johnny whispered. "So sorry…"

Johnny released Willi when her tight grip loosened. However, when she leaned back slightly, her hands still on Johnny's waist, he held her hips, never letting go, since she did not pull all the way back.

Slowly she lifted her eyes to meet his again. "Don't be sorry," she whispered. "Never be sorry. I will not do that to you. I realized, just now, that you truly are, and always will be, Johnny Oneshot, as much legend as real. And I would never take that away from you… or me… or the rest of the universe. I love you. All of you. In all your guises. With all your quirks. I love…"

Her words faded, and she once again laid her head on Johnny's chest and gripped him tightly. But only for a moment. Then she stepped back, stood on tiptoes, and kissed him. And then kissed him again.

Willi suddenly grinned when Godiva/*Lady Paladin* spoke.

Godiva/*Lady Paladin*: "Captain Anderson to the bridge."

Sidney and Clyde were not the only two people that shared a look, with one whispering, "Who is Captain Anderson?"

Evie heard the murmurs from those on the bridge behind her. She simply grinned. Her brother still had some secrets from the others on board. She frowned then. And, apparently, from her, she suddenly suspected.

Since Godiva/*Lady Paladin* had not indicated an emergency, Johnny took the time to change out of his flight suit into ship's clothing. Not without some interference from Willi. She seemed determined to annoy him in the most pleasant way. Finally, he stepped back, took both of her hands in his, and looked at her face. "You. Will. Stop… Correct?"

Johnny winced just a bit when he realized the last had come out as a question, and not the command he had intended.

Willi stood there, tilted her head slightly, and looked at him. She finally grinned. "Well… Since you put it so nicely. I suppose I will have to. I will meet you on the bridge." With that, and a tug of her hands, she pulled away and left Johnny to his task.

The questions began immediately when Willi entered the bridge. "Who is this Captain Anderson?" Sydney asked. "Did Oneshot bring someone on board from those Ecronian ships?"

"What?" Willi asked. Looking rather confused.

"Godiva just requested a Captain Anderson to come to the bridge," replied Major Echart.

"But that's…"

Before Willi could finish, Johnny entered the bridge. "You requested my presence, Godiva?" Johnny asked.

"Wait…" Syd and Clyde exchanged another glance, and then looked at Johnny again. "You're Captain Anderson?" Syd asked. He looked at Willi for confirmation, rather than Johnny.

Willi grinned. "He sure is. Oscar John Anderson." When the others looked a bit shocked, she added, watching Sydney closely. "Yes. **THOSE** Andersons."

Sydney's eyes got wide. He stared at Johnny.

"Willi…" said Johnny, rather hurriedly.

But Willi was on a roll. She needed to make up some time with the teasing she had not been able to get in lately. "Yes, sir. Those Andersons. Of the Quincannon family." When she cut a look at Johnny, she quickly looked away, ignoring the look he was giving her.

"Your sister, brother Sydney, is married to Sir Dunigan Quincannon. AKA, Johnny Oneshot."

As Johnny tried to calm Sydney and Clyde down, and keep Cherokee from exploding, while Evie looked on with a grin, Janet leaned over slightly toward Bill, who was still in the Command Chair. "Kind of blows Telstar, Protector of the Sector right out of the competition, huh?"

Bill frowned at Janet, but she just laughed and turned back to her console.

"I will deal with you later," Johnny said, shooting a look at Willi that made her blush. She quickly took the co-pilot's chair and activated the console.

Johnny took the Command Chair when Bill stood up and handed over the con. Bill stayed, taking up a seat at one of the other, currently not needed, consoles.

"Yes, Godiva. You requested my presence?"

Godiva/*Lady Paladin*: *Yes, Sir, Captain Anderson. We are still on a course toward Zero, Zero, Zero and accelerating.*

"Yes," Johnny replied. The communicator had appeared in his hand. Willi frowned. She still had not discovered where he kept the thing. He looked up again. "That is correct. You have concerns, Godiva?" he asked.

There was a pause, most unusual with the AI.

Godiva/*Lady Paladin*: *I do, Captain. I have been accessing my historical memory banks. There are statements within them… Many statements, Captain, that Zero, Zero, Zero should not be approached under any circumstances.*

"I am aware, Godiva. What is our current position, distance to Zero, Zero, Zero, and ETA at current acceleration?"

The AI immediately replied:

Godiva/*Lady Paladin*: *In thirty seconds we will be at negative thirty-eight decimal nine nine three, negative three hundred twenty-one decimal four seven six, zero decimal eight three one. Distance is seven decimal six three nine light years. ETA is four years, five months, twenty-seven days… Correction.*

There was silence for a few moments, and then the AI spoke again. The voice sounded strained.

Godiva/*Lady Paladin*: *Correction… Correction… This… This is not possible… I cannot calculate an ETA. Not a correct one. It continues to change… keeps getting sooner and sooner. This is not possible…*

"Cease calculation, Godiva. You have confirmed what I needed to know. Pilot, change course to rendezvous with *Trinity Home*, based on her last known course and speed."

Johnny glanced at Sydney, Clyde, and then Willi. "Since it seems we have found Miss McKendrick, I believe her brother and her friend would like to get her home so her mother and the rest of the family does not worry."

Laughter erupted. Everyone was relieved they were through pirate hunting, and heading for home.

But, not unexpectedly for Johnny, a short time later, when Cherokee had a few minutes to talk to Johnny privately, Cherokee said, "Hey, Boss. Ship is all patched up. Good as new. It would take a magnifying glass to see the repairs. If I do say so myself."

Cherokee started to remind Johnny about the flight recorder in his Dominator II. Cherokee did not have access to it, and if Johnny intended to prevent the automatic transfer of the recordings from it to *Lady Godiva's* systems he would need to do it right away. Without a qualm, Cherokee decided to not bring up the subject.

Johnny waited a moment, but Cherokee did not speak. Though he did look like he wanted to do so. "Yes, Cherokee?" Johnny asked.

"Well… I was wondering…" He looked over to meet Johnny's eyes. "Are we truly calling off the hunt for pirates? They are more out there, you know… Many more… And other… dangers to the Confederation."

The sardonic smile appeared on Johnny's face and Cherokee almost grinned. But managed to maintain his stoic demeanor. Even after Johnny said, "Why, you are probably right, Cherokee. It would be a shame to let this craft sit idle. Or plow around the galaxy on pleasure cruises. Wouldn't it?" And Johnny winked.

At least Cherokee thought he did. But he had to turn away quickly to keep Johnny from seeing the huge grin Cherokee could no longer keep from forming.

Johnny shook his head and headed toward the gravity wheel air lock to join Willi. He was stopped again. This time by Major Butler. "Johnny… Captain… Sir…" Bill shook his head. "Too many names, kid. Anyway, I wanted to double-check about what our status might be upon our return."

"I see," Johnny said. "And by the way, you can refer to me as Johnny, when circumstances do not indicate otherwise." Johnny looked at Major Butler's earnest face for a moment.

"That would be up to you, would it not?" Johnny asked, but continued immediately. "I am not sure what your plans with the Space Navy are currently. Or, more accurately, when we get to a point where you and Major Eckhart can transfer to a Naval vessel."

Bill basically sighed. Though he did straighten up quickly and look at Johnny. "I have not decided. And I do not think Janet has either…"

Just then Janet joined them in the corridor. "Janet has not what either?"

Bill started slightly. "Um… Decided what to do when we get back to Space Navy territory."

Janet looked at Bill for a long time. At least it seemed like a long time to Bill. She looked at Johnny then. "I am not sure, honestly. I expected the search for 'Willi' to take a great deal more time. I thought we would be aboard for quite a while."

She glanced at Bill, but immediately turned back toward Johnny.

"Hm…" Johnny said, trying to look thoughtful. He had already made a decision after the first long talk with Willi after they headed for *Trinity Home*. "I seem to remember that you both were on what could be an open-ended leave. I'm not sure how either of you would feel about staying a while longer as temporary crew aboard *Lady Paladin*…"

Another quick look between the two majors, and both looked at Johnny again, and both nodded.

"I could do that," Bill said.

"Sure," added Janet. "Nothing really better to do. Could take a break from the Navy for a while…"

"That's settled then," Johnny said. Without further conversation, he drifted into the airlock and headed up to join Willi.

"You were right, Willi," Johnny said when he entered their one-gee cabin in the gravity wheel. They both want to stay." He grinned. "Not sure if it is stay with the ship, or with each other."

Willi grinned back. "I am sure. Now. What can we do about Clyde… and Sydney, I guess?" she asked, trying to look dismayed at asking her brother to stay with the ship, too.

"I have no doubts that their commanding officers would be more than willing to let them stay on extended special assignment. One Miss Goodkind can be very persuasive." Johnny grinned.

"You?" Willi asked, finding herself a bit surprised. Which surprised her even more.

"Oh, no. There is only one Miss Goodkind. The real one. I am sure you will run across her one day." Johnny did not add that he was sure that one or the other of the women, or more likely both, would make sure of it.

Now sure that they would have the crew they wanted, when they headed back out to fight for the security of the Confederation, in their own way, they began to plan their 'real' wedding.

"Are we really going to have to have a royal wedding…" Willi was not sure how she felt about that. She smiled. "As long as it is to him…" Her eyes went to Johnny Oneshot, man of many names, and even more talents.

It was not until almost twenty-four hours later that Johnny remembered the flight recorder in his Dominator II. And it was way too late to do anything about it. Since Willi, and the others most likely, had seen it, from the thunderous expression on Willi's face, and the looks the others gave him, when she came onto the bridge…

THANK YOU FOR READING!

If you enjoyed this book, we would appreciate your customer review on your book seller's website or on Goodreads.

Also, we would like for you to know that you can find more great books like this one at www.CreativeTexts.com

MEET THE AUTHOR

Jerry D Young was born at home, in Senath, Missouri July 3, 1953. At age 5 the family rented a small farm house on an active farm 40 miles southwest of St. Louis. While the family weren't farmers, they lived something of a homestead type life, raising a milk cow, sometimes two, and calves, a pig or two, chickens, and the occasional goat. Along with the stock, a large garden helped to feed Jerry's three brothers and two sisters for several years. Fishing and hunting contributed to the pantry, as did foraging the wild edibles on the property.

At the age of 14, the family, minus a brother and two sisters that were now adults and on their own, moved back to Senath. Having been encouraged from an early age to read, Jerry was a regular patron of the Senath Branch Library. A love of a good story was born within him, and shortly before graduating high school, for a lack of stories that he liked at the library, he began to write short vignettes, and started taking notes for stories that he wanted to tell. Jerry eventually began to write in earnest and now has more than 100 titles to his credit including Prep/PAW stories, Action/Adventure, and a few of the romance type stories that first got him started.